TEMPTING REBEL
PRINCESS

ALLURING RULERS OF AZMIA
BOOK THREE

MAHI MISTRY

Tempting Rebel Princess
Copyright © 2021 Mahi Mistry

All rights reserved. No part of this book may be reproduced or transmitted in any form or by any electronic or mechanical means, including information storage and retrieval systems, without written permission from the author, except for the use of brief quotations in a book review.
This book is a piece of fiction. Names, characters, places, and incidents are the product of the author's imagination. Any resemblance to actual events, locales, or persons, living or dead, is coincidental.
This book is licensed for your personal enjoyment only.
This book may not be re-sold or given away to other people. If you are reading this book and did not purchase it, or it was not purchased for your use only, then you should return it to the seller and purchase your own copy.
Thank you for respecting the hard work of this author.

Published by Mahi Mistry
Cover Design by GermanCreative
Proofread by Roxana
ISBN e-Book: 978-93-5437-727-3
ISBN Paperback: 978-93-5473-226-3

"And if the devil was to ever see you,
   he'd kiss your eyes and repent."

— FAROUQ JWAYDEH

Dedicated to all the kinky readers who love reading filthy, steamy romances.
This one is for you.
Hold on to your panties.

PART I

"I want you to hurt me."

1

ZARA

I did not want to be a Princess.

The constant thought rang thorough me, sighing at the cluster of men who kept glancing at me. I looked at Safiya, my maid, who was busy rating princes and Royals on their looks while my two personal guards stood two steps behind me. They followed me everywhere I went, except my room. They were ordered by my brothers, Zain and Khalid, the Sultan and Prince of Azmia, for my protection.

It's not that I hated being a Princess. There were perks, but the cons of being one outweighed the pros.

I hated being looked at as some kind of conquest. The way the hungry eyes of men from noble families looked at me, their sons, sheikhs and princes eyeing me like I am just an object waiting to be sold to the highest bidder.

"I want to get out of here," I mumbled, sipping on the bubbly champagne. My stomach and back itched from the tight fabric of the lace corset dress. Safiya had cinched it too tightly to show some cleavage, despite how small my breasts were. No doubt the dress was beautiful and perfect for a

Princess with a heavy skirt, but at that moment, it annoyed me because I wanted to rip it off and scratch my back.

"But it's your birthday party, Princess Zara," Safiya frowned, her brown eyes blinking at me. "Don't you want to have dinner, eat spicy food, cake and open the expensive presents all these people have gifted you?"

Her eyes were shining like stars, in awe at the corner of the Court Room where a pile—no, a mountain of presents with big boxes wrapped in pretty, shiny gift papers were kept together. I scoffed, seeing royal security in their suits guarding the presents.

I dreaded the moment I would have to open them and accept the luxurious clothes, dresses, blouses, that would be released in next year's fashion show, tailor made by the designer with gold jewellery, personalised for me, Zara Al Latif, the Princess of Azmia.

My eyes flickered to my eldest brother, Zain, sitting on the throne where father used to sit before that night. I rubbed my wrists, glad to see the pale skin soft without any marks. Khalid prowled towards him with a glass in his hand, smirking and taunting him while Zain glared at him playfully.

Their happiness mattered to me more than anything. They had saved me from a monster and it had tainted them to their soul. Saving me had made them afraid of their past, so much so that Zain didn't want to get married.

I could see the irritation behind his obsidian eyes, the same way the constant staring and attention irritated me from the royals in the crowd. Khalid didn't mind. He and Zayed, Sheikh of Azmia, his close friend, liked the attention.

"Found anyone yet?" I asked Zain, saving him from the batting lashes and flirting, lacing my arm around his elbow and walking with him on the marble floor designed in beautiful, tangled patterns.

Even though it was my nineteenth birthday party and New Year's Eve celebration, we held the for Zain so he can find a suitable bride and the future Sultana of Azmia. If I had to describe his preferences after living with him under the same roof for nineteen years, I would say he was a rock. He didn't like women or men or any other genders. I had never seen him flirting and if I did, it would be a miracle.

Meanwhile, Khalid had different women in his room most of the time. I had learned my lesson to always knock and enter after seeing two of his conquests sprawled naked on his bed, kissing and doing *other* stuff while he was, thankfully, in the shower. I may or may not have run to the library and looked for some books that mentioned two women or three people in the act of intimacy.

Who knew that could happen? Certainly not me.

Being a Princess, I was sheltered and coddled since the day my mother, Isabella, announced that she was pregnant with me. The only time I had ever been physically alone was in the washroom. Sometimes Safiya insisted to ready my bath with oils and dresses and even scrub my back before special events like that day. I didn't mind being nude with her in the bath, she was just a year older than me and the closest person I would consider as a friend.

That was why I wanted to go out. Sneak out of The Golden Palace of Azmia and into the Capital Street, go to the club and maybe kiss a stranger. I wanted to be reckless. Do something impulsive and have fun.

I was nineteen and haven't kissed anyone. Well, I had, once, but it was awful. I didn't want to kiss a boy with fumbling fingers and gentle lips. I wanted to kiss a man who knew what he was doing. Who knew how to mould a pair of lips together and feel the rush of adrenaline.

The kind of kiss that makes a Princess forget who she is just for a moment.

Unfortunately for me, I can't outright tell my brothers that I want to go out and kiss a man. It would create a lot of argument. That was why I would sneak out *tonight*.

As soon as Zain agreed to allow me to go to our club (because we owned the club, it was only for royals and celebrities, Khalid would be there) I rushed to go to my room.

"Going somewhere, Princess?"

My eyes widened, and I halted hearing his silky voice. It felt wrong, but I couldn't help feeling the hate and the giddy feeling of having a crush whenever he was around.

I glared at him, at his charming smile, the dimples and the dark curls. "What do you care, Zayed?"

Even after his rejection at my advances when I was thirteen and girlish and naïve that a Sheikh like him could ever want me back, I had tried my best to push away the attraction I had felt towards him.

"You're Khalid's little sister, Zara," he had said in a calm voice under the roof of a stable, the horse neighing as tears burned my eyes.

"But I have liked you for so long!" I had complained, stomping on the dirt like a spoiled princess who demanded to be loved back by a twenty-six-year-old man who was a Sheikh and best friend of my brothers.

"It's a silly crush, it will go away." He had the same patient voice, melting chocolate eyes. "I see you as my little sister. I apologize if my actions made you think otherwise."

I had cried, turning away from him and grabbing the stable boy my age and kissing him in a tack room so I could feel what I wanted from Zayed. But, of course, it was utterly wrong and felt awful, apologising to the flustering boy and running back to the palace to cry the heartbreak away in my room.

I blinked at the long hallway lit with small golden chandeliers, my room only a few steps away from him. Zayed walked towards me, my body straightening up. I didn't have that silly crush anymore. After ignoring him for a year, I had grown a conscious and realised that even princesses aren't loved by everyone, no matter how pretty they are.

"I care plenty, Zara," he said, noticing I wasn't with my maid or guards. "Where are you going?"

I narrowed my eyes at him and crossed my arms. "I am not telling you."

He looked at me, at my defiance, and smiled. Zayed whispered as if someone might hear us in the empty hallway, "If you are going to sneak out of the Palace, use the gate on the East and go to the *Sayih* Club in *Naureen* Street. It has tourists and your brothers won't think you'd be there."

I swallowed the lump in my throat. Okay, I know in my heart I don't have that crush anymore, but I enjoyed talking to him because he treated me as his sister, which he could spoil with mischief. I had learnt most of my pranks from him.

"Why are you telling me this?" I demanded. "What's in it for you, Zayed?"

One of the things princesses learn when homeschooled by three brotherly royals and an old advisor: Never accept gifts from royals because they always have an ulterior motive that will benefit them.

Those gifts I received? From designers and royals? They would have an invitation to their show in London, Milan or New York for more publicity. Royals will have more invitations for me to visit their palaces and mansions and ask for my hand in marriage.

"I have taught you so well, haven't I?" Zayed grinned, standing straight. "But I promise you I don't have any ulterior motive. I want you to go out and have fun but still be safe."

He lifted his hand, and I saw a shiny new black phone. Probably the latest model.

"What's this?"

"A phone."

"I can see that, but why are you holding it? Are you showing off your new phone—?"

He signed and handed it to me. "It is for you, silly. I want you to press this button thrice as soon as you feel you are in danger or need my help. It has mine and the number of your brothers, your maid, guards and even Rahim's number."

Rahim was our advisor who mostly acted as our cool uncle. "Why Rahim's number?"

"If you cause a fire or kill someone, call him, not me. I will panic."

He said that with a grin.

Zayed had caused a fire in the Palace running in the hallways and since then he was banned from ever running on the palace grounds. He still won't tell me how he did it and won't share his secret. Rahim had helped control the situation while we all evacuated the Palace. He was also present that day… that night when my brothers saved me, killing our father. He had handled it all and took care of us in a way true father would.

I looked over the phone, unlocked it and noticed it was brand new. I never needed a phone. If I wanted to get the latest gossip, I could ask Safiya and look around her phone when she was with me. I didn't have any use of it. I never needed to call anyone or had anyone to message. I took pictures with my own DSLR and read books in the library, painted with Khalid in his art studio, studying in Zain's study room or ride a horse from one of the stables Zayed owned.

But Zayed was right. If I go out of the palace alone, I would need one. To take pictures and call him if I needed anything.

"What's the number of this phone?" I asked, wondering if someone would ask for my number like I see on TV shows and movies.

Zayed chuckled, ruffling my hair and quickly moving his hand, when I glared at him. My dark hair was wavy and thick, so they turned into a mess when ruffled.

"Do you plan to give it to someone?"

"Maybe."

He looked at me, waiting for me to break under his stare. *Ha! He should have known better.*

I squared my shoulders and asked him for the phone's number again and smiled when he told me.

"Don't do something I wouldn't do," Zayed said when I moved towards my room.

"No problem." I grinned, looking over my shoulders, "That's a pretty comprehensive list."

A SMALL GRUNT MADE ITS WAY PAST MY LIPS WHEN SAFIYA helped me remove the enormous dress I had been wearing.

"Are you sure you want to do this, Your Highness?" She asked, her voice low as I jumped out of the lacy, puffy fabric that pooled around my ankles.

I nodded, removing the corset. "I am sure, Safiya, and how many times do I have to remind you to call me by my name? We are almost the same age," I said, raking my hand through my hair. She opened her mouth to argue, but I said, "No. It's my birthday so you have to call me by my first name when we are alone. Understood?"

"Yes, Princess. Er, Z-zara."

I grinned and went behind the ornate wooden screen to change into the stunning cream coloured backless dress I had seen in a fashion magazine Safiya had been reading. I had to get it and as my birthday, the fashion designer had it customised for me. The dress felt like a soft hug from the richest silky fabric, its thin straps comfortable on my shoulder. It ended on my thighs but had a slit that reached to my inner thigh. *Scandalous*. Something a Princess wouldn't wear.

My fingers nervously fidgeted with the material even though it clung to my body with my back on display. I had bought it to wear it for the party held in the Golden Palace, my home, but knowing there would be so many royals, sheikhs, sultans and princes, my confidence had wavered. I didn't want them to see me in that dress. It didn't matter that my brothers, the Sultan and Prince of Azmia, would do anything to protect me. I didn't want to be seen as a conquest or a challenge for them.

I wanted to be seen like a nineteen-year-old celebrating her birthday and New Year.

"Help me with the zip please!" Safiya said, just as I stepped out of the screen.

"Aw, you look just like a princess, Safiya!" I cooed and helped her with the zip.

"Look who's talking. You look stunning in the dress. I am quite jealous," she muttered when I straightened the fabric of the dress I was wearing moments ago.

When my eldest brother Zain, the Sultan, allowed me to go to our club, I knew I had to try. Try to have a night off from being a princess. I didn't want to be coddled and protected safely, which I knew would happen if I went to the club we owned. Knowing Khalid, the Prince, would be there didn't help. He would make sure no men made any eye-contact with me and if they stared at me for over five seconds, he would threaten to pull his eyeballs out.

I had seen him threaten a man once when we were out in the market. "No one gets to stare at you like that. You are the only Princess of Azmia and my little sister," Khalid had said with no ounce of regret after I scolded him for threatening the stranger.

Today's my lucky day. I won't be a Princess tonight. Just a nineteen-year-old, sneaking out of her house—er, palace, to go to a club.

"Please don't do anything stupid," she said, pinning two strands of my hair on the crown just how she does her hair every day. I liked it. It made the sharp features of my face stand out.

"Define stupid," I answered, applying a red lipstick. It made the beauty mark on the corner of my upper lip look more enticing. I wished I could dress up like that every day.

"Don't get arrested. Don't threaten someone. Do not even try to help a stranger when they ask you for direction," she threatened, her usual soft tone gone.

"Why not? They need my help—"

"*Zara*," she said. "You are terrible at giving directions and if you are looking like that, the only thing that stranger would want is a direction towards your bed."

I pouted.

"Princess, are you ready?" The guard knocked on the double doors of my room as Safiya and I rushed to wear heels.

"Just a moment!"

I strapped the nude sandals on my feet as Safiya wore flats with rhinestone that worth more than the club I would go to. I safely tucked a sheer dark veil across her face so the guards wouldn't know that Safiya was pretending to be me for a night. I was sure she would extremely enjoy the attention she would get while I would wander around the capital on my own.

"Will you be safe?" She asked, watching me wear a coat to hide the dress.

"Of course."

"You won't be a Princess outside the palace, Zara," Safiya said, her brown eyes softening. "No one will recognise who you are. Please don't get killed."

"I promise I won't get killed." I hugged her. "Now quit worrying about me and have fun for the night."

The feathers of the mask on my face kept tickling my nose, but I had to wear it until Safiya was safely seated in the Rolls Royce waiting for her. The guards frowned at the sheer veil, but they hurried behind Safiya when she walked ahead of them, leaving me alone in the palace's hallway.

I could hear the musicians playing instruments in the Court Room. My brothers would be busy engaging with the guests.

This was my only chance.

So I turned, a grin on my lips and went to the gate on the East, towards the *Naureen* Street.

2
HAYDEN

I swirled the auburn liquid in the glass, loud pop music blasting from the speakers as people's laughter echoed in the background. The cute bartender with glasses slid a tissue paper towards me, her baby blue eyes gazing at my face as I took a long gulp of the alcohol, relishing in the burning sensation it left in my throat.

"Are you visiting for the first time?" She asked, her voice and accent thick, just like others I had met in Azmia.

"First time on the land," I replied, trailing my finger around the rim of the glass, eyeing her curvy figure and looking at the crowd partying on the stage.

I had almost travelled all the countries because of my job but I had never seen a celebration of a New Year's Eve like this. Fireworks were going off outside. Everyone was dressed for some type of occasion, and the entire capital was decorated with expensive orchids.

"Why is there so much celebration?" I asked the bartender over the music after she strutted towards me in her high boots after serving shots to the loud group of men.

She wiped the marble counter in a way that showed off

her cleavage, her eyes gleaming with emotion I knew too well.

She wanted to fuck me.

I gave her a small smirk and tugged at the cuffs of my shirt, letting her entertain me and I might just take her up for a quickie.

"It's for the Princess's birthday," she said. "She is turning nineteen tomorrow, so the Sultan and Prince have invited royals from all over the continent to celebrate."

"Good for her," I scoffed, emptying the glass of whiskey and licking my lips. "So much for a nineteenth birthday." I shook my head, remembering how I had celebrated my nineteenth birthday almost a decade ago. Just one beer passed around me and my troop in a camp outside the border of Baghdad in Iraq.

She continued with a smile on her face. "Sultan Zain personally donated a lot of food, clothes and gold to everyone who earned minimum wage. Rumours say that Princess was with him, but no one knows for sure."

I tilted my head at her, frowning at her sentence.

"No one except the royals knows what she looks like. She is the daughter of late Sultan's second wife, half-sister to both Sultan and Prince, but they treat her like their own blood. Her mother was English, so the few people who have seen her know she has skin as pale as the moon and during one event, a royal was threatened to have his eyes removed by Prince Khalid because he looked at the Princess the wrong way."

My brows raised at the threat. I had a little sister too, but I wouldn't go around threatening to remove someone's eyeballs if they stared at her for too long.

It seemed like her protective brothers spoiled and coddled the Princess.

The bartender continued, leaning in, "Some say that she is

too ugly to be a Princess so they have kept her hidden while others say that she might have been born without nose but I don't believe that rubbish."

I chuckled, "People have a lot of time on their hands to think about some nineteen-year-old girl."

She nodded, ready to voice her opinion when she was called for more shots by the group of men. I clenched my jaw, hating the way they leered at her. I reminded myself to relax. There were guards on every corner of the club and besides, Azmia was one of the safest countries.

I admired the work of royals who looked after their own land and people—*woah*.

My thoughts came to an abrupt halt. Blood thrummed in my veins, my breathing getting a little faster watching a beauty walk inside the club. Her wide eyes blinking up at her surroundings.

I licked my lips, shamelessly staring at her. *Ethereal*. That was the word that I would choose to describe her. From her long, thick dark hair falling down in waves to her heels that strapped up her pale calves. She was absolutely stunning. Her legs were endless and my filthy mind wondered how they would tremble and shake wrapped around my shoulders when I eat out her pretty pussy.

Several heads turned towards her, checking her out just like I did, their eyes burning with lust and envy.

I raked my hand through my hair, noticing every curve of her bare skin in the illuminated lights. Her beige dress clung to her lithe frame, draping over her breasts with thin straps, flaunting modest cleavage with the hem reaching her thighs. I bit my lip at the scandalous slit of her dress on her left leg, ending on her inner thigh. My gaze narrowed at the silver like thread around her thigh when she moved, some type of golden body jewellery.

I averted my blue-grey eyes from her ample breasts to her

slender neck where I wanted to leave hickeys. I could easily hold her by her neck, pushing the hem of her dress to her waist and watch her beg and whine, wanting me to touch her.

I took a sharp intake of breath, looking at her face. *Enchanting.* Her face was innocent, young, with sharp cheekbones that matched perfectly with her elfish features. Her two big dark eyes blinked curiously at her surroundings as she licked her red lips nervously.

Fuck.

Her lips looked so soft and full that I wanted to savour them in a sweet kiss before pushing her on her knees, watch them part and stretch around me.

Shuffling on the stool, I caught the sight of a beauty spot on the corner of her upper lip as she smiled, flashing her perfect white teeth to the bartender. She was a couple of stools away that I couldn't hear her. A dimple formed on her cheek when she talked.

Who are you?

Ignoring the urge to march towards her and drag her to my suite if she was interested, I ordered another glass of whiskey. She seemed way too young for me, anyway. Blinking innocently at the crowd and fiddling with the hem of her short dress.

Was she even legal? I shook my head at the dirty thoughts and decided it would be best for me to go back to my suite alone and call it a night.

"What's that?"

I turned towards the girl in beige, walking towards the stool near me and pointing at my drink with her manicured finger. Her voice was nothing like I had imagined. It was husky, sweet with a heavy English accent. I wondered how it would sound in the morning.

Keep it in your pants.

"It's whiskey neat," I answered, intrigued by her. And her erotic voice, her sexy body.

Her hazel-brown eyes looked from my face and the glass filled with auburn liquid. She called the bartender and ordered the same.

I raised my brow at her. *Well, someone was being bold.*

Leaning back on the stool, I watched her face scrunch adorably when she took a sip. My curiosity turned to amusement.

"Is it sweet?" I asked softly, her eyes flickering to be as she nodded at me.

Poor Princess.

I pulled a peach flavoured candy from my suit pocket and held it up for her. "Here."

Her gaze narrowed, leaving her glass untouched. "My brothers warned me not to take candies from strangers."

I chuckled. How adorable. "Suit yourself, Princess."

I unwrapped the candy and was about to lift it to my mouth when her nimble fingers held my wrist.

"I didn't say I don't want it," she said, standing so close to me that my pants brushed with her bare legs. I watched her face when she leaned down, the tips of her long hair brushing my arm. Her lips wrapped around the candy, her tongue licking my fingers teasingly before she pulled back, her heating gaze meeting mine.

I tilted my head to the side, studying her. *Hmm.* She was curious about me, innocent, judging by the way she entered the club but… daring, judging by her dress and her behaviour.

"How does it taste, Princess?" I asked, playing along with her. If she could enter the club, then she was definitely legal.

Her eyes gleamed when she stared at me. Humming, she shrugged her dainty shoulders and perched herself on the stool across me. Her bare thighs brushed against my knees when she sat, the hem of her dress inching dangerously high. I shamelessly stared at the golden, dainty chain of diamonds wrapped around her inner thigh. It might be some type of body jewellery that I was not familiar with, but just one look at it on her pale thigh and I wanted to fuck her with just that thing on.

"You didn't answer my question." I uttered, my voice deeper than before.

"It's not as sweet as I thought it'd be." She tucked a lock of thick hair over her ear. "How old are you?"

I answered with a small smirk, "I'm twenty-nine, Princess—"

"Why do you keep calling me Princess? I'm Zara."

Such a pretty name.

"Nice to meet you, Zara. I'm Hayden and I want to call you Princess because you look like one. Minus the dress, of course."

She took a shaky breath, her legs crossing over each other as I sipped on my whiskey, finishing the drink and watching her push her long dark hair over her shoulders. Her arms and legs were toned with slim muscles. Maybe she was a dancer?

"What's wrong with this dress?"

"*Tsk.* There's nothing wrong with it, but pretty princesses like you don't go to clubs wearing a dress like that without a goal, Zara," I said, her cheeks turning light pink as she looked away from me. "How old are you?"

"I'm nineteen."

Fuck. Ten years—

"You're right," Zara continued, staring straight at me.

"Hm?"

"I have a goal."

"I'll take a wild guess and say that it's related to stealing my candy and sitting here, talking to me."

"Yes, Hayden." She licked her lips. "And I did not steal your candy. You offered it to me."

Fucking hell.

I wanted to hear her say my name again. Hear it rolling out of her tongue when I have her heels over my shoulders with my co—

Zara leaned closer and whispered, "I want to have sex with you."

3
ZARA

"I want to have sex with you," I whispered in his ear, his expensive musky cologne wafting in my nose when I leaned back to see his expression.

My breath got caught in my throat when I looked at him. There was handsome and then there was... *him*. Hayden.

Being a Princess, I had met several handsome princes, sheikhs and rulers, but their beauty came from expensive procedures, surgeries and regular care. Not like Hayden, whose rugged features made my thighs clench. His broad nose slightly crooked as if someone had dared to punch him. His stubble peppered over his sharp jaw, his cheekbones high, his wavy sandy-brown hair styled perfectly, matching perfectly with how sophisticated he looked.

His blue-grey eyes widened, only for a fraction of a second, before they pinned me to the spot. My heartbeat slowed and increased. I felt hot all over my body. His gaze was hot. The heat radiating from his powerful body made me squirm on the chair, a shiver rolling down from my body to the spot between my legs.

Hayden noticed it.

He came closer, his handsome face, his deep eyes pinned on me. "Are you playing with me, little Princess?" He purred. The deep rumble in his voice made me clutch the hem of my dress in a fist.

I started stuttering because he made me nervous and excited. "I… I am not playing with you, Hayden. I want to have sex."

I whispered the last part, looking around to see if my brothers hadn't noticed my absence, and called the guards and police to search for me everywhere. I hoped that Zayed would take care of them.

"With a stranger?"

His voice made me look at him. He was watching me as if I was a piece of a puzzle, assessing me with his intense eyes that seemed playful just a few seconds ago. Even though he was a stranger, I felt I could trust him. Trust him… to have sex with.

"Yes. I know your name is Hayden and that you like me—"

"I never said I like—"

I raised my chin, "I wasn't finished." He stared at me for a few seconds and nodded for me to continue. "You didn't say it, but the way you look at me says otherwise, Mr Hayden."

"It's Knight," he replied.

"What?"

"My last name. Hayden Knight. But I prefer Hayden."

"Hayden Knight…" I said out loud, my cheeks turning warm.

Hayden sighed as if he was frustrated. "Zara, I'll be honest. I want to fuck you." I took a sharp breath when he continued, "But you are nineteen. I am a decade older than you. Why not ask someone who is of your age?"

There it was again. The men around me wanting to remind me how little and small I was.

"What's with that judgmental face?" He asked, raising his brow.

"I already tried asking someone my age, and I didn't like it." I looked away from him, remembering the time in the shed with the stable boy. I hated I asked him, of all people. Shaking my head, I paid the bartender with tip and stood up from the stool.

"It was a mistake to ask you. Apparently, you are too much of a pussy to talk to a nineteen-year-old. Have a good night, Mr Knight."

I walked away from him, his musky cologne that reminded me of the ocean, strutting towards the crowd dancing on the stage hoping that I can enjoy a few more minutes in the club before I go back to The Golden Palace.

What a Birthday Night it was turning out to be.

Hayden

WHAT A FEISTY LITTLE PRINCESS.

I smirked, enjoying the way Zara had riled up and walked away, leaving a trail of her sweet perfume. I wanted to follow her, hold her dainty wrist, drag her to the nearest alley and fuck her before taking her back to my suite and spend the entire night pleasuring, using and fucking her lithe body until she passes out.

But I held back. She needed some time to cool off. I was as feisty as her when I was nineteen, if not more, and I use that in training and occasional sex.

"Can I ask your hotel room number?" The cute bartender asked, her eyes averting to my muscled forearms when I rolled up the sleeves of my light Armani blue shirt. It was one of my favourites.

I noticed the previous group of men who looked more

like a group of frat boys following my Princess with a wolf whistle into the crowd. Looking back at the bartender, I gave her a hefty tip.

"Sorry, darling. Not today."

Looking at her wide eyes when she took the tip, I knew she didn't mind it one bit. She seemed really nice to spend the night with, but I was curious about Zara. When she had entered, I figured it might be her first time at a club. She seemed innocent, naïve, sweet, but the way she talked with me with her flustered face and sharp tongue, I knew she was anything but that. I wanted to know her. Especially her body.

Was her innocence an act or was she really a poise, sweet girl?

Only one way to find out.

I walked to the center of the dancing crowd, unbuttoning the top two buttons of my shirt when the DJ lowered the sound of music to announce that New Year's countdown began in a few minutes. I eyed the people, ignoring the glances of women in short skirts and dresses to look for a certain vixen.

It was easy to locate her with a group of frat boys trying to circle her. Clenching my jaw, I was ready to step in, but paused when I noticed the Princess didn't need my help. She stayed calm and collected, talking to them as their faces fell, some turning angry and calling her names as they turned and left her alone.

That's my Princess.

Staking claim already?

Ignoring my thoughts, I walked to her, watching her body move to the rhythm of the music, the light smile on her lips that didn't reach her eyes.

Was she sad? That I rejected her?

I wasn't looking forward to spend the night with an innocent girl who just wanted some experience. I was ready to sleep alone in the bed that night, but the way Zara dared me, wanting to rile me up made me curious about her.

"Hey, pretty Princess," I crooned in her ear, my breath tickling the shell of her ear as she shivered, turning to face me in the small space.

Someone pushed her while dancing, her front body flushing against me as I protectively wrapped my arm around her waist, her wide eyes blinking up at me.

"What are you doing here?" Zara asked, licking her lips and trying to straighten up when people started cheering.

"Tonight's your lucky night, Zara."

"Why's that?"

I smirked, pressing her body against me and noting the way her pulse increased. I trailed my hand down to her lower back and held her close, whispering in her ear,

"Because I am going to fuck you, Princess."

4
HAYDEN

"Because I am going to fuck you, Zara."

When I said that to her, I didn't think I would receive such a response from her. Her brown eyes gleamed at me, they almost seemed hazel with the neon lightening, her palms sliding up to my shoulders and pressing herself closer against me. I took a sharp breath, feeling her soft breasts press on my muscles. She wasn't wearing a bra.

"You will?" She asked with a hopeful smile that reached her eyes. Her beauty spot making it hard for me to meet her eyes, but I managed not to gawk at her full lips.

Some men liked either breasts or ass.

Me? I liked lips.

There was so much you could do with them. Kiss them until they are pink and swollen, make them drool around my fingers, watch them stretch around my girth and hear the sweet sounds of moans and whimpers when you fuck them.

And I, Hayden Knight, was a fucking goner for Zara's lips. They were perfect. Her bottom lip fuller than the top, they even shaped a small heart, and they looked so soft that the sadist in me wanted to ruin her red lipstick and bruise them. Just a little. Then kiss them better.

"Really, Hayden?" Zara asked, as if I had offered everything to her. "Really, you will?"

I liked her pleading. I liked it a lot.

I cupped her cheek, caressing her cheekbone with my thumb, her skin soft and warm. "Beg me again when we are in my suite and I will think about it," I said, my voice husky and low, only audible to her with all the cheering around us.

Her eyes scorched as if the challenge excited her. I knew she wouldn't let me take charge in the bedroom. Zara seemed like a girl who asked for something and it was served on a silver platter for her. She demanded something and received tenfold.

If she wanted me to fuck her, then I would make her beg for it. Beg for my fingers, my mouth, my cock. I would not spoil her, only if she was a good girl and let me take care of her.

The countdown started for the New Year's Eve, her eyes flickering away from me to see the people huddle closer to each other, counting down the numbers.

"Hayden?"

I peered down at her.

"Will you kiss me?"

"Of course, Princess." My eyes softened. "Anything you want me to do."

Anything she wanted me to do? Calm down, Hayden. She is a stranger.

With great lips.

I leaned down, kissing the corner of her lips, feeling her take a deep breath. "This beauty spot of yours…" I whispered, licking its soft skin and kissing it, "It drives me fucking insane, Zara. You have no idea how much I want to see you take me."

"See you… take me?" She asked, and everything about her voice and question portrayed pure innocence.

"3… 2…"

I pulled back a little, noting the flush on her cheeks. Her willingness to sleep with a stranger, getting excited by it.

"Are you a virgin, Princess?"

The lights of the club had dimmed for the countdown, so I could only see her silhouette and feel the warmth of her body. I could feel her increased heartbeat against my shirt.

"Yes, Hayden."

Fuck.

I am going to Hell.

"Happy New Year!"

I threaded my fingers in her hair and claimed her lips, swallowing her gasp of surprise when I wound her closer to me. Claiming her body against me as I kissed her. Sweetly and softly at first, willing her to relax, trailing my hand from her hair to hold the back of her neck. I squeezed slightly, a sweet moan eliciting from her lips.

I lost it.

Parting her lips, I swallowed her sweet moan, lowering my other hand to her back and feeling her warm skin shivering. I tasted the sweet contrast of whiskey and peach, the candy she had stolen from me before. Our kiss turned deeper, more passionate, and I relished in the feeling when she tried to hold on to my shirt, grabbing it with needy fingers, wanting to get rid of it as if she didn't care we were in public.

I pulled away, trying to calm my breathing, and watched her flushed cheeks and swollen wet lips while the entire club was hooting and awing at the fireworks outside.

"Are you okay?" I asked, pulling her closer and protecting her head when people went crazy with their cheers as if it was Fourth of July.

She nodded against my chest, "I want to do it again."

"Needy girl," I chuckled softly and held her hand. "Have some patience. Come on, my hotel is few blocks away."

"Hotel?"

"My suite. Unfortunately, I am a gentleman and I don't plan to fuck you in any alley." I looked over my shoulder, my eyes noting the small smile on her face. I liked her smile. "I want to take care of you, Princess."

"Don't be—" she shook her head, cupping her mouth to stop herself from saying anything.

I narrowed my eyes and asked about it as soon as we were alone. I held her close when we walked out of the club, watching the night sky lit up with fireflies and the sounds of airplane flying over the buildings as people burnt candles from their roofs and cheered.

"Must be some kind of Princess if people are celebrating her birthday more than the New Year."

Zara tensed for a few seconds and cleared her throat. "Yep, must be. Where's your hotel again?"

"*Tsk*, you need to learn patience." I nodded at the grand hotel. "Just over there. But before we go there, hand me your phone."

"What are you doing?"

"Taking our picture," I said as a matter of fact and with a tug on her waist to pull her closer, I clicked our picture. I was looking at the camera, Zara was looking at me with fireworks as our background. My eyes were dilated and her lips were parted in surprise. I handed the phone back to her.

"Send that to your friend or someone you trust with my suite number and hotel address," I ordered her.

Zara blinked at me and back at her phone. "Okay, I will do that."

I watched her send it to two people, getting an instant message from someone, but I didn't want to pry. I had to make a call, so I nodded at her and called the Colonel to ask about the departure. As a Navy Seal Officer, I couldn't talk about the projects, meetings and missions out loud, especially around a stranger, no matter how pretty she was.

Zara

I TRIED NOT TO OGLE AT HAYDEN'S BACK MUSCLES AND FAILED miserably. Even with a shirt, I could notice the way his muscles tensed, his jaw clenching as he talked formally to someone on the phone, the veins on his forearms... I was practically drooling.

I didn't think he would take up my offer to have sex at first, but I was so happy and relieved when he agreed. The way he demanded me to send the address of his hotel suite number and our photo, I knew I could trust him. Zayed had messaged me instantly, promising me to take care of myself, and he would wake up Hayden with a knife to his throat if I wasn't alive or missing the next morning.

Zayed was being silly. Hayden didn't even know I was the Princess of Azmia and the reason why people were hooting and celebrating. It was strange for me. Spending my eighteen birthdays inside the Palace, I never noticed that people of Azmia cared so much about a girl who they had never met or seen.

I touched my lips, remembering the kiss. They still tingled with the memory of being savoured, licked and bitten by Hayden. It was one of the best kisses I had ever had, despite I had only ever kissed one other boy than him. Despite that, it had made my knees buckle and my belly tighten with need. I had never felt that way before.

"There you are! Prancing around the street and all alone."

I turned, sighing at the boys who were trying to flirt with

me in the club. I had threatened them with life in prison, I wasn't lying, and get their eyeballs removed, I wasn't lying about that because if Khalid knew what they were trying to do, he would gladly remove their eyes for me. They had left me alone, but they were back again because they didn't understand the word 'no.'

"You disgust me," I said, crossing my arms. "Didn't your mothers teach you any manners? Frankly, if I was your mother, I would be ashamed to give birth to such waste of space."

One of them got angry, marching towards me and trying to intimidate me, but I stood my ground. I had seen a worse monster than him and got hit by him.

"Who the fuck you are calling that you bitch?"

I picked at my nails. "Apparently, you lack common sense as well. I don't wish to waste my breath on your existence so I will be leaving."

Yes, I would leave but I would call police on them too. They were drunk and annoying, cat calling any women who walked past them.

"Oh, no, you don't!" One of them sneered and grabbed my wrist just as I was about to turn.

I glared at him and the hand that was holding my wrist. I mentally thanked my brothers with all the training for fighting and defending myself as I twisted my hand, his entire arm turning with mine and punched him on the neck until he groaned loudly, dropping on his knees, coughing loudly and cradling his neck.

Others backed away from me. My eyes narrowed at the man wailing because his neck hurt. I hadn't even hit him that hard.

"What happened?" Hayden came by my side. "Are you okay?"

"We are sorry," one of the scared guys said, holding up the guy who was moaning in pain and rushing away from us.

"Did he did that to you?" Hayden stepped closer, his eyes on my wrist which I was covering with my fingers. "Show it to me."

His firm hand closed around my forearm, his hold firm but gentle when he lifted it to see the red finger marks where the guy that held me. His nose flared, his jaw clenching as he caressed the marks with his thumb.

"I-It's nothing," I stammered, the feeling of his thumb on my skin, stroking me like that with an intense look on his face, did something to me. Especially to my lower parts. "I took care of it."

"I could see that," he said, lowering my hand and entwining our fingers. "It was impressive, but don't lean your upper body too much while you are punching someone."

"Noted." I glanced at him when we entered the hotel. The man at the registration bowed at us, the huge golden chandelier casting little golden lights around the marble floor. "Been into a lot of fights?"

God, my brothers would kill me if they ever found out that I was with someone who enjoyed fighting.

But Hayden didn't seem like that. He seemed more… put together. Professional.

Oh, fuck, what if he is a hitman?

"Come on, this is my suite…" he paused at the elevator door. "Unless you have changed your mind?"

"Are you a hitman?" I blurted.

His face changed from confusion to amusement. "I wouldn't necessarily call my job as a hitman."

I pressed myself back on the elevator, my skin prickling with its coldness. Hayden paused the elevator, my breathing increasing as I thought of a way to… *to what?*

Why was I enjoying this? *What the hell is wrong with me?*

He crowded around me, his musky scent, his lean, muscular body closing around me. Trapping me.

"Does it scare you, Princess? That you are about to let a stranger do dirty things to you and you are going to enjoy it even though he has killed people before?" He whispered, his blue eyes so dark that they looked obsidian.

"H-How many people?" I asked, taking a sharp breath when he held my hands over my back, stopping me from turning on my phone. I shivered when his hand tightened around my wrist.

Hayden smiled and leaned down. I closed my eyes, waiting. My teeth pressed into my bottom lip when his warm tongue licked the pulse of my neck, his voice guttural as he whispered, "Too many to count."

I tried to squirm, but his hold stopped me. Red alarms that fired up in my head with those men before didn't fire up when I was with Hayden. It seemed fucked up, but I trusted him.

Why else would he be cautious about my age and make sure someone knew where I was going with him?

"No," I licked my lips and raised my chin, meeting his eyes. "I am not scared of you, Hayden."

5
ZARA

Hayden loosened his grip on my hands and stepped back. He didn't say anything and raised his hand for me to accept it. I looked at him and his calloused strong hand, muscles and veins prominent all over his arm. He was giving me a choice and space to tell him *no* and go back to my home, the Golden Palace.

I didn't want to be alone on my birthday, I wanted him.

I accepted his hand, relieved to see his expression soften when he led me to his suite. He opened the French double doors, inviting me in as I awed at the luxurious interior.

But I was more interested in him.

Hayden had just hung his suit, which I noticed was Tom Ford—the man has good taste, a hitman or not—on the wooden coat hanger and asked me if I wanted something to drink or eat. I shook my head, stepping towards him.

"I want you to kiss me," I said, my tone more of a demand.

His dark eyes slid to me, his index finger tapping my nose. "Good things come to good girls who are patient, Princess," Hayden said, his voice rumbling down my body.

Good girls. Princess. I was going to melt if he kept teasing me with his words.

I pouted and sat on the island, removing my heels, and watched him. His back was towards me as he looked into the fridge. I licked my lips, watching him as his deltoids and muscles move, his shirt stretching over his broad shoulder when he pulled out a water bottle and an icepack from the refrigerator.

"What's that?" I asked, looking at the shiny wrapper inside the freezer.

"It's a popsicle," Hayden answered, turning towards me. His eyes narrowed to my clattered heels.

"You have a sweet tooth," I smiled. "I want to eat it, can I?"

"No, you can't," he said, closing the fridge and pointed at my shoes. "Not until you keep these heels by the door and be nice. Then I might let you have it."

"Are you serious?" I asked, crossing my arms.

"Very serious, Zara," he said, holding my hand and putting icepack on the redness those fingerprints had left. "Be a good girl and put those shoes where they belong. I don't like mess."

"It doesn't hurt," I said, my voice fueled with annoyance because I didn't understand how can someone be caring yet so... demanding at the same time.

"Still, let me. I didn't like the way he held you."

I watched his handsome face and bit my lip when he stepped back, pointing to my heels again. From what I knew, he liked to be in control and everything in place. Put together. Almost perfect.

I wanted to tease him and ruffle his feathers.

Shrugging my shoulders, I uncapped the bottle and said to him, "If it bothers you so much, you do it."

I kept my eyes on him as I drank water, licking my lips and swaying my legs, trying to hide my smile.

Hayden crossed his arms and leaned back on the marble counter. "Stop being a fucking brat, Zara, and put those heels away. Don't make me repeat."

My thighs clenched, and blood pounded in my ears.

"Or what?"

He tilted his head. "Or I will spank your ass until I bruise it and you won't be able to sit properly for two weeks."

Spank my ass? My cheeks reddened. No one had ever talked to me or address me like that before.

"Maybe… I'd like that," I heard myself say, surprising myself.

Since when did I enjoy being spanked? Since I met Hayden.

"Zara," he said in a warning deeper tone that scared for a moment. *Okay, he is not kidding about it.*

I grumbled, "Fine, fine, I am doing it." I slid down the island and picked up my shoes, stomping towards the double doors. "Don't need to act like a fucking dad," I said and kept them near his polished dark shoes.

I gasped when I felt him behind me, pushing me against the door, his face close to me. "Watch that pretty little mouth of yours before I fuck it, Princess," he threatened, pressing his body against me so that I could feel every hard muscle on his toned chest.

Biting my lip, I squirmed, wanting to feel him more and touch him. His eyes read my emotion, the neediness in my eyes and body, how I was begging to be touched by him.

"What do you want, Princess?" Hayden asked, his voice softer.

"I want you to hurt me," I breathed, staring into his eyes. They were a dark, sexy shade of blue. They compelled me to do terrible, dirty things to him and for him. Things I had never imagined I would ever want, but… there was something about him that made me want to be just Zara.

Not the Princess who had her own castle, who ate with a golden spoon every day, who was spoiled rotten from the day she was born.

No. With him, I just wanted to be Zara, a woman who wanted to be pleased and do the pleasing.

"Where do you want me to hurt you, Princess?" Hayden asked, a hint of a smirk on his lips as his eyes gleamed with unknown emotion.

My lips parted, but no words came out. *He wants me to make the first move.* He wanted to make sure I wanted *this* just as much as he wanted it, even though I was ten years younger than him.

The thought of this man, this handsome, sexy man wanting to hurt me because I told him to, scared and excited me.

It was thrilling.

"Here." I placed his calloused hands on my breasts, still covered in the satin fabric of the beige dress. His eyes darkened, his face becoming sharper when he clenched his jaw. I licked my lips, sliding his hands to my waist. *Lower.* "Everywhere."

His nose flared, pulling his hands away from my touch as he glared at me. I took a sharp breath when he pressed closer, my back against the closed doors of his hotel suite.

"Don't mock me, Princess. I will bruise your lips, kissing them, fucking them until you cry," he rumbled, swiping his thumb over my bottom lip. His hand lowered to my neck, wrapping it around my throat. My eyes widened when he pressed lightly, my pulse getting slower as anticipation and pleasure burned through my core. "I will choke your slender neck. Just. Like. *This*. Making you hold your breath until you cum for me."

I gasped, tears blurring my vision when he lowered his hand to hold my breasts. I blinked at him, at the sight of his large palms holding me roughly.

No one has ever touched me like this before. As if they were claiming me with their touch, their words.

I never wanted him to stop.

"You like this, Princess?" He asked, his voice gruff with desire. He squeezed my breasts until a whimper tore out of my lips. As if satisfied with my answer, his hands lowered to my thighs, yanking the hem of my dress over my hips and between my legs.

I held my breath, staring at him through my half-lidded eyes, waiting for him to be rough with me.

But he didn't.

Hayden ran a finger against my drenched underwear, from my slit to the pleasure nub, rolling the pad of his finger around it. He leaned closer, his musky scent wafting in my nose as he whispered, "I will spank you *right here*, Princess. Get your clit red and swollen before I stretch your pretty little cunt with my thick cock. I will fuck you hard and rough and won't stop until you scream. You know why?"

"W-why?"

He pulled back, trailing his finger over the side of my cheek, the same finger he had between my legs. I could smell my feminine musk on it. My inner thighs clenched, wanting to rub against something. Anything.

"Because you *begged* me to hurt you, Princess."

I gasped when his fingers clenched around my hair, tugging them back and pulling me closer. I felt the hardness of his length against my legs and I knew he wasn't kidding about stretching me.

"You can leave right now, Zara, or stay here and allow me to hurt you."

I didn't even give it another thought.

"I want to stay."

He tugged my hair harder until it hurt. His ocean eyes

narrowing on my face, "Then for this night you belong to me."

The dominating tone made something click inside of me. As if that was what I wanted for the longest time after being caged and coddled as a Princess. I could have whatever I wanted, but not... *this. This pleasure, this need of getting hurt through pleasure, because who would ever hurt the Princess of Azmia?* No one but him. *Hayden.*

He didn't know I was a Princess.

He *wanted* to please me. Hurt me.

I wanted him to please me. *Hurt me.*

My stomach dipped as if I knew the answer even before he had asked me. I felt my pussy moisten when I sealed my fate and said, "My answer is yes, Hayden."

His hold on my hair loosened, but he didn't let me go. No, I didn't think he would let me go until next morning. I didn't think I would complain even if tied me up on his bed and held me captive.

Bringing his face closer, he crooned, "Such a pretty Princess." He smiled and there was nothing sweet about it when he whispered, "I'm going to enjoy breaking you."

Breaking me? He wanted to break me?

I licked my lips, not understanding why such words from him made me wet. There was definitely something wrong with me.

His lips closed around mine, and despite his tone and filthy words, the kiss was sweet. Caring. His large hands cupped my face, removing the diamond pins from my hair and running his hand through my hair. I relaxed and melted in his arms, humming and gasping into his sweet kiss when he held me up in his arms.

I didn't realise we were in the master bedroom until he sat on the edge of the bed with me straddling his lap. My cheeks burned, and I wanted to hide my face when we pulled away.

"You're so beautiful." Hayden gazed at me as if he was in awe. His fingers tucking a strand of hair over my ear. "Like an angel."

If it was possible, I flushed more, looking around his room because I couldn't handle his sincere look.

"What is that?" I gasped, looking at the corner of the room, walking towards it and touching it.

"That's my uniform."

I gaped at him and the… uniform. The white soft fabric full with medals and the golden eagle trident.

"You're in Navy?" I asked, trying to hide my nervousness. I was in a room with a stranger who was a soldier of another nation. If Zayed was here, he would laugh at me.

"Yes," Hayden's voice was much closer, his warm breath caressing my neck, his hands on my waist. "I am a Navy Seal Officer."

Even better. I thought sarcastically.

I swallowed the lump in my throat and realized what he meant by killing people. "You've killed people because you are a soldier?" I asked, my voice soft as I dropped my hand from his uniform and turned around.

He nodded. His eyes had a lost look in them. The same look that I had seen in my brother Khalid's eyes when he remembered the night he had killed our father.

I held Hayden's hand and smiled up at him. "I am glad you are not a hitman, Hayden." Leaning up on my toes, I kissed the corner of his lips, feeling the graze of his stubble.

"Hm," he laid me down on the bed. The mattress dipped when he hovered above me. "You should be, Princess. Now tell me, what have you done before?"

I felt parched when he leaned back on his heels, unbuttoning his shirt. His light tan was beautiful, his muscles tensing and flexing when he unbuttoned the last button and kept it on while my eyes drank over the marvelous sight of his toned abs.

Hayden looked… delicious. With his sandy brown hair, his lean muscular frame, and those piercing eyes pinned on me, I would die of overheating.

"I asked you something, Zara."

It took me a while to clear the hazy lust fog Hayden had put me under as I blinked at his face. "Huh?"

He smirked, knowing full well the reason behind my distraction. His hands glided over my legs, caressing them mindlessly, toying with the golden diamond chain on my thigh. Should I tell him it was worth over a million dollars with real diamonds? *Nope, probably not the right time.*

"You told me you are a virgin. I want to know what you have done so far."

"*Oh,*" I bit my lip and felt shy. He seemed so experienced compared to me, yet wanted me to tell him what I had done.

Sensing my nervousness, he kissed my knee and said softly, "I want to know so that I can take care of you, Princess. Be gentle and not hurt you."

I frowned at him and leaned up on my elbows, "But I don't want you to be gentle."

Hayden chuckled, pinching my thigh. "I know, you dirty girl. But I don't want to hurt you in a way that causes emotional or physical damage."

I didn't understand what he was talking about, but I trusted him to take care of me.

I sat up on the bed and looked at my lap. "I have kissed and almost ended up having sex… but I stopped."

"You said he was your age, right?" Hayden asked, putting a finger on my chin and making me look at him.

I nodded. A stable boy, the same person I had kissed.

"Can I ask why you stopped?"

I fumbled with my dress and answered quickly, "Because it hurt."

His hand froze on my calf as he asked quietly, "Did he hurt you?"

I glanced at his face, at the anger in his eyes, and shook my hand. "Oh, god, no. *No*. Not like that. I… I stopped because it hurt during… uh, um, penetration."

He sighed and nodded at me. "He must have skipped foreplay. Foolish boy."

"Is that all you ever did?"

I nodded. "I want to try everything."

He raised his brow, "*Everything?*"

"Yes."

"Good girl. Remove your dress and get naked."

6
HAYDEN

Her hazel eyes widened, her fingers fumbling with the straps and the zipper. Her nervousness was a physical living thing in the room, especially since she had seen my uniform. When other women noticed that or my military pendant, they wanted to climb me on the spot.

But not Zara. She had frozen as if sleeping with a Navy Seal Officer was the last thing she wanted.

I wanted to know why. I would have thought she was a spy if it wasn't for her nervousness and the honesty and sincerity behind her words. No, she couldn't be a spy even if she tried. She was sweet and innocent.

And I wanted to taint her.

"Come here." I pulled her onto my lap, claiming her full lips and lowering the zipper of her dress. I groaned in her mouth at the feel of her warm skin, moving my palm lower on her back and removing the straps of her dress.

Her hips rocked as if her body was excited for what was coming next. I tried to calm myself down, but Zara must have felt the bulge and gasped, trying to grind on it.

I let her play with me, her fingers in my hair, soft hands sliding from my neck to clutch my shoulder. Her expression was of pure lust and innocence. She wanted more, but needed my help.

Poor thing.

"Need my help, Princess?"

She nodded, releasing her bottom lip from her teeth. "Please."

"Such a needy slut, hm?" I whispered, noting her reaction to my words. Her eyes widened, her thighs clenching as she stared at me with parted lips.

I caressed her waist, her expensive dress rumpled on her body. "How did you feel about that, Zara?"

"About?"

"Being called a slut, Princess," I said, enjoying the way she gasped when I pulled her on top of my hardened member, moving her hips with my hands. I felt her wet underwear on my pants, my fingers digging into her skin.

Zara murmured something, and I didn't hear it.

"Say it louder, Princess. Yes or no?"

Her cheeks, nose and ears were flushed, but she covered her face with her hands, making me stop my movements and smile at her. She was so fucking adorable.

"I liked it," she whispered, her voice muffled.

I gently pried her hands away. "There's nothing wrong about enjoying being called names during intimate moments. Some like being called sweet things and some like—"

"Degrading things?"

I stroked her cheekbone. "You can tell me to stop, Princess, and I will."

Zara closed her eyes, and I let her think about it, caressing her cheeks and her body. With a deep breath, she opened her eyes and said, "I want to try it."

I smiled, giving her a small kiss on her lips. "That's my good girl."

Her cheeks flushed, and she started rocking her hips on me, her eyes getting heavy lidded. Fucking hell. I was getting harder and harder by the minutes, watching her move over me, rubbing herself shamelessly on my bulge.

Holding the hem of her dress, I tugged it upwards, removing it. I swore at the sight of her naked body, her dark waves falling around her as her cheeks turned ten shades redder. I moved her hair back to look at her. Her perky breasts heaving up and down, her pink nipples poking towards me. I ran my hand down her flat stomach, watching her suck in a sharp breath towards the small white lace covering her pussy.

I lightly traced the lace with the pad of my index finger, enjoying the way she squirmed on my lap, clenching and grinding herself on me.

She pleaded, "Hayden."

I flickered my eyes to her face. The neediness and lust in her eyes was prominent. "What do you want, Princess?" I asked, my voice guttural when she humped me through her underwear, making me twitch in my pants. I wanted to unzip and free myself, move her thong to the side and slide inside her in one thrust.

"I want... *more*," she whispered in a breathy voice.

I nodded, understanding what she wanted, and rubbed my thumb on her bottom lip, clenching my jaw when she parted her lips, sucking it in her mouth.

"Have you ever sucked a cock before, Princess?" I said, pulling out my thumb from her lips, caressing her needy little body. I loved touching her soft skin that smelt like sweet but exotic perfume. I loved how responsive she was to each little touch.

"No…" she trailed, her eyes lowering to see the prominent hard-on in my pants, and licked her lips.

"Do you want to?"

Her wide eyes met mine as she nodded slowly, "But I… haven't…"

I hushed her, petting her hair and kissing her lips softly. "You say the word red whenever you want to stop, okay?"

Zara looked confused but nodded, frowning when I stood up, leaving her on the bed with her drenched underwear. The golden chain on her thigh as I ran my finger through it.

"Come and stand here for me, Princess," I said, my voice a little demanding to test her. She looked at me and slowly made her way to the centre of the room where I was standing and stood across from me, almost naked. I could see the way it affected her, her breathing becoming shallow, her eyes glazing with lust, licking her lips as I kept my eyes on her face, her legs squirming with anticipation.

The surrounding air became thick with sexual tension and a waft of feminine arousal. She was as aroused as I was, if not more judging by the way she eyed my hands when I removed my belt from my pants.

"What do you say when you feel uncomfortable, Princess?"

"Red."

"That's my sweet little slut."

Zara

HEARING HIM ADDRESS ME AS A GOOD GIRL AND PRINCESS DID something to me. But hearing him call me slut made me want to do terrible, dirty things that I had never imagined.

Maybe it was because I was a Princess of one of the most

powerful countries in Middle East. Growing up, no one had ever dared me to talk back to me except Zayed. Even then, it was a brotherly teasing. Not even my own brothers argued with me and spoilt me because of how our father had treated us.

I, Zara Al Latif, Princess of Azmia, was extremely turned on when Hayden Knight called me his sweet little slut.

He stepped closer, my hands curling into fists as I tried not to wrap myself around his hot body, kiss him and tell him everything else could wait, but I needed him inside me at that moment. But he had other things in his mind.

I took a shaky breath when he asked me to raise my hair from my nape. His eyes drifted lower when I did. I blushed when he licked his lips because it made my breasts arch up higher. I had never been naked in front of a man before, a man like Hayden Knight. It was odd that he was still wearing his unbuttoned shirt and pants while I was naked except for my underwear. But I didn't mind the tease and anticipation. I knew he would do everything to please me and him.

My eyes widened when he wrapped his leather belt around my neck, telling me to let my hair down as he swiftly moved it through its buckle and tugged slowly. My feet moved on its own at the small pull on my neck, my hands landing on his chest for support.

Holy shit.

"Hm, I think you like this. Being collared and leashed, don't you, Princess?" Hayden crooned in my ear, wrapping his hand around the belt and pulling it down in a way that my knees buckled and I had to kneel but keep looking at him. My walls clenched as I nodded up at him, too humiliated, embarrassed, and aroused to say anything.

He gave me a small, sexy smile. "I knew you would."

I felt too hot under his gaze, too small and vulnerable. My eyes averted to the boner in his pants, at the size of him and looked away. That was my mistake. I gasped when he tugged on the belt, my neck craning up at him.

"Don't look away from me, Princess." His voice was soft, but it was laced with a warning.

I nodded.

"Be a good girl and stay here. I will be right back."

I frowned, watching him walk out of the door, eyeing his ass and blushing furiously. I looked down at myself, kneeling on the marble floor, naked and turned on with a belt cinched around my neck that lay between my breasts, its leather hot and warm on my skin.

My clit was throbbing, and I wanted to touch myself. I knew how to do it and it brought me pleasure, but I never could orgasm just from touching myself and I was too scared to use my fingers inside me. But the thought of Hayden crooning sweet and dirty words in my ear, hovering above me and sliding himself inside me brought me immense pleasure. I wanted to have sex with him. I couldn't *wait* to have sex with him.

"You are such a pretty sight, Zara." My head snapped towards Hayden who was leaning on the door frame, watching me with a small smile.

I looked at his handsome face, his tousled hair, the glimpses of his abs from his shirt and said, "So are you."

He chuckled lightly, my stomach tightening into a coil hearing his soft husky laugh. It was the most arousing thing I had ever heard from him. Yet.

"You wanted to eat this popsicle, right?" He asked, showing me the white popsicle that was already melting from the top.

"Yes," I answered with a confused face. "Do you want me to eat this right now?"

I mean, if watching a naked woman eat an ice cream in front of him did it for him, then I am okay with it.

Hayden shook his head. "It's not for you to eat, sweetheart."

Holding the end of the belt again, he pulled me to the corner of the room as I crawled after him, biting my lip. *Fuck.* Another thing to add to 'I didn't know I enjoyed this until I tried it' list. He stood near the bed, plopping a pillow on the ground, and asked me to kneel on the pillow.

"This is your first time, so I don't want your knees to hurt. Does that feel good?" He asked, raising his brow and caressing my cheek.

"Better," I nodded, not knowing my knees were hurting until I knelt on the soft pillow.

"Good," he pulled on the make-shift leash and pointed at the mirror. "Now see how beautiful you look being my princess slut."

I shivered at my reflection and his words. I looked nothing like the Princess from a couple of hours ago. My dark hair fell over my shoulder, the tips of my breasts were flushed and there was a distinct gleam in my eyes. I met his blue eyes as he stood across from me, tall and looming over my body. I had never met anyone who excluded sexual energy like he did. His demeanour, his words, his eyes, his body, everything about him, made me want to turn into a puddle and do everything he wanted me to do.

That scared me.

"Open your mouth, Princess," he said, my eyes moving away from the mirror.

Something cold dripped on my bottom lip and I licked it, humming at the sweet taste of vanilla. My eyes widened when I saw it was the popsicle.

"You are going to suck this for me, Princess. I am going to make you practice on this popsicle and if you behave like a good girl, I will reward you, *hm?*"

I nodded blindly, looking at the popsicle. It was tapered at the front and straight from there, but it was girthy. I shifted on my knees, wondering why the hell a popsicle was making me hot.

It wasn't popsicle thought, it was *him*. Hayden. Turning the innocent sweet ice cream into such a filthy task for me to follow.

"Don't bite it off. And if you want to stop, tap my thigh." I nodded eagerly, licking my lips when he leaned it closer against my mouth. "Part your lips, Princess. Let me teach you how to suck a cock."

7
ZARA

Meeting his glittering blue eyes, I parted my lips and waited for him. The coldness was the first thing that I noticed, and the sweet taste of vanilla seeping into my mouth, stretching my lips. I sucked on it instinctively, loving the way it melted on my tongue. Pulling away, I licked my lips and looking at Hayden's lust fuelled eyes, I dipped closer and licked the popsicle. I imagined how he would feel on my tongue, in my mouth... inside me.

"Just like that, Princess," he praised, tugging on the leash as he pushed the popsicle inside my mouth deeper and deeper.

My hands found purchase on his thighs, trying to support myself as I kept sucking. I hummed when it melted and dripped on my breast. Its coolness tingling against my nipple.

Hearing Hayden curse in his deep voice made me look at him. His eyes were half-lidded, cheeks flushed and jaw clenched as if seeing me like that bothered him, turned him on. I dug my fingers into his thigh, watching his eyes widen a little when I thought of every way I could please him more. I pulled back, swirled my tongue around the melted ice cream, licking its length, wishing it was him, sucking on its tip and stroking his thighs, feeling the muscles of his legs tense.

His nose flared and pulled on the leash, sliding the cold ice cream deeper inside my mouth. I gagged, tears gleaming in my eyes.

"Don't tease me, Princess," he warned, not moving an inch. "Look at me and relax your throat."

I whimpered, tapping his thigh at the uncomfortable feeling. He pulled it back instantly. He knelt in front of me and removed the belt from my neck and cupped my cheeks.

"Are you okay, Zara?" He asked, wiping the tear. "Did it hurt?"

I licked my lips and answered, "It felt… uncomfortable."

"It's okay, Princess, you did so well," Hayden whispered, kissing my forehead and helping me up.

"But I wanted…"

He raised his brow, waiting for me to finish.

My eyes flickered at the reflection of both of us in the mirror. How different I looked. With my pink, swollen lips and white vanilla melted on my nipples.

I didn't blue or stutter when I said to him, "I wanted to do more. Sucking the popsicle and then… *you*."

His eyes darkened, his eyes lowering to my neck. I shivered when he grazed his fingers on my neck where his belt was moments ago. "Isn't your throat sore?"

I shook my head. "Please?"

Narrowing his eyes at me, he hummed, asking me to sit on the bed with my back against the headboard. It felt more comfortable than being on my knees.

"Keep your legs spread," Hayden ordered, his eyes blazing with hunger when I did. I jumped, clenching my legs when he spanked my inner thigh. "Wider, slut."

Oh God. That voice again.

I spread my legs wider, gasping when he slid his finger over my underwear at the centre of my sex. "Tap my thigh if you want to stop, okay?" He asked, his voice stern.

"Okay," I nodded, my voice a little breathy.

I hummed when he asked me to lick the popsicle before sliding it between my lips, my eyes meeting his, my entire body scorching under his gleaming blue eyes. It was as if he was imagining that it was his cock that I was sucking on. I burned more at the idea.

His fingers pressed over my clit, making me jump at the shiver of pleasure. A muffled whimper tore out of me when he spanked my pussy through my underwear.

"Who told you to stop sucking?" Hayden glared at me. "Keep using that pretty mouth and keep me pleased."

His fingers brushed over my burning sex. Oddly, more turned on after that little spank. Instead of replying, I did what he asked, the popsicle half of its size than before, so it was comfortable when he slid it deeper, his eyes on my face with his fingers rubbing me teasingly.

I bucked my hips towards his hand and groaned, squeezing my eyes shut when he spanked me again. My clit throbbed to be touched when he repeated his actions.

"Don't be greedy, Princess," he crooned, kissing my thigh. "Greedy girls don't get fucked."

He... was so filthy. His words. I would never have thought that he was a Navy Seal with his dirty words. But feeling like a normal person, a normal girl around him, made me wet. If he had known that I was a Princess of Azmia, he would never dare to call me his slut. But I enjoyed the play.

Hayden pulled my thong to the side, my legs trying to close because I felt incredibly shy, but he stopped, holding my thigh and gazing at my sex as if it was a work of art.

"Such a pretty pussy my Princess slut has," He whispered softly, sliding his index finger over my slicked folds as I moaned around the popsicle that he had pressed against my tongue. "So pink, already dripping wet and clenching at nothing."

He looked at me, licking his glistening finger and groaning at the taste of me. I squirmed and whimpered, his words, his actions, Hayden himself melting me inside out. I had never wanted someone so badly. I *never* wanted something so badly.

"You are begging for my mouth, my fingers, my cock, aren't you, Princess?" He teased me, nipping at my earlobe as cold ice cream dripped over my breasts, his hands holding me in place against the headboard. His fingers slowly rubbed over the clit, both of our eyes trained on his powerful hand as he achingly rolled his digit around my pleasure nub.

Hayden

"So pretty all wide and open for me to use, *hm*," I whispered, my eyes roving over Zara, her flushed pussy as I teased her, keeping her on the edge and watching her suck greedily on the ice cream.

She was so fucking hot that I might just come inside my pants without her touching me at all.

Remembering the reaction of her body after being spanked, I lifted my palm and spanked her right on her clit with just a little pressure. Her entire body reacted, arching up as she groaned and clapped her mouth shut with her wide eyes.

I stopped my actions, concerned if I accidentally hurt her and looked at her.

Then I saw her mouth move, her flushed face looking away, and chuckled. "You bit the popsicle, didn't you?" I asked, moving her hair behind her ear as she nodded shyly.

"It's okay, Princess," I said, teasing her. "But please don't bite my dick or I'd have to punish you."

I removed my shirt, her eyes darkening as they roved over my muscular figure and stopping on my side. Her fingers grazed the scar on my abdomen.

I pinned her hands above her head and answered, "I got this after being stabbed twice... they were a rough couple of weeks."

Her throat moved as she licked her lips. "Did it hurt a lot?" Her voice was a lot smoother than before, a little sultry than before. It did something to me.

"Yes, it did. I remember crying a little when the doctor removed the jagged knife from my body." I cringed at the memories.

"Jagged knife?"

"Yes, the piece of shit stabbed me twice and left it like that." I said, not discussing further about how I had killed him. "As much as I would like to tell you how I overpowered him, I don't want to talk about it when you are naked and soaking for me, Princess."

Zara licked her lips and arched her body towards me. "I want to kiss you," she murmured, gazing at my lips, trying to wriggle free of my hold.

Instead of letting her go, I pressed myself against her, spreading her legs with my leg and feeling the softness of breasts on my chest.

"You know how to beg, Princess," I purred in her ear, kissing her beating pulse on her neck, biting the pale skin. I wanted to mark her because one night with such a vixen like her wouldn't be enough. It would never be enough. I was selfish and wanted more of her. All of her if I could.

So I sucked the sensitive skin in my mouth, licking it until she made the sweetest needy sounds from her full lips. "Please, please, please, Hayden. Kiss me," she begged, her eyes pleading me while her heated sex rubbed against my thigh wanting some friction.

Humming, I kissed down to the valley between her tits and sucked one nipple into my mouth. I groaned at the sweet taste of vanilla, remembering how she had made a mess while sucking on a popsicle. I gave another thrust, biting and licking the other nipple until they were both red.

I pulled back, proud of myself to see the pink hue of hickies forming on her neck and breasts. Her brown eyes looked like molten gold in the dim light of the suite, her full lips whining and pouting at me as she squirmed on her back, wanting me to kiss her. How could such a sexual being be a virgin was still a mystery to me? But as fucking bad as it sounds, I was glad that she was choosing to have sex with me.

I cupped her throat, having her attention on my face when I slowly bucked my hips against her, making her feel how hard she had made me. Her lips parted and her eyes widened. My cock throbbed at the sight.

"Will you let me fuck your pretty face if I kiss you, Princess?" I asked, fondling her breast and pinching the nipple while slowly teasing her, grinding into her.

I knew if I removed my pants and boxers, she would crawl and do it without asking me to. But there was something sexy about the way an innocent yet sexual being like her would say those words to me. I found her consent, the way she would accept to suck my cock, extremely erotic.

"Yes," Zara nodded, her raven hair fawned on the silk pillows. "Use me as you want, but please touch me, *kiss me*, Hayden."

Her sweet words were my undoing. I wanted to own her, fuck her and take her back with me to the states.

Ignoring those scary thoughts, I pressed my lips against hers, sighing when she moaned against my mouth. Her lips, her tongue, her mouth, everything tasted sweet like vanilla. I relished in the coldness of her mouth from the popsicle, deepening our kiss.

I let go of her hands to cradle her small frame in my arms, pressing her back into the mattress. She gasped when I gave a small thrust against her pussy, my stiffened member pressing against the confines of my pants, wanting me to tuck her soaked underwear to the side and slide in.

Panting, I pulled away first, watching her frown at my retreat. Yes, she was definitely very needy. Before I could say anything, she was on her knees, kissing down my neck, my collarbone. Her cold fingers trailed over my shoulders, my back, my abs, as if she couldn't get enough of me. Just like I couldn't get enough of her.

"Easy there, tiger," I hissed, holding her by her hair when she licked and bit my nipple.

Her eyes twinkled with mischief when she gave it one more lick before her cold lips trailed down to my scar. I took a sharp breath when she kissed it softly.

Swallowing the lump in my throat, I said, "Unbutton my pants and pull me out, Zara."

Blinking up at me, she nodded, her fingers fumbling with the button and gently lowering the zipper. I watched her long lashes, her slope of her button nose and her pouty lips as she worked. I hadn't lied when I had called her beautiful. She looked like an angel with her elfin face and halo of dark hair. I was going to taint—I had already tainted the pretty angel.

Her fingers lowered my dark boxers and gasped softly when my cock sprang free of its confinement. The look on her face... of shock and surprise and awe made me twitch.

"It moved!" Zara said with wide eyes, looking up at me expectantly.

This girl...

8
ZARA

I didn't know dicks could move on their own, so when I saw the little twitch on Hayden's cock, I was extremely surprised.

He let out a throaty chuckle that had me awing at him again. It was truly illegal to have so many pretty genes in one human being. I had heard from Safiya that male gentile couldn't be pretty, some outright scary. So, I had prepared for my reaction, but Hayden's cock was, dare I say, beautiful. It was clean shaven, longer than the average with enough girth that I knew I would feel him everywhere when he'd fuck me. The shaft lined with veins, his balls heavy, and the tip was leaking with glistening pre-cum that had me licking my lips.

"If you keep looking at me like that, Princess, I will cum all over your face," Hayden whispered, his voice deeper and sexier than before.

I met his blue eyes and asked, "T-teach me how to touch you, please you."

He swore, caressing my cheek, "Such a good little slut, my Princess."

My pussy clenched hearing his dirty words as I leaned into his calloused palm. He gave me a small smile and took my hand, wrapping my fingers around his shaft, feeling the warm, velvety skin. He showed me how to move my hand, but I couldn't fit my fingers around his girth and that made my breath shaky.

"Don't squeeze too hard or too softly. *Fuck*—yes, just like that, Princess," he groaned when I experimentally squeezed him and moved my hand back and forth. He was hard and soft at the same time. I wanted to touch him more.

Shuffling closer to him, I licked the pre-cum from the head, humming at the sweet, tangy taste. He elicited a throaty groan that had me blinking up at him. His eyes were half-lidded as he watched me, biting his lip with his hand lightly holding my hair. Meeting his dark blue eyes, I licked the tip again and took him in my mouth, sucking on it.

"Fuck," he moaned, his hold tightening in my hair as he pulled me closer. "Do that again, Princess."

The sound of his moans was all the encouragement I needed as I kept moving my hand over his length while sucking, licking, and swirling my tongue around his head. I supported myself with my hand on his thigh, feeling him clench his muscles as he shivered.

I had never felt more powerful and aroused knowing I was the reason behind his throaty groans, curses, and his shaking body.

"That's my sweet slut," he whispered, gazing at me as I tried to take him deeper in my mouth, remembering how he had taught me to relax my throat and keep breathing with the popsicle. "Look in the mirror, Princess. Look how fucking beautiful you look, letting me fuck your mouth like this."

I whimpered when he slid deeper, drool seeping out of me as

he made me look at the reflection in the mirror right across the bed. He was on his knees, hair disheveled, shadows falling over his abs with his cock inside my mouth. I moaned, clenching myself when I saw I was almost on my fours, grabbing his thigh with my lips stretched around him and a hazy look on my face.

I didn't look like the Zara I knew.

"You don't look like a Princess, do you?" Hayden whispered as if he read my mind. He tugged at my hair and pulled out of me, a string of saliva following me. Hayden made me look at him as I gasped for breath.

"Answer me." His hold on my hair tightened. "What do you see in the mirror?"

"I don't look like a Princess," I said in a small voice.

I moaned when he smacked my ass, the sound ringing in my ear as my skin scorched with tingles making me wet.

"Then what do you look like, Zara?" He said in my ear, his breath warm and teasing. "Look in the mirror and answer me."

The girl in the mirror had her long hair tousled as if she had just woken up, but I knew it wasn't the real reason. Her hair was like that because it was grabbed, tugged, and pulled. Her lips were pink and swollen, her cheeks flushed and glowing with a hazy look in her dark eyes that I had never seen before. Her pale neck and breasts were peppered with small hickies, as if someone had marked her roughly. And she had loved every part of it.

The scent of our musky arousal was wafting in the air. I met his piercing blue eyes that were looking at me as if I was someone special to him. Someone he could play with, call names, yet care for. It made me shiver.

"Answer me," he said again, his voice low and smoky. "I won't ask again. What do you see in the mirror? What do you look like?"

"I look like a slut," I said and breathed out, turning to look at him. "Your slut, Hayden."

He claimed my lips in a kiss, pulling me and holding me close to him as he made me breathless with his lips. "That's right," he whispered between the kiss, "You are my slut, Princess."

I moaned in agreement, kissing him again, but he pulled me down, holding himself against my lips. I parted my lips for him and whimpered around his girth.

"Open wider, come on," he encouraged me in his smoky, deep voice. "I know you can do better, Princess."

I nodded, wanting to do better and please him more. Taking a deep breath, I relaxed my throat, making my jaw click when he slid deeper inside me.

"That's my good Princess," Hayden breathed and held my hair with his both hands, slowly moving inside my mouth until I was deep throating him, tears blurring my vision.

I whimpered, my fingers digging in his thigh, remembering to tap it if I wanted to stop it. Despite it being uncomfortable, the sounds he made encouraged me to trust him and let him do whatever he wished.

Slowly, he pulled out, allowing me to breathe a little. "I am going to fuck your pretty face as I promised, Princess," he said, wiping a tear from the corner of my eyes.

I nodded, sucking on his tip when he slid inside me once more. I kept my throat relaxed and breathed through my nose when he moved back and forth inside my mouth, increasing his pace just as his breathing increased.

Moaning, I squeezed my eyes shut when I felt myself gagging, his shaft and length too big for me.

"Oh, is it too much, Princess? You are already gagging, *hm?*" Hayden taunted me, his voice hoarse. "But this is what you wanted, isn't it, my innocent slut? You begged me to use you and fuck your throat like this." I moaned, tears spilling out of my eyes when I blinked at his face.

His jaw was clenched when he slid inside my mouth, holding me there. "Seeing you cry on my cock with your pretty lips stretched like this pleases me a lot. So be a good slut and gag until I am satisfied, Princess."

My brain stopped working as I nodded, letting him use me however he wished. I had never felt the intense rush to make someone orgasm like I did with Hayden, despite my lack of experience. I *wanted* to be his good slut, his good Princess and make him cum.

"So. *Fucking*. Pretty," Hayden groaned, fucking my mouth with each thrust. His hand cupped my face, making me flicker my eyes at his flushed face, his eyes pinning me to my place.

I gasped and frowned at him when he pulled out, his dick throbbing. He didn't let me speak and raised my mouth to kiss me. I gave in immediately, kissing him back.

"I can't wait to fuck your little virgin cunt, Princess," Hayden whispered, stroking himself and straightened up. I stared in awe at his hand wrapped around himself.

"Open your mouth and pull out your tongue for me," he ordered as I kept watching him.

My cheeks burned with embarrassment and arousal as I pulled out my tongue, looking from his blue eyes to his cock. His legs were trembling, his abs clenched as his hips jerked with a low groan. My eyes widened and squeezed shut when a coat of thick cum landed on my lips, my tongue, and inside my mouth.

I quickly swallowed it, looking at him through my half-lidded eyes as he petted my hair. He sighed when I leaned closer and licked his hand and his dick clean, humming at the taste of him.

"Show me," he whispered, gazing at my lips when I licked them clean.

I parted my lips, showing him my empty mouth.

Hayden hummed, "Good girl."

I sighed in his arms when he pulled me over his body, stroking my back with my legs straddling his hips.

"How do you feel, Princess?" He asked, cupping my right cheek and rubbing my left cheek with his shirt.

I blushed, realising that he was cleaning his own cum from my cheek. I slid my hand over his muscles and said truthfully, "Very very horny." Meeting his clear blue eyes, I said, "I want you to fuck me right now, Hayden."

"Needy brat." He let out a soft chuckle and pinched my nipple, enjoying the way I moaned. "I meant emotionally, Zara. I want to know if I said anything that hurt you."

"Hurt me?"

"I addressed you as a slut and made you accept it. Are you having second thoughts about it? Do you want to slap me? Cry?"

His hand gliding on my back was really distracting, but his eyes were concerned, so I knew he was serious about it.

I shook my head. "I don't feel like crying or slapping you. I..." I blushed and looked at his abs as I answered, "I liked it."

"Don't look away when we are talking," he ordered, cupping my face. His eyes softened as he shook his head at me, "*Tsk*, look at you. An innocent virgin who is into degradation kink."

My cheeks warmed with blood as I squirmed on his lap. "Stop teasing me and touch me, Hayden."

"I won't hold back, Princess."

"I don't want you to."

9
ZARA

His pupils dilated hearing my words and rolled me on my back. I bit my lip when he spread my legs, his large hands sliding over my legs. Leaning down, he kissed me sweetly, teasing me until I was grinding on his bulge. He lowered his kisses on my neck, cupping and fondling my breasts while I writhed underneath him.

"Hayden," I whined, threading my fingers through his soft, thick hair.

He hummed, kissing down my stomach, holding me down on the bed as my legs spread on its own to accommodate him. The sight of such a handsome man kissing my body made me moan, the mirror showing off the beautiful sight of his back muscles and deltoids moving when his lips lowered to my abdomen.

I wanted him so badly that it was hurting.

As if reading my mind yet again, he pulled back to remove his pants and boxers, leaving him naked. I licked my lips at the sight of him, wondering how he would ever fit inside me.

But it seemed like Hayden had other things in his mind when he grabbed the lace of my underwear in his hand and tore it away from my body. I gasped at the sound of fabric tearing and closed my legs at the burning sensation.

He glared at me as shucked away the torn lace. "What did I tell you about hiding yourself from me, Zara?"

"You tore my underwear," I said as a fact, my cheeks red and legs still closed.

"And?" His eyes narrowed to my legs. I gasped and groaned when he pushed my legs away, smacking my inner thighs. "If you want to stop, you say the word red. And if you move your legs again or dare try to hide yourself from me, I *will* tie you up and tease you all night."

My stomach clenched at the hot threat. I raised my brow at him and said, "They taught you that in the Navy?"

His eyes darkened, and I held my ground even though I was a bit horny, scared to know what he might do next.

"You don't want to know what they taught us what to do with innocent little Princesses like you, Zara," he said, holding my legs spread when his fingers slid over my slicked lips and dipped inside me, stretching me as I winced at the little pinch of pain.

His voice was like velvet, smooth and deep, dripping with sweetness when he crooned, "Oh, does it hurt my Princess? But you can handle two fingers, *hm*."

I bit my lip. My walls clamped around him as he fucked me with his fingers, much bigger than mine when they filled me. He kept a pillow underneath my hips that gave him more access to my burning sex.

Hayden looked at me with his deep blue eyes and said, "Keep your legs spread or I will spank your cunt until you beg me to hurt you, understood?"

I nodded quickly, clenching my walls around his fingers

that were still inside me. I watched him lean down, kissing my inner thighs softly, and I sighed, melting into the mattress. He had spanked me everywhere that I was burning for him, but his lips and tongue licked every inch of my skin where he had spanked me with a gentle caress while his fingers curled inside me.

I was putty and needy within seconds, feeling the pleasure bubbling inside me when he licked everywhere, except where I wanted him the most.

"Please, Hayden," I begged, touching my own breasts and squeezing them when his eyes darkened, his face between my legs. "Stop teasing me."

"Pinch your nipples for me, Princess," he murmured against my pussy, his warm breath making me shiver. "Play with your tits while I make you feel good, okay?"

I hummed in agreement, blushing at the squelching sounds when his fingers fucked me. It was erotic to hear it, and look at Hayden's handsome face when he stared at my pussy as if I was his last meal.

"Your pussy looks so fucking good stretched around my fingers, my Princess slut," he groaned, his lips kissing my clit as I moaned at the soft touch. "I can't wait to fuck you and see how you fit me inside you."

"Oh, God," I gasped when he licked the dripping juices, my clit and sucking it in his mouth as his fingers fucked me faster, the scent of my feminine arousal all over the room.

"I bet that boy didn't lick you here at all, did he?" Hayden rumbled, slowly lapping his tongue from my lips to my clit, flicking it as I bucked on the bed. He hummed at my reaction, "Did he suck your pretty pussy like I did?"

"N-No," I shook my head. "Hayden! I… I—" I tried to get away from him, but he held me tighter, not allowing me to move away from his face.

But he slowed his ministrations, caressing my shaking thighs and said, "Let it go, Princess. I want you to cum before I fuck you. I want to taste you."

I was so embarrassed for my thoughts, but I figured that Hayden was a grown man and I could tell him.

"But I feel like... like I will..." I stuttered, wanting to hide under the blankets.

Hayden raised his brow, "Like you will pee?"

My face burnt red with humiliation as I nodded, wanting to look away from him.

He kissed my stomach. "You won't, Zara. Just relax yourself and let me play with your sweet pussy." I let out a soft moan when the pads of his fingers pressed against a sensitive spot inside me. "Yes, just like that, Princess. Let me make you feel good, yeah?"

I nodded, my eyes on him when he lowered himself. The sight of his face moving over my flushed sex made me feel hot, his hands, lips, tongue and fingers playing with me, teasing me on the edge. The pleasure built again and that time I let myself enjoy and relish in the feeling because even though I had never played with myself like that before, I trusted Hayden.

A half scream and half moan tore out of my lips when his hand smacked my thigh before moving my legs over his broad shoulders. *Holyshit.*

"Show me how pretty your tits are, Princess, play with them for me," Hayden rumbled. The reverberations of his voice sent shivers of hot pleasure down my spine.

I played with my breasts, enjoying the way he licked me and sucked my clit harder. I realised that he must feel the same way I did when I had sucked him before. The way I got aroused when I pleased him.

"Cum on my fingers, Princess," he groaned, and my eyes flitted to the mirror across the bed to see his hips move.

My lips parted in surprise as I watched his ass clench. Was he grinding on the bed? I raised my hips and asked for more at the sight of him and looked back at his face when he ate me out.

"Such a sweet, needy slut, all wet and dripping for me," he whispered, his tongue replacing his fingers as my fingers pinched my nipples.

Hayden had to hold my stomach down when he licked me, his fingers fucking me once more with his lips around my clit as he sucked. His digits curled inside me as I squeezed my eyes shut at the explosion of pleasure that rocked through my body, making me whimper and squirm underneath him.

My toes curled as I grew hot and feverish, pleasuring ache flooding and gushing through my sex. My voice was unrecognisable as I panted, white fiery lust rolling out of my body, warm tears trailing down my face as my body trembled with the after waves of the orgasm.

From far away I could hear Hayden's sweet words, his gentle caress as he soothed me down, but I was still drowning in the clouds of pleasure.

Hayden

I MADE MY WAY UP ZARA'S SHAKING BODY, PRESSING SOFT, sloppy kisses on her stomach, tits and her face until her half-lidded eyes opened up, her lips parted as she panted up at me. I trailed my fingers over the apple of her cheek, wiping away her tears.

She looked so fucking beautiful with her flushed, glowing face. Her feminine taste was sweet and tangy, and I wanted to eat her out again and again. Make her sit on my face, overstimulating her until she cries or passes out.

"How are you feeling, Princess?" I asked, tucking her hair that framed her face. I had to remind myself that she was inexperienced. Be gentle with her.

Zara hummed, pressing her face in my hand. She looked blissed out and so beautiful and perfect that I wanted to take a picture of her and save it on my phone. But we had not discussed about it so I remembered every inch of her face at that moment.

I didn't know that she would cum apart like that on my fingers and mouth. The sounds she had made ringed in my ears, making me twitch. I controlled myself from grinding on the bed again like a horny teenager. Again.

I never thought I would be so fucking turned on by someone that I would hump a fucking bed. I like pussies. Period. But I would do anything to get Zara's taste again.

Ignoring the possessive thoughts, I focused on her shaking little body, soothing her with sweet words and telling her how fucking proud I was.

"You did so well, Zara," I kissed her cheek, tasting the saltiness of her tears. "Watching you fall apart on my fingers and mouth was so erotic. I'm so proud of you for coming like that."

Her hands ran down my body, and I tensed when her legs wrapped around my torso. Her hazy eyes blinked at me, cheeks flushed and face glowing with pleasure and lust as she asked in the sultrier innocent voice,

"Will you please fuck me, Hayden? I… I want to be full of you."

Fuck. Fuck. Fuck.

All rational and logical thoughts abandoned me hearing her words and gaping at her sexy, innocent face, her full lips, and that hot fucking beauty mark on her top lip.

I asked in a guttural voice, "You want to be full of my cock, *hm?*"

Her face dipped, her hands running down my back and making me hiss with pleasure when she pushed my ass so that my length brushed over her bare cunt.

I lowered my hand to her pussy. "*Tsk*, you are dripping wet, Princess. Aren't you sore?"

"No," she blurted. "Not sore at all. Please, I want you."

I should just hold her hips down and thrust inside her, cum inside her, make her orgasm and breed—

No, you fucking asshole. She is a virgin.

I ignored the primal part of my brain who wanted to do terrible things to her and pulled away a little, my fingers rolling her swollen clit, keeping her on the edge. If she was a virgin, my main priority should be to make her forget about the pain she might feel in a few moments.

"Give me your hand," I ordered. She lifted her palm wordlessly as I held it and brought it down on her pussy, under my hand and watching heat creep up her neck.

"Seeing you blush like that makes me so fucking hard, Princess," I whispered, rubbing her own fingers over her clit. Teaching her. "Have you ever touched yourself before?"

"I have but..." Zara licked her lips, watching my hand move over her fingers that rubbed her clit. Her eyebrows scrunched as she tried to continue, "B-but not this well."

I hummed, bending her legs so her knees faced the ceiling, setting the pillow comfortably under her hips. "Keep rubbing yourself for me, okay, Princess?" I eyed the golden diamond jewellery on her thigh, seeing it tighten, and caressed it. "I want to fuck you in just this. Don't remove it."

She nodded, biting her lip and watching me get up from the bed. I loved the way her eyes dropped to my naked body. I might or might not have flexed a muscle or two. It felt good to know that she was as attracted to me as I was to her.

But my face fell when I looked at the box of condoms I had brought with me. I forgot how I had been travelling since my last mission and had dumped the box inside the suitcase without reading its expiry date.

"Hayden," Zara called me, her voice breathy. "What happened?"

I walked back to her, awing at the beautiful sight of her small fingers pleasuring herself and making a mess on the bed. Fucking hell, I had the sexiest being on the bed with me and expired condoms.

"You look so sexy touching yourself in front of me, Zara," I said, running my hand over her body, her soft breasts and legs. I couldn't keep my hands off of her. I had to touch her and get as much as I could from her because I felt selfish and the need to keep touching her. "But we can't have sex tonight, Princess."

"What?" She stopped her ministrations, her eyes alert as she sat up. "Why not?"

Someone was upset. *Well, that makes the two of us.*

I showed her the date on the unused box of condoms. "It's expired."

Her shoulders drooped, and it was adorable to see her bottom lip jut out a little. Then she looked at me expectantly. "I am on pills. I know... I met you tonight but I-I am clean. I tried having sex last year, and we had used condom but I promise—"

"Calm down, Zara," I said, putting the box on the nightstand and sat across her. Both of us as naked as the day we were born. "I trust you that you are clean. I had been on a mission recently, so I am clean as well. In fact, I got tested last week before arriving here."

"Then let's do it," Zara grinned.

I chuckled at her excitement. "Princess, you shouldn't trust someone's words so easily. Especially a stranger."

"Why not? You took care of me till now." Her voice softened as she said, "I trust you, Hayden."

My heart stumbled at the sincerity behind her eyes and sweet voice. Swallowing the lump in my throat, I nodded, not knowing how to respond to her. "Thank you for trusting me, Princess. But, see my test results just to give me a peace of mind."

"If it makes you feel better."

She looked through the negative results of the photo I had captured on my phone and said, "See? I know you are clean. Now, can we please—*oh*."

I looked down at the screen to see what had made her sound surprised. It was a picture of me with my brothers in our Navy Seal Uniform just after the mission was over and we had scored a victory.

Her legs closed, and she squirmed on the bed, clutching the phone tightly.

I took away the phone from her, ignoring her gasp and pressed her down on the bed. "You are getting turned on looking at that picture, aren't you, you dirty fucking girl?"

Her breasts brushed against mine when she nodded, biting her lip. "You look incredibly hot in that uniform. I wish you would wear it for me."

I raised my brow. "Demanding, are we? What else were you thinking about looking at that picture, Princess?"

Her eyes widened as she shook her head. "Nothing."

She was such a terrible liar.

"Nothing?" I asked softly.

Zara shook her head. "Nothing."

I pulled back and held her legs apart, my eyes flickering at her wet pussy and glaring at her. "You should know by now that I hate liars, Zara. Tell me—" I spanked her cunt, holding her legs open when she groaned. "*What*. Were. You. Thinking." I added three more smacks, one harder than the other as she whimpered, bucking against my arm as her sex turned a bright shade of red.

"And don't even think about lying right now," I continued, soothing her heated sex with the same hand I had spanked her with. "I want to know what my dirty little slut was thinking that got her dripping wet."

10
ZARA

I squirmed, feeling the wetness seep out of me at his dirty words. *This man has a way with his mouth.* Literally.

"I was just..." I started, paused at how weird it would sound, and looked away from his blue eyes. "It's embarrassing, Hayden."

"Princess, if it was embarrassing, you wouldn't be so turned on right now," he purred, knowing exactly how turned on I was when his hand stroked me, soothing my scorching sex. "You can tell me. Come on. I want to know what you were thinking."

I knew that if I used the safe word, he wouldn't prod, but somehow, I didn't want to use it. Swallowing the lump in my throat, I nodded. "Seeing you... and the other soldiers in that uniform made me wonder—" my legs clenched at my thoughts, heat creeping up my body. "Wonder how it would feel surrounded by all of you. Naked."

I squeezed my eyes shut, wanting to hide my face in a blanket when Hayden's body move against me, his hard muscles felt delicious against my soft skin.

"Look at me." His fingers trailed over my face, waiting.

I opened my eyes, waiting for him to be disgusted or laugh. But he didn't. Instead, his pupils were dilated, heat glossing over his eyes.

"Are you into gang-bangs, Princess?"

"Gang-bangs?" I questioned.

Hayden pulled back, his fingers softly caressing my body. I liked how he couldn't stop touching me. "Wanting to be fucked by a lot of men or women, sweetheart," he shook his head with a grin. "I'd never think you'd be into—"

"*No.*" My face burnt as I shook my head wildly, "No no no, I am not into the gang-bang or whatever. One person is enough for me. And that's just a fantasy, anyway. I don't want that to happen for real."

Hayden nodded, "Of course, Zara. Maybe you are into exhibitionism." Looking at my confused face, he continued, kissing my knee, "Being naked or fucked in front of someone... *or* many people."

He chuckled when I made a face. "There's a word for it?!"

"There's a word for every kink, Princess."

I hummed, trailing my fingers over the veins of his forearms. Meeting his eyes, I shyly whispered, "Then what are you into?"

"*You,*" he answered, kissing me softly on my lips. "Very much into you. But if we are talking about kinks, I like to humiliate and degrade. Sometimes..."

I kind of figured that Hayden would like that because, despite being a Princess, I was into humiliation and degradation. But he stopped what he was going to say, looking at me and shook his head.

"What?" I asked. "Why'd you stop? You were going to say something."

"I can't say that to you, Princess," he said.

I frowned, sitting up. "No, tell me, Hayden. I want to

know what you were going to say. I told you about that picture. I want to know about whatever you are into."

"Princess…"

"Tell me."

Hayden sighed, "I feel like I am tainting you by saying this…" I blinked at him as he took a deep breath and continued, "Sometimes, I enjoy doing a role-play of consensual non-consent. It takes a lot of trust and a safe word, gesture to even try it, but seeing the element of fear and anticipation on my partner is arousing. Given they are into it, of course."

His cheeks had a light blush when he finished, waiting for me to react. I tilted my head at him and asked, "You were making it sound as if you had a weird fetish. But…" I swallowed the lump in my throat. "I like the sound of it."

Hayden exhaled sharply. "Good. It is just a fantasy as yours is. Now lay down on your back and spread your legs. Show me that pretty pussy of yours."

I bit my lip, and leaning up, I kissed him instead. Humming into the kiss, I slid my hands over his pecs, shoulders, and hair. His hands gripped my ass, squeezing them when I kissed his sharp jaw, his warm breath caressing my face when I licked his earlobe, feeling him shiver.

With a small bite, I whispered in his ear, "Make me Hayden."

His hands trailed up from my back to my shoulder as he looked at me. "Say that again, Princess."

I knew it was a warning, but hearing the deep edge of his voice stirred something inside me. I smiled at him and repeated, "I said, make me, Hayden. Didn't you hear me —*ooh!*"

"Fucking *brat*," he whispered harshly, kissing me and forcing his body on top of mine, pressing me down on the soft mattress and pinning my wrists above my head. "You love to tease me, don't you, you little slut?"

"Yes," I nodded, spreading my legs and groaning when he pumped two fingers inside my dripping heat. "Please... want... you."

"Look at you," Hayden chuckled. "Can't even form a coherent sentence and I haven't even fucked you yet, Princess." I whimpered when he pushed his fingers—the ones that were inside me moments ago—in my mouth, making me lick them clean.

"Do you think your cunt is ready for me, Princess?" He asked, parting my legs and trailing a finger over my entrance. "Ready for my cock, *hm?*"

I raised my hips, begging him, "Yes, yes, Hayden. Please don't make me wait anymore."

He propped up my hips with a pillow beneath my hips and asked me if I was comfortable. I nodded quickly, shivering with anticipation and licking my lips when he palmed his length. I licked my lips, remembering how big and girthy he had felt inside my mouth.

Hayden hovered above me, lining against me as his lips pressed against mine in a soft, gentle kiss. "It might hurt, Princess," he said. "And I promise I will make you feel better, but if it hurts a lot or you want to stop, at anytime, you just have to say the word red, okay?"

"Okay," I replied breathily, wounding my arms around his strong shoulders.

I watched him bite his lip, the intense look on his face making me clench with anticipation when he pressed closer, the bulbous head of his cock sliding inside me. I gasped, digging my fingers on his back when I felt his shaft stretching me as he pushed slowly.

"*Fuck,*" he breathed out. "You are so fucking tight, Princess."

Tears gleamed in my eyes as I cried out, "You are too big." I was burning up from inside out, maybe splitting in two. I winced, trying to clench him, his guttural groan making me shiver.

"*Princess…*" he choked out, his face flushed. "D-don't clench me. I will cum and I am not even fully in."

He wasn't even fully in? I was going to die. I didn't want to die. Not like this. Not by a co—

Hayden pinned my wrists down, "Hey, look at me, Zara."

I did, biting my lip from crying when he stayed still, half inserted inside me. I felt overwhelmed by the sheer size of him. Even though I was dripping wet, it felt too much. *He* felt too much.

His other hand lowered between our bodies and slowly rubbed over my clit, making me gasp at the small bubble of pleasure. "That's it, baby," he purred. "Focus on me, okay? I will fuck you good, I promise, Princess."

I nodded, trusting him and relaxing even when he had pinned my arms above my head, rendering me helpless. He started moving, rocking his hips as I whimpered and whined when he slid an inch inside me. More and more as I groaned and squirmed, his hold on me tightening.

"Shh, Princess, it's okay," Hayden crooned in my ear, his hot breath fanning on my cheeks. "You're doing so good, taking my cock in your virgin pussy. So pretty stretched out like this, *hm*. You can take it."

His voice was so soft and gentle, pinning me on the bed when his muscled body moved over me, fucking me slowly until he settled inside me in one slow thrust. I groaned, and he grunted when he filled me to the brim, my walls stretching out and enveloping him, clamping him tightly.

"H-Hayden," I panted. "Please, move… I…"

"Hush, Princess," he said, kissing me on the lips and trailing his hand down my face, allowing me to move my hands and slide them over his back. "Let me stay inside you until you feel better, hm."

He kissed the corner of my lips, his cock throbbing inside me as his fingers teased my clit. I moaned with the increasing pleasure, trying to squirm away and move my hips for some friction, but Hayden didn't let me.

"Doesn't it feel good, Princess? Being so full of my cock, hm?" He whispered hotly, groaning and kissing my neck when I clenched him.

I agreed with a shaky breath, "I-it does."

"That's my good slut," he said, caressing my cheek with a small smile when I leaned into his palm. "Are you feeling better now that my cock has warmed you up?"

My cheeks burned as I nodded. "Better but... horny. I want you to move and fuck me. Please."

"*Tsk*, such a demanding Princess. Wrap your legs around me."

I gasped when I felt him go deeper with my legs around his torso.

"Good girl."

A soft moan slipped past my lips when Hayden moved, dragging himself back and thrusting inside me in a slow thrust. His sharp breath and low grunts made it more erotic when he clenched his jaw, fucking me slowly and deeply.

"*More!*" I gasped out, clenching him with each thrust.

Hayden slammed inside me, my eyes squeezing shut at the pleasure building inside me. The sounds of skin slapping against each other surrounded us with our heavy breathing and the scent of arousal and sex in the air.

"Look. At. Me," he gritted out with each thrust, wrapping his hand around my hair. "Yes, watch me fuck you, Princess. Look how well you take my cock, you sweet slut."

I whimpered, holding his forearm when I watched myself stretched around the girth shaft of Hayden's dick. I moaned, flickering my eyes from his handsome face to where he was fucking me between my legs, my hips rising to meet his thrusts, my pussy pink, flushed and swollen with the stimulation.

"Come here," he demanded, his chest heaving when he pulled out of me, leaving me empty as I clenched around nothing.

I felt weak when he turned me on my stomach, slamming his full length inside me in one thrust, making me cry out.

"*Ah!*" I moaned when his palm spanked my ass, his other hand wrapping around my hair as he slammed inside me from behind.

"Christ, look at yourself, Princess," he groaned, his voice deep and smoky when he lifted me, his chest against my back. "Look in the mirror. See how fucking beautiful you look while I am fucking you."

"Oh God." Tears burned in my eyes when I saw the reflection of both of our naked bodies across the bed in the mirror.

The way my breasts moved with each thrust, the way I held on to his forearms, his large hands pinching, slapping and fondling my flushed breasts with his other hand on my hair, forcing me to look in the mirror. My eyes were glazed, my face glowing and blushing with my pouty lips parting with gasps of pleasure as Hayden fucked me. My thighs trembled and shook, watching his handsome face, his blue eyes roving over my body. He made me feel so desirable and sexy. I wanted him so badly.

"I am going to make you cum just like this," he whispered, kissing my neck and wrapping his hand around my neck, pressing lightly in a way that had me clamping around him.

He groaned, the sound of his pleasure sending shivers down my body. "Fuck yes, Zara. Keep clenching me like a good girl and see yourself cum, okay? See how beautiful my Princess slut looks."

I hummed in agreement, watching his other hand lower down my stomach to my clit and slightly applying pressure on it. I bucked in his arms, his hips moving behind me when he continued to fuck me while rubbing me and choking me with his hand.

"Squeeze your tits for me, pinch them," he growled, the pace of his thrusts increasing as my pleasure peaked higher and higher.

I cupped my breasts, still looking at the mirror at how erotic we both looked together. I looked like Zara. Not at all like a Princess. Princesses don't get fucked like sluts. They have sex wearing their tiara crowns. But with Hayden, his soft voice crooning dirty words while he fucked me made me feel like a slut and a Princess. Even if it was a role-play and it was just a kink.

I adored every second of it, relished in it and basked in the feeling of being fucked like that.

"Hayden," I moaned, clutching his forearms when my body shook, exploding around him. Light blinded my vision and tears burned my eyes as I held onto him for support, the orgasm rocking through me.

When I came back, I was on my back with Hayden hovering above me, his hold on my neck tightening when he jerked, clenching his jaw as he groaned, thrusting deep inside me and coating my walls with his climax. I had never seen anything sexier than Hayden orgasming like that. The way he had lost control, just a little, to pin me down and fuck me relentlessly to chase his own pleasure.

I licked my lips when I felt the warmth of his orgasm inside me, his head looking up from my breasts, his clear blue eyes zeroing on my face.

"Hi," I whispered, raking my fingers through his sandy brown hair, brushing them back. How could anyone look so handsome?

Leaning closer, Hayden brushed his lips against mine.

"How is my pretty Princess feeling?" He murmured, slowly pulling himself out with a low grunt.

I blushed, feeling our release slid out of me, his blue eyes gleaming with lust when he looked up from between my legs. "I am feeling tired," I said, licking my lips before he gets any other ideas. "You exhausted me."

"I am glad I did," Hayden gave me a small smile. "Stay here, I will be right back, sweetheart."

My heart swelled hearing him call me sweetheart. As he made his way to the ensuite bathroom, I eyed his gloriously muscled body. That man was inside me, fucking me moments ago. I could feel the emptiness inside me and shivered.

Leaning up on my elbows, I frowned at the glistening release from my legs.

"Didn't I tell you to stay still?" Hayden said, my eyes blinking up to meet his. He was wearing boxer—*boo*—as he crawled on the bed with a wet towel. I jumped when he spread my legs and cleaned me up, stroking my inner thigh and knee with his other hand.

"I could have done this myself," I murmured, ogling at the focused look on his handsome face.

His blue orbs flickered to me. "I know. But I want to clean the mess I have made."

I bit my lip and nodded, trying to relax when he cleaned me, kissing my knee and walking back to the washroom. I kept looking at him, my eyes heavy-lidded with exhaustion and… strangely enough, adoration for Hayden. He had been attractive from the beginning, asking me what I wanted, showing me and teaching me, giving me both pain and pleasure before having sex with me.

I didn't want the night to end. I wanted more time with him.

More of *him*.

11
HAYDEN

I sighed, splashing cold water on my face to calm my raging thoughts. I didn't expect it to be that good. But it was. I cursed under my breath just at the thought of Zara lying on the bed with her rosy cheeks and doe eyes. Even if she was a virgin, the sex with her was the best I ever had. No, not just the sex.

This entire night was one of the best I ever had.

I didn't want it to end. *Ever.*

"Are you kidding me?" I asked myself, looking down at the bulge in my boxers. She had wrung me dry. *Twice.* Once in her sweet mouth and then inside her warm pussy. Yet my dick had other thoughts and was ready for more rounds.

Shaking my head, I calmed it down and walked out of the washroom. Zara was checking her phone sitting on the bed, her dark hair trailing down her pale body, which was covered in pink hues where I had spanked her or held her too hard. Hickeys covering her neck and breasts.

I did that to her.

Male pride surged through me as I stepped closer, her

eyes flickering to me as she gave me a small smile. The beauty spot above her lip begging to be touched.

So, I leaned on the bed and kissed her lips. Her dark eyes were half lidded with exhaustion and gleaming with post-coital bliss.

"How are you feeling, Princess?" I asked, kissing down her cheek, her phone long forgotten somewhere on the bed when her fingers curled in my hair. Fuck, I loved that.

"Much better," she gasped when I bit the soft skin of her neck.

I pulled away, licking my lips. "Aren't you sore?"

Her cheeks burnt. I knew the answer. "A little."

Before I could ask her to take a warm bath with me, her stomach interrupted us with a loud growl. Her eyes widened as she hid her stomach as if it would stop another growl.

"*Tsk.*" I shook my head at her, raking my fingers through her tangled hair. "I can't have my Princess starving. What do you want to eat?"

I asked and called the hotel service, ordering us some burgers with fries and milkshake because that was what she wanted. I ordered a cake too when she disappeared into the washroom and smirked when she winced, walking slowly.

Yep, she was definitely sore.

Our food was delivered by the time she stepped out, wearing my shirt that was too big for her. The jewellery that was around her thigh was placed on the nightstand, its diamonds gleaming in the light.

I twitched in my boxers at the sight of my shirt reaching her thighs, the sleeves rolled up on her arms because it was too big for her.

"You can keep that shirt," I said when she sat down on the bed, crossing her legs across me with the food between us. "It suits you much better."

Her cheeks flushed as her eyes landed on the blueberry cake. "You ordered a cake," Zara said, surprise on her face.

I shrugged, licking the frosting from my finger. "I thought you would like it."

I served her burger, and fries as she cleared her throat, blinking her eyes at me. "I love it, thank you," she whispered.

Her words were softer as she spoke, as if I had bought her a ring instead of a cake. I shook my head and bit into the delicious burger, ignoring the calories it had. I could use a cheat day.

We talked about each other while we ate and slurped on the thick milkshakes. Zara was homeschooled her entire life. She liked horse riding, painting, photography, animals and wanted to get out of Azmia for her university.

"Forgive my interruption, but you don't have the natural accent of the people of Azmia," I said, frowning at her. "I thought you were a tourist when we met before."

She shook her head. "I was born and raised here. I... well, my mom was from England and I was raised by English tutors."

Ah, she came from money.

"I am surprised that you haven't travelled if you had the funds to do so," I said, watching her lips when she slurped on the milkshake through the straw.

Keep it in your pants, Hayden. She is sore.

But her mouth isn't—

Jesus Christ, this woman was going to give me blue balls if she kept being so sexy all the fucking time.

"I have protective brothers," Zara replied.

I narrowed my eyes at her, remembering how she had handled herself. "Did they teach you how to fight like that?"

"Of course, it is compulsory—" she paused, her eyes wide as she looked at me and cleared her throat. "I mean, it is necessary for me to know how to protect myself. You know?"

She was saying the truth by emitting the real reason. If she had to learn how to protect herself, then it meant that she came from old money.

I had heard of Navy Seals retiring and getting involved in service as bodyguards for the rich. People like her and her family. I wouldn't be surprised if she had talked with one of her guards when I was in the washroom. But would her parents and protective brothers even allow her to be out with strangers during New Year? *Wouldn't that be too risky?*

Knowing she didn't want to talk about her fighting skills and why she had to learn them, I asked her about horses. She beamed, talking about the name and species, which one was her favorite to ride and which horse had an attitude.

"Do you see this?" she asked, pulling up the shirt and pointing at the lightly darker skin, which looked like an old wound on her lower back.

I nodded, eyeing the back of her spine and remembering how she looked on all her fours when I fucked her from behind.

Zara didn't notice the lust in my eyes when she continued, "I once snuck out to ride Malak. He is a new horse and everyone kept saying that he had an attitude so I wanted to tame him and test him." She finally pulled down the shirt, her eyes gleaming as she said, "Malak not only allowed me to feed him, but ride him as well. Unfortunately, he panicked and pushed me down."

"You got injured?" I asked, not knowing how a girl like her could tame a stallion with an attitude. I was surprised that she wasn't scared of horses after such an event.

"I did and had to hide it from my brothers about it," she said cheekily, finishing her fries.

Her brothers, *hm*. Didn't they seem too overprotective?

Does that sound like someone? *Me.* It sounds like me

because I have a little sister of her age too, but I don't give her too much curfews that she has to sneak out of the house.

Zara had gone quiet, staring at the bedsheet.

I flicked her nose, her eyes narrowing at me as I asked, "What's going on inside that pretty head?"

"I didn't bleed," she said, shuffling on the bed. "I heard that women bleed after their first time."

"Princess," I said, pinning my eyes to her concerned face. "Women only bleed when their hymen breaks. Sometimes they don't even have a hymen. You mentioned horse riding, so I wouldn't be surprised that it was already broken. Stop worrying about that and finish your food."

"So bossy," she murmured under her breath and took a big bite of her burger.

As she finished her food, I talked about my work discreetly. I couldn't just tell her about what my mission was to stop by in Azmia while the Navy ship was docked on the shore of the capital. I told her how I got into the Navy. Talking about my father, who was an ex-Colonel and didn't want me to follow his steps because of what he had witnessed.

"He must care about you..." Zara whispered, sadness lacing her voice.

I cleared my throat. "Far from that, actually. He wanted me to become a doctor or a lawyer after our mom walked away. He became different, and I was the one who took care of Ivy." At her raised brow, I answered. "My sister. I wanted to give her a good example and be better than my father. So, I joined the Navy Seal and became an officer in less than a decade."

Her cheeks reddened when her eyes flickered from the uniform to me. "That's impressive. You must have worked hard for it."

"I did." I wanted to see how she would react if I wore the

uniform for her, do some role-play and fuck her in it. She'd definitely enjoy it, that's for sure.

I tried my best to remember that she was a virgin moment ago, and I had done more than enough to cause her soreness. We ate the blueberry cake. I glared at her when she made obnoxious moaning sounds as she ate it, giving me a cheeky smile in return, as if she wasn't doing that on purpose.

Taking the blue dessert in the golden spoon, I lifted it to her lips. Her hazel-brown eyes twinkled as she parted her lips and I fed the cake to her.

But some of the frosting fell between her collarbone, her eyes widening at me. Leaning closer, I licked the frosting from her skin, humming at the sweet taste.

"Messy girl," I whispered, meeting her burning gaze and kissed her clumsily, holding her close.

But, being a sensible gentleman, I pulled away before it could lead to other things. "Are you hungry?" I asked, clearing the bed of the empty plates.

Zara licked her lips and crawled towards the edge of the bed where I was standing. She stared directly at my crotch, covered in boxers, and blinked up at me with her not-so-innocent eyes.

"A little," she replied, her soft fingers sliding across my hips, making me shiver.

I narrowed my eyes at her, wondering what happened to the shy vixen. Holding her wrist, I stopped her. "Not now, Princess. You are sore."

"But my mouth isn't," she argued, a frown on her face.

I cupped her jaw and arched her head at me. "It will be after I fuck it for as long as I want to. Stop being a slutty brat and do what I tell you."

Her eyes scorched with anger as she pulled away from me, grumbling under her breath. I ignored it and asked her to follow me to the washroom. She did, stomping her feet on the ground.

Even furious, she looked adorable, wearing nothing but my shirt. I wanted to bruise the angry pout from her lips with a kiss.

"Brush your teeth," I said, pointing to the plain toothbrush offered by the hotel.

She eyed me and the toothpaste I offered to her. "Are you serious?"

I deadpanned. "Yes, Zara. Brush. *Now*."

She took the toothpaste, eyeing me from the corner of her eyes as I looked at our reflection in the mirror, standing beside each other. She was tall, but she reached my shoulders, frowning at the brush.

"You do this after defiling every virgin you meet?"

I winked at her. "Only the special ones, Princess."

Anger faded from her eyes as she looked away, brushing her teeth. Now that she mentioned it, I had never done it with any women. Not once. I don't know why I even offered to brush teeth with her. Maybe because we had eaten and my nighttime routine forced me to remember brushing my teeth that I offered it to her.

Nope. Something was very wrong with me.

Because she had behaved without making any other advances on me, I stripped her of the shirt on the bed and kissed her everywhere. Massaging and caressing everywhere I had spanked her, marked her with more hickies, saying sweet words in her ears and snuggling her close to me.

I relaxed in the bed, her arm around my abs as my fingers trialed over her soft hair that smelled like sweet vanilla. Even though she might be rich, I liked that she smelt of vanilla. Exotic yet feminine. Even though she was nothing like it.

Zara was anything but that. She portrayed the image of a

tempting Princess looking for some fun and do something little rebellious.

Kissing her hair, I fell asleep beside my tempting rebel princess.

Zara

I HUMMED IN MY SLEEP, SHUFFLING AND RUBBING MYSELF against the hardness that felt too good to be true. My fingers tightened over warm and hard skin, a sigh escaping my lips when I moved, settling over the stiffened—

"Having a wet dream, Princess?"

A deep husky voice whispered in my ear, making me flutter my eyes open. I blinked sleepily at the bluest eyes I have ever seen and smiled at the sharp face of Hayden who peered at me through his half-lidded eyes.

"Wet… dream?" I asked, my voice heavy with sleep as I looked down at his chest. I was straddling his hips, his back against the headboard as he ran his hands down my back.

He hummed, the throaty sound rumbling through his body making me tremble. "You were rubbing yourself on my thigh making small whining sounds," he pinched my cheek. "It was adorable and woke me up."

I bit my lip, shuffling until my bare sex brushed against the throbbing hardness over his boxers.

"I am sorry I woke you up," I said, not sorry at all.

His eyes narrowed, "You don't seem sorry at all." I gasped when he pushed me over his length, rubbing me over him.

"More!" I moaned, scrunching my hands in a fist and grinding over him.

Hayden shook his head, smacking my ass lightly. "Always greedy for more, hm? Aren't you sore, Princess?"

"No." I shook my head, kissing the hot skin of his neck and leaving a hickey on his collarbone. "Please, fuck me, Hayden."

He stopped me from humping him and cupped my face, his blue eyes soft. "Are you sure you don't feel sore? I don't want to hurt you."

"But I want you to."

His eyes darkened and his jaw clenched as he shook his head. "Not like that, Zara. I want to hurt you in a pleasurable way but I don't want to cause you any harm or bruise you."

Swallowing the lump in my throat, I held his hand on my cheek and said, "It's okay, Hayden. I am asking you to hurt me. I want this."

His pupils dilated as he pulled me into a sweet, passionate kiss, leaving me breathless for more. His muscles chest heaved as he pulled away, my hands tugging down his boxers.

I licked my lips at the sight of his proud length, at the big girth of his cock and the glistening pre-cum.

Hayden beckoned me on his lap, holding my hand as he instructed me how to position myself over him, my knees on either side of his strong hips.

"Come on, Princess," he whispered. "Ride me. Take me inside your wet cunt and ride me."

I bit my lip at his dirty words, squeezing his hand as I looked down between us, lining the tip of his cock against my slit and glancing at his flushed face.

Just one look at his face. I knew he was holding back.

I didn't want him to hold back.

I was the Princess of Azmia, I could take whatever he had in store for me.

Licking my lips, I slowly moved my hips over the crown of his head so that my slicked lips coated him while sending jolts of shivers from my clit to my toes. I repeated my moments, my breathing laboring as he glared at me, his fingers digging in my hips.

"Stop being a tease, Princess."

I ignored him and moved my hair over my shoulder, his sapphire eyes lowering to my breasts. I cupped them in front of his face, sweeping my fingers over my nipples, squeezing them, pinching them and playing with them while teasing both of us with the slow movements over his tip.

"Teasing slut," he whispered. A groan slipped past my lips when he tugged at my hair. I whimpered and moaned when he moved his hips, topping me from bottom and impaling himself inside me. My sore walls clenched him desperately as I blinked at him through the tears.

"What did I tell you about teasing me, *hm*, Princess?" He mocked, holding my hips and dragging me over his length. Back and forth. Back and forth. Back and forth.

"P-please," I cried out, squeezing my eyes shut when he slammed inside me, brushing against the sensitive spot that had my toes curling.

His palm landed on my ass, spanking me. "Then be a good girl and ride me, Princess."

I nodded, blinking at him and keeping my hands on his shoulders. I slowly slid up and then down, gasping at the fullness and clenching him tightly. Hayden groaned, the sound so husky and deep that I wanted to hear him again. I repeated my actions, slowly circling my hips as he guided me, his voice guttural and throaty.

"I like your voice," I gasped when he told me how to ride him.

I swear I saw his cheeks flush when he pulled me closer, his warm breath caressing my neck, his lips on my cheek. "I like your voice too, Princess. Now keep riding me and make yourself cum."

Nodding, I moved my hips like he had told me to. "Like

this?" I asked, my thighs shaking at the strain, but I kept repeating the move.

He hummed, dipping down and sucking my nipple under his hot mouth. I sighed and ran my hand through his hair when he nibbled at my breasts, kissing them, squeezing them until they both had pink hues spread across them.

"I fucking love your tits," he grunted, pinching the nipples and wrapping his hand around my throat.

I closed my eyes, holding his wrist and getting lost in the pleasure of riding him, clenching him, feeling his legs shake and abdomen clench. The sounds of our gasps and groans with the slippery sound of our sex and skin slapping surrounded in the room. The air was musky and cold.

"Open your eyes and look at me when you cum," he ordered, tightening his grip on my neck, making me whimper.

"I... I can't," I gasped, tears threatening to spill from my eyes when the strain of my legs took me away from the pleasure.

"*Tsk*, my Princess slut can't even ride my cock properly without needing my help," he teased, settling himself deep inside me as I squirmed, feeling his entire length throb inside me.

"Please, Hayden." I said, trying to move over his length, but he held me, not allowing me to move.

Holding my chin, he tilted it up to his face. His eyes seemed almost onyx when he whispered, "Poor Princess. You know how to beg with your pretty mouth, don't you? Haven't I taught you any manners, *hm*?"

Tears burned my eyes at the tone of his deep voice and the way humiliation burnt through my body, arousing me as my walls clamped around him.

No one would ever dare to talk to me like that. No one but him. He didn't know I was the Princess of Azmia, Zara Al

Latif. But it aroused me knowing that I enjoyed the way he played with me, humiliating me, degrading me and pleasuring me all at once with his words.

It was, in some sort of fucked up way, powerful to know that I, a Princess, enjoyed it and wanted more of it. Knowing well it was all sort of mental stimulation.

Licking my lips, I looked at him and said in a sweet voice. "Would you please fuck your Princess slut, Hayden? I... I can't do it myself and I need your help. Please help me and fuck me. *Please?*"

Pride rolled through me when I felt him shiver at my words, the corner of his lip turning into a smirk as he caressed my face. "If my pretty slut begs me so desperately, how can I deny her, *hm?*"

I hummed, brushing my lips against his and gasping when he slid out of me only to slam back inside. I clutched his shoulder when his arm wrapped around my waist, slowly fucking me with his deep thrust. Topping me from bottom and groaning dirty words against my neck, making me see stars.

I cried out against his skin when I came, thrashing in his arms and trembling when he released inside me. His warm seed filling me up once again, his low grunt pulling me out of my aftershocks as he caressed my back.

Humming, I went lax in his arms, my body limp with exhaustion when he kissed my face, murmuring sweet words that lulled me into deep sleep.

12

HAYDEN

"You did so well, Princess," I said, kissing her hair when she sighed, her body relaxing against mine.

When her breathing evened out, I took a peek at her face and bit back a small smile. It seemed like even the innocent vixen had her own limits, and I had effectively fucked her to sleep.

I slowly slid out of her and gently tucked her on the bed, hating to walk away from her soft, warm body, but I had to clean myself and her. We both had made a mess.

After cleaning myself and her, as much as I could, in her sleepy state, I came back to the room. A smile crept up at my lips at the adorable sight of her sleeping naked on the messy sheets. Her dark hair was fawned on the pillow, her pale body covered in red hues where I had spanked her and held her too hard with hickeys all over her body.

I did that to her.

Male pride surged me as I stepped closer, noticing the shadows of her long lashes on her cheeks. I trailed my fingers on her cheek and held my breath as she curled around the pillow, her lips parting a little.

Fucking adorable.

Swallowing the lump in my throat, I took a step back. I didn't do adorable. I did sexy and stunning. Not adorable. *No. She is too young, and you have tainted her too much. It's just a one-night stand, Hayden.*

I lied to myself, sliding on the bed and covering her with a blanket, tucking her in. I wanted to take her in my arms and protect her from the harsh realities of the world. The ones that I fought. My hand covered the stab wound on my abdomen as I looked at her.

No, even if I wanted, I couldn't have Zara in my life. She was too young and full of life. She hadn't even lived through her twenties yet.

But I could spend another day with her, ask her to show me around Azmia. I wanted her company. It was the least I could have from her.

I checked my phone to let my close friend, Aiden, know that I would stay in Azmia for another day. But my hopes died because I had been commanded to return to the ship early in the morning.

Zara hummed in her sleep, leaning closer to my body, seeking warmth as her lips turned into a sleepy pout. Fuck. I didn't want to leave her alone. I didn't want to get out of the bed and leave.

Swallowing the lump in my throat, I ran a hand through my hair. Throughout the past decade, I had learnt that our choices make us who we are. It had been grilled deeper during the training.

If I chose Zara and spend time with her, it would make both of us happy and we would get to know each other better. But it would mean that I don't value or respect my colonel or my job. All the early morning, late night training, the people I had saved and killed during the missions wouldn't matter if I decide to stay.

Kissing her forehead, I stood up, getting dressed in the quiet night. I wore a fresh shirt and eyed the hickeys she had given me. It was going to hurt so badly when they disappear. I was going to miss her terribly, and I hadn't even left the damn room yet.

What the fuck, Hayden? Since when did I start being soppy as shit?

Shaking my head, I wore my suit. My luggage was packed and ready as I glanced at the naked sleeping beauty on the rumpled bed. I had hung her expensive dress in the closet rack. I was confused seeing her name on the label of the dress in black and gold. She would be upset if I had ripped it off of her.

Thank God, I hadn't.

Walking closer to her, I brushed her hair away from her cheek. Taking the dark marker from the nightstand, I gently pried the blanket from her stomach and awed at the red flush on her breast.

Focus, you horndog.

With a deep breath, I pressed the tip of the blank ink to the pale skin of her stomach and glided it over her skin. Satisfied, I leaned back, growing hard in my pants at the sight of her skin marked with what I had written. Kissing the red flush on her ass, I tucked her in and pulled away before I demand a quickie from her.

Glancing at her one last time, I opened the door and left the hotel suite with a single hair pin to remember her by. I couldn't have anything more than a one-night stand with her. I have to remember that.

Zara

I woke up groggy, my entire body sore as if I had run a fifty miles marathon with sunlight streaming down the window curtains, warming my body. Yawning, I stretched my limbs, wincing at the throbbing soreness between my legs.

Biting my lip, I sat up on the bed looking for the reason of the delicious soreness of my sex. It was surprising that despite the initial shock and surprising of waking up to the aching, I desired him.

In fact, I wanted him more than ever.

"Hayden," I called out, rubbing the sleep from my eyes and looked around the empty bedroom.

Disappointment crashed through me when his lean, muscular frame didn't appear in the suite. Maybe he was showering? I guessed, even though I hadn't heard the shower running.

Frowning, I leaned against the marble sink of the bathroom.

He had left. Hayden had left without waking me up.

I tried not to gasp at my reflection in the mirror. I was naked, but I hadn't noticed the black words until now. Swallowing the lump in my throat, I patted down my mussed-up hair and splashed some cold water on my face, careful not to wash away the ink.

"Okay, calm down, Zara. Deep breaths," I whispered, limping to the bedroom and standing across the full mirror across the bed. The one where he had made me watch myself sucking him and later fucking me in front of it.

My flushed nipples pebbled just at the mere thought of the night before. They were sensitive and marked with the red hues of hickies. Just like my collarbones, my stomach, my hips and even my inner thighs.

Brushing my fingers down the hickeys, I stopped to admire his penmanship on my skin.

'Be ready for my call, my pretty Princess slut. H'

A sigh escaped my lips when I stared at the words longer. I had given him the phone number but still, he had left his own number on my skin, just below the *H*, reminding me that I could contact him if I wanted.

Glancing at my phone, I opened the camera app, blushing when it focused on my face and the writing on my stomach. Sunlight provided the natural light as I took a few pictures with the rumpled sheets of the bed in the background. I crossed my thighs in a way to hide my sex and my hair covering the tips of my nipples.

Arousal and lust rushed through my body as I swiped through the pictures I had taken. I wish Hayden was here. Maybe he would like those pictures...

A knock interrupted me. Covering myself with a robe, I opened the suite door to the delicious smell of pancakes. Thanking and tipping the room service, I ate alone on the bed that smelt like sex and Hayden.

He had ordered me breakfast before leaving.

Hayden will call. He had promised me. Written it on my skin. He will.

The shrill ringtone of my phone made me jump as I scrambled to get it.

"Hel—"

"Where the fuck are you, Zara?" Zayed asked, his voice a little too loud.

"In bed."

"Whose bed?" He sighed. "Never mind. Do you know what time is it? Khalid is waiting for you to come out of your room and it won't be long before Zain notices your absence and the entire country is looking for you."

"Give me a break, Zayed. I am tired. It was my first night outside the palace and... I can handle my brothers." I lied, looking for my dress.

Ahan! Hayden had been kind enough to hang it up in the closet and even left me his own shirt.

I shimmied inside the dress, jumping to zip it up.

"Don't even start right now. Safiya is panicking in your room because she thinks your brothers will behead her for not taking care of you and I am worried that I might get my precious nuts nailed by Khalid if he finds out I helped you sneak out." I was shocked to hear the concern in his voice. "Even I can't get out of this one."

He was Khalid's best friend and one of the most charming yet annoying person I know. If he said that he can't get out of this one, then I knew he meant it.

"Okay, okay, okay. Can you send a car or a cab to the hotel? I will be down in five."

Taking Hayden's crumpled shirt and heels in my hand, I left a hefty tip on the counter for the room service because I knew they would have a field day cleaning the bedroom. They deserved it.

"Already waiting for you, Princess."

I sighed and ended the call, leaning back on the elevator. I licked my lips at the reflection, noticing how different, yet similar, I looked. My cheeks were flushed, and I had to use my hair to cover the hickeys on my neck and collarbone. My brown eyes flowed differently and even though I was still the Princess of Azmia, I felt different. Better.

Glancing down at my palm, I clutched the diamond hair pin. I had two of them with me last night, but I only found one just before I left the suite. It had real diamonds as well, but I didn't have the time to find the other one.

Despite knowing Hayden Knight just for a day, I missed him. I wonder if he would miss me too and call me.

Hayden

"Yes, sweet. Are you eating on time? Don't depend on instant noodles all the time. It's not healthy for you," I said on the phone, nodding at one soldier who was in a uniform, ready to start the engine of the ship.

The early morning sky was still dark, but the view of Azmia's Golden palace was marvelous through the ocean. It shimmered like true gold, even in the dark.

"Yes, Hayden. I am hoping to get a scholarship, so it's okay to pull a few all-nighters. You know I want to get out of here," Ivy said, her voice light.

"I know, Ivy." I continued, hating I wasn't there to help my sister. "I promise I will be back as soon as I can."

"It's okay, I am proud of what you are doing." Relief washed over me to hear her say those words. She was one of the most important people in my life, the only proper family I cared about, so hearing her say those words made me want to do better. "I will wait for you. And... Aiden."

I chuckled, hearing her say my best-friend's name. "You haven't met him in years. He has only gotten worse."

"Who the fuck are you talking about, you man whore."

I didn't need to turn around to see who the deep voice belonged to as I leaned against the railing of the ship, looking at the dark waves splashing against the surface of the ship.

"Tell Aiden I said hi. I have to go. I love you, bye!" Ivy said quickly, her voice high pitched as she ended the call in a hurry.

I frowned at the phone and turned around to see Aiden. We both had similar built, but he was a bit on the leaner side as he wasn't a part of the Navy Seal. He specialized in psychiatry, so he trailed along with me sometimes on the mission, helping the soldiers who had PTSD.

"I was talking about you. Ivy said hi." I eyed him and his

usual formal attire that comprised a shirt and pants. No suits like me. "Where were you last night?"

"I was working on a thesis unlike you." He removed his glasses and leaned beside me. His dark hair and piercing grey eyes looked sharp. "I thought I would have to come and get you from the hotel this morning because you didn't reply to any of the calls. Was it that good?"

I looked away, at the phone where I had Zara's number saved and now the only thing that connected me with her. I thought of her innocent doe eyes, the fire in them, her elfish vixen face and that fucking beauty spot above her lips. Her sweet voice and soft skin.

"No," I answered. "It was better."

"Don't fall for it, Hayden," Aiden chuckled lowly. "It was a one-night stand. Like the million others."

"No, it wasn't." I glared at him. "Does it feel like a one-night stand when you fuck Addison?"

His face hardened hearing about his on-and-off girlfriend. I had crossed a limit, but I didn't care.

"It *is* different with her. We have known each other for years."

"I wanted to spend another day with her instead of standing here right now. You would have understood if what you have or had with Addison was real."

"Hayden," he said in a warning. "Don't talk about her like that. We have been through this. And don't you dare compare her to whoever you spent the night with."

I couldn't do it anymore. I had to tell him.

"At least Zara was innocent and wanted to fuck me because she was attracted to me, Aiden. Did you ever think why Addison is still not committed to be with you after all these years? Because she only wants you for—"

"*Don't*. Say. It."

"Your money." I ignored the way his nose flared, but he

was my friend and if I didn't tell him how stupid his decision was related to his relationship, then no one will. "I am sorry for hiding this from you, but the night she broke up with you for the first time? She showed up at my apartment, drunk and crying, asking me to have sex with her."

His face paled as he blinked at me. "You are lying."

"I wish I was, Aiden." I shrugged. "I called her a cab and left her in the hallway. That's why I couldn't see you for a week because I felt guilty for the break-up until I saw you both together—"

Aiden punched me.

Pain rang through my cheek and I clutched my jaw as I glared at him, his fist. "What the fuck was that for?" I hissed.

"For being a lying piece of shit."

"I am not lying, you dickhead." I said, punching him right back as others just ignored us. Yes, we fought a lot, and it was common that no one but only Ivy tried to stop us. But sometimes, it helped release the testosterone.

"That hurt," Aiden said, rubbing his nose and rolling his shoulder. "You are asking for it now."

"You are slacking," I replied and continued. "Break up with Addison or I am calling her right now to tell her you are gay."

"But I am not—"

I raised my eyebrow.

He closed his mouth. "That was one night."

I shrugged and called her on-and-off girlfriend slash ex. She picked up on the first ring. "Hey, Hayden. I never thought you would call me so late at nig—"

"Aiden's gay and madly in love with me."

"Shut the fuck up, Hayden."

I, like a true best friend, ignored Aiden.

"What?" Addison's voice was filled with horror.

"Yes," I said sadly, turning away from Aiden, who was

trying to take the phone away from me. I pushed away his face. "He confessed to me last night with a ring and I said no, but I don't think you should be with—"

Aiden ripped the phone from my hand and spoke. "He is drunk, sweetheart. I will—"

I tried to snatch it back, wrestling him against the railing. I gaped when the phone slipped from his hand and fell in the ocean. I stared at it. The dark waves of the ocean.

"It was your fault," Aiden grumbled, fixing his shirt and hair as if he hadn't just thrown my phone into a fucking ocean.

"You are dead."

That was the only warning he received when I wrestled him on the floor, punching him and fighting him before the soldiers had to interfere, pulling both of us away. We were scolded by the Colonel and given extra rounds and service at night on the ship.

"I have to eat soup for next three days just because of you," Aiden complained, an ice pack on his swollen cheek while we monitored any suspicious activity in the ocean at night.

"I can't see from my right eye," I shot right back. He had given me a black eye. "I can't believe you dropped my phone. I had her phone number saved on it."

"Stop sulking like a baby. Surely it wasn't that good that you had to fight me."

"It was the best sex I ever had, Aiden," I answered truthfully. "Not just the sex, man. I can't get Zara out of my head. She was enthralling."

He snorted, throwing a paper ball at me. "Look at you using big words for a one-night stand. I don't ever remember you mentioning someone you liked, so this is new."

I flipped him the bird and took notes of our location with a squinted eye. "I wanted to call her tonight," I said to myself.

Maybe have a phone sex with her, ask her to finger herself while—

"Gross, stop making that face in front of me," Aiden complained. "I don't know why you are whining about her number. Didn't you give her your number?"

I smirked, remembering the numbers and words I had written on her body.

"I will take that as a yes, then. Quit worrying about it. She will call you if the feeling was mutual and focus on the altitudes before we get scolded again."

Aiden was right. Even though I had lost her number, Zara still had my number. All I have to do is wait patiently until I get her call or message. I could do that.

I could wait patiently. If it meant hearing her voice, then I could wait.

13
ZARA

Hayden didn't call me that night. I had to make up an excuse of food poisoning to my brothers for not meeting them at the dinner and ate alone in my room, clutching the phone and waiting for his call.

"Why are you sighing like that?" Safiya asked from the lounge chair, flipping through a magazine as I sat on the settee of the low table on the balcony of my room. Water in the pool rustled with wind as the sun disappeared down the sand dunes, painting the sky orange and blue.

"Sighing like what?" I asked, looking down at my sketchbook. My cheeks burnt noticing the soft curves and hard definitions of two bodies. Since when did I sketch nudes? Especially of me and Hayden.

Safiya closed her magazine and looked at me. I squirmed under her heavy gaze. She had scolded me when I met her after her night of being a princess in my place and forced me to shower because, according to her, I reeked of men. I didn't bother to correct her that it was just one man. *Hayden.*

"Don't tell me you miss that stranger."

I shrugged, not replying to her and glancing at the phone.

I was gathering up my courage to call him when Safiya leaves me alone.

"Oh my god, you totally miss him!" She groaned. "You went out of the palace for one night and fell in love."

"It wasn't love," I grumbled, hating the way I felt disappointed that it was true. "I don't know what it was, but I liked him. I enjoyed the night I spent with him."

Safiya giggled, "I figured that out the way you limped yesterday. Prince Khalid will be so livid if he found out that you went—"

"Why would I be livid, dear Safiya?"

I froze and her eyes widened when I looked over to the open double doors of my room to see my brother standing near my bed, frowning at the dress I had worn that night.

Did he find out? That I had snuck out of the Golden Palace on my birthday wearing that dress. *Oh, God.* Did he find out about Hayden and was holding him as a prisoner in the dungeon? Is that why he didn't call?

No. Stop thinking. Act like you have done nothing wrong. Be calm.

"P-Prince Khalid," Safiya scrambled on her foot even though he waved her off as she bowed to him, her cheeks red. "I was just…" she trailed off, mouthing 'hothothot' and fanning herself over his shoulder when he walked towards me.

Khalid eyed my sketchbook as I subtly changed the page to the sunset I was previously working on. I didn't have the energy to give him any explanation why I had been sketching two people having sex. The way he and Zain had taught me sex education at eleven had traumatized me enough. Khalid had painted each painting with labeled body parts and Zain had demanded me to study and remember them while Zayed had taught me about using protection with a dildo and an actual vaginal toy.

Zain and Khalid had banned him from visiting me or live in the palace for a month after that.

"You can leave," I told Safiya, who was ogling the back of my brother and drooling. I had told her he would never return her feelings because I had never seen him in a relationship before, but she had argued that she never wanted a relationship with him or anything. He was an eye-candy for her.

Yes, I wanted to bleach my ears after hearing that.

Khalid hummed, flipping through my old sketchbook, his dark eyes averting to me and narrowing at my face. "What was your maid talking about, Zara?"

He knows something or else he wouldn't enter my room to talk about it.

There was no beating around the bush about it.

"I snuck out of the Palace on New Year's Eve," I said, meeting his stare head-on.

His jaw clenched as he leaned back on the settee. "Were you alone?" He asked.

"No," I said and continued with the half-lie. "I wasn't alone, but I fell off the horse and hurt my inner thigh."

More like I rode Hayden, who was hung like a horse a little too hard.

Shut. Up. Brain.

Khalid's face morphed into concern. "Did you see the doctor? Is it serious? And why didn't you tell us?"

I cleared my throat. "I didn't see the doctor because it wasn't serious. Safiya helped me. I can walk properly now."

"Is that why you weren't present at the dinner yesterday?"

I nodded, closing my sketchbook and making sure my hair covered my collarbones. If he noticed any hickies on my neck, he would make sure he finds Hayden and do something terrible. There was protective and then there was Khalid. He had been like that ever since that night when I was six.

He had promised to take care of me and he would do anything to make sure no harm came to me. Even kill our own father when Zain couldn't save us.

I loved him and Zain. They were my only family, but I didn't like the way they took care of me by being so overprotective.

"Did anyone know you were out of the palace and roaming around the capital unguarded?" Khalid finally asked, his voice deep and stern. He was angry, but he was controlling himself. I knew he would send his team of security to find out who I was with and if I was safe as soon as he walks out of my room, but he was holding back himself for me.

"Yes, Zayed knew—"

He stood up, "That son-of-a—"

"*Sit*. Down." I ordered my brother, glaring at him.

His nose flared as he glared at me right back. I kept my chin high, remembering how Zain handled his meetings with the council and other countries being a Sultan. He had taught me to never lower my head or eyes for anyone and always be calm, as if you have the upper hand in everything.

Khalid sat down in his seat. "Whatever you have to say, do it right now, Zara. I am furious with Zayed and disappointed in you."

Hurt bloomed in my body, and my heart thudded loudly hearing that from him. *How could he say that?* He loved me.

I looked away from him, forcing my voice not to quiver. "Never say that to me again without listening to my choices. It was supposed to be my birthday and not a way to find a suitable bride for Zain. A political move."

"We are Royals, Zara. Our entire lives are political mo—"

"Then I don't want to be a Princess!" I said, glaring at him. His face morphed into a shock and something else. I sighed as relief washed over me, saying the truth, "I don't want to be a Princess, Khalid."

"You don't... you don't mean that."

"I do. I never asked to be a Princess. I never wanted to be one. It has brought me, you, Zain and what little family we have in this palace, but it came with a cost." Hot tears blurred my vision, remembering the sobs of my mother, the screams and the way my own father had hurt me. I had never told my brothers about it because I had been afraid and scared. I would take that pain and secret to my grave.

"*Zara...*" Khalid's voice was raw and filled with anguish. He shook his head, "I don't know what happened when you went out, but this is not you. I am going to find out what happened unless you tell me right now."

"Don't do that. Can't you trust me, your own sister, when I said nothing important happened?" I couldn't have him find out about Hayden. He didn't even know that he slept with Princess of Azmia. I didn't want him to know that. For him, I just wanted to be a nineteen-year-old-girl without any royal titles and terrible past.

"I trust you, Zara, but not the person who was with you. There must be a reason you are acting like this," he said, standing up.

I followed suit. "He has nothing to with this! I have been thinking—"

His eyes narrowed at me as he turned around. "The person was a *he?*"

I snapped my mouth shut. *Uh-oh.*

He took a step closer and color drained from his face when he whispered, "Is that a hickey?"

My hand covered my bare neck.

I might die today.

"Did you spend a night with someone? A boy?" Khalid asked, blinking at me. His voice had gone soft.

I didn't reply. The doors of my room opened, but we didn't turn to see who it was.

"Hey sexy bitches. Did you miss your daddy?"

"That's gross, Zayed," I said, side-stepping from my fuming brother who was going to explode at any moment. I patted Zayed's shoulder. "Thank you for saving me. He is going to combust any moment so I—"

Zayed ignored me and gasped dramatically, even cupping his cheeks as he eyed my neck. "Are those hickies?"

"There is more than one?!" Khalid asked, glaring at me when I ducked behind Zayed.

"It wasn't my fault!"

"Was it with that hunk—"

"*Not*. Now. Zayed," I gritted through my teeth.

"Get out of the way," Khalid growled at his best friend, who I was using as a physical shield. "I will scold you later, but first I need to talk with Zara. Come here!"

"*No*." I answered, pushing Zayed at him, dashing towards the doors of my room. I only turned back to see Zayed groan when Khalid punched him and ran down the hallway of the palace, hiding myself in Grandma's room.

I was safe here for a while. Before Khalid finds out exactly who I slept with.

"Hello?" I said, holding my breath and tightly clutching the phone.

It was midnight, and I was safe in my room. Khalid had sent me a message that he had emergency matter with Zain but he would talk to me as soon as he could as a brother first and then as a Prince. That meant he would try to ground me.

After dinner in grandmothers' room who praised me for my skills of sneaking out and sleeping with a stranger, I decided to end my frustration and call Hayden. Safiya had told me to wait for his call instead, but I didn't care. I had told her to go to sleep in her own room.

"Yes, munchkin. You want someone?" A woman with a heavy twang in her tone asked while chewing on a gum.

I glanced at my phone and checked if I had dialed the correct number. I had.

"Um, can I talk to Hayden? I am Zara."

I heard some shuffling and the loud noise of someone yelling in the background and throaty laughter.

She continued, "We don't have any Hayden's here, but he can be anything you want, hon. Hayden, Jaden, Garon, anything and anyone you want."

I squeaked, "I am sorry, what?"

"Oh, you want something specific like role-play? Yeah, we do that here too." I heard the pop of her gum as she added, "It will be fifty dollars for an hour and an extra fifty if you choose role-play. Another fifty if you want to add cuddling after."

"I am sorry, it must be a wrong number."

She giggled, "That's what they all say before calling us again at Twinky's escort."

I ended the call, blinking in horror at my phone. A shudder ran through my body as I recalled the phone conversation.

What the absolute fuck? Did I just call an escort agency?

I rechecked the phone number Hayden had written on my stomach and frowned. Disappointment crashed through me as I sat on my bed, lying back on the soft mattress as I eyed the diamond chandelier on the ceiling.

Hayden had given me a number of escort agency.

I didn't know whether to cry or laugh.

PART II

"Are you my sweet Princess slut, Zara?"

14

ZARA

TWO YEARS LATER

"Are you sure this fits me?" Ivy asked, her fingers pulling at the hem of the dress. "I look…"

"*Beautiful*," I interrupted her. "You look stunning. Stop stretching the fabric with your fingers and here… you might like this one."

She took the perfume bottle of *Delicate Dew* from my hand. Ever since my brother, Khalid, engaged to Valeria, I received a lot of perfumes launched by her brand.

"Oh, this smells so sweet." Ivy applied it with a shy smile as I met her eyes in the mirror's reflection.

We were in her old childhood room, all ready for her father's surprise event. Since I had moved to San Diego a month ago, she had invited me and asked me to get ready with her.

I had met Ivy when I was in Australia, still hell bent on travelling the world with a camera and a backpack, treated like a commoner than a royalty. She was the same age as me and I had made a friend out of hers when I was bar tending at a club. A guy wasn't leaving her alone while she was minding her own business and I had stepped in. Since then, she had stayed in touch with me, helping me move into a small house in San Diego that I bought with my money that I had been saving up.

"You look like my father is going to get an aneurysm after seeing you." Ivy beamed at me. "I mean that in a good way. He would never expect me out of all people to befriend you."

I let out a light chuckle. Her strained relationship with her father was one of the reasons I liked her as a friend. He had been neglectful all her childhood, especially after her mother left her and her brother. Her father only stepped in when he wanted something of familial value, like lunches, dinners, his parties, and she couldn't do anything about it because she was a sweetheart.

"Twenty bucks and I will tell him I am here to tell him I want to marry you," I said in a serious tone, looking at her baby blue eyes. They always seemed familiar to me, as if I had seen them somewhere.

Ivy's cheeks turned warm, and she shook her head. "I couldn't do that to you. Besides, he already knows who you are."

"Really?" I asked, running a hand through my short pixie hair. I liked the platinum white dye on it more than ever. I touched up my subtle makeup of dark-winged eyeliner, red lipstick, and blush with some mascara. Despite living in Sri Lanka, Australia and even San Diego, I had not changed a shade in my skin color. My skin didn't want to tan, and I had given up on the thought. But it made me blend in better. I didn't look like a royal. I looked far from a royal.

Ivy hummed, looking through the pictures on her old bookshelf. It was their old house, and no one lived here anymore except her father, and occasionally she would find his girlfriend when she visited. She lived at her brother's house, even though he was never there whenever I went to meet her.

"He told me he would like to meet you. A photographer who is travelling around the world. And exactly how I befriended you."

I shook my head with a small smile, fixing the strap of my black body con dress. It suited me well, and it was the only piece of clothing that I owned and could wear to a family dinner.

I handed her a small bottle of whiskey that I had in my handbag. "Here's to hoping that we can survive this dinner."

She would moan to me every time after her lunch with him. I had told her multiple times she should not go, but she wanted to have a chance of having a normal father-daughter relationship.

I could relate. I never knew why my father, Salman Al Latif, sneered at me, calling me a witch or a monster every time I tried to play with him when I was a kid. Avoiding me like a plague and hurting my blind mother in a way that she would clutch me on her lap, crying and whispering to be a good girl.

"Let's go, Zara."

I blinked out of the memories and smiled at Ivy. The photo frame she had been seeing caught my eye. It was Ivy and her brother as kids and some other kid standing beside them. He was holding her in his arms as if he was about to raise her to the sky and tickle her with an infectious grin on his face. He had similar eyes to Ivy in the photo, the bluest I had ever seen.

"That's Robert. He is always busy with his work nowadays. Come on."

She tried to hide the sadness in her voice, but I could hear it well. She missed her brother. I turned back to see the boy's features, but it was an old photo with a grainy texture. I closed my eyes and shook my head.

It's not him. I will never meet him again.

The event was taking place in the backyard of their old house, which, to me, didn't seem old at all. It was built like a small manor with slopping roof and old walls.

There was a buzz among the people wearing suits and dresses, greeting Ivy with a big smile and their smile going half when they looked at me, eyeing me like I didn't belong there. After being used to the same reaction several times, I didn't let it bother me. I was here to support Ivy and eat free, delicious food.

"I will bring you something to drink," I said to her over the light music playing in the background and went to look for some alcohol.

"Hey sexy," a voice drawled over my shoulder.

A chuckle escaped my lips as I removed his hands from my waist, looking at his charming smile and blond hair. "Not now, Noah. We are at a family dinner."

I thanked him when he handed me a glass of champagne from the server.

"And when has that ever stopped you, my darling?" I rolled my eyes at his fake British accent, trying to mock me playfully for having the English accent. It had stuck with me growing up, hearing both my brothers speak in the same accent as they had studied in London most of their life while I was homeschooled.

"If you are lucky, I will call you after this," I said, checking him out and mentally removing his three-piece suit that clung to his muscular tanned frame. "But why are you here? I thought you would be busy partying or having an orgy. Or both."

He was a friend of Ivy, but Ivy denied it when he came to talk with us while I was visiting Ivy at her university. After getting a number out of me, we had discussed that everything was for fun, just what I wanted. I couldn't handle a romantic relationship. I never been in one to begin with. So falling for someone or develop some feelings was the last thing in my head.

"Parties and orgies can wait when I have my beloved darling waiting for me to rescue her at such a boring dinner—"

"Noah!" Ivy walked towards us, her long hair brushed over her back in waves. "I thought you wouldn't come."

Noah grinned at her, "Of course I would come when you invited me so graciously—"

"You begged me to invite you."

"And I was just telling Zara what a wonderful dinner it is. Want some hors d'oeuvre?"

Ivy ignored him, "Help me."

"I can be of any help, my sweet Ivy." Noah batted his lashes at her.

"Put a sock on it," I said to him. "She asked for my help and go talk with someone else. Those cougars have been eyeing you for some time. Shush!"

He pouted when we left him on his own. Ivy had invited some of her college friends too because, according to her father, it was a very special event, and he wanted to make Ivy happy.

"Father, this is Zara Kent. Zara, my father, Matthew Knight." She introduced me to a tall man with salt and pepper hair, his stubble white but still in shape for his age. His eyes looked at me and instantly I could see why Ivy would come vent to me after her lunch with the man.

His eyes were cold and empty. They already marked me as unworthy of his attention and even his daughter's after seeing me.

"Hello, nice to meet you. Ivy had told me about you." His voice was gravelly, and he didn't hide the way he was judging me, putting me in a categorized box in his head. "Where are you from again?"

"I am from Azmia," I replied with a small smile.

I hadn't told Ivy that I was a Princess of Azmia because I didn't think it was necessary and I had been told by my brothers to keep a low profile and try not to tell anyone who I was, as it would jeopardize my safety. If I told Ivy, she would have to sign NDAs and the security of Azmia would keep tabs on her and run a background check on her family. I didn't want her to go through that. I wanted her to know me as Zara. Not Zara Al Latif.

"Ah, it's in Middle-East."

"It's also known as one of the most powerful country in Middle-East. A country, the only country, I believe, that bleeds gold. *Matthew*." I said in a clipped voice, raising my chin a little and sipping from the glass of champagne, meeting his cutting stare. If he was going to judge me, I couldn't care less about it, but no one can belittle the country my elder brother, Zain, ran while I was present.

"Oh, look, I have been dying to introduce you to her." Ivy clutched my arm and forced a smile at his father. "Wonderful talk, dad. Waiting for the big surprise."

She dragged me away from him and as soon as we were out of the earshot, I said, "I need a bottle of champagne."

Ivy burst into a soft laugh, making me smile as she introduced me to her university friends. They were interested to know about my travels and why I had majored in photography and how my freelance photography was going on. I was more than happy to talk about it, asking about their semester, knowing how hard Ivy studied to get good rank and get a scholarship for masters in the University of San Diego.

Noah was talking to, but he had his arm loosely wrapped

around my waist as if he was trying to signal about our relationship to everyone.

"What's up with you?" He asked when he saw me frowning at his hand.

"I would like it if you didn't touch me in front of everyone."

His eyes turned mischievous, "Remember that time when we were at the fair, I had—"

"*Noah*," I said. "I am serious. We are just… sleeping together."

"Ouch. Here I thought I was becoming your friend."

Before I could reply, Ivy's friend Olivia asked me if I wanted to join her to grab more drink from the bar. Yes, the backyard was so big that they had a bar setup, and if I listened closely, I could hear some splashing in the pool. The crowd was getting bigger, and it was only a matter of time when they would announce the dinner.

"You're from Azmia, right?" She asked. "Ivy couldn't stop talking about you when she came back from her vacation."

I smiled, nodding at her. "But didn't you transfer last month? I don't know why you changed from the University of Melbourne to San Diego."

"I had a rift with one professor and came back to my hometown."

I asked her about her previous university and how it was like living in Melbourne, its weather, when my phone rang.

I cleared my throat checking the number and said to her, "I am sorry but I have to take this."

"No problem," she smiled, her eyes kind as she gave me space to pick up the call.

"Where have you been?" Zain, my elder brother and the Sultan of Azmia, asked as his way of greeting.

"Nice to talk to you too after a month, dear brother." I shook my head with a smile. "I thought I gave my monthly updates to Khalid. He is a worry wart so please don't pick that off of him."

He scoffed. "I am not a... worry wart. We are just looking out for you, Zara."

His voice warmed me and instantly, I missed the cool warmth of living with them at the Golden Palace and having sweets Nasrin made for us.

"I am fine, I promise. I have a good friend here and I am bonding. Socializing. Being... an adult, I guess. I have rented a house. Can you believe it?"

"Yes, I can. You can rule the world if that's what you wanted."

I giggled. *Of course, he would say that.*

"I called you for a reason, Zara." His tone changed. He was back to being a Sultan talking to a Princess. Not a brother talking to his sister anymore. "I need you to be careful."

I pressed the phone closer, looking around. "Careful?"

"Yes. Do you have a gun Elena gave you for your twenty-first birthday?"

I had it in my handbag, but the thought of ever using it made me freeze. "Of course."

"Good. I have security surrounding your house and you. Discreet, of course. But I need you to make sure you can protect yourself, okay?"

I didn't like the sound of it. How carefully he was choosing his words.

"What is happening, Zain?"

"Khalid's wedding is in two months. Aya is two and there had been some troops that tried to attack Maahnoor."

"What? Why?" Nasrin, Zain's wife and the Sultana of Azmia, was from Maahnoor. It was previously nemesis with Azmia, but when they both got married, it dissolved the hate with love.

"Not sure why. Sadiq handled it well, but we all have to be careful. You should be thankful that I am not sending Zayed to pick you up and have you here in the Palace. Khalid is constantly with Valeria and I am afraid of keeping Aya out of my sight for one minute."

"First of all, if you sent Zayed here, I would pretend not to know him and ignore him. Second of all, Khalid is always with Valeria because he is whipped by her. And you are a father of the most precious baby in the world, Zain. Of course, you would feel that way."

People were getting closer to the tables arranged, and I didn't want to miss out on appetizers. My stomach was grumbling loudly.

"I have to go Zain."

"Keep me updated and remember about the securities. They are for your protection," Zain reminded me.

"Yes, yes, I remember," I paused, looking at the smiling face of Ivy as she talked animatedly. "But please don't run any background checks on any of my friends."

"*Zara*," he warned.

"Please. She is my only close friend. I don't want to break her trust like this."

"I will try, but please be careful."

I started walking over to the crowd, opening my handbag to check if I had the gun and pepper spray. "Yes, yes, I will be careful. Love you, bye!"

I heard his distant 'love you and goodbye' as I ended the call, turning to keep my phone in the bag, when I stumbled into someone.

"*Oh…*"

"I am so, so sorry!" I stared in horror at the champagne I spilled on a white crisp shirt. "I wasn't looking where I was going. I am so sorry!"

"It's okay," the man pulled the wet shirt away from him,

his defined muscles transparent through the shirt. *Well, damn.* My eyes travelled up the chest to look at him.

"*You...*"

My mouth parted, my heart beating fast and throat going dry at the sight of him. It couldn't be. After two years, I am meeting him here out of all the places. The same piercing blue eyes, same sandy brown hair, the sharp jaw with stubble and high cheekbones.

"I am sorry?" He asked, furrowing his brows as he tilted his head and stepped closer. The wave of nostalgia hit me like an ice bucket when the scent of his musky cologne wafted in my nose.

I couldn't say anything. I was nineteen again. Wearing an imaginative tiara on my head, knowing I am a princess and should be treated as such, blushing and stammering in front of a handsome man who wanted to kiss me and take me up in his suite. Teach me dirty, filthy things, humiliating me in a way that felt pleasurable, ruining me for any other man and taking care of me in the sweetest voice. Buying me a blueberry cake, making a fake promise of calling me and leaving me alone.

"Zara?" His tone changed, his voice huskier as his pupils widened, his intense gaze looking at me. *At my soul.*

"Who?" I asked stupidly, trying to compose myself and pretend that it wasn't me.

He took another step. We were an inch away from each other. Almost touching each other. My body was aware of him, the heat thrumming in my veins just at the sight of him. My body remembered him. All the ways he had made me feel.

"I will recognise those lips in my sleep. Your eyes. This beauty spot..." he said each word like he hated me, as if he was angry with me. His eyes glaring at the corner of my top lip where the beauty spot was.

I covered it. It was the one thing I had gotten from my mother. I would not stand there listen to him complain about something on my body and skin that I cherished.

"I looked for you everywhere," he whispered, holding my wrist, his touch burning my skin, and moving my hand from my mouth. His eyes pinned me to the spot, a predator assessing his prey. I couldn't move even if I wanted to. My stomach clenched with anticipation. "But I found you in my own home, little Princess Zara."

15

HAYDEN

A FEW HOURS AGO

A small grunt escaped my throat as I pushed the heavy weights from my body, focusing on my breathing despite the heavy soreness of my arms. One more round, and I am done. Just one more.

Breathing deep through my nose and slowly pulling the heavy weights down to my chest. Holding them there for two more seconds, I pushed, exhaling through my nose and keeping the bar on the rack. I sighed, taking the face towel and wiping the sweat off my brows.

"How's it going, man?" one of the veterans, Jim, clapped my shoulder as I drank some water mixed with a protein shake.

I nodded at him, "Doing alright, Jim. How are the kids?"

He smiled just at the question, and I knew he was doing well. "They are little stubborn shits but Mary and I couldn't be happier." His expression said it all. I tried not to make a point of looking at his prosthetic leg when he sat down beside me on the other bench press.

"Tell Mary I loved her cookies. Take care, soldier," I said, standing up as he grunted in reply through his weight lifts.

After sitting in a sauna for a while, I walked out of the gym into the hallway, nodding at the young soldiers who saluted me after seeing me. I had served for my country and I had served well.

But I didn't want it to be over so early.

I thought bitterly, standing outside the shooting range and hearing the muffled noise of single gunshots. Taking a deep breath, I opened the door with my ID card, the heavy metal door unlocking as I stepped in.

The scent of metal, gunpowder and smoke hovered in the air, people talking to each other, wearing enormous glasses to protect their eyes and headset for their ears. I took a few steps, mentally counting the victory of stepping inside after... after that day. I had puked and retched before that day whenever I tried to enter it.

The doctor had said it was normal for soldiers like me and I shouldn't force myself to try. But I couldn't just sit and watch.

I eyed the various dark guns on the wall. Rifles, pistols, shotguns, carbines, assault rifles... My chest tightened and my breathing sped up as I tried to swallow the lump in my throat when flashes of images rolled through my head.

Dessert. Sweltering hot as men shouted. My brothers, my soldiers. My ears ringing with the pounding of blood and screams. I tried to navigate through the dangerous mission, the sounds of gunshot increasing and increasing until my ears went numb. Sticky blood dripping down my head into my eyes as I panted, wiping my eyes, my muddy gloves covered in blood. A shout of 'Watch out!' came from my mouth, but it was too late. The blast had thrown me away, my head hurting as I slipped into unconsciousness.

I blinked, staring at the rows of guns looming down at me. I had walked up to them and I was touching the trigger of one pistol. I remembered my friends, their families, and their funerals after that blast. The silent cries of widows, their children's face gleaming with tears as they watched coffins after coffins lowered to the ground. While I stood there, fighting off dizziness and telling them how brave their father was.

Brave. What a strange fucking word. I was anything but brave when they awarded me, attaching yet another medal on my uniform that felt heavy and suffocating.

Holding down the breakfast I had in the morning, I rushed out of the shooting range, out of the building for training new soldiers, and into the streets of San Diego. I breathed the cool air and tried to calm down my heartbeat.

'Point ten orange things in this room, Hayden.' I could hear the soft, lilting voice of my psychiatrist in my head as the ringing in my ear kept bubbling, my breathing getting heavier until I slowed down enough to count the orange-colored things in the street.

The traffic lights in the road's corner. That man's shirt. I kept counting, distracting myself until I reached ten. Slowly, my body went back to its normal breathing and heartbeat pattern. I had calmed down the panic. I was okay. I was in San Diego now. Not Iraq.

My phone started ringing as I made my way to my car and accepted the call from my little sister, Ivy, as I sat in the car.

"If you don't come this evening for the dinner, I will never forgive you and no amount of sushi will make up for it."

I smiled hearing her voice and started the car. "I told you, I am busy."

"No, you are not."

"But Ivy—"

"No, you are not busy, Hayden Robert Knight. Because I said so."

I didn't reply. She only ever called me by my full name when she wanted me to listen to her. She always called me by my middle name, Robert, a habit that she had picked up from my father. But I only ever allowed her to address me from my middle name.

"Please," her voice turned soft and I could hear someone in the background, one of her friends maybe. "Don't leave me alone tonight. I need my big brother."

"You can't pull that big brother card every time, Ivy," I warned her, but I couldn't ignore it. I knew I would be stupid to leave her alone tonight when my father was having a surprise dinner party. Neither of us knew what he was up to and wouldn't share the 'surprise' even if we tried to ask and tell us separately. No, he wanted to announce it publicly.

"I am your sister, so I can. Wear a suit, okay?" The feminine voice of her friend rang through the call as I stopped at the red light. "Yes, Zara! Wait for me."

That name.

"Who's Zara?"

Just the sound of her name brought goosebumps all over my skin. My body going tight with tension and remembering the night I had spent with Zara in my suite in Azmia. I had been whipped and regretted that I didn't ask for her last name, and even leaving the suite before she woke up.

"Who, Zara? That's my friend I told you about, Robert," Ivy said. "She's the one who flew from Australia, short pixie hair, nose piercing. Just rented a house? You should listen when I am talking."

My shoulders drooped hearing her description. That's not her. It couldn't be her. It had been two years, and she hadn't called me. I had moved on and I was pretty sure I wasn't going to meet *that* Zara in San Diego, of all the places.

"Yeah, yeah. Have fun, I will see you tonight."

"Bye!" The call ended just as I reached my home, parking the car in the garage.

I don't want to go to the stupid surprise dinner event at my father's house, but I have to.

Shaking my head, I went through the contact and called Jane. She was one of my recent dates and asked her if she would be busy after midnight. If I was going to be in the same place as my father for more than an hour, then I would need something or someone for a release afterwards. Even though it had been years, I could try.

"Your sister is really sweet," Jane whispered, her arm pinned over my elbow after introducing her to Ivy.

"She is," I said, eyeing the crowd and ignoring the tightness in my stomach. "Are you hungry?"

Her bright brown eyes looked at me. I had known her since I was twelve when we went to same school. We had hooked up in our teenage years and stumbled into each other at a grocery store when I came back from Iraq. She was single and, just like me, wanted something that didn't involve feelings.

"I am famished, but if you plan to take me to KFC, then I won't complain."

I smiled at her. "I just need to talk to my father and then we can leave."

My eyes averted to the people surrounding the man who looked just like me, but older and less handsome with salt and pepper hair with the stubborn frown on his lips which made him look stern. I narrowed my gaze at the tall woman beside him, holding his arm and whispering something in his ear that made the frown leave his face. Just for a moment.

I had never seen him gaze at our mother like that.

Jane excused herself to go to the washroom while I planned to tell Ivy why I must leave early. The hushed voices of the people were getting on my nerves. A headache was already forming—

Oh.

I tilted my head to the side as I saw a woman in a black short dress by the bar. The crowd faded into smoke. My attention zeroed in on her. Her short platinum hair, tucked perfectly behind her ears, few strands framing her face. The golden hoops and piercings above them glinted with light as she talked with someone on the phone. I didn't care to look. I was occupied by her.

I felt my hair rise on the nape of my neck at the awareness of knowing her. I wanted to erase all the distance between us, my fingers aching to touch her, talk to her.

Her long legs, pale and toned, donned in elegant dark heels. Her lithe frame as she moved, whispering. She was ten steps away from me, but I noticed the way her brows scrunched and relaxed, her pert nose high and pillowy lips moving as she talked rapidly.

I know her. I remembered her from somewhere.

That slender neck, her elfish face, sharp cheekbones and angled jaw with that dimple on her cheek. Fuck, I knew her. My body remembered her.

Who is she?

Why is she here?

Before I could comprehend, I was walking towards her, wanting to know. Know her name, hear her voice. See her look at me as she talked, give me that dimpled smile. I wanted to be the one she gave attention to.

"*Oh...*"

Cold wetness seeped from my shirt to my skin as I looked down. I hadn't even noticed that I was holding a glass of champagne. The woman in black was apologizing furiously, her voice sweet but husky with a bit of English accent. Her voice was filled with sincerity, as if she had bumped into me.

I looked at her face. Inspecting her when her lips parted, the beauty spot above her lips, her golden-brown eyes, that looked little bit of green and yellow and grey with all the lights, widened. They blinked at me, her lashes long.

"*You…*" she had whispered in shock and surprise. With anger, I noted.

I didn't care. She looked beautiful. And I remembered her.

She pretended that I didn't, but of course, I recognized her. I told her why. The anger burning in her eyes as she cupped her mouth when I glared at the beauty spot above her lips.

Silly girl.

She didn't know I was glaring at it because I was afraid that I couldn't handle myself seeing her after two years. That I wanted to lock her up in a room and kiss her senseless, bite her slender neck and lick that beauty spot that made me lose control just at the mere sight of it. Her *lips*. Fuck, how I remembered and dreamt of those lips.

"I looked for you everywhere," I said, pulling her wrist away from her mouth. Her pulse had increased. I eyed her pretty face. She had gotten even more beautiful since the last time I saw her. "But if found you in my own home, little Princess Zara."

She took a sharp breath as if I had struck her. I frowned. "Don't call me that."

"Why not?" I shook my head. "Doesn't matter. *You…* you are here."

"You didn't—" she stopped whatever she was going to say and closed her mouth.

"What?" I took a step closer and looked around. "Let's go somewhere. I need to talk to you."

"I… I don't," Zara said. Her eyes were wide and there was a flush on her face. "I don't want to talk to you, Hayden."

I swallowed the lump in my throat, looking at her again. My heart was pounding in my ears. "I like your hair."

She nodded curtly.

I didn't like whatever that was churning in her head.

"I didn't what, Zara? My phone fell in the ocean and I lost your number. I regret that I didn't stay with you that night."

She exhaled sharply as she bit out, "I am glad you didn't."

I looked at her. The woman who had infatuated me. Her appearance had changed, yes, but in a way, she was just the same.

I took another step. She didn't move back, peering up at me with her closed off brown eyes. I had hurt her. Somehow, in those two years, I had hurt my Princess so terribly that she wished I had stayed.

"You have always been a terrible liar, Princess," I said, my warm breath caressing her cheek.

"Hayden, there you are."

I clenched my jaw and took a step back, the sweet musky scent of her making me slid my hands into my pockets to control myself.

"Jane, why don't you sit at the table? I will be right back." I said tersely, her brows raising as she looked over my shoulder at Zara's frame and gave me a small smile, leaving us alone once again.

"Now—"

"Don't talk to me," Zara said, her eyes lined with kohl, glaring at me as she away.

I would be mistaken, but I might have heard a little tremor when she said that.

Sipping on the last bit of champagne, I smiled to myself. Two years and she still couldn't lie.

Meeting Zara was the last thing I would have imagined

coming back to my old house. But I was more than glad that I did. I had to ask Jane to cancel our plans that night and for the foreseeable future because I would be damned if I didn't have my sweet as sin Princess writhing beneath me again. Begging me with those lips and moaning around my length.

16
ZARA

You have always been a terrible liar, Princess.

God, fuck him and his handsome as ever face.

If I put anymore force on the heels while walking, I was sure I would break them. But I was angry. Frustrated, and a bit sad. At the man-who-must-not-be-named and at me. After two years, changing my hair, the way I look, everything I had tried, and I still hadn't changed.

I was still a weak Princess who was living in a small rented house instead of a Palace. That's the only thing that had changed. Nothing else.

"I saved you a seat, sweetcheeks!" Noah called out, the round tables where everyone was already siting around in their own little groups.

Ivy sat with us, her group of friends with three chairs empty.

Before I could ask Ivy about the man-who-must-not-be-named, she stood up, a grin on her face as she looked over my shoulder.

"Robert! Zara, come on I will introduce you to my brother."

What? No!

But she was oblivious to my expression and turned me around to face him, my nose flaring at the sight of him. Hayden nodded his head at me, a small smirk curling at the corner of his lips. God, I wanted to smack it off of his face. How dare he look handsome as ever, especially with a champagne drenching his shirt?

"Zara, this is my brother. Hayden—what happened to your shirt?"

Hayden smiled at me, mischief twinkling in his eyes. "I got bumped into a pretty girl, that's all."

My cheeks flamed. With anger. Nothing else. I was angry.

"Weird," she muttered and continued. "This is Zara, the friend I made in Australia, the one I was telling you about."

Ivy talked about me to him? *Doesn't*. Matter.

"Oh, that friend!" He grinned and, taking a long step closer, he wrapped his arms around me.

My entire body froze with the initial shock of being in his embrace again. My skin scorching and remembering that night with him as I tried to relax, fighting off the urge to hug him.

But Hayden was ruthless. He pulled me closer, tightening his arms around me, his palms on my lower back, and I was burning and aching where he touched me. His warm, hot breath caressing the shell of my ear when he whispered, "Hey, pretty stranger."

"Let go of me." I hissed, scrunching my hands on his back, but it must have seemed like I was hugging him back. The scent of his cologne and musky aftershave was all around me, and it was unfair that he smelt so divine. Like the ocean and sloshing waves, calm yet strong.

"Now, now, that's not how you used to beg, Princess," he said, pulling away, raising his brow at me and stepping back.

My lips parted, my eyes wide at his face when he

remarked something to Ivy, how glad he was to meet her close friends. I was barely out of my shock when the same gorgeous woman in emerald dress walked up to him, whispering something in his ear that made him look at her and give her a sincere smile before turning back to me.

I swallowed the lump in my throat and looked away. I didn't need to know why he was flirting with me when he was with her. Still, I hung on every word he said, introducing her to Ivy. That the woman's name was Jane, and they knew each other since middle grade.

Thankfully, I was saved by the announcement of dinner as all the guests sat down on their chairs, servers in suits bringing out the appetizers. I knew Ivy and her father were loaded, especially the way Ivy had a touch of naivety towards her. Similar way I had until I realised that the world outside the Golden Palace of Azmia was not always flowers and tiaras.

As Ivy talked to Jane, I felt a tremor run through my body, his looming presence behind me. "I love your dress, Princess. But you look way beautiful with nothing on. Except that body jewellery, of course."

I forced my legs to stay still and took a deep breath. "And you'd look better with a tape on your mouth."

He raised his brow. "Kinky, are we?"

I exhaled sharply, looking at his blue-grey eyes. With as much force as I could muster without getting attention of others, I stomped—*hard*—on his shoe.

I was glad to see his expression change when I moved back and sat beside Noah, kissing him on the cheek with a smack of lips. "Thank you, darling," I said in a sweet tone as he grinned boyishly at me.

Ivy sat on the other side of me, then her brother, whose face was red and blue eyes dark whenever he looked at me.

Beside him sat Jane, who was speaking to her friends and making a pretty good impression on a date.

"Why do you call your brother Robert?" I asked Ivy, ignoring his daggers on my face.

"Because that's his middle name and I have always called him by his middle name. What's the matter?" Ivy asked, leaning close. "Did something happen between you two?"

Oh, nothing much. Other than he had raunchy, kinky sex with me on my first time in his hotel suite two years ago, promising me to call me, broke that promise, left his suite before I was awake, broke my heart and then pretended that he had not given me a male escort's number and a few minutes ago he tried to flirt with me even though he has a date.

I chuckled, rolling my eyes. "What? *Pffsh*, no. He has... very weird hair. That's all."

Yes, I was a bad liar when it came to Hayden.

"Weird hair?" Ivy frowned, looking at her brother's hair while he grinned, talking to Jane.

"Yes," I said curtly. "It's all... golden and brown. It's weird. Never mind, this soup is delicious."

"Are you coming over to my house?" Noah whispered when the servers cleared out empty plates of dinner, replacing it with sweet smelling chocolate tiramisu.

Seeing the glint in Noah's eyes, I knew what he meant. But the house was filled with unpacked boxes and I needed some space after meeting Hayden tonight. I would have never thought that he would turn out to be Ivy's brother. Or that I would ever meet him again.

I shook my head. "Sorry, Noah. Not tonight. I still have to unpack."

"Maybe I can help you with it?" He asked, raising his brow.

I thought about it, my eyes wandering around and

landing on him. Hayden. I frowned at his glare and looked away, even though I felt him burning holes in my skin.

"I will call you tomorrow if I need your help," I said to Noah, with a smile, and stood up, excusing myself to use the washroom. I had too many drinks, and it was time for nature's call.

As the event was in the backyard, I had to walk from the gardens to the pool by the sliding doors and use the common washroom in the hallway of the house. Someone knocked on the door when I washed my hands.

"Just a moment," I replied and tugged down my dress a bit more. The fabric was cotton and silk. It was one dress that I couldn't leave behind in Azmia. It had my name engraved and stitched on the label on the back, tailored by one of the few famous designers who designed the clothes of Royals when needed. Me being one of them. But I didn't want anyone to know about it.

I fixed the thin straps and opened the door. My eyes met the familiar stained shirt first and then the handsome face with blue orbs.

Oh, no.

Before my reflexes could kick in, Hayden had already stepped inside the washroom, locking the door and leaning on it. In the golden light, shadows fell on his face, making him look like a villain with sharp edges of his cheekbones and jawline.

"What are you doing?" I asked, trying to maintain a distance between us and crossing my arms, but it was difficult. Behind me there was an empty bathtub and, on the side, there was a vast mirror with a sink and cabinets.

I had nowhere to go. I hated the thrill of rush that spiraled down my body.

"Are you dating that kid?"

I stared at him. *Kid?*

"Don't tell me you were planning to fuck him tonight," he said, making himself comfortable, leaning on the door and blocking my exit.

"Even if I was, Hayden, it would be none of your fucking business," I said in a firm voice. I had enough of him. "You left giving me a wrong number, writing it down on my skin, without calling me once. It's been two years. It shouldn't matter to you even if I have an entire orgy."

I tried to move and open the door, but before I could touch the knob, Hayden moved quick as a snake. I gasped and exhaled sharply when he pinned me against the sink, standing behind me and holding my right hand over my lower back.

"Hayden—"

"*Tsk*, still a fucking brat," he crooned in my ear, my eyes pinned on the mirror across me. They were wide, not with fear but with anticipation as I wiggled, trying to have some space between us, but that made him clench his jaw, pressing his hips against me, my hand tightened in a fist as his hold tightened on my wrist.

"Behave now, I haven't even touched you properly and you are already squirming, Princess."

My throat bobbed as I swallowed loudly, a gasp leaving my lips. His eyes met mine for a flicker of a second when his fingers lowered to my thigh, touching the hem of my dress.

"Is that what you say to Jane?" I glared at him. "That she is a brat one moment and a Princess a second? Pin her down and tell her to behave? Does she like it—"

Hayden let out a low chuckle that sent shivers down my spine. "I would watch that mouth of yours, Princess—"

"I told you to stop calling me that." I groaned, pushing back with all my weight, catching him with surprise.

But he was stronger than me and even though all the

years of martial arts and training I had received as a Princess, he was a soldier. A Navy Seal Officer.

Hayden had me in his arms once again, pinning my back to the edge of the sink, my chest flush against his as he gazed down at me as if I was the treasure he had been looking for years. I stopped struggling. I knew I was stuck.

Willingly. At his mercy.

"So beautiful," he whispered in awe, his finger tracing my cheekbone, lowering down to my lip. I shivered, parting my lips when he splayed his warm fingers on my cheek, shaking his head with a small smile. "Pity, you are still a Princess slut, *hm?*"

I gaped at him, pushing him on his chest, but he didn't budge. Instead, he lifted me onto the marble counter and parted my legs to step in.

Holding my chin in his hand, he made me look at him. "Tell me you are not dating that boy."

Something in his tone made me want to acquiesce. "I am not," I said, forcing the words out. Despite my anger, I scrunched my hands around the collar of his shirt, pulling him close. "Are you dating Jane?"

"I don't date, Princess."

"Good."

I tugged on his collar just as he cupped my cheek, our lips clashing together.

17

HAYDEN

I had lost the number of counts I had imagined her soft pillowy lips. Kissing them, biting them, claiming them. Of her arms wrapped around me, urging me closer and parting her soft thighs for me.

I had squeezed my eyes shut, shivering and swallowing the sweet hums of her. Her fingers were in my hair, keeping me close, as if she was afraid I would pull away. I was scared that if I opened my eyes, it would be just another dream. I would wake up in my bed, dark, cold and alone. That her warmth would leave me. The aching press of her body, gently rocking against me, would disappear.

A groan left my lips when I felt the metal on her tongue and pulled her closer, squeezing her hips with my other hand. She had her tongue pierced.

"*This...*" I murmured between the kiss. Eyes closed and kissing her beauty spot. I could trace it with my tongue even if I was blind. "This feels like a dream," I breathed out, her hot breath brushing against my jaw as her hands fidgeted with the collar of my shirt.

"Kissing me?" She asked, despite the sultry tone of her voice. It was innocent and shy.

With a deep breath, I opened my eyes. Zara was still there, beautiful, with wide doe eyes staring at me. Her full lips were swollen with a pink hue from the kiss, and her pulse was throbbing against the gentle caress of my fingers.

Fuck, this woman.

How could she ask that when I was trembling in her presence?

I shook my head, light dimming in her eyes as she looked down at the button of my shirt she was playing with. I held her wrist before she could pull it away and pressed her palm against my heart, let her feel what she was doing to me.

"All of it, Zara," I confessed. "Having you here pressed against me, holding you and kissing you. It all feels like a dream. I am afraid that as soon as I walk out of this door, it will end."

Her lips parted, my eyes dropping to them. I cursed, pressing my thumb against the bottom of her lip before sliding two fingers inside her mouth, feeling the press of a small metal stud against them. My cock throbbed in my pants at the sight of her smudged lipstick, her lips sucking my finger with her eyes on my face.

I lowered her hand from my heart down to my chest. Lower until she could feel me throbbing through the fabric. Her thighs, that were parted for me, tensed.

"This is what you do to me, Princess," I said harshly, fucking her pliant, hot mouth with my fingers, watching her drool for them. "You *wreck* me."

I replaced my wet fingers with my lips, kissing her lips once again. Tasting her cherry gloss and lowering my kisses down her neck, biting the soft pale skin until she arched up to me, letting out a sweet moan that made me want to fuck her like an animal. Do some not-so-gentlemanly-things-to-her.

"Hold your dress for me," I ordered, pulling back to see her fingers fumble with the hem of her tight dress. I pushed it above her inner thighs and held her waist when she lifted it up her hips, offering me with the beautiful sight of her black lace thong. It delighted me to see a wet spot on them.

"How many piercings do you have?" I asked, brushing my finger over the stud piercing on her belly button.

"Why don't you find out?"

That was a challenge I was more than glad to follow.

Gazing at her under the dim glow of light, I was in no hurry, touching and licking every part of her bare skin with my eyes. Her cheeks and lips flushed, golden hazel brown eyes gleaming with lust, her short hair tousled up, with her slender fingers holding up the hem of her dress. Her thighs were parted, thong soaked as she shivered, sinking her teeth into her bottom lip and squirming on the cool marble of the sink.

"Are you my sweet Princess slut, Zara?" I crooned, trailing my finger on her leg, her soft ankles strapped in black heels.

Her eyes widened, a sharp inhale of breath as her fists tightened on the material of the dress. I had caught her off guard. She wasn't expecting that.

My palm glided up her inner thigh when she didn't reply. I pressed my thumb on her pulsing clit, taking a sharp intake of breath, feeling a stud through the soaked fabric of her wet underwear. A tremble of shiver passed through her body as she tried to close her legs, my other hand keeping her legs parted.

"A clit piercing, *hm?*" I teased her, pressing the piercing on her clit over her as she bucked. "Dirty fucking girl."

I hushed her when she whimpered, kissing her softly, stroking her pussy with my two fingers, her hips moving and pressing herself against my hand, wanting more friction.

"Come now, Princess," I breathed, looking down at her

soaking thong, rubbing her warm, slick juices on her clit, feeling her scorch for more. "Don't be greedy."

Her back flattened on the mirror, her short hair distracting me. They suited her too well. Her hand trailed down my shirt to my throbbing semi, cupping it through the pants and flickering her eyes at my face with a lick of her lips.

Fuck.

"I am not being greedy, Hayden," she whispered, her voice as soft as sin. "You are. Locking us both in here, kissing your little sister's friend under your father's roof when you have such a pretty date." Her words were sweet, teasing, her palm rubbing me, back and forth, until I was hard as a rock.

I realised what she was doing. Zara was the same woman, but she had changed. Grew up into a wonderful, seductive creature who I would gladly do anything for.

Smirking, I leaned down and kissed the corner of her lips, sliding her thong to the side and dipping my two fingers inside her. I relished the soft gasp of her lips as I moved my fingers back and forth, curling them to hit the sensitive spot that had her clutching my arms with a shiver.

"Tell me something, Princess," I whispered hotly against her cheek, the sound of lewd wetness of her cunt echoed in the bathroom over her panting. We were both flushed, Zara more so when she heard it. But I kept my pace, pumping my glistening fingers inside her, her velvety walls clenching them with each thrust. It would be so fucking easy to unzip my pants and thrust inside her warm heat. But before that…

"Does he make you blush like I do?" I asked, my tone husky yet fuelled with angry lust. A moan tore out of her throat and I cupped her mouth, her eyes widening. "*Sh*, you don't want your friend or that boy to hear how good I am making you feel, do you?"

Zara shook her head, raising her hips when I slid my

fingers out of her. Removing my hand from her mouth, I ignored her small whimper and spanked her right on her flushed, glistening pussy. The white stud of her clit piercing gleaming in the light.

"Does he make your toes curl like I do?" I asked, landing one more smack. Right. On. Her. Clit.

She groaned, her thighs trembling.

Her lips parted willingly for my fingers that smelt like hers. It was an erotic sight to see her suck all her feminine essence. My cock throbbing hard for her.

"Answer me, Zara."

She shook her head, her golden earrings glinting. I slid out my fingers from her mouth and ordered, "Say it."

Her cheeks flushed more.

"No, he doesn't make my toe curls like you do, Hayden." There was a tremor in her voice that I wasn't expecting. Her expression of lust changing to a broken one. *Fuck, what had I done?* I wanted to wrap my arms around her and make everything alright. "But he doesn't give me broken promises like you. Or hurt me."

I didn't want to hurt her. But it seemed like I had done just that.

"*Zara...*" my voice trailed off, seeing her look away from me as she straightened her clothes, trying to get away from me.

"What broken promise? I tried to call you and my phone—"

"Save it," she glared at me, unlocking the door of the bathroom. "And to answer your previous question, *no*, I am not your fucking princess slut. Don't touch me again."

Zara, her eyes burning a hole in my heart, stepped out, closing the door shut as I blinked at the empty space where she was sitting moments ago.

How the hell did I manage to fuck it up that badly?

I needed to talk to her. I could handle of not touching her ever again, but I wanted to make things right. Whatever I had done. I didn't want to be a disappointment to her, of all people. God knows, I already was one in my father's eyes since the day they had forced me to retire from Navy Seal Officer.

But not with Zara. I will talk to her. I can't have my Princess mad at me. I will make things right.

18
ZARA

I went straight to our table and sat beside worried Ivy and concerned Noah. They both knew something was wrong as soon as they saw my face, but I told them it was nothing to be worried about.

I ate the dessert, ignoring Hayden when he walked back, whispering something in Jane's ear and avoiding looking in his direction. I was probably being childish, but he had given me lost hope. My nineteen-year-old self was so saddened that I had been angry at myself and chopped my hair with craft scissors in my room. I had hated how vulnerable and emotional he had made me feel that I was willing to change myself.

Nasrin, my sister-in-law, had helped. I had moved on from him with time, never expecting to see him again, and as soon as we were alone, he brought up all those memories. I should be angry at him.

"Slow down, Zara," Noah whispered, his hand on my waist when I swallowed the white wine. It was my fifth glass.

"I'll be fine, you cutie," I said, smiling at him.

Ivy chuckled. "She's tipsy. I almost forgot how cute you get when you get tipsy."

"You are adorable," I said, poking her cheek.

I winced when something buzzed through the speakers, someone speaking in the mic as everyone shuffled in their seat to look at Ivy's father, a beautiful woman in his arm as he introduced her to us. I only paid attention because the servers had stopped serving wine and food and even Noah seemed intrigued. I glared at Hayden's perfect sandy brown hair when he moved to hear his father.

"Me and Whitney, this enchanting lady, have decided to get married this December—"

I was shocked when Hayden stood up, anger rolling off of him in steam when Ivy, who looked as if she was about to cry, held his arm. *What was happening?*

Noah filled me in with hushed whispers. Hayden and Ivy's mother had left them when Ivy was barely a year old, leaving Hayden to look after his sister because their father neglected them. He had been dating Whitney for a year, but neither Hayden nor Ivy knew *this* was the surprise their father wanted to share publicly without telling them first.

Their father talked some more as people applauded and congratulated them. Except our table. Hayden stormed off in the house and Ivy was so shaken that she had to clutch the table.

"I-I will be right back." She forced a smile.

I remembered the events held at The Golden Palace, the exuberant gowns I had to wear, talk to guests, charm them. Let old sheikhs and their sons flirt with me while forcing a smile. I always had my brothers and Safiya to rely on.

"I will come with you," I said, standing up and holding her arm. I dragged her away from the backyard.

We were alone in her room and it didn't take over five

seconds to see her face crumble and her arms wrap around me. My heart hurt for her, hearing the sobs.

"He is... he is so selfish, Zara!" she cried out as I sat us both on her bed, patting her hair. I let her vent, hearing her sniffle and talk about how neglectful he was of her and Hayden.

"Do you want me to take you back to your home?" I asked. It would mean Hayden's house too, but I didn't care about him at the moment. Ivy needed me, especially after hearing about her father's marriage, which would happen in a couple of months.

She sniffled as I wiped the streaks of mascara from her cheeks. "You would?"

"Of course, Ivy. Staying here is the last thing you want, right?" She nodded. "Good, stay here. I will be right back."

I closed the door behind me and sighed, leaning back on the door. It was going to be a long night.

Hayden

"How much more selfish could you be?" I asked, trying to hold back the anger as I glared at the back of my father.

It was dark and cold in his study, the place covered with books, desk, old chair and an old computer. He hadn't even tried to make a slight difference in his living when we left. Pathetic.

"Loving someone is not selfish, Hayden," he said, looking over his shoulder at me. "I would watch your tone if I were you."

"Oh, for the love of God," I pinched my nose bridge. "Ivy is crying in her room because of you. And it's not the first time she had done this, you know that?" His back froze, hearing about his daughter. He had at least tried to improve his relationship with her, but it didn't matter when he didn't care to tell us about it.

I looked at the old frame of me and Ivy on his desk. He was staring at it, too. My toothy grin as I was about to raise my sister in the air. I could almost hear her shriek of laughter trickling down my ear.

"Do you care about us, Matthew?" I asked, looking at him and sliding my hands in my pocket. The champagne had left a stain on the shirt, but I didn't have any suitable shirts to change into in my old room.

He didn't answer for a few moments. "I am your father, of course, I care about you."

I scoffed. "You are a terrible liar. Being a sperm donor has nothing to do with caring about us—"

"*Hayden!*"

His throaty voice echoed in the study. I smiled at him. At his angered face.

"You have been nothing but absent in our lives since that woman left us," I said, referring to the woman who had given birth to me and Ivy. She didn't deserve to be called mother, neither did my father. "You both neglected us. Did you know I stayed up with Ivy when she had a fever? I took care of her and made her finish her homework and went to her teacher parents' meeting because the only parental figure that was in our life never fucking cared."

His blue eyes had gleamed, and I hated I had the similar ones.

"If you had cared, dad," I said, "you would have told your children and tried to talk to them about this so-called lovely woman you are marrying. Don't expect either of us at the wedding. Congratulations."

I ignored when he called me back and slammed the door behind me, marching towards the kitchen. I leaned on the marble island and took a few deep breaths. Shots and gunshots rang through my ears, the urge of surviving and adrenaline kicking in as they increased, hot blood dripping down my right eye—

"Are you okay?"

The voice seized me back from the panic attack when someone touched my shoulder. I moved so quickly that Zara took a step back from me, her hand going to her heart. "Jesus, I just asked if you are okay or not, no need to scare me like that."

"Yes, sorry." I exhaled slowly, blinking away from her. "I am fine."

"*Liar*," she said, opening the fridge and offering a bottle of cold water. "Drink this."

I took it from her, wondering why she was helping me. When I was taking a sip, she looked down at her heels and said, "I know you were going to have a panic attack, Hayden." I stopped drinking and looked at her. "I… I am sorry for what must have caused them, but you don't have to lie when someone asks about your wellbeing."

We were silent for a long moment.

I spoke first, "Did you…?"

"Yes," she said curtly, and I knew she didn't want to talk about it. I wondered what could give someone like her a panic attack? What had happened? The idea of someone ever hurting her emotionally made a lump in my throat. I ignored the urge to ask her about it and make sure she was okay.

"How is Ivy?"

"She cried. A lot. I need to drop her home so I will be—"

"*Stay*," I ordered, her eyes meeting mine. "I will drive her back and… drop you home."

She frowned at me, crossing her arms. "Then what about your date?"

I took a step closer to her, her gaze steady on my face. I loved how she never backed down from me. It made me want to do terrible things to her. "Jane is not my date. My father invited her family because they are friends. You should stop being a jealous brat for once and meet me outside with Ivy."

Zara gasped when I walked away from her. A small smile tugged at my lips when I heard her say, "God, I loathe you."

IVY WAS NOT IN THE MOOD TO TALK WHEN I DROVE THE CAR, Zara sitting beside her, her expression full of worry and concern for my sister. I was glad that Ivy had made a friend like her who she could trust. Growing up, she was very shy and quiet, getting bullied in the school unless I stepped in. I was very protective of her and even though she had very few friends, she went alone for her vacation in Australia.

I wanted to ask how they met, as Ivy never told me the details. What was Zara doing in Australia?

"I will come with you," Zara said when we stopped by my house. A two-story suburban house with a small backyard that I had bought for me and Ivy so she could live as comfortably as she want when I left San Diego for work. It would not happen soon, but I wasn't planning to buy another house so soon.

As soon as they were out of the car, Ivy whispered something in Zara's ear, hugging her as I made a call to Aiden. He must be with Addison, but I wished he would pick up. I needed to talk to him and maybe get some drinks if he was up for it.

"Are you sure you want to drop me home?" Zara asked, "I can call a cab—"

"Sit your cute butt down." I turned on the engine of the car and gave her a look. "I told you I would drop you home."

I heard her a grumble 'Bossy' under her breath as she sat

on the passenger seat, wearing the seat belt. I averted my eyes from her bare thighs to the road and drove carefully with the directions towards her apartment.

Zara asked me about my military service, and I grew tense.

"I... t-they asked me to take a leave after the last mission," I said in a clipped voice. I couldn't tell her more even if I wanted to. I cleared my throat. "I was the only survivor, and the PTSD doesn't help either. I could be called retired at this point." I refrained from telling her about how bad it was. How I couldn't sleep without waking up with nightmares of that day and not even able to use a fucking gun.

"I am sorry, that must have been hard for you." There was genuine sincerity in her voice when she glanced at me.

I pulled at the collar of my shirt, unbuttoning the top button to let me breathe. I desperately changed the subject. "What about you? You wanted to become a photographer two years ago."

Zara smiled, and for a second, the world disappeared when she looked at me like that. I paid attention to the road. If I didn't, I was sure I would crash us just looking at her.

Fool. I was turning into an utter fool.

"I did. But I needed to see the world, so I travelled to Sri Lanka, Australia and met Ivy. I was in London for a couple of times and decided to move here for a while. I work as a freelance photographer right now. I mostly take portraits."

Zara had a smile on her face the entire time she talked about her travels and her job, which felt more like passion to her. I was delighted that she was doing well, so well.

Just to tease her, I asked, "Do you take boudoir pictures?"

Her cheeks bloomed with color as she narrowed her eyes at me. "As a matter of fact, I do. Mostly women in lingerie or nude, depends on what the client wants."

I raised my brow. "I don't know who I am jealous of, you or the women who you take pictures of."

Zara squirmed on the seat, crossing her leg as we waited in the traffic. The night sky was clear, with a full moon.

"Sometimes there are couples too with men, so Noah helps me out with it."

My hands clenched on the steering wheel, the knuckles turning white as I bit out, "He helps you with boudoir shoots?"

"Of course, I don't want to be alone with a strange man standing buck naked. He helps with the lighting—"

"Wouldn't that make them feel more awkward?"

"I tell them beforehand and there's a contract so they know what they are getting into."

I hummed, imagining a dark room with a flag of light as Zara takes pictures of people in lingerie—

"Have you ever gotten your pictures taken?" I asked.

"What do you mean?"

"Your boudoir pictures, Princess."

Zara didn't reply for a few moments. I glanced at her and I was curious to know why her entire face had gone red. "I… I took some of them."

I wanted to see them.

"Who took them?" I asked, my voice heavy all of a sudden.

"I did. I took them on my own."

The car grew silent as I let my mind wander. Sexual tension between us was a living, breathing thing and it only grew when I stopped the car outside the small house she was renting. It was a pleasant area, but I was worried about her safety. The garden was overgrown with weeds and the color on the wall was getting cracked, almost peeling off.

"Did your phone really fell in the ocean?" Zara asked in a soft voice, blinking at me with her doe eyes.

"Yes, Zara," I said, recalling that bitter day on the ship. "I was going to call you or send you a message when I was on a ship. My friend, Aiden, had a little fight with me and the phone dropped into the water. I couldn't retrieve it even if I wanted to."

"*Oh.*"

I noticed the throbbing pulse in her neck and asked, "Why didn't you call?"

Her fingers fumbled with each other. Her ears turning pink. "I did. A lot of times but... you gave me a number of male escort agency."

I couldn't help but laugh. "What?"

She glared at me. "See? You think that was all a joke—"

"No, Zara!" I stopped her from opening the door. "I didn't give you a number of male escort agency. Why would I do that?"

"I don't know, you tell me!"

I stared at her. "Zara, I gave you my number. In fact, I wrote it on your stomach."

"I remember." She swallowed the lump in her throat. Unlocking her phone, she went back to that day and I was surprised to see that she didn't have any more pictures before that day as she scrolled and stopped to show me the picture she had taken.

My cock throbbed in my pants, looking at it. She truly had a gift for photography. She was naked, standing across the mirror and holding her phone. The tips of her tousled hair brushed against her pink nipples, her face flushed and eyes glazed. Sunlight filtered through the curtains fell on her smooth skin covered in hickies, the black words on her stomach. I licked my lips at the soft curve of her thighs, hiding her pussy.

Fuckfuckfuck.

I diverted my attention to her stomach, to the number I

had written. "Well, it spells my number. What did you get wrong?" I asked, furrowing my brow.

"It doesn't!" Zara said, her eyes wide as she opened a keypad typing the number. My heartbeat increased a little when I saw that she had memorised it despite her thinking it was a number of male escort agency.

"That's a zero."

She gaped at me. "It's not."

"It is. That's a zero." I said, pointing to the closed loop on the picture she had taken.

"That's a six, Hayden," she said. Her black coloured nail pointed at the line. That must have been my mistake. "*See?* That's a six."

"I guess, that looks like a six."

She ran a hand through her short hair that fell in a perfectly smooth wave, making her look like some sort of sexy pixie fairy. All she needed was wings.

"Don't tell me I dialed the wrong number just because you don't know how to write a zero."

"*Shh,*" I hushed her. Taking her phone from her hand, I typed my number and gave myself a miscall. I handed it back to her. "You can stop whining now that you have my number."

Her eyes gleamed, and she looked embarrassed. Shaking her head, she opened the car door, but before I could point out the seatbelts, she tried to get up, her butt sticking back to the seat. She mumbled, 'Oh my God' as she tried to unbuckle the seatbelt.

I let out a soft chuckle, amused by her actions, and helped her. Zara was adorable.

"Thank you," she murmured, fixing the hem of her dress.

I leaned closer, cupping her cheek to make her look at me. I made a note of the slope of her pert nose, her high cheekbones, brown doe eyes, elfish face and the sweet lips.

Stroking her cheekbone with my thumb, I whispered, "I missed you, Princess."

Her lips parted, but she didn't say anything, her eyes averting from my lips to my eyes. I thought she would kiss me. I wanted her to kiss me, make the move. But she didn't.

She pulled away, opening the car door and walked away.

19

HAYDEN

I wanted to make sure Zara entered the house before driving away. Frowning, I leaned closer when I saw someone in a suit walking towards her, hair blond. I remembered that guy. Ivy and Zara's mutual friend, Noah. The guy she was sleeping with.

My hands clenched into a fist when they talked, too far for me to hear anything or even read lips. With horror, I saw her leading him inside and closing the door behind them.

"*Fuck*," I cursed, wanting to punch something or go in there and do some not-so civil or gentlemanly things to Zara. I dialled Aiden's number again, a headache forming in my head. But he didn't pick up.

When it went to voicemail, I said, "Call me. It's color red." Color red was one term we had made up to let the other person know when things were looking terrible.

I glanced at Zara's house and drove away. I didn't want to stay outside her house like a creep and hear… whatever they were doing inside. I told myself that it didn't matter. Zara and I had just met tonight. We hardly knew each other. It shouldn't matter.

Zara

"What do you mean you can't come?" I complained to Ivy, who was hiding underneath her covers.

It had been two days since I met Hayden and he hadn't attempted to call or text so neither had I, albeit disappointed. I was standing in Ivy's room. Thankfully, Hayden was at the gym.

"I... feel groggy," Ivy grumbled through the blanket. A loud sniffle and a grunt as she moved. "I think I got food poison. I can't be sick now. I have exams in a week. Zara," she popped her head from under the blankets. "Please make me healthy again."

I pouted at her. "I wish I could do that, love. You need to rest for a couple of days and you'll be as good as a horse."

"What about the photoshoot?" She asked, her voice trembling and baby blue eyes blinking at me.

Oh God, she was going to cry.

"I will work something out, don't worry."

I had a few portrait photoshoots to take today, but I needed one more person's help to move the lights and be with me. I would have asked Noah, but he wasn't in good shape since that night he had come over. I didn't want to bother him. Ivy had promised a week ago before I booked the client, but it seemed like I would just have to lift some extra weights and be safe on my own.

"Ask my brother. He will help."

Just the thought of it made me shiver. I shook my head when I heard footsteps in the hallway. Hayden leaning on the door.

Speak of the Devil...

"What do you need my help for?" He asked, drinking some sort of green smoothie.

I licked my lips at the sight of sweaty Hayden. I had almost forgotten how good he looked underneath the suit. *Almost*. His muscles were bulging, the sweat glistening on his brow made me think of some not so nice things. Like his body hovering above mine, his lips whispering dirty things.

"Nothing!" I said, standing up from Ivy's desk chair and picking up my handbag. "Take care, love, I will—"

"She needs your help with a photoshoot," Ivy said calmly to her brother. I was stuck in the room. Hayden was too big for me (haha) to squeeze around the little space and escape. "I promised her I would help, but I got food poison."

"I told you not to eat that Chinese food last night, didn't I?" Hayden said to Ivy with narrowed eyes, his tone brotherly 'I told you so.' He glanced at me, checking me out as the tips of my ears warmed.

I was wearing tight black shorts with fishnets and a cropped white blouse that emphasised my décolletage. Dark chunky Doc Martin that I had thrifted to complete the outfit. I had barely put on any mascara and lip tint, but I had washed my hair that morning and I smelled rather nice.

"Give me ten minutes."

He turned to his room and closed his door. A few seconds later, I heard the shower turn on and my face turned red. I avoided looking at Ivy as I talked to her about anything, trying my hardest not to imagine how he would look naked under a shower. His muscular body dripping with water. Did he have more stab wounds? I hope not.

"He can be an asshole sometimes, but I promise you, he's a good guy, Zara," Ivy said.

I met her eyes and tried to offer her a smile. She was so sincere with me. Trusted me so much. Yet I couldn't find the courage to tell her that I am a Princess. I couldn't tell anyone about the truth or else my safety would be concerned. Not Ivy, Noah, and *especially* not Hayden. He was in the Navy. I don't know what he might do if he finds out.

Nope, he can never find out. I might tell him if we were in Azmia, in the Golden Palace, surrounded by guards.

But not alone. I was scared of he might do. He might hurt me emotionally and break my heart in a few words. I hated he had so much power over me and I couldn't do anything about it.

Hayden eyed my car suspiciously. I narrowed my eyes at him. I hated to admit it but he smelt fresh with his musky cologne and the lingering scent of his aftershave. His hair was still damp. His untucked light blue shirt fitted his broad shoulders and tapered waist, sleeves rolled to the elbows with darker jeans and shoes. He almost looked normal in a casual wear.

"Is it safe to ride that creature?" He asked, lowering on his knees to check the tires.

I scoffed at him and sat in the driver's seat. I know it's not the best car out there, but it is the only one I could afford with rent and moving around with the money I earned myself. I had driven my baby all around San Diego, and she had kept up with me for a month.

"Are you coming or not?" I asked him, hiding my wince when the passenger door cranked open, a sound of nut falling somewhere in the car when he sat down. His weight was probably double than me and the car slanted towards him.

I ignored his wide eyes and turned the key for ignition.

"Let's take my car—*oh fuck*," he swore, clutching the seat belt when it started with a jolt, moving forward.

I hit the brakes just in time because I was used to it by now. Truly, it was a great car.

"See?" I grinned at him, hitting the accelerator and driving us to the location of the photoshoot.

It was an old abandoned factory, and the clients were mostly teenagers in groups who wanted to take early pictures for Halloween that was in a few weeks. Their mothers had already paid for the shoot, so they hadn't joined them. Hayden followed me silently, asking me if it was safe when we met up with a group of four girls who couldn't stop ogling at him.

If Hayden noticed, he didn't pay attention and helped me set up the soft box lights. Sun was still out, but it was cloudy and I didn't want to take chances with the lightening.

When Hayden was speaking to someone on a call, one girl with olive skin tone and a sexy witch outfit came up to me. She glanced at his back and asked me, "Are you two dating?"

Despite my blush, I shook my head, checking the pictures I had taken so far. "No, we are not. He's… really old."

Real classy, Zara.

Her eyes widened. "How old?"

I thought about it. "Hmm, maybe thirty-two or thirty-three?"

"That's not old!" She exclaimed. "You should ask him out."

I offered her an awkward smile and went back to taking pictures. I showed them most of the results on my laptop, their grinning faces making me happy when they left. The actual work would start now, as I had to edit them and send them the photos they wanted.

"I am sorry, I didn't know it would take so much time." I said to Hayden, alone in the dark abandoned factory. The sun was about to set and all we had eaten was granola protein bars until the girls ordered pizzas for all of us. *Bless them.*

"It's alright, Zara. I offered to help."

We had packed most of the things when he suddenly asked, "Did you sleep with him?"

I frowned, turning towards him. "Sleep with who?"

"*Noah,*" he bit out, his blue eyes dark. "Did you sleep with him when I dropped you home?"

So he did see me with him.

"It's none of your business, Hayden."

I turned back to carefully put the lenses of the camera in the bag when I felt his presence behind me. The hair on the back of my neck rose, goosebumps skittering all over my body.

"Answer me, Princess," he whispered. I clutched the old creaky table when he pressed against my back.

Oh, fuck, why did that feel so good?
Body, please don't betray me.

"Did you fuck him?"

Clenching my jaw, I said. "Yes, he fucked me really good, Hayden. I hoped you would hear my moans and drive away—"

He thrusted into me, the friction of his rough jeans grazing my skin and whispering harshly into my ear, "You. *Fucking.* Slut."

A whimper tore out of me, my stomach tight with arousal and anticipation. *God, what the hell were we doing?*

Turning around, I blinked at him. I was just planning to tease him, not have him play rough with me. I couldn't handle that. I would melt.

But Hayden had other things in his mind.

His hand wrapped around my short hair and tugged at them until my lips parted, a gasp echoing in the empty room. I squeezed my eyes shut when he pushed a knee in between my thighs, making me grind on his thigh, moving my hips with the belt loops of my shorts.

"Look at me when I am making you feel good, you dirty girl," he commanded, his hand lowering from my hair to my neck, wrapping his fingers around it.

"What do you want?" I cried out, clutching his shirt, when wetness gushed out of me, his thigh still pressed against me.

His eyes were gazing at my face with an unknown emotion. Shadows falling on his face as he leaned closer.

"Beg me to touch you, Princess," he whispered sweetly, as if he wasn't choking me lightly, kissing the corner of my lips.

"*No*," I shook my head, but my body betrayed me when I pressed against him, moving my hips over his thigh.

He smirked, looking down at where I was grinding on him. "No, *hm*? I had almost forgotten what a brat you are."

"I… I am not a—"

"*Tsk*," he said, glaring at me. "I didn't ask you to speak."

I glared back, wanting to pull away from him, smacking his chest. "Let go of me," I said, gasping when he pinned my wrists on my lower back and bent me down on the table. I squirmed, trying to move away when he pressed against me.

"Listen to me, Zara."

"I don't want to listen to you—"

"I don't want to hurt you so stay still for fuck's sake."

"*How sweet*," I said sarcastically, glaring at him over my shoulder. "You don't want to hurt me and holding me against my will."

"If I slide my hand under your shorts right now, your pretty cunt would be soaking wet, Princess." I squirmed when his palm squeezed my pussy through the shorts. I hated how my toes curled with that little squeeze at his dominating and threatening tone. "So shut the fuck up and hear me out before I have to make you listen to me with my cock in your mouth."

I froze hearing his words.

"You are a piece of shit."

"End things with him. Noah."

His breath was brushing against my neck as I held back, snapping at him.

Taking a deep breath, I lifted my leg and stomped on his toe before he could notice.

"Fucking hell, Zara." He grunted, "Not again."

I pushed back at him and wriggled out of his grip and despite my efforts, I knew he would let me go. I rubbed at my wrists, shooting daggers at him.

Just one word, that's what I would need to say to get him into the jail of Azmia.

Pushing those angry thoughts, I took my camera bag and walked away from him while he groaned and tried to make sure I hadn't made him bleed. Good. Doc Martin was multitasking.

"Zara!" He called for me.

I knew I wouldn't be able to ignore him for longer, so I turned around and said. "We didn't fuck. He helped me unpack my things until he broke down crying because his parents had called him that his father has a lung cancer." I breathed out. Hayden's expression changed as he looked away from me, clearly embarrassed. "He is my friend and I won't end 'things' with him just because you entered my life out of nowhere. Stop being such a possessive piece of jerk. It's *not* attractive."

I turned, but remembered something. Marching towards him, I said in a firm voice, "If you ever hold me against my will like that again, I will aim for your balls next time."

20
ZARA

I made sure all the lights and bags were placed properly when I heard his footsteps getting closer. My breathing and heartbeat had finally calmed down. I had realized that I may or may not have exaggerated snapping at him, but the way he could so easily get close to me scared me. Not physically, but emotionally, mentally. It had been difficult forgetting about him two years ago. I didn't want to repeat that, but if Hayden kept trying to get close to me, I... I wasn't sure what would happen.

He didn't even know I was the Princess of Azmia.

"I am sorry, Zara," Hayden looked at me, his blue eyes gleaming at me as the sun setting behind him. The wind ruffled his hair as he swallowed the lump in my throat. "I got jealous—*no*, I am jealous of Noah for knowing you so well. Physically and as a friend. I won't touch you again without your consent and I am sorry."

He repeated it once more, redness slashing over his cheeks and neck. I stared at him for a while and said, "Apology accepted. Please move out of the way. I need to get groceries for dinner after I drop you off."

"I will come with you," he announced, sitting in the passenger seat. Slowly this time, as if he was scared that another screw would fall.

"I can get my groceries myself," I said, remembering the time when I had first gone to buy groceries. I was shocked to see that beans cost two dollars.

He played with the radio, but when loud static buzzed through it, he shut it off. "Of course you can. But it's getting late and I don't want you to go alone."

I hid my smile and continued driving.

"DID YOU GET EVERYTHING?" HAYDEN ASKED, LOOKING OVER my shoulder when I checked my Notes app for the list of 'Need to Buy ASAP.'

I hummed, "Asparagus, hummus, cheese, tampons, tomatoes, garam masala. Oh, shoot, I need to get tampons. I will be right back."

But Hayden insisted on following me. He pointed at the one which had heavy flow and asked, "I get this or the average flow for Ivy. What's the difference?"

I ignored the flutter in my stomach at the mention of how he buys his sister tampons.

It is a normal thing to do, Zara. Even your brothers bought them for you.

"Heavy flow is for the first couple of days and average flow is for the last few days," I answered, adding them in the cart, which he also insisted on carrying. He was full on 'forgive me' mode, even though I had already forgiven him.

Hayden raised an eyebrow when I added a box of condom in the cart but commented nothing. While we waited at the checkout, Hayden sneakily added a box of chocolates to scan.

"For you, Princess," he said, making me blush when the cashier looked at us both with heart eyes.

"You both look so good together," she said, accepting his card when I mentioned I was paying.

"You didn't have to do that," I complained to him. "These are my groceries and you are here because you helped me—"

"*Zara*," he said my voice in such a sweet, intense way that I had no choice but listen to him. "It was my choice to come with you and pay for the groceries. I am not asking for anything in return. Why don't you go start the car? I will bring these bags in a few."

I nodded hazily and made my way to the parking. As I had predicted, it was extremely cloudy, the night dark and airy as I walked. I quickly became aware of how alone I felt and—

A big hand clamped around my mouth, their arms going around my hands and dragging me towards a dark van. My heart pounded in my ears as I struggled to breathe, trying to elbow or stomp their feet. But the person was way too large, and I felt weak.

My voice was muffled when I tried to scream. The sound of my shoes dragging on the asphalt made me realize how real it all felt. I was getting kidnapped in a shady parking of a grocery store.

"Stay calm Princess Zara Al Latif. We don't want to trouble Sultan Zain or Prince Khalid with the news of hurting you."

My entire body stiffened hearing my name. My brothers' names. *This person... whoever he was, knew I was the Princess*. They were going to kidnap me and try to use me against my own family.

I opened my eyes wide, grunting and biting the palm of the culprit with as much force as I could. He yelped, his hold on my mouth and arms loosening as I elbowed him hard in the ribs. I exhaled sharply when I kicked him in the balls. He was wearing a ski mask on his face and I was about to yank it away from his face when someone pushed me away with so much force that I grazed my knees on the rough asphalt.

I blinked through the gleaming tears to see two men looming over me. I heard my name being called and the men disappearing from my view as his voice got closer and closer.

What if they hurt him? No. I couldn't live with that.

Hayden

I WALKED TOWARDS THE CAR, WONDERING WHERE ZARA WAS. I had asked her to go first because I wanted to buy her a pizza which if she allowed, we could have together in her old car.

"Zara!" I called out, wondering if she was pranking me.

I heard tires screeching and frowned at the large vehicle. It was a van, dark in color, my eyes narrowing to note the number plate because I had a gut feeling it was something bad. Leaving the grocery bag and the pizza by Zara's car, I rushed to find Zara.

It was easy to find her. She was on the floor with her knees bruised as she covered her face. *What the hell had happened?*

"Zara," I breathed out, kneeling across from her. "Princess, what happened? Are you okay?"

She moved her hands to look at me and it wrecked me to see her brown eyes gleaming with tears. I took a sharp breath when she wrapped her arms around my neck, a broken sound of my name tearing out of her throat.

"Oh, baby," I cooed, taking her in my lap, hugging her tightly as she hid her face in my chest, crying softly. I rubbed her back, breathing in the scent of her shampoo and trying to notice anything strange on the cars or by the asphalt.

"You are okay, Princess. I got you, I am here," I whispered, thinking back to that van and why it had changed the gears so fast when I had called out her name.

"I am so sorry, Hayden," she said, pulling away and blinking up at me. Tears had slid down her cheeks and I gently wiped them with my thumbs.

"What are you apologizing for, silly?" I looked down at her knees. They were minor bruise. I clenched my jaw, thinking who would dare to harm her and push her down. "How did you bruise yourself? Is everything okay?"

She sniffled and nodded, biting her lip when she saw her knees. Her fishnet was torn up.

"Hold on to me," I said, picking her up and taking her to the car. Thankfully, Zara had a small medical kit in the dashboard.

"I tripped really badly," she whispered, not looking at me when I cleaned her wound, gently applying the ointment on her knees with cute cat bandages.

I peered at her and straightened up. She was sitting on the hood of her car with her long legs draped down as she avoided looking at anywhere but me.

I knew she was lying. Zara couldn't injure herself like that, even if she tripped. Someone had pushed her. Hard. But I nodded and smiled, asking her to sit in the passenger seat while I drove.

I didn't tell her, but I had asked to come with her to the grocery store because I had seen two large and strange men following her. They had at least five inches on me with muscled bodies and darker clothes. I couldn't leave Zara alone and go talk to them or show them my Navy Seal ID to scare them off.

At first, I thought they were normal people when I had come home from gym to see them talking on their phone and looking away once I glared at both of them from the porch. I stayed on the porch until they moved their car, making a point.

But no, they had followed us to the abandoned factory. The same dark SUV was waiting by the trees when we had left to get the groceries. I knew I needed to stay close to Zara, wondering who those people were.

Were they trying to get to me through her, or was it about Zara?

"You got us a pizza?" Zara asked excitedly.

I glanced at her with a small smile. "Yes, that's why I asked you to go ahead. I wanted to surprise my Princess."

Her expression faltered just for a second, but it was quick enough for me to notice. It was about her then. She was hiding something and someone had hurt her. Had they hurt her before? *Who would dare to do that?*

My jaw clenched as I stopped the car at my house, wondering if I could ask her to come inside and stay in Ivy's room or the guest room for tonight. I didn't trust those two men. I didn't want her to stay alone.

But I didn't need to when I noticed a car on my porch.

"What the hell is he doing here?" I said under my breath.

"What happened?"

I looked at Zara. "That's my father's car. He is in my house."

I got out of the car, so did Zara. "Do you mind if I come inside?"

"Not at all, Princess."

PART III

"You have a dirty little mouth.
I am going to fuck it."

21

HAYDEN

The lights of the living room were on. Zara followed me wordlessly. I looked over my shoulder to make sure she could walk properly without hurting herself. She offered me a small smile, and I quickly looked away.

"Ah, Hayden... and Ivy's friend," my father said, standing up from the couch. "I am glad you are here."

I glanced at Ivy, who had a blanket around her with heavy bags under her eyes. Zara walked towards her, ignoring my sister's concern about the bandages on Zara's knees.

"Why are you here?" I asked my father. "Ivy, you need to rest. Go back to bed. Did you eat?"

"I had some chicken soup."

"Hayden, Ivy, I need to talk to both of you," my father said, looking at Zara.

Zara stood up, "I will leave then—"

I stopped her. "Wait in Ivy's room. I need to talk to you." *About the two men who had been following you and might have hurt you.*

Zara peered at me from under her lashes and nodded

slowly. My sister and father looked at me as if I had grown another head when Zara went upstairs.

"Please hurry with whatever you want to say."

I sat down on the other armchair as one of them was occupied by Ivy. Dad looked at us both, making us both nervous when he said, "Whitney and I had booked tickets for Almas Peninsula. To have a small one-week vacation before the marriage."

My jaw clenched as I leaned back on the chair, flickering my eyes to my sister and making sure she was okay with him going on.

Of course, my father didn't care. He kept talking. "Unfortunately, she has gotten ill. Doctors are saying it's a flu, and she has a heavy fever. It will take another week for her to recover."

"And?"

He sighed and looked at me. "We can't cancel the tickets and Almas Peninsula is a rather lovely place. We had a private cabin booked, planned trips and everything." He looked at us both. "So we decided to give the tickets to both of you."

Silence fell in the living room.

Ivy spoke first. "I can't go. I am sick and I need to prepare for my exams."

"Yeah, I don't feel like—" Before I could finish, my sister interrupted me. "But Zara likes to travel."

I stiffened, staring at her. *Does she know? Does she know I had slept with Zara when I was in Azmia two years ago?*

Dad nodded at us both. "I was hoping that you both could travel together, but it's alright. These are the tickets and details so if you decide to go, it's up to you."

He kept a white envelope on the coffee table. I felt Ivy glaring at me but I ignored her.

"I am... sorry for that day," he said, looking at his hands. "I didn't… I didn't consider both of your feelings when I should have told you both about my intentions of marrying Whitney."

We didn't say anything at all and it was awkward for all of us. A sincere apology from him was the last thing I was expecting. Ivy was busy staring at the envelope, and I knew she couldn't wait to open it and check the details.

Almas Peninsula was near the Middle-East and it was famous for its diamond mining. It was also one of the most expensive peninsulas that was famous for its lovely weather, calm beaches and beautiful tourists spot.

I would be bummed if I didn't get to go but I didn't want to go without Ivy. Aiden had called me the next day after the dinner at my father's house and despite being surprised by my meeting with Zara, he had mentioned that he was extremely busy. He had his own marriage coming soon, and I had promised to help as much as I could. Not to mention, he was a therapist, so needed his own time to make sure he remains sane.

"Alright, then. I will see you two later."

Father left with a clipped smile, and as soon as the front door closed, Ivy sprang up and opened the envelope.

Ivy rattled on. "Two airplane tickets. Seven days stay in a cozy cabin by the forest to get the view of both trees and the beach. A day of hiking and leaving the Almas Peninsula by—a yacht?!"

I sighed, rubbing my temples and went upstairs to check on Zara. When I opened the door to Ivy's room, I paused at her sleeping form. *She's adorable*.

With light feet, I made my way towards the bed and removed her shoes. She made a small whining sound when I draped a blanket over her. Her lips were pursed in a stern pout as I tucked her hair behind her ear. *How could someone ever think of harming her?*

When I straightened up and looked in the mirror, I had a smile on my face. Shaking my head, I turned off the lights and went downstairs.

"You need to share your bed with Zara tonight," I announced to Ivy, who was busy reading the travel guide. "She fell asleep."

She kept down the guide and glared at me. "Why were her knees bruised?"

"She tripped."

"Okay, did you two have fun today?"

I narrowed my eyes at her. "No, I was just helping her with her work. It wasn't… that fun. Why did you mention Zara and me to go there? I would rather ask Aiden."

She shrugged. "Her home is closer to the peninsula and because she loves to travel."

"But you can come with me, Ivy. You will be healthy in no time and you're already a scholar—"

"Doesn't matter. The dates match with the days of my exams. It's next week. I won't be able to come and you know how much I hate the ocean."

I pursed my lips and looked at one template of the travels. It was about a cabin. Warm pictures of it during the day and night, the interior cozy with one bedroom, kitchen, living room with couch and books. There was no television, which I preferred.

I wouldn't complain about living with Zara in such a close space. There was also that thing about those two people and God knows how many others stalking her. If I could take her with me and maybe find some sort of evidence, her case would be much stronger.

"I am going to bed. Don't you dare eat pizza or you will get sick again," I ordered Ivy when she pouted and went to my room. A night's rest would make me think better the next day.

Before going to bed, I checked my phone to make sure all the motion sensors that I had attached on the porch and front door were active. I checked the live footage of the front and back of the house. There was a grainy film over the live feed, but other than that, no one was around the house.

As soon as I had bought the house, I wanted to make sure Ivy could stay here without me for months without worrying about her safety. I didn't dare to run check up on any of the neighbours or her friends, but the cameras outside the house and motion sensors were a necessary precaution.

Especially if someone was stalking Zara.

Zara

"I told you why I can't go, Ivy." I kept the books that I had collected on the bookshelf on the corner of the apartment. It was looking cozy, not barren and cold anymore. Ivy made herself comfortable on the couch and looked at me with her big blue eyes.

It was her third day of trying to make me agree on the one-week trip to Almas Peninsula with Hayden. From her perspective, it looked like her friend and brother would go together, get two cabins and enjoy the time of their life.

But what she didn't know was that we had slept together two years ago and the enormous bubble of sexual tension when we were in the same room.

"Give me a good reason you can't go or else I will kidnap you and strap you to the seat of the airplane."

She looked cute when she was angry. I ignored her threat and sat down on the couch, the diary of my mother in my hands. She was blind, but she had a maid she trusted to write for her. The pages of the diary had turned warm, a bit rumpled, but the wording and the beautiful handwriting were readable.

"It's so pretty," Ivy whispered in a small voice.

I smiled reading that day's entry. She told how tiny I felt in her arms. It was one of my favourite entries when she had recorded me growing up in different pages. It made me remember the scent of her, sweet cinnamon, her cold hand on my shoulder, her sweet voice.

I almost told Ivy about the day I played hide and seek with my brothers and maids, and soldiers. The Golden Palace was fuelled with laughter and chorus that night until I cried and made a fuss that I had won because I was the youngest.

But I remembered I couldn't tell Ivy about it. Share those memories with her because she didn't know I was a Princess. Even if I told her, she would push me away. Call me a liar and walk away from me.

So I didn't say anything. Maybe I should tell her about the reason I couldn't go with Hayden.

"Ivy," I said, turning towards her. "I need to tell you something."

"Is it about Hayden kissing you—*oops*," she cupped her mouth when I gaped at her.

"How did you know?!"

"You guys weren't that sneaky at father's house," she smirked, flicking her hair over her shoulder. "Not to mention Hayden had your shade of lipstick on his neck. I may not look like it but I notice everything."

I ran a hand down my face and leaned back on the couch. "Ivy... it's not just that."

"You know," she leaned beside me. "I love you both. I don't mind you two being together but—"

"We slept together."

Silence fell between us and I was a coward to notice her expression when she muttered a small 'oh.'

"Two years ago. In Azmia," I added. I had told her about the mysterious stranger who had slept with me and broke my heart. "Hayden was that mysterious stranger and I didn't know I would ever meet him again until... you know."

"*Oh my God*," she whispered to herself, her wide eyes blinking at me. "It was my brother? Oh my God. Why didn't you tell me sooner?"

"*Ivy*."

"I knew something was going on between you two and it makes so much sense!" Why was she grinning? Why was she happy? "Then it's decided that you are going—"

"Ivy. Which part of him breaking my heart went over your head?" I shook my head. "It is silly now, of course. I am over it but me and Hayden can't be together."

"Why not?"

Because I am a Princess of Azmia and he is a Navy Seal.

"Because I am not ready for a relationship."

"Zara, forget about my brother for a while, okay? Think about Almas Peninsula. You are getting a chance to travel to such a pretty place for free. Why don't you go there?"

I didn't have the heart to tell her that we (me and my brothers) owned the Almas Peninsula. It was under our country and I had travelled there when I was sixteen. For free because I am Zara Al-Latif.

I forgot to mention that there was a jewellery shop named after me because the owner loved how pretty I looked.

"Please think about it. Hayden is already packing because he has nothing much to do."

"What do you mean? Isn't he a Navy Seal Officer?"

As I had imagined, she looked away when I asked about his job. "He... hasn't been to work or missions since the accident in Iraq." Her voice had turned low and almost inaudible. "Psychiatrist and his colonel decided it would be best for him to retire because of his PTSD. It was very hard for him, going to all of his friends' funerals."

I swallowed the lump in my throat and. Looked down at my lap.

"All he had been doing was going to the gym and going out for drinks since he came back." She held my hand. "Until that evening. He hasn't come home drunk since then and I think it's because he likes you."

"Ivy, if he likes me, then it's a fine reason I shouldn't go. I don't want to lead him on when I have nothing to give or offer him in return."

"You are overthinking it, Zara," she said and stood up to grab her ringing phone and silent it. "I need to work on an essay tonight. And you need to pack for the trip to Almas Peninsula, okay?"

I hated how weak I was when it came to her.

I nodded slowly, "Okay."

"I knew you would come around!" She grinned. "See you soon."

I sprawled across the couch and stared at the ceiling. If I have to go to that island, I need to call either of my brother and give them an update on my situation. Which meant they would ask about Hayden and run a background check on him. Khalid was way too smart and if he found out that Hayden was in Azmia two years ago, he might also find out where I had snuck to that night. He would do anything to bring Hayden to Azmia and arrest him, or worse, invite him to the Golden Palace and keep a close eye on him.

"*No*," I said in horror, sitting up.

I couldn't have any of that. If Hayden found out about me... it would be terrible.

22

HAYDEN

The last thing I expected to wake up to on the day me and Zara were supposed to leave for Almas Peninsula were the pictures of us together. I don't mean the happy Instagram filtered pictures that couples take. No, the pictures were from the evening Zara had bruised her knees and I had taken her in my lap, hugging her.

I clenched my jaw, looking at the few different angles from the exit of the parking lot. That meant that it could be the person who had pushed her. I wasn't sure.

Why would someone take our pictures like this? Did Zara have stalkers?

Setting up the phone with my laptop, I tried to trace the unknown number but as I had imagined, I couldn't find the correct IP address as its location kept changing within every ten seconds. These people were good.

The message alert popped on my phone. It said,

Stay away from the Princess.

I frowned at the text for a second as the entire text and pictures vanished from my phone. Clearing evidence already. What the hell were they talking about? *Was this some type of sick joke?* But Zara wouldn't go so far with it. She was crying that night and it had made her panic. Whatever happened that night hurt her. These people could be stalking and trying to hurt Zara.

"Hayden Robert Knight!" Ivy knocked on my door. "You need to go pickup Zara or you'll be late."

Sighing, I shut my laptop. I need to stay closer to Zara for the entire trip and make sure no harm comes to her. I needed to find out what she was hiding and why there were two people stalking her. A scary thought flitted across my mind. *What if there were more than two people?*

Ivy had her exams, so she was going to her university and I had to pick up Zara from her house. The weather was windy, as it was already November.

When I had first met Zara two years ago at the club, I knew she didn't fit in with others. She looked innocent with an air of elegance around her. As if she had been told to walk with her chin high and back straight. Come to think of it, I had never seen her slump either.

"What am I thinking?" I muttered to myself. She had mentioned two overprotective brothers. Where were they? What did they think of Zara being stalked by two or more people? Did she know about them? Had she told her brothers?

What if she was loaded and they are stalking her to keep her as a hostage for ransom or to do something worse? There must me some kind of motive to stalk someone and threaten the person who had held her on his lap making sure she was okay.

No matter what happens, I needed to stay close to her. *Make sure she's safe.* That's all. Nothing more to it.

Zara had packed one luggage and was wearing a cute dress. By cute, I mean, if I bend her over, I would easily eat her out, flipping her dress over her waist.

We filled the drive to the airport with silence and the occasional talk about what we were going to see at the Almas Peninsula. I had read most of the travel blogs last night, so I wasn't worried, but she seemed nervous.

"Why did you decide to move here?" I asked her, playing it off as a casual question when, in reality, I wanted to know the reason behind moving here when she could stay in Azmia.

"I wanted to get out of Azmia, travel a bit, see the world and stay in San Diego for a while."

Hm, it was a sincere answer, but it still made me suspicious of her. Or her reason for moving away from home.

I showed my ID at the airport security, telling them about the two pistols I was carrying with my license. Zara was wide eyed, but I offered a relaxed smile when they checked my bag, making sure the firearms were empty in a hard carrier.

"Do you…" said Zara as soon as we were out of the earshot, "Always carry guns with you?"

"Yes." I peered down at her and, just to tease her more, I wrapped my arm around her waist. "Is the little Princess scared?"

Zara narrowed her eyes at me. "I am not little. Or scared of guns." She looked away. "I just… I wasn't expecting that you would have them on your vacation."

"It's a force of habit. I like to make sure I can protect myself and the surrounding people at all times."

She didn't meet my eyes, but her cheeks were flushed.

I had to force my attention on something else and read a book about some Saint while she worked on her laptop, her fingers flying over the keyboard, editing the pictures efficiently. Despite the book, which was boring, I couldn't keep my eyes off of her even though I tried. My shoe accidentally brushing against her boots, her lips forming a stern line as she worked, her pert nose flaring when she had to undo a revision.

Fuck. I was going to like her if I kept acting like a stupid teenager.

The silence between us was much awkward after sitting in our seats on the plane because it was just two of us. No one else was travelling to Almas Peninsula in the middle of November. Or we were just lucky.

"Are we alone—"

"Looks like it," I said, turning around to see the all the seats were empty.

The air hostess greeted us personally, and we pretended to be a couple when they brought us a bottle of champagne. We gladly accepted it and smiled when she stood there looking at us.

"Oh, honey, my neck is really sore, could you please move..." Zara grumbled, our knees knocking together as she moved in her seat to support her neck.

"It was because you kept editing on your laptop for an hour straight, darling," I said to her, helping her fix her neck pillow. "I told you to take a break and stretch, but no, why would you ever listen to me?"

"I was fine, but you kept poking—"

"Gosh, you two are such an adorable couple!" The air hostess beamed at us and left us alone while we gaped at her.

I quickly moved away from Zara, and she did the same. We didn't speak a single word to each other until it was time for dinner. Zara was taking a peaceful nap when I gently patted her awake and sat through her tiny whimpers, which I was getting used to when she woke up.

Zara was a very vocal person. If she didn't like something,

she would sigh in disappointment, if she was angry, she would grumble under her breath, if she was sleeping and woken up by someone, she would whine and whimper as if we had done a horrible crime waking her up.

"This sucks," she whispered to me when I sipped the tasteless soup from a cup.

"So I have noted."

"It's too bland."

"Yes."

"Are you going to answer me in monosyllables the entire trip?"

Sighing, I looked at her and pointed at the sachet of salt in her plate. "You might try adding that."

"Oh," she mumbled, picking at it. She might be hazy from the sleep. "I didn't notice."

"Hm."

When I was making my way to open the sandwich, I watched in horror when Zara dumped the entire packet of salt in the soup and stirred it.

"What are you doing?" I asked, scared for her mouth when she took a sip, her expression turning to dread. She coughed loudly, her eyes tearing in the corner.

I took the cup away from her and gave her mine. "Drink this." I shook my head at her, staring at the soup that must be floating in salt. "Who told you to dump the entire thing in here? You are insane."

"You told me," she said in a small voice, gingerly taking a sip of the soup I offered her. She hummed, taking a big sip.

"You are such a Princess," I said to her, ignoring the soup she had made. Just looking at it made my tastebuds shrivel in protest.

"What is that supposed to mean?" She asked.

"Nothing. Eat your food."

"If I had known you would be such an annoying travel

partner, then I wouldn't have agreed to this," Zara said without looking at me. "But thank you for the soup. I can at least feel my tongue now."

"*Christ,*" I whispered to myself.

The air hostess was extremely polite when she took our empty plates including the cup full of soup and gave us sweet dates to eat, offering to put a romantic movie for us to watch while we cuddle.

We, of course, rejected her offer as politely as we could.

"When will I get to sleep on a bed again?"

"See? Princess." I said to her, answering, "Tomorrow afternoon if we are lucky. If you didn't know, Almas Peninsula is twelve hours from San Diego and we have to take a cab to reach our cabin, which will take another hour if the weather is on our side."

She didn't reply for a few moments. I checked to make sure she hadn't fallen asleep. "Can we get two cabins instead? Or does it have an extra room?"

I smirked at her. "Why? Scared of sleeping on the same bed with me?"

"I think it would be a better idea if we maintain our distance from each other—"

"Why?"

"Because..." she trailed off. "I don't want to be in a relationship right now. Even though I am attracted to you, I... I don't w—"

"Zara, I get it," I said. "Even I am not ready for a relationship. God, the last time I actually dated somebody was in high school."

"You don't date?"

"I never needed a reason to date. I mean, I knew I wanted to be in a military so I didn't date seriously. Now," I shrugged, my heart pounding in my ears, "although I have time, I don't know where I want to settle. And with who."

Zara hummed, but didn't reply. We left it at that. Talking about my sad dating life had made us both awkward yet again.

As a gentleman, I let her go to the bathroom first, seeing her talk with an air hostess as I checked my phone. I hadn't received any more pictures of us together from her stalker. I was checking a few emails when Zara came back, her cheeks flushed and dewy under the dim glow of airplane lights.

God, I wish I could kiss her lips, I thought.

I wish I could stop being so weird, I added to my thought.

23
ZARA

I had been embarrassed to even think that Hayden would ever want to date me. He had said that he dated seriously someone in high school. That too for a week. He was not someone you could settle with. Even Ivy had mentioned the night before the trip that it might be hard to convince Hayden for a relationship.

But, as a grown woman, I had pushed those thoughts away.

The weather was warm in Almas Peninsula. We were both stiff limbed and jet legged for trying to sleep for a few hours and cheerily woken up by the air hostess. I had been so shocked waking up from the deep sleep that I had clutched Hayden's arm as if it was my life support.

"He should be here by now," Hayden murmured, checking his phone for the cab that would take us to the cabin.

"We can get an Uber," I said, hiding my yawn in a fist and looking around at the scenery. Cool breeze made me shiver despite how hot I felt standing under the scorching heat.

"Come on." His hand wrapped around my wrist, dragging me to the white van. For a moment, I forgot about the events of the evening go to the photoshoot and stared at his hand, nicely shaped long fingers with clean short nails. *Veins*, my mind blurted at me, my body joining in. He has veins on his hands and *oh*—forearms too.

How sinful.

"Zara."

I snapped back to reality and blinked at Hayden, his blue eyes on me. "Are you okay?"

"Of course, why wouldn't I be?"

"You muttered 'How sinful' when we passed by a lovely gay couple holding hands."

With wide eyes, I looked over my shoulder towards the two men who had a 'We are on a honeymoon!' sign on a cardboard cutout. "I was… I didn't mean them. I was thinking about something else."

He gave me a suspicious look and nodded to the white van. He said something about the cab driver loading our bags in the trunk.

Was Hayden behind that attempted kidnapping in the parking lot? No, he wouldn't do that. There were two or possibly more men. And if he was, he would know who I am, but he didn't. He couldn't do that.

I was silent, sitting inside the van and sighed in relief when the cab driver showed up, Hayden sitting beside me. He offered me a sandwich he had bought for us when we landed. It was stuffed with healthy vegetables and mayonnaise. I ate it without complaint.

We had decided that it was easy to pretend to be on a honeymoon than explain our situation to other strangers. So we went along with it.

The sun had set by the time we reached the cabins. The air was fresh and cool as our cabin was located near the shore. There was a small empty dock nearby our cabin as we walked through the small sandy path.

"Finally," Hayden groaned, stretching his arms over his head. My eyes travelled south, ogling at the tan skin of his muscled torso when his arms were raised.

I glanced away from him, his perfectly sculpted Greek body, to the cabin we would live in for the next week. We had mutually decided that we were too tired to ask for another cabin.

It wasn't completely made of dark wood. Three steps leading up to the black door, a heart-shaped with rose petals was made in the hallway, which Hayden and I ignored. It was spacious enough for two people with a cozy living room, a small kitchen and a bedroom with just one bed and a bathroom.

We shared the comfort of the bed with each other for the night. I hated the idea mostly because I liked to cuddle my body pillow while sleeping. But I didn't have a body pillow there and Hayden was the last person I wanted to cuddle with.

Because if he cuddled me... it would mean something. I wasn't ready for that.

"It is very cozy," I announced, smiling at the photo frame of a baby elephant in the living room, just above the couch.

"Why don't you go shower? I will cook something up for both of us." He left to check the fridge and the cabinets in the kitchen before I could ask if he needed my help.

AFTER THE WARM SHOWER AND CHANGING INTO SWEATPANTS and a tank top, my stomach grumbled loudly when I entered the kitchen. I eyed the delicious pasta with the equally delicious sight of Hayden.

His sleeves were rolled up to his elbows, he was barefoot, his hair was tousled, and he was wearing an apron that said

'Kiss the chef.' I was feeling generous, so I walked up to him and leaned on my toes to give him a peck on his cheek.

His pupil dilated as he gave me his full attention. "What was that for?"

I pointed to the apron. Looking around the kitchen, I cleared my throat, "Anything I can help with, chef?"

"Yes."

Hayden leaned closer, my back hitting the marble counter when he trapped me with his arms on either side of me.

What was he doing?

"What are you doing?"

I couldn't handle the way he looked at me with his intense blue eyes. As if he would rather have me for his dinner than the food he had cooked for us. The worse thing was, I was so weak for him that I would agree if he said he wanted to have me for dinner.

"What if we don't agree to a relationship," he started, his voice firm and husky that made me clenched my legs. "But we agree with other things?"

I didn't reply. I was going to melt with his body heat so close to me. *I don't want to touch him. I don't want to touch him. I don't want to touch him.*

"What do you mean?"

"I am attracted to you, Princess. I hope I had made that clear in that bathroom." Flush creeped up my neck and my cheeks, remembering the things he had done to me, fucking me with his fingers, keeping me on the edge.

"You did," I breathed out, trying to understand what he was trying to do.

"If we are both attracted to each other, then why don't we come to an arrangement of—"

"Do you mean sex?"

He blinked at me and pulled back a little. It surprised me to see red flush on his cheeks as he cleared his throat. *Oh, my...* Hayden Robert Knight was nervous. *Who would have thought?*

"Yes. If that's what you want."

I controlled myself from agreeing to him quickly and throwing myself on him by looking away and inspecting our dinner. Instead, I maintained my dignity and said, "Yes, I agree with it," I said. "But, I want to take it slow."

"Slow?"

"Yes. Slow. As much as I would like to have sex with you on the floor, I am not ready to just jump into that, you know."

"You want me to fuck you on the floor?" He was smirking. Of course he was. "*Kinky.*"

I deadpanned. "Look who's talking."

He walked towards me and bopped me on the nose. "Fine, Princess. I agree to take it slow with you, too. How about we start now?"

I gave him a slow nod as he gave me way to sit on the padded sitting area for the low dining table. The knuckles of his fingers brushed against mine, making me shiver when he sat across me.

"Is it okay if I..." Hayden reached out his hand, hovering it above mine and looking at me with a look that said hold-my-damn-hand-please.

I smiled, clasping my hand with his, entwining our fingers together. "Like this?"

He nodded, his thumb making different patterns in my hand. It was an odd feeling to hold his hand. It felt more intimate than anything I had ever done. It felt real and before I could overthink it, Hayden asked me about my dating life.

"I haven't been in a relationship. Ever."

"It's hard to imagine that."

"I... I tried dating, but I liked sex more than that. It was less work and with travelling, I wasn't ready to commit myself with long-distance."

I took a bite of the pasta and wondered why I felt anxious yet warm at the same time. I had never talked to anyone about dating or why I didn't want to. For obvious reasons, I had refrained from telling him about the actual reason was that I was a Princess of Azmia.

If I enjoyed being in a relationship with someone and, *worse*, fell in love with them, then I would have to tell them the truth about me. If they still want me after knowing my truth, despite being it a secret for a long time, then I would have to introduce them to my family. Khalid and Zain would stop at nothing to be thorough in their background check and be overprotective. It would be a miracle if someone would want to be with me, even after all that.

But the idea of someone loving me felt so strange that I couldn't accept it. If you love someone, you are ready to suffer for them. If they lie, you suffer wondering if it was the right decision to trust someone. If they love you more than you love them, you suffer with the guilt. If they die, you suffer until you die.

Love meant suffering. That was all there was to it.

Hayden had gone to shower after dinner while I insisted on doing the dishes because he had cooked for both of us. He was looming in the kitchen until I threatened him to sleep on the couch if he didn't let me do the dishes.

I jumped with a hand on my heart when I heard the lightning thundering outside. I had read about the weather of Almas Peninsula. Sometimes it would rain with thunderstorm at night and feel like dessert in the morning. My knees shook when the sky boomed with more lightning.

Flashes of images of that night ran through my head. The thunderstorm and wet marble when my father had dragged a six-year-old me, still sleepy, to his room, babbling something angry. My maids or guards hadn't questioned him, and he had led me to his room.

Ordering me to accept the betrothal when I was so so sleepy and scared at the strange red look in his eyes that I had started crying. Sobbing with big fat tears trailing down my cheeks when he threatened to kill me if I didn't follow his command. He was full of greed and anger. He was insane. Wanting me to accept my future to be someone's betrothed just so he could have more gold than he needs in his palace.

But Khalid and Zain had saved me.

I covered my ears, squeezing my eyes shut and focusing on my breathing when lightning had stricken the sky. I hated thunderstorms and lightning.

Khalid was so angry, but Zain, my eldest brother, was the one who scolded my father, telling him to let go of my hand. I had hugged Khalid, closing my eyes and trying to ignore the shouts and cries and thunderstorm. Khalid had shielded me behind his legs when the noise became too loud and I was too scared to even cry, just hot tears streaming down my face.

'I won't let anyone harm you, Zara. You are my sister.'

Khalid had told me they would protect me, and I had believed him. Even if my father yelled at me that I was a monster and a witch. Someone born out of jealousy and anger and greed that stole his wives from him in a plane crash.

But I had felt nothing but some strange sort of relief when Khalid had plunged my father's sword through his heart, the blood of my father splattering across my cheeks, my white nightgown and the beige walls of his room.

I had hugged Khalid closer and thanked him. I had thanked him for killing our father and told him it was okay until Rahim and Zayed had arrived.

"*Zara!*"

I shook my head when he leaned down across me.

"Zara, what happened?" He asked again, his voice soft. "Why are you on the kitchen floor?"

Another lightning struck and my entire body jumped, locking itself with fear. I didn't want to open my eyes, scared that it was all a strange dream.

"*Oh you*," he whispered in the sweetest voice, and my heart clenched at the sound. "I am going to touch you, okay?"

His arms wrapped around me, cocooning me to his body heat. The smell of fresh ocean and warmth spread over me when he took me somewhere. His muscles tightened when I trembled in his arms, hearing the lightning once again.

Hayden kept me close, my butt touching the soft mattress of the bed as he laid me down. But I was so weak that I kept my arms around his waist, his fingers running through my short hair.

Another lightening struck that made me shiver.

I don't know why he wasn't complaining and calling me a coward. I am sure he had other things to do then coddle someone like me.

But still, he kept his hand on my head and allowed me to hide my face in his tee shirt that smelt like fabric softener and ocean.

"You don't like thunderstorms?"

"Hate them." I shuddered. "Too loud."

"Poor Princess," he said, running his hand down my spine. His voice wasn't mocking or teasing, he was sincere.

Hayden must have hit his head in the shower, or it was his long-lost twin that was actually… *nice*. Yes, that must be it.

When he tried to get up from the bed, I clutched my fingers on his tee shirt. "Zara, I am not going anywhere. I will just go grab my Kindle, okay?"

I peeked my eyes open and the dim glow of light made everything felt warm in the bedroom. I nodded slowly, his gaze soft and hot. It reminded me of hot chocolate. If hot chocolate were blue like his eyes.

Sliding under the blankets, I muttered, "I am sorry, this... this wasn't how you would have imagined your first night of vacation to be like."

Hayden sat beside me on the bed. "No need to apologize, Princess. It is not what I would have imagined, ever, but I am not going to complain."

"Why not?"

"Because I get to snuggle you, silly."

My cheeks reddened, my body relaxing and trying to focus on him rather than the—fucking hell. I clutched the blanket and stayed still, hoping the lightning would stop and let me breathe.

"What do you want to read?" He asked, wrapping his arm around me and pushing me flush against his chest. I was almost lying on top of him.

He must have not seen how red my face was as he scrolled through the fiction section on Kindle.

"I am not in the right position to read."

"I will read it to you."

I couldn't miss a chance like this.

"Romance," I said in my best I-am-scared-of-lightening-please-read-me-something voice. Then added, "With some steam."

Hayden pinched my butt. "Naughty girl."

I pinched his arm or tried to. His skin was hard and soft at the same time, made with muscles and tears of children, probably.

"How about this? *The Duke and The Princess*," he said, surprising me with a shirtless cover of a faceless Duke and the heroine in a scandalous red corset dress.

I was busy reading the blurb, but he turned the page on

the screen and had started reading it. I sighed, melting over him, and listened to his rumbling husky voice.

"'You shouldn't be here,' the Princess whispered, her rosy cheeks flushed. The sight of a man like him was too much for a virgin maiden like her—" Hayden paused. "Did I really just read that?"

"*Shh*," I whined. "Keep reading. It's getting to the juicy part."

"Only if you promise to recreate this with me afterwards."

"Only if you behave."

Hayden took a deep breath and continued, "The poor princess didn't know that a man who had barged in her chamber at such an odd hour was none other than the Duke she was thirsting for. She thought of him as a stable servant. A handsome, stable servant. 'What are your intentions?' The Princess asked, her voice quivering when he prowled towards her.

'I…' The Duke, who had thought that the poor woman in nothing but a white dress was a maid, held her arm, 'am going to ravish you.' Stop grinning like that, Zara. This is…"

"Exciting?"

"No."

"Romantic?"

"For the love of—"

"Arousing?"

He glared at me, his blue eyes steely and cold. "No, it's none of that. I wonder why the author started the book like this. They clearly don't know who they are except judging from their clothes and wanting to sleep each other."

"It is fiction. These characters must have fantasised about having foreplay and sex like this, so in their mind, they have created the person that doesn't exist and accept whatever happens afterwards with character growth."

Hayden sat up and looked at me, his gaze intense. "But

doesn't it feel wrong in some way? What if we had first met, and I thought of you as some maid and you thought of me as that stable boy?"

"It's not about us. That is fiction—"

"Would you have been thrilled to have sex with me if I had introduced myself as a Navy Seal as soon as we started talking?"

No, I would have run away.

"Well, of course." I asked, "Would you have been thrilled to have sex with me if I had introduced myself as a Royal Princess?"

His gaze was warm, and it made me aware of how close we were. "Yes, maybe. I am not sure. Even if I had taken you to my suite, knowing you are a Princess, which I wouldn't as a Seal, I wouldn't dare to bring kink between us. Like that night."

I swallowed the lump in my throat and laid down on the bed. "See what I mean…" I mostly said that to myself. If Hayden had known I was a Princess, he would have had sex with me. Probably missionary and call it a night. He might have even dropped me back at the Golden Palace after it was over.

"But you aren't a Princess and these characters are Royals." Hayden was staring at his Kindle again.

Yeah, right.

"So you think they should tell each other what they are born into before they bump uglies?"

"Bump uglies?"

"Not the point, Hayden."

He thought for a moment and nodded. "Yes. Sex is about trusting your partner and being comfortable with each other. If they can't communicate about their actual identities to each other, then I am not sure if the relationship would work out between them despite how good the sex is."

"What if they are ashamed of what they are born into and didn't ask for the royal titles attached to their name… and just wanted to live a normal life and have kinky sex?"

I held my breath when he replied, "I guess I could try to empathise with them but I would still prefer if they told each other who they are." My heart dropped in my stomach when he settled beside me once again, "We are still on the first page, they might tell—"

"I think the lightning stopped," I whispered, getting on my knees on the bed and seeing the view outside. The dark sky was clear of clouds with a full moon, stars twinkling.

"You don't want to read anymore?" Hayden asked.

I turned towards him and gave him a sad smile. "Sorry, I feel like sleeping."

He nodded and called me over. He turned off the lights, holding the blanket for me as I slid beside him into his arms. I nuzzled my face into his chest, breathing in his scent.

"Princess?"

"Hm?"

"Don't kick me in the sleep."

24
HAYDEN

Next morning, I woke up without nightmares. With sunlight streaming down my face and a soft body pressing against my chest. I hummed, breathing in the scent of sweet vanilla, my lips curling into a smile as I pulled her closer. As I had expected, she let out a small whimper.

I opened my eyes, her short platinum hair gleaming in the sunlight as she squirmed, pressing her cute butt against my crotch. If she wanted me to wake up, it was working.

But I was a gentleman of my word. Zara had wanted to take things slowly and grinding against her and waking her up with my fingers in her underwear would not be considered slow.

So with a lot of self-control, I pulled away from her, her lips parting as if my movements had deeply disturbed her. I let her clutch a pillow and watched her in awe when she leeched around it. The blanket was all over the bed. I gently untangled her legs from it and tucked her in, letting her sleep for a few more minutes until I got ready.

We had planned to go to the beach in the morning

through a hike. The sky was clear, and it seemed like a perfect day for a hike and a swim on the beach. I would never mention it aloud, but I was looking forward to see Zara in a bikini.

"You're awake," I said, finding Zara in the kitchen, cracking eggs and adding chopped chives in a bowl.

"Hm, I woke up—" she turned around, her eyes dropping to my chest while I patted my damp hair with a towel. "Go wear some clothes."

"I am wearing clothes," I said, tugging the grey sweatpants over my hips. "My eyes are up here, Princess."

"Why are you wearing that?"

I didn't know whether she was complaining or in a complete glee.

"Wearing what?"

"Those…. Those *disgusting* grey sweatpants." Zara licked her lips when I crossed my arms.

"You are objectifying me in your head, aren't you?"

Her cheeks flushed with embarrassment, and she looked away, applying butter on the pan and making eggs. Her silence was enough of an answer.

I took mercy on her and ruffled her short hair because they looked soft and extremely pet-*able*. She gave me an adorable frown while serving eggs in two plates.

We ate our breakfast at the low table, Zara maintaining her distance and not looking in my direction with color on her cheeks.

"I didn't know you had a tattoo."

I looked at the eagle with the rough sketch the artist had made. "Yeah," I cleared my throat, blinking out the past. "I got it done after coming back from Iraq."

Zara's hazel doe eyes peered at the dark ink and met my eyes. "That's really sweet of you. I am sure they were… or are grateful to have you."

I didn't know what to reply. *How could she just say those deep, meaningful words that made me want to cry and just smile at me as if nothing had happened?*

I wanted to ask if kissing was allowed at that stage, as we had already cuddled all night. But I didn't want to seem too desperate. Even though all I could think about was grabbing her face and pressing my lips against hers.

Shaking out of my thoughts, I cleaned the plates and got ready for the hike. I wore dark shorts and a loose half-sleeve white shirt. At the last moment, I had a gun with me. Just in case something terrible happens and I—

I can't even pull the trigger. *What the fuck was I doing?*

Doesn't matter. It could be useful. Maybe Zara could use it. Just the thought of having it made me feel better than leaving it behind.

"Here," Zara stopped me before we could step outside the cabin, handing me a sunscreen.

"I already applied it, thank you."

Her face coloured and she looked away. "Can you help me?"

I raised my brow. Touching her skin and rubbing sunscreen on it, massaging it? *How could I let such a chance pass?*

I took the sunscreen, and she turned around. She was wearing a flirty dark dress that minced around her waist and draped freely, reaching her thighs. I held my breath when she removed her dress, shaking her hair, leaving her in a black bikini and shorts.

Fuck, fuck, fuck.

I had a semi just seeing her back and the beautiful arch of her spine. How would I manage to take it slow for a *whole fucking week?* Oh, good, *please remove the only string that was holding your bikini together. Why don't you?*

I glared at her pale bare back and took a coin sized sunscreen.

"We don't have all day, Hayden," Zara said, looking over her shoulder as I prepared myself to touch her skin as if I was a teenager.

I tsked at her and rubbing the sunscreen in my palm, I applied it on her nape, lowering hands down her tensed back that soon relaxed and melted into my hands. I watched it arch, licking my lips.

"You seem very tense," I said, moving my fingers in a circular motion over her shoulders. Zara couldn't hide her gasp. "Your muscles are so tense, Zara. When was the last time you got a massage?"

"Two years? *Oh fuck.* Hayden… if you don't stop now…"

I leaned closer, brushing my nose against the shell of her ear. "Or what, Princess? Don't you want to lie back naked and let me give you a massage, *hm?*"

She nodded slowly, leaning back in my hands.

I purred in her ears, "Such a good girl." I knew how much she enjoyed being degraded and praised. A perfect match for me.

"What… are those?"

I had stopped, turning her around and pointing at her breasts. Zara frowned at me and looked down. "These are my breasts, Hayden. Most mammals have them," she said like a teacher talking to her student, tying the string of her bikini.

"N-no," I, Hayden fucking Knight, stuttered, "I know what breasts are. I meant…"

I vaguely moved my hands over her chest when she picked up her dress.

"Oh, you mean my piercings?"

Piercings. She had piercings. Every—*fucking*—where.

"What..."

I was a mess while Zara ignored me and wore her dress with a cute beach hat. But I was still staring at her breasts. She had them pierced.

"As much as I like you staring at my girls, we will be late for our hike and swimming in the ocean. Come on, I want to try famous prawns of Almas Peninsula. They get sold out before noon. We need to hurry."

Zara left the cabin as I slowly wore the small backpack trailing behind her. I had never been with someone who had their nipples pierced and, knowing that Zara was walking around in a bikini underneath her dress, I was going insane. My head was filled with filthy images of licking her nipples, biting them, playing with her piercings until she groaned and fucked her breasts.

I was going insane and Zara was definitely testing my control when we were midway through our hike, half drenched in sweat and takin sips of water now and then. I stayed close to her, glaring at other travellers who walked past us. They wanted to talk as soon as Zara, but as soon as they looked over her shoulder at me, they hurried away.

"Oh, wow, it's empty," Zara muttered, disappointed that we were the only ones at the beach in windy weather.

"It's because we are here in November." I said, removing my shirt and eyeing the waves of the dark blue water. The sand was cold. I was glad that I had applied sunscreen and so did Zara. She looked like she would have burnt more than me.

Averting my eyes from the sand to her toned waist to her perky breasts with pierced nipples covered in black bikini made the tips of my ears pink. I couldn't even think. Her belly button, a small silver stud, glinted in the sunlight.

"My eyes are up here, Hayden," Zara's sultry voice rang in my ears.

"How many piercings do you have?"

She replied without thinking. "Ten."

Nine piercings—my nose flared as I glared at her back when she confidently walked towards the ocean, water hiding her body with each step.

Two on her ears each. Her nose. Her tongue. Two on her nipples. One on her belly button. Finale one on…

I made a grunt like sound that must have been what a caveman ready to mate would have made. Zara has definitely changed, a tempting little rebel Princess. That's what she was.

When I swam with her in the cool water, she seemed like a mermaid underneath. Her hair white and blue, her pearl like skin glittering with sunlight as she swam lazily, as if she belonged in the water. It was her kingdom, and she was a Princess… maybe a Queen. I was a mere by-watcher or a Knight protecting her from God knows what. She didn't seem to need my protection.

"Come on," Zara stopped me, flicking water on my back. "Help me, Hayden!"

"Picking seashells is a child's—"

She didn't let me finish. She splashed more water and when I turned around to glare at her, she was grinning at me.

"Stop being a party pooper and let's pick seashells together."

"Why would I spend my precious time—"

Of course, Zara didn't let me finish. She held my wrist and dragged me towards the wet sand, bending down to pick up a white seashell.

"You need to loosen up sometimes," she said to me in a calm, soft voice, opening my palm and giving me the shell with the sweetest smile.

I took it and pulled her closer with an arm around her waist. We were both wet with water and I felt the small press of her piercings on my skin. My palm cradled her chin as I brushed my lips abasing hers.

Water from my hair fell on her forehead as she closed her eyes, cinching her hands around my neck and whispered, "Kiss me, Hayden."

"Say it again—"

As always, Zara didn't let me finish.

Tipping on her toes, she claimed my lips in a soft, sensual kiss. Humming at the taste of salt water and licking my lips with a teasing grin before biting my bottom lip. With a small growl, I squeezed her ass and kissed her. I ran my tongue over her full lips, over her pierced tongue and swallowing the little moans she made.

"We should..." I said between our wet, clumsy kisses. "Stop..."

"Why?" she asked, trailing her kisses down my jaw, nipping it softly and kissing my throat that had me groaning. "I don't want to stop, Hayden."

Her voice was as soft as a whisper. She was a mermaid. A siren. Luring me with her voice and pretty face, full of desire and awe that had me throbbing for her. The need to feel her, touch her everywhere, and fuck her overpowering my senses.

"I want to see all your piercings," I said, my voice distant, deep and husky.

Her pupils dilated when she pulled back a little, adjusting the strap of her bikini on her shoulder that I was the culprit of. "Buy me the prawns and then I will think about it."

25

ZARA

Hayden bought me the prawns. We dried off with towels and I wore my dress back while Hayden kept his shirt unbuttoned. It was hard to see so many men and women check him out, with his damp wavy hair, sunglasses and low slung shorts that showed off the vee of his hips.

But I maintained myself, controlling the carnal urge to tug at the collar of his shirt and kiss him, feel his calloused hands on my body. I was the one who had said I wanted to take things slow. I could keep my hands to myself for a little while.

"Can't you please hurry?"

I ignored his voice and glanced at the various toys for children in bright colors. I picked up a remote-controlled toy car and wondered if Aya, Zain's daughter and my niece, would play with it. She was at that age where she loved anything that was bright, colourful, and could hold her attention for a few minutes.

"Zara, don't tell me you want to buy this."

"Why? What's wrong with it?" I asked, paying for the car and held the box in my hand. If Aya didn't like it, then I was sure Zayed would. He was a child in a man's body, after all.

I grinned at his stern, surprised face and said, "It's not for me. It's for my niece."

"*Oh*," he said, trailing behind me as we took the hiking route to get back to our cabin. Sun was on our heads with our shadows falling above us on the ground. "I didn't know you have a niece."

I bit my lip, not sure how I should reply. I knew all about his family because of Ivy. I had even met his father and his soon-to-be-wife.

"I never told you about my family."

"Except that you have two brothers."

"Yes, well, Aya, is the daughter of my eldest brother. My elder brother is getting married soon so I will go back to Azmia next year."

He hummed, which made me glance at him. He looked deep in thought and I wondered if I had blurted something regarding my family that he figured out the truth about me.

This was why I needed an NDA between us. But it felt awfully selfish to ask him to sign some papers just so I could be a Princess with him and he can keep my secret, worrying about his life.

"Don't you miss your life in Azmia?" Hayden asked when we reached the cabin.

I stared at him. *Did he know?*

"I... I miss the horse riding," I started because I knew I had told him about it when we had first met. "The spicy food and sweets. Mostly, I miss my family."

Hayden nodded. His eyes were cold, but it didn't seem like he had figured out who I was. But I knew I needed to be careful around him and hold my tongue. I had been reckless the night before while he read me a book and asking him all sorts of personal things, pretending that it was all about the book and characters of *The Duke and The Princess*.

"What are you thinking?" I asked, very aware of how silent and calm Hayden was with a cool look on his face.

He gave me a small smile and shook his head. "It's nothing. I want to go out and see some stores down the road." There were a few of them set up by locals just before entering the small alley that led to our cabin.

"Do you want me to come with you?" My fingers felt clammy and there was a weird nervousness in my stomach.

"It's alright. I won't be long." He was already by the door when he looked over his shoulder and said, "You have my number now, don't you?"

I nodded, and he left, closing the door behind him, the cabin silent with the white curtains on windows flowing from the wind.

It's okay, Zara. He doesn't know. If he had, he would have either tried to kill me or demand me to call my brothers or, worse, walk away from me.

Which he just did. *Oh fuck.*

I took a shower, washing off the sweat from the hike and worked on the Halloween photoshoot at the factory. Once I had sent the last files to the girls, I looked up from the blue light of the laptop to see that it was evening already. The sun had long set and crickets were chirping by the trees outside.

Hayden still hadn't arrived.

I leaned back and saw a text message on my phone. It was from the Royal service. We had our own private message and email service so that no one can hack it and we can maintain our privacy through the royal network.

It was from Zayed. Khalid, my elder brother, was frowning at the plate of sweets in front of him and they both seemed like they were sitting at the low tables of the dining hall at The Golden Palace. Zayed's caption read,

I hope you are not dead xoxo

Rolling my eyes, I started typing. It was just like him to send a picture which had no context related to the caption. So I sent him a picture of Zain, my eldest brother, scowling at the sky when we had been in a desert, riding horses together.

Unfortunately, no. You still can't have my tiara of Princess of Azmia, Zayed. Suck it up.

I ended the text with a sunglasses emoji. He had been eyeing my tiara, made of twenty-four carat gold, that was locked safely in my room ever since I had been crowned as a Princess. Khalid had warned me to keep it safe because Zayed had stolen his Prince's crown and returned it the next day when Khalid threatened him to ban him from The Golden Palace.

Zayed sent me another text. A blurred photo of my dear brother Khalid, who was about to either punch Zayed or smack him. I giggled at the angry face and wondered how he took the picture and if he really punched him.

You didn't give us update for last week. We are worried xoxo

I wondered if he knew what xoxo meant, but decided to leave it. Sending a picture of a sad duck, I replied,

I am busy.

What, petting ducks?

Yes.

Get me one. I shall name him Steve.

Need to go. Bye.

He sent me a pouting emoji. **Tootles!**

Just when I was saving the blurred picture of Khalid, the front door opened. I froze at the tall figure and slumped back on the couch when I saw it was Hayden closing the door behind him.

I said nothing until he stepped into the dim light of the cabin. His hair was mussed up as if he had run a hand through them a lot of times. He seemed tired, but his gaze was piercing as ever when they landed on me.

"What have you been up to?" He asked, his voice deep and rough. My body warmed hearing it despite how odd he was acting.

I waved my hand around the laptop nervously. "Editing photos and all. Where were you?"

He placed a paper-bag on the small kitchen counter that had a wafting aroma of spices, my stomach grumbling, reminding me that I hadn't eaten anything since the lunch with him.

"I walked to the stores down the road and talked to them about this place and I got us a yacht to go visit a—"

"*Wait*." I stood up, blinking at him, confused. "You bought a yacht?"

Hayden tilted his head at me and leaned back on the counter, crossing his arms in a way that the short sleeves of his shirt stretched around him. *Yes*, I thought, *you and me both*. Looking away from his deliciously distracting muscles, I forced my eyes to pay attention to how nice the wooden floors looked.

"I didn't buy a yacht. I rented it, Zara." I felt him walking towards me. My stomach clenched with bubbling anticipation when he tipped my chin towards his face. "I want to take you to see where they used to mine diamonds."

"That's it?"

I held my breath when his eyes dropped to my lips. Hayden moved closer, his lips brushing against my cheek, the touch leaving me burning and aching for more. It was soft with the slight graze of his five o'clock shadow that had my toes curling on the wooden floors.

"I want you alone with me," he whispered in my ear, almost inaudible as he pulled away. "And do everything I have wanted to do... slowly."

My eyes burned until I remembered to blink. "I am alone... here. Um, with you."

His hand brushed down my neck, to the low neck of the tank top I was wearing without a bra. His pupils dilated, his blue eyes darkening when he noticed it. Licking his lips, he pulled away his hand, making me barren without his touch.

"I know, but surrounded by water, you are alone with me. No one is there to disturb us... and I have heard that people like grand gesture." I was shocked to see that color had creeped up his neck to his cheeks. "Yacht is a romantic gesture, isn't it?"

I parted my lips to reply that I would love to go with him, but he had already closed himself in the bathroom. Seconds later I heard the shower turning on. I grinned, cupping my mouth and doing a happy dance with a small squeal.

Hayden Robert Knight was embarrassed and blushed because he was going to take me out for a date on a freaking yacht. I melted on the couch, giggling once again as I thought about how wonderfully romantic it would be. All alone with him...

"How does he know how to maneuver a yacht?" I said to the ceiling and shrugged. Must be trained in the Navy Seal, I suppose. I didn't need to tell him I had a license as well.

But why take me to a yacht out of the blue? He had been awfully silent since the lunch and I thought he figured out who I was. *What if he plans to take me to the yacht and murder me because I am a Princess?*

I shook my head, my heart falling in my stomach. Hayden would never do that. If he had rented the yacht and tried to kill me, then it would be like leaving bread crumbs to the killing spot. He was smarter than that.

Hence, he was not going to murder me on a yacht.

I moaned, taking a bite of *manakeesh*, a bread sprinkled with cheese, ground beef and herbs also known as *zaatar*. It had the perfect level of spiciness that melted on my tastebuds.

"This is the best food I have ever eaten." I swallowed the contents in my mouth and looked at the name of the restaurant Hayden had brought that delicious goodness from. I noted the name and planned to talk to their owner via email or let Zayed know about them.

One of the benefits of being the world's first anonymous Princess was that if I liked local and small businesses, then I could try to help them with more publicity just by sending Zayed, Sheikh of Azmia, to that place. Him because he doesn't like to work and when he tries to do it, he gets banned from Zain's study or the Palace.

"No need to moan about it," Hayden replied, finishing his *manakeesh* and patting his mouth with a tissue. His damp hair slightly curled over his forehead, making him look younger. I wondered if he looked like that when he was a quarterback during his high school year, if he dated cheerleaders and nerds and anyone he found interest in that week.

"What's going on in that head of yours?"

"I was wondering how you were during your high school years."

He visibly cringed, making me snort. "I am glad that you didn't meet younger me. I slept around a lot, thinking I was the King of the high school because I was great in sports and aced all my academics. I thought everyone loved me and all the rubbish teenagers think."

I tilted my head. "I guess it is natural that you wanted validation from your peers because of your parents, no offence."

"Since when did you start psychoanalysing people?"

I blushed and looked down. "Sorry, that was out of my line."

"Yes, it was." He paused. "But its okay, Princess. I don't regret anything except the prom night. It was horrible."

"Tell me about it."

Hayden's blue eyes gleamed as he kept his forearms —*veins*. Arms. Veins. *Must. Not. Lick.* When I found my brain working, I forced my eyes on his face. "If I tell you about the prom, then you need to tell me something equally embarrassing."

"Deal."

"Okay," he sighed with disappointment, as if he couldn't believe he was sharing his embarrassing story with me after eating world's best *manakeesh*. "My prom date, Julie Andrews, was really hot, but she had an ex who kept trying to hit on her the entire night. I got drunk, went to after party with her which, surprisingly enough, was at her ex's house."

"I don't like where this is going."

"You and me both," he deadpanned. "Anyway, we were all drunk and sweaty from the dancing and she dragged me to a bedroom, proceeded to..." he moved his hands, color on his cheeks. "You know... and she asked me if I wanted to have a threesome with her friend."

"*Oh*."

"Don't look at me like that. I was eighteen, full of hormones and alcohol and said yes because I thought her friend meant a woman."

I cupped my mouth. "But it was her ex."

He sighed, running a hand through his face. "It was her ex."

I tried to hide my choked laugh with a cough as he glared at me. "I didn't have a threesome with them. I got the fuck out when he entered the room as if he was waiting for her signal." He shuddered as if the memory haunted him.

"That's not even that embarrassing, Hayden," I said with a grin on my face.

"Now it's your turn, Princess."

Do I really have to spill that in front of Hayden? By the looks of it. *Yes*. "I had a crush on my brother's best friend."

He looked horrified. "Oh, no."

"It was stupid, really," I nodded solemnly. "He cared for me like his own sister, but I got that caring mixed with romance and like a spoiled child, I demanded him to return my feelings."

"*Christ…*"

I continued. "When he rejected me, I thought he was joking and tried to make him jealous… thirteen-year-old me went ahead and—I can't believe I am saying this—kissed a guy my age."

Hayden cupped his mouth, his eyes wide.

I was shaking my head in disappointment. "It was bad. *So* bad. I cried for two weeks straight after that evening."

"Is that why you moved to San Diego?" Hayden asked after a while.

"*Har har.*"

"Well, I didn't think anyone could top my embarrassing moment, but you won fair and square." He clinked my glass with his, sipping on chilled white wine.

Hiding my smile, I finished my dinner and kept our empty plates in the sink. Cold air breezed through the open window, curtains flowing. The calm, serene atmosphere made me feel grateful that I was here with Hayden. I had thought I might regret it later, having to spend awkward silence with him, but Hayden Knight was surprising. And the more I learned about him, his embarrassing moment, the more I wanted to spend time with him.

But when I walked into the bedroom, the last thing I was expecting was to see Hayden holding a gun.

26
ZARA

"What are you doing with that gun?" My voice was sharp because I was scared. Not sure of the gun or the person holding the gun. I eyed the weapon like it was a living, breathing fire dragon.

Hayden looked up from the thing in his hand. *No, you perverts*—I meant the *gun*. His fingers still tinkered with it while his eyes were on me, and that made me really uncomfortable.

What if it was loaded, and he accidentally shoots at me and I accidentally die and then he accidentally gets executed for accidentally killing the Princess of Azmia which he accidentally didn't know I was?

Yes, I was terrified and nervous... and strangely liking the way his hand held the... gun—*gah, body, not now!*

"I am cleaning it," he nodded at the bed. "Come, sit here. I will show you how to clean it."

"No, thanks!" I squeaked.

"*Zara.*" There it was again. His voice. Deep and rough and so husky that it made my bone tremble. Either with arousal or with fear, I was not sure, and I was too darn of a coward to find out. "I am not going to hurt you or won't let anything hurt you. Come. Here."

Fuck me for falling for his patient blue eyes, the endless depth of them that I didn't know when I was sitting across from him, cross-legged with a—*oh my fucking God*—gun between us on the white sheets.

"It is quite easy and calming, you see," Hayden started, asking me to repeat his actions when he removed the bullets from the clip. He showed me where the safety was and the other small duster like cleaning equipment he had to clean it.

I leaned in and followed his instructions on how to clean it. I was holding the gun and held my breath when he cupped my hands, teaching me how to wipe the metal. His smoky voice rumbling through my ears to down my body.

"Like this?" I whispered, my voice barely audible.

His eyes flickered to my face, noticing I was paying more attention to his face and his lips than the gun. "Yes." His voice turned guttural. "Just like that, Zara."

I nodded, averting my attention to the gun once again when I felt the bed dip near me, the warmth of his body beside me. So much closer than before.

"I want to kiss you, Princess," Hayden said, still working on cleaning the bullets and placing them expertly in the clip as if he could do that while he was sleeping. Just seeing that trick of his hands skilfully handling a gun made something churn in my belly, making me all warm and fuzzy.

"Why… why did you left so suddenly this afternoon?" I asked, gently keeping the gun on the bed so that its nozzle faced away from both of us.

"Because." I looked at him, his face raw and full of emotion, eyes clouded with lust. "If I didn't, I was afraid that I would lose control…"

"And?"

My breathing got heavier.

"And… I might not be slow with anything that I do to you."

My lips parted, eyes lowering to his lips as I licked mine, tasting the raw sexual attraction we had for each other. I asked, "What sort of things?"

"*Filthy* things." His deep blue eyes became stark, pinned on my face. "The kind of things that a Princess such as you shouldn't hear about."

I frowned, blinking at him. "Then…" I licked my lips and shuffling so I could get closer to him. "Can you show them to me?"

Hayden didn't reply for a while, the silence filling the room making my blood thrum with excitement and anticipation. That was the one I had been chasing since the night I had met him two years ago at a club. The raw, vulnerable feeling of trusting each other and baring our truest desires to each other.

I had never felt like that with anyone before.

"You have a dirty little mouth," Hayden whispered, slowly caressing my cheekbone. His touch was soft, but his words were harsh. "I am going to fuck it."

An aching pulse throbbed in my pussy as I bit my lip. I had missed it. The blunt way he always asked and demanded things from me in the bedroom.

"Are you…" I took a deep breath and looked into his hooded eyes. "Are you going to hurt me?"

"A little."

He didn't hold back when I whispered, "Please do."

His lips crashed into mine, our bodies blending into one when he cradled my head, moving his face to deepen the kiss. All types of lewd, sloppy sounds echoed in the room, but neither of us cared. We kissed and kissed and *kissed*.

Whimpering into his mouth when he played with the metal stud on my tongue, biting my lip and kissing down my throat. His hands were shaking where he held my waist, his cheeks flushed, his eyes dark and feral.

"Fuck, I wanted to kiss you for so long," he said, his voice thick with arousal when I moved my hands over his arms, feeling his muscles tense and move when he removed my tank top over my head, baring my breasts to him.

Blood rushed my cheeks at the way he looked at them. He seemed in complete awe, his lips parting as he just stared and stared.

"Hayden," I breathed out, covering myself.

His eyes snapped at my face, glaring at me. "Don't you ever cover yourself in front of me, you understand?"

I nodded, wide eyed and too horny to let his demanding tone bother me. When I didn't make a move to move my hands away, he pried my wrists down and kept my hand on the mattress. His warm breath brushed over my hard nipples, cold metal barbells straining against them.

"Touch me," I begged him. "Please."

"Let me take my time," he murmured, his hands roving over my waist, settling on my ribs, his thumb fitting right under my breast. "Weren't you the one who wanted to take things slow?"

"Not this slow!"

Hayden cupped them, his hands feeling just right, squeezing them as I gasped, arching into his warm touch. "What did I tell you?" He asked, taking immense pleasure in fondling my breasts, twisting my pierced nipple until I groaned, squeezing my eyes shut. "Have patience, Princess."

Biting my lip, I watched him through my half-lidded eyes when he pushed me down on the bed, kissing me on my lips before latching his lips on my burning peaks. Soothing them with his tongue and soft lips until I was putty in his hands, trying to squirm and undress him.

"I want to see you too."

Hayden ignored me, removing my sweatpants and underwear until I was naked beneath him.

He cursed, "Fucking knew it." I made a low, embarrassing sound when he spread my legs apart. "Look at you…"

Hayden

I HAD NEVER SEEN A SIGHT LIKE HER BEFORE AND I WAS SURE I never would.

All flushed and pink and swollen. Wet with desire with a little white stud on her clitoris. I pushed her thighs apart, gazing at her pussy like it was my last meal on the earth and spreading her open with my fingers, groaning at the sight of her wetness leaking.

"I want to tie you up, Zara," I confessed. "And do terrible, filthy things to you."

The sweet fool moaned and raised her hips towards me, her brown doe eyes wide. "Please do."

I shook my head, pulling away from her. My entire body was thrumming with want and need. My hands were shaking. "I… I can't."

She leaned up on her elbows, looking like a little devilish angel with gleaming white short hair framing her face. Her sharp elfish face and flushed pale skin with piercings glinting in the light.

"Why not?"

"Because I won't be able to stop."

She didn't reply for a while, her breathing as heavy as mine, my eyes sloping down to her perky breasts, pierced nipples hard with a pink hue. "Then don't."

"Zara." I stared at her, shaking my head.

"Please, Hayden," she sat up, crawling towards me in such

a suggestive way that had me trying to pull away from her, but I was stuck with a wall behind me.

"W-we can use safe words."

"Princess, Zara... you are... I." I stopped and closed my eyes. I couldn't even fucking say anything with her naked and all pretty in front of me. I took a deep breath and without looking beneath her chin, I said to her, "I haven't been with anyone since we last slept together."

"You haven't?" Zara asked, her voice low. "But... it's been two years."

"I know."

"Why not?" She shook her head. "I am so sorry, that was a bit rude of me to ask."

I swallowed the lump in my throat, forcing myself to look at her face, her beauty spot above her lips even when she moved, raking her nimble fingers through her hair.

"What I am trying to say is, we need safe word, safe gesture and *fuck*—Zara, I don't want to hurt you." I was pleading her, my hands clenching the sheets because it scared me to hold her, hold her too tight that I might—

Her eyes blazed with something. Maybe it was determination or anger. "I am not some fragile doll that I would break if you touch me. I got my clit pierced. I can... I can handle you. *Us*. Don't torture both of us just because you are afraid." She paused and looked at me, "Unless, of course, you don't want to have sex right now then I completely—*mffh*."

I kissed her. The taste of her lips on mine was the sweetest sin. She looked too distractingly beautiful with her bare face and light dark shadows and her warm stern eyes that I had to kiss her. Cradling her face in my palm and moving my lips against her until we both relaxed on the sheets.

"Trust me, Princess." I ran my hand through her back, her

breasts pressing against my chest. "I want to fuck you. So bad that it is all I have been dreaming out since I met you."

"You dream about me?"

"Yes, but I prefer *this*—reality—more." My eyes trailed down her body. "I would have never imagined that you would have piercings. It's perfect. *You* are perfect."

Her hand slid down from my neck to my chest as she peered at me through her long lashes. "I promise I will say the safe word, red, if I want everything to stop. But please, Hayden, if you are as ready as I am… I want you to hurt me."

Zara always had a way with her words. It was one of the many things that I liked about her. So if she meant what she had said, which she always did, then I would offer it to her.

I wrapped my hand around her slender throat, pressing against her pulse light that her lips parted, lust pooling into her dilated hazel-brown eyes. "You want me to hurt you, Princess?" I purred, teasing her with a question and pinching her nipple as she whimpered.

Zara nodded, muttering a soundless plea.

Laying her down on the pillows, I spread her legs to see she was already dripping. "*Tsk*, look at you, already making a mess on the bed when I haven't touched your cunt," I lightly smacked her inner thigh, her skin flushing when I soothed the burn.

"You'll be a good girl for me, right?" I asked, meeting her eyes, my heart thudding loudly in my ears. I splayed my hand on her leg, trailing it up with the goosebumps skittering on her skin as she shivered, gasping softly when my thumb played with the stud on her clit, rolling it softly. "Be my good Princess slut, *hm*?"

"Yes, Hayden," Zara moaned, her voice hitching in her throat when I pulled away.

27

ZARA

It was the way he said it. Every time. Hayden called me and owned every part of me when he called me his own Princess slut. The way he played with my degradation and praise kink, touching me like I was *his*.

"Good girl." I visibly shivered, almost panting for him to touch me when he made sure my legs stayed spread. "Play with yourself for me, Princess."

I nodded, licking my lips when he pulled away. Sliding my hand between my legs, I watched him and slowly rubbed my clit, the stud piercing on it. It hurt a little, the type of pain that brought pleasure.

"Look at me, Princess," Hayden whispered, closer to me than before. I was delighted to see him shirtless. His tattoo, his perfect tan, and his muscles were a feast for my eyes. The way his bulge formed a tent in his sweatpants made me rub faster, saying his name and shivering when my legs closed.

I cried out when his palm landed on my inner thigh. "Keep your legs spread, Princess."

Biting my lip, I looked up at him, and my lips parted

instantly. My hand stopped moving. I stiffened. "Hayden," I whispered, too scared to move.

"Who told you to stop?" Hayden asked without looking at me as he removed the safety of the gun and slid his eyes to me, pointing the nozzle my way.

"Hayden... I..." I couldn't speak. My back was stiff, the cold nozzle pressing against my chin. I whimpered when my neck craned as he tipped my head back. His eyes were so blue and dark.

"I asked you something." His voice was low and thick. "Who told you to stop touching your pussy, Princess slut?"

I shook my head, eyeing the gun he was still holding against my chin and lowering to my throat as if it wasn't a weapon. I pressed my back on the pillows, trying to support myself, my hands numb against the sheets.

"N-no one told me to stop. But you are holding a gun."

"And?"

"*Hayden...*"

"Use a safe word or spread your legs."

"But you—"

"*Now*."

His tone was firm, his eyes unreadable and cold and blue. Was this one of his ways of hurting me? Shoot me and then fuck me? God, no, what the fuck I was thinking? He could lose his job as a Navy Seal if he shot an innocent civilian. Especially if that civilian was a royal anonymous Princess. He had told me that he wouldn't do anything to hurt me or won't let any harm come towards me. Maybe that was just another one of his kinks. A fucking gun.

Exhaling a shaky breath, I spread my legs and closed my eyes. The cold nozzle of the gun was a living thing between the valley of my breasts, against my hammering heart.

"Open your eyes." His tone was soft that made me trust him.

As soon as I opened them, looking at him, I cried out when he spanked my pussy. I covered my mouth and groaned, trying to move my hips for more against his repeated thwacks when he pressed the nozzle against my skin, making me aware of the gun.

"Why are you doing this?" I asked, blinking through the tears, feeling the delicious sting of pleasure and pain burning on my sex, spreading into warmth and melting into a puddle of wetness.

"Because you begged me to hurt you, Princess." His answer was all I needed to bite my lip, touching my sensitive clit, staring at him. His eyes softened, and he pressed his lips against my forehead, making me hum with pleasure.

The gun stayed on my heart until he ordered me to edge in front of him, spanking my thighs each time my legs tried to close. It was a pleasurable torture.

"I... I can't," I gasped, so close and tethering on the edge of the orgasm when Hayden trailed the gun over my breast, circling the nozzle around my areola.

"Yes, you can. Hold your orgasm for me for a little while, Princess," he whispered, his hand gliding over my leg, keeping it spread when it trembled. "I promise I will make you feel good."

Feel good. Yes, I knew exactly what he meant by that. Even though I was angry after he left that night, leaving me alone, I had lost the count of nights when I would touch myself and think about how Hayden had made me feel good and sleep after exhaustion of my orgasm.

I could do it, I could stay on edge even though my fingers were drenched, and I was probably making a mess on the sheets. There was constant fear and adrenaline rushing through my body and brain at the sight of his gun rolling around my breasts, playing with my nipples.

I groaned, jumping when Hayden spanked my pussy, the

pleasure of the burn spreading with warmth all around the sensitive nerves.

"*Tsk*, look at this." Hayden was staring at the glistening juices coating his hand. He pressed his hand against my lips and I greedily licked it clean, sucking his fingers in my mouth, watching his eyes dilate. "You get excited every time I spank your cunt, don't you, Princess?"

I licked my lips, humming at my taste. "Yes, Hayden."

"Open your mouth—*no*, keep moving your fingers over your clit, Princess. I want it swollen and red."

I parted my lips, my pussy clenching around nothing when he slid the gun over my neck, to my jaw, to my lips. I stopped, begging and pleading him with my eyes, watching blue eyes turn so dark that they almost looked onyx.

"I told you I would fuck your mouth," he purred, his other hand moving to my thigh, spanking it. "Keep fucking yourself, *you naughty brat*, and open your mouth. *Wider…*"

My brows scrunched when I squirmed, moving my fingers in circles around the clit as Hayden gazed at me. His face gave off nothing but lust. Remaining calm while I was shaking so badly that he had to hold my thigh.

"Tap my thigh twice and everything will stop, Princess," he reminded me. "Anytime you want."

He had taken care of me that night. A stranger. He wouldn't dare to shoot me while I… while I…

"Open your eyes, look at me and part your lips wider."

He knew what I was going to before I could do it. Taking a deep breath, I met his steady gaze, my eyebrows furrowing when he slowly slid. The cold metal of the gun inside my mouth.

I had imagined I would start crying, lock up with fear, and utter the safe word. But I didn't do any of those things because Hayden was looking at me when he made me gag on a gun whose trigger was brushing over his index finger.

"Open wider, come on, I know you can do better, Princess." He encouraged me, reminding me to breathe when I kept rubbing myself, juices gushing out of me as Hayden kept exploring and playing with my limits.

The metal felt sturdy and hard against my teeth, my tongue trying to lap against it as I whimpered and groaned around it, moving my hips as if to want more.

"That's my Princess slut," Hayden whispered in awe, his blue eyes glittering at me with a soft gleam. "Look at you. Sucking on a gun while you touch yourself, just because I told you to."

Hayden took my wrist and licked my fingers with a low grunt that made me clutch the sheets. I wanted him so badly. I hummed when his thumb rubbed tiny circles around my clit.

"Look in the mirror."

My eyes met the reflection of a flushed girl, drooling around a gun while Hayden's strong hand held it. His fingers rubbing over my clit and spanking my pussy from time to time to keep me warm and on the edge, playing with me and teasing me. My piercings glinted in the light and it was such a strange sight to see that I moaned around the gun, forgetting that it was a weapon and could kill me within seconds.

Hayden finally pulled the gun out of my mouth, my saliva coating it when he said in a haughty tone that I had made such a mess of a gun when he had cleaned it few minutes ago.

I wiped the drool from my chin, licking my lips before whispering to him, "Hayden, please... I want to feel you inside me."

"Aw, look at you, I haven't even played with you yet." He was mocking me, but it still sent a jolt of arousal down my spine.

"Please..."

He cupped my face, wiping the tears that had leaked from my eyes. Slowly rubbing his thumb on my bottom lip, he asked, "What does my Princess need?"

"*You.*"

"*Tsk*, you need me where, Princess?"

"Everywhere."

Hayden pushed his thumb inside my mouth, and I latched onto it, sucking it, licking it. "In your mouth?"

I nodded, repeating his words when he pulled away his thumb.

Biting my lip, I leaned back on the pillow when he removed his sweatpants and boxers. I greedily took in the marvelous sight of Hayden. His lean muscled body, made like a Greek God with broad shoulders, a tattoo and tapered waist with abs. I swallowed the lump in my throat at the sight of his powerful thighs and his throbbing, hard cock.

"Come here," I whispered, wanting him on the bed, pleading for him to hurry and crawling towards him.

"Is this what my sweet slut needs?" Hayden asked, pumping his length with his hand when I reached the edge of the bed, staying on my knees across him. I was in awe at him, watching the pre-cum leak out of the head of his cock.

"Yes." My voice didn't belong to me anymore. It was sweet and husky. "*Please*, yes."

"Then take what you need, Princess," he whispered, raking his hand through my hair and pulling me closer until I could palm him, stroking him slowly, peering at him through my lashes.

He felt soft and hard at the same time, his skin hot as I licked his shaft, the ridges of his veins and pressing my lip piercing at the sensitive underside of his cock. Hayden swore, his hips jerking and hand tugging my hair when I swiped my tongue at his head before sucking him inside my mouth.

I moaned at the tangy masculine taste of him. With my hand stroking his balls as I took him deeper into my mouth, I felt an odd sense of power and arousal. The things I was doing to him were making him moan and groan like that, making his muscular legs shake and hips thrust because he felt so out of control by my actions that he couldn't help but acquiesce.

"God, Princess, that is so good," he groaned deeply, the rumble of his voice rolling down my spine to between my sex. I took him deeper, breathing through my nose and deep throating him. "Fuck, baby, you are such a good girl. My sweet slut."

I hummed when he opened his eyes to look at me. His eyes were glazed, cheeks and neck flushed with a red hue as he panted, watching me pleasure him, suck him like he had taught me all those years ago, making me watch and practice in front of a mirror.

"Such a pretty Princess slut," he whispered, caressing my cheek with my mouth full of his throbbing cock.

I pulled back to take a deep breath before dipping my head again. His hand stayed on my hair, guiding me on his girthy length. "*Fuck... oh, fuck,*" he was moaning, whispering my name when I repeated my actions with his help.

His fingers tightened in my hair. "I am going to cum in your pretty little mouth, but don't you fucking dare swallow it, you sweet slut." I moaned when he leaned down to tweak my nipple. "I want to see it slither down your pierced nipples."

I nodded as much as I could, wanting to make him release as I pumped my mouth on him. I needed him to cum, however he wanted to.

Hayden grew rigid and, pulling me close, he made a low groan, spilling inside my mouth. Tears streamed down my face, but I stayed put, digging my fingers in his thigh when he pulled back, his warm cum sliding out of my lips, down to my neck and nipples just like he wanted.

"Such a good, pretty Princess," Hayden whispered, taking a step closer and lifting my chin and kissing the corner of my lips while my body grew hot with him coating me.

He pulled away and looked down my body, so did I, getting wetter at the sight. "Look at you," he said affectionately. "My cum dripping down your pierced tits, you are my sweet cum slut." I bit my lip, clenching myself tightly when he ran his hand through my breasts. "I like you covered in my cum," he said, his voice rough and heavy, rubbing his seed over my stomach and thighs as if he wanted to mark me everywhere.

His crystal clear eyes met mine, a warm glow on his face. Cupping my face, he gently wiped my mouth, making me suck his finger clean and pulling it free. Leaning closer, he bent and kissed me, humming as if he was the most satisfied person on earth, licking and biting my lip and pushing me down on the mattress, savouring my lips like a savage man.

My hands wrapped around his shoulders, holding him as he made out with me. I let out a soft moan, feeling him harden against my inner thigh. I tried to grind myself on him, but he pulled away.

"You have been such a good Princess," he whispered, pinning my wrists on the bed and settling himself between my legs.

I glanced down at his length, trying to move and have him rub against me, just a little. But he held me back. "Please, Hayden."

"*Shh*, have patience, love."

Biting my lip, I nodded, relaxing under his touch as he asked me not to move my hands as his glided over my body, kissing my neck. I melted in the mattress, sighing with pleasure when his deft fingers pinched and tweaked my nipples, his hot tongue on my stomach, his lips kissing my belly button, lightly tugging at the piercing.

"You smell so fucking good, Princess." His large hands spread my thighs, gliding his hand over them. Licking his lips, he eyed my pussy as if I was the meal he would ever have. His fingers gently teased my sensitive clit, sliding his fingers over my slicked lips to get them wet before dipping two fingers inside me.

I clenched around him, raising my hips and scrunching the sheets. He smacked my thigh, his dark blue eyes flashing at me. "Good Princesses don't get greedy. Stay still and let me make you feel good."

I whined at him, but caved in under his commanding eyes. I eyed his body, the sweat sheeting on his smooth, chiseled skin. The tattoo on his shoulder, the way his abs tensed when I moaned his name, his fingers moving in and out of me until I couldn't hold it anymore.

"Oh... *fuck*, Hayden!" I tried to hold on to something, anything, grabbing the sheets and wrenching them as my legs trembled, my body shaking with the edge of the orgasm.

"Hold it, Zara," Hayden said sharply, pausing his movements as I cried out. "*Sh*, take a deep breath and don't cum until I tell you to."

I cupped my mouth and tried to take a deep breath, controlling the tittering orgasm, focusing on his warm hands rubbing my thighs, holding them softly. His deep, rumbling voice when he praised me. 'Such a good Princess slut', 'So proud of you', 'My sweet Princess.'

When I opened my eyes, Hayden was licking his fingers clean, the ones that had been inside me moments ago, making a low groaning sound that had me clenching. He eyed me and, leaning closer, he spread my legs with his shoulders, keeping them over them. I moaned at the sight, his handsome face between my spread legs with my legs over his shoulder.

His warm breath was so close to my heated sex. I whimpered, shivering when he blew cold air, teasing my clit with the tip of his tongue, playing with me.

"Need... *more*," I gasped out when his fingers moved over my entrance, his lips wrapping around my pleasure nub, flicking the piercing with his tongue and, kissing it, toying with it, slowly sucking it while he inserted his digit inside me.

"*Hayden*," I let out a soft moan, biting my lip when he pressed his hand on my stomach when I tried to buck my hips against him. He was so controlling and demanding.

My walls fluttered around him, clamping his finger in a grip when he inserted another, all the while making out with my clit with his eyes closed as if he was having the time of his life. I moved my hands down my body, remembering his cum on my nipples, and groaned, wrapping my fingers around his thick hair.

Hayden opened his eyes and looked at me, his eyes cloudy and deep and burning with lust, his tongue lapping at my pussy as I rubbed myself on his dirty mouth. His name kept bubbling out of my mouth with little pleads, begging him for something... something more.

"So fucking delicious," Hayden hummed against my sex, my toes curling over his back. "Such a pretty pussy. All wet and dripping for me, right, Princess?"

I nodded, crying out, "Yes, all for you, Hayden. *Pleasepleaseplease*."

"I love when you beg, my sweet slut." He pecked my clit and leaned back, keeping my feet back on the bed. His fingers moved inside me, back and forth, back and forth, pressing against the sensitive spot that kept me on edge. "You want to cum, don't you, Princess?"

"Yes!"

"*Tsk*," he shook his head, a cruel, mischievous look on his face. "So fucking horny and greedy. Maybe I should keep teasing you for a few days—"

"Hayden, please, *no*, I can't handle it. I want to cum so bad."

I was going to cry or kick him. Or both.

"How bad, sweetheart?"

He was playing with me, by the glint in his eyes, I knew he was playing with me. But he knew I liked it. Craved it.

"I will…" I panted. "I will do anything."

"Anything you say, Princess?"

I nodded, blinking at him.

"What if I want to fuck your cunt with this gun?"

He wasn't serious—

My lips parted in a soundless moan when his fingers curled inside me. I whimpered and groaned when he kept my legs from snapping shut, fucking me with his fingers.

"Imagine, Princess," he crooned, pressing his fingers down to hold my thigh. "How horny are you that you would do anything for me… even fuck a gun, *hm*?"

"*Hayden.*"

"My sweet Princess slut," he said, his voice lowering an octave. "I want you to cum, baby. See you climax."

I peered at him through my half-lidded eyes, shamelessly grinding myself on his hands as he kept sliding his fingers inside me, his thumb pressing against the piercing of my clit and rolling it around while his lips moved against the shell of my ear.

"Say that you belong to me, Zara." His fingers curled inside me. "Say you are my Princess slut."

"*Yes.*" I was gasping because I was falling and falling and falling. "Belong to you, Hayden. I'm your Princess slut." I wrapped my arms around him, holding on to his shoulders when I exploded around him, convulsing and shaking with his name on my lips.

When I came to, his arm was securely wrapped around me with my body pressed against his. The ache in my pussy was simmering, and I felt so hot and hazy that I wasn't sure which year it was, let alone the month.

"Welcome back, sleepyhead," Hayden whispered, his eyes soft as he ran his hand through my short hair. "You were out like a light."

I didn't have the energy to roll my eyes at him. "Thanks to you." My voice was sultry and husky.

"Are you okay, Princess?" His eyes flickered to my body as he raised himself on his elbows, his gentle hands holding my waist as he looked at me with concern in his eyes. "I didn't hurt you, did I?"

I cupped his jaw and kissing him on his lips. It was a peck, but it was soft and warm, everything I ever wanted. "No, you didn't. I told you I can handle myself."

He still wanted to be sure as he spread my legs, making me blush when he inspected me like that, making me feel so vulnerable and... *open*. I winced when he touched my clit and moved his hand back, looking at me.

"You seem very sensitive."

I swallowed the lump in my throat. "The piercing... ever since I got it, I have been extremely sensitive."

"Is that so?" His eyes lit up, and I didn't like it. "I would have loved to over-stimulate you now but my Princess needs her rest."

I bit my lip, stretching and sighing on the bed as he got dressed. I pouted at him when he wore his boxers and sweatpants, ignoring my request to help him out and flicking my nose before going to the washroom.

"I am twenty-one years old," I said in a firm voice. Well, as firm as I could manage with him, cleaning my chin, neck and breasts with a warm towel. His other hand softly caressing my waist. "I can clean—"

"Don't make me gag you."

"*Hayden!*"

He flickered his eyes at me. Down to my mouth as he smirked, "What? You would enjoy it. It would be a treat for me to see you like that."

I blushed and looked away from him. I am going to blame him for many kinks he had introduced me to, for tainting my innocent virgin head and for... being such a hot, handsome, caring... *something*. Despite spending so much time together, pleasuring each other and being intimate, we hadn't discussed what were we to each other.

"What's troubling you?" Hayden asked, walking back to bed and turning off the lights to slide under the blankets with me.

I wondered if it was the right time to bring up a topic of... relationship. But I had sucked a fucking gun in my mouth and had one of the best orgasms of my life. Because of him.

"Was that gun loaded?" I asked.

He turned to me and opened the nightstand drawer to show it to me. I held it and it was weighted, but I knew there were no bullets in it.

"I told you, I would never hurt you, Princess," he kissed my hair. "I removed the clip without you noticing. I wasn't expecting that you would agree to it."

I flushed, thinking more about it. "I wouldn't dare to but... I don't know... it's *you* so." I shrugged and turned away from him. My head was still fuzzy with the release of hormones, so I was being emotional and I didn't anthem to see that. He had already hurt my heart, even though it was not intentional. He had.

His hand wrapped around my waist when he snuggled

behind me, maintaining his distance so that my back pressed against his strong chest, but our hips were not in contact.

"I understand what you are saying, Zara." He thought for a moment when I relaxed under the weight of his arm around my ribs, his fingers softly stroking my breasts.

Fuck it.

I turned around and looked at him in the dark, blinking at his face. "What are we doing, Hayden?"

His hand froze on my skin. "What do you mean?"

I tugged the blanket to my neck. "*This*. Kissing, flirting… almost having sex."

"In case you need me to remind you, we just had oral sex, Zara."

"Yes, but you told me you don't date."

"Why is that a problem?" He asked, taking a deep breath. "You told me yourself that you sleep around. Won't you go back to Noah when we get back?"

My heart sank at his words as I faced the ceiling. "Do you want me to?" My voice was barely a whisper.

He didn't reply as the seconds passed by. Minutes.

"Then why did you make me say those words? That I belong to you?" I was angry all of a sudden. Sitting up on the bed and trying not to get overwhelmed.

"Do you want me to tell you the truth?" He sat up to, still not looking at me.

"*Yes*."

"Because I want nothing else than that, Zara," his voice was full of guilt and anger. "I hate that whenever I see you around someone, I get jealous. I don't want to get jealous because the truth is that you don't belong to me. You are your person and I… I like that I get to have some sense of control over you when we are intimate. Like *before*."

I had never seen Hayden like that before. Stammering and not meeting my eyes when we talked.

"What are you saying, Hayden?"

He finally looked at me and the emotions in his eyes, the gleam in them, took me by surprise. "I want you, Zara. *All* of you. Every inch of your body and soul. I don't want you to fuck around. I want you to fuck me and share your embarrassing stories. I want to take care of you, but hurt you too." He closed his eyes and breathed out, "I want you or… nothing."

28

HAYDEN

"I want you or... nothing."
What the fuck did I just say? Was that the right time to disappear under the blanket and ignore Zara? Maybe lock myself in the bathroom and take a cold shower with clothes on. I felt embarrassed and so fucking naked, even with boxers and stripped pyjamas.

"Hayden..."

This was it. Zara would say, *You are a possessive jerk, leave me alone. I wouldn't have kissed you if you were going to be so emotional about it.* And then she would put on her clothes and walk out of the room, leaving me confused and sad and hurt on the bed while I wondered if it was because I didn't have sex with or if my tongue game wasn't that strong.

But I had made her orgasm twice, hadn't I? Oh fuck. Was she faking it?

"I would... um, like that." Her cheeks flushed as she looked at her lap. My eyes travelled down the curve of her spine. "I haven't done this before. You know... belonging to each other. All or nothing, although I felt the same way, but if I haven't experienced it before so I don't know how it woul—

Why are you looking at me like that? Did I say something wrong?"

I blinked at her and took her palm in my hand. I ran the pads of my fingers through her thin fingers, her black coloured nails, pressing her palm against mine and entwining our fingers together. She squeezed my hand as I brushed my lips across her knuckles. It felt electrifying. The sparks and the feeling bubbling in my chest, making my stomach flutter.

"Even I don't know this works, Princess," I said truthfully, holding her gaze. Her liquid brown eyes with dark rings. "But I want to *try*. With you."

She slowly nodded, looking at our hands, and smiled at me. *Fuck*. Her smile. I wanted to kiss it. Every night and every day. "I want to try this, too. Whatever this is. Let's take it one day at a time?"

I hummed, brushing her short hair and tucking the loose lock behind her ear. "One day at a time." I agreed, kissing her forehead.

Even though I might not have a future in Navy Seal or any military service. I couldn't care less about money. I had earned my fair share and saved up enough to last my second generation. I could try for something else. I had many options with my medals on my uniform. But for the moment, I wanted to try being the best I could be. For Zara. One day at a time.

I BIT MY BOTTOM LIP WHEN ZARA LET OUT A WHIMPER, HER thighs shaking as I pressed her closer, the small arch on her back and the way she clamped around me making me heady.

"H-how... long?" Zara managed to utter when I kept gliding my hands on her bare skin, skimming my fingers through her nipple piercings and pressing a soft kiss on the crook of her neck.

I lazily eyed the laptop screen that was in front of her, her fingers frozen on the keyboard. "Did you finish your work?" I asked, soothing the tremors on her legs for sitting on me for the past half an hour.

We were bored, and I was extremely horny while Zara was working. So I proposed an idea of cockwarming to her. Zara had blushed and stuttered but caved in, promising not to tease her too much while she worked.

I, of course, had obliged and let my sweet Princess sit on my throbbing cock that was hard as rock inside her warm heat. I had to tighten my hands in fists and shift on the couch to keep myself from combusting around the constant clench of her sopping pussy.

"It's almost done—*oh*, Hayden!" Her back flatted on my chest and I wrapped my arms around her when she quivered. "You're... you are going to make me come if you keep moving."

Poor thing was already panting and pawing at my hands as if she didn't know she wanted me to leave her alone or touch her more.

"*Tsk*," I whispered, lowering my hand over her abdomen, trailing my fingers over her hipbones and making her shiver. "I haven't even fucked you, Princess."

"But you have been inside me for the past half an hour."

I lightly spanked her clit, tightening my arms around her when she trembled, letting out a long gasp. "*Shh*, Princess. Finish your work and then we will go out."

"Go out? I don't want to go out, I want you to fuck me."

"Greedy Princess." I let out a soft chuckle and purred in her ears, my hands on her breasts, pinching and tweaking her hard nipples, pulling at the piercings. "If you behave, then I will think about fucking you."

She made a low grumbling sound and shifted herself on my lap—oh sweet heavens. That felt so fucking good. Lewd sloppy sound came from our unison when she sat up and looked at me over her shoulder with a mischievous glint in her eyes.

I awed at her beauty, her short hair, her dark hooded eyes, the way soft blush spread over her cheeks and nose.

"Or I can just ride you *like this…*" Zara trailed off, spreading her legs more and supporting herself on the couch. She slowly started moving, little gasps making their way out of her pretty mouth.

I sat up and halted her movements, pressing her down on my hard length by holding her hips. She whimpered, being stretched to the hilt and full of my throbbing cock.

"Finish your work and then we will play if you behave like a good girl." My voice was firm as I held her thighs apart. "And because you are being such a needy slut, riding me like that, I will spank your thigh and sopping pussy each time you try to close your legs. Understood, Princess?"

She nodded, her short hair brushing my cheeks when I kissed the hammering pulse on her neck. "I… understand, Hayden."

"Get back to work, Princess."

I went back to caressing her sinful body, brushing the pads of my fingers over every inch of her skin and smacking her thighs or clit whenever her legs trembled and tried to close. Her fingers would move either too quickly on the keyboard or she would freeze with a breath hitching her throat whenever I slid myself deeper inside her, pressing the flat of my palm on her abdomen, making her feel how full she was.

"D-done," Zara breathed out after a few minutes, shakily closing her laptop. "Hayden, please fuck me now. I am—"

"Good girl," I murmured in her ear, wrapping my hand

around her neck and lowering my other hand between her legs. "Keep your legs spread like that and stay still, hm?"

She nodded, leaning back on my shoulder and closing her eyes as I slowly played with her swollen clit. Her piercing brushed against my fingers as I increased my pace, her wetness growing and making me twitch inside her. Her little moans grew as I kept my hand on her throat, keeping her in place and rubbing her while I was balls deep inside her.

"Do you want to cum, Zara?" I asked, kissing her cheek when she opened her eyes and gazed at me. "Do you want me to fuck you in the middle of the day, on a couch, you naughty Princess slut?"

"Yes," she moaned, her hips bucking and clenching me in a tight grip, making me tremble. "Please, Hayden, I need you."

"I know, Princess." I increased my pace and soon enough, she was coming all over me, the walls of her pussy spasming around me, making me edge. I groaned and pulled out just in time to release all over her stomach and breasts, shivering with her.

We held each other and calmed down enough to sulk on the couch together, messy and wet and flushed from the orgasm.

"That was…" Zara trailed off, my arm draped over her waist.

"*Yeah.*" I whispered, kissing her on the lips.

When we woke up from our nap, it was evening, and the weather looked cold and gloomy. We were both sticky, so we took a quick shower, which ended up with a long make-out session until I pinched her butt, reminding her we have to go out.

"Let's go out."

"Hayden." She looked at me from the mirror and paused with a palmful of body lotion.

"I'll buy you anything you want."

Zara considered it for a moment. "Anything?"

"Yes, Princess. I can't spend one more minute inside this cabin... unless we both are naked in the bedroom, of course."

She pouted at me. "Fine, you are buying me the most expensive dish in Almas Peninsula."

"Yes, ma'am."

I wore a white shirt with pants, eyeing her naked body while she got dressed. She even made a show, fondling and massaging the lotion onto her breasts for a few minutes until I ordered her to get dressed.

"Help me zip up the dress."

I held my breath, seeing her wear golden hoops in her ears. My fists clenched at my side as I stiffly walked towards her, trying not to meet her eyes, and slowly zipped her dress. It was black in color that fit her lithe frame, ending on her thighs.

She looked too good. I didn't want anyone staring at her.

"How do I look?" Zara twirled, grinning at me as she fixed the collar of my shirt and wore black sandal heels.

Fucking beautiful.

But I glared at her breasts, the material of the dress fitting her so perfectly that I could notice the outline of her piercings if I stared too hard.

"I can see your nipple piercings through that dress." I slid my hands in my pockets, standing straighter than before, even flexing my muscles when she glanced at me.

"Then stop being ungrateful." Zara said in such a bland tone that had me gaping at her. She didn't notice. She was busy buckling her heels and walking out of the room to find her handbag.

Did she just...

I followed her, holding her wrist and turning her around, pressing my lips against her, swallowing her gasp when my hands squeezed her breasts, my thumb and finger pinching her nipples through the dress. Her hands wrapped around my shoulder, pulling me close, grabbing my shirt as our kisses got heated.

"Am I being grateful enough?" I teased her bottom lip, licking it and pulling back to see her molten eyes.

"*Mhm*." Her eyes travelled down to my body, licking her pink swollen lips. "Let's stay naked in the bedroom."

I let out a low chuckle and pulled back. "Not at all, Princess." I glanced at her breasts, her hard nipples poking through the dress, and sighed. Flashing my eyes to her face, I asked, "How do you feel about body writing?"

She frowned at me.

I remembered I had written on her skin once. Two years ago. "How did you feel when you saw my number on your stomach… right here?" I brushed my thumb over her belly.

"Oh… with *H*?"

I nodded, adoring the way her cheeks flushed. "I… I liked it." I could sense she wanted to add something and waited for her to tell me. Pursing her lips, she took a deep breath and said, "I didn't want to remove it from my skin whenever I took a bath. I like that… that you wrote it and it made that night not feel like a dream."

My lips wrapped around hers, kissing her to make her feel that what she had said was a huge deal for me and I would do anything for her. Anything at all. Even make that a reality, once again.

Even if the bedroom was closed and I couldn't wait to have her, I pecked her lips, slowing down. Our warm breath mingled with each other. "What if I wrote something on your skin right now?" I asked, keeping my eyes on her face and hands on her waist. "Would you like that?"

Her lips parted. "Like what?"

I thought about it for a moment. Cupping her perky

breasts, I rubbed my thumb over her right nipple. "I will write my name here. *Hayden…*" Flicking her left nipple, I whispered, "My last name here. *Knight* with a *S*." Lowering my hand to her stomach, I gazed at her, "And *Princess Slut* right here."

Her eyes were clouded with lust, blinking at me slowly as the tips of her ears turned pink. I felt her stomach clench and the way her thighs tried to rub against each other. She was aroused, but she hadn't consented to it.

I pulled my hand, "Maybe when you are more comfor—"

"Please." Zara held my wrist. "Do it. I… I want you to write that."

Zara

HOLYSHIT. MY TEETH SUNK INTO MY BOTTOM LIP WHEN Hayden spanked my ass, glaring at me.

"Stay. Still."

He had me perched on his lap—*no*, his thigh, with a marker on his hand while I scrunched my fingers on the hem of my dress, holding it up above my neck. I was aching and wet and so so horny. I was scared to make a puddle in my underwear and soak into his expensive pants as I tried to stay still.

But it was considerably difficult with his palm stroking my breast mindlessly, the cold tip of thick black marker moving across my pale skin. I felt so dirty and small and hot. Just like that morning when I had first seen it. Wore my dress and went back to the Golden Palace. Having guards and maids bow at me while hiding the dirty secret of having *his* number on my skin. A letter *H* on my skin.

"I know you are soaking wet, my sweet Princess slut."

Hayden closed the marker, pulling me closer to him by looping his fingers on my thong. I whimpered, the feel of his pants rubbing against my clit, giving me the friction I needed, making me cream more. "But I don't care. Do you know why?"

I shook my head, clenching and unclenching, when his glittering blue eyes gazed at my body as if I was a painting that he had created.

"Because I want your pretty cunt dripping for me this entire evening." I arched up to him hearing his dirty words. So perfectly said in his deep voice, as if he was talking about the damn sky and not my pussy. "And when we come back, I want to lick you and if you behave, make you cum on my mouth."

"Just your mouth?" I pouted, cupping his jaw.

I gasped, grinning when he spanked me playfully. "Greedy Princesses who don't behave don't get to cum at all." He warned, pinching my nipple. "If you want something else, you know how to beg. I have taught you some manners, haven't I?"

"*Ass.*"

He spanked me again, glaring at me. "Badmouth me once again and I—"

"You are an ass."

I glared right back at him and cupped his length, stroking him slowly through his pants. "I want to fuck you and I know you want to fuck me too, but you keep—"

"Have patience." He held my hand and looked away with his cheeks pink. "And we can't have sex right now because I don't have condoms."

I pulled back, blinking at him. "Really? Again?"

In all honesty, I was both touched and angry. Touched that he never thought he would need them and angry that he didn't think he might need them if he wants to have sex with me. But then again, he had asked me to cockwarm him and I had gladly done it without protection because I was on pills.

Hayden sighed and stroked my cheek. I loved how he could be rough and sweet in a matter of seconds. "I told you, I didn't want to have sex with anyone else but you. And I thought you would rather… you know, with someone else…"

"*Hayden.*" I cupped his hand on my cheek. It was warm and soft. "I don't want to have sex with anyone other than you." Then I added, "I… I am still on pills so… we could. I am clean. I got tested before arriving here."

He nodded, his throat bobbing as he swallowed. "Me too. I…" he shook his head and looked at my breasts. "I can't think with these in my face."

Before he could tug my dress down, I handed him my phone. "Take a picture." At his surprised face, I said with warm cheeks, "I want to remember it. And I look pretty hot like this, don't you think?"

His voice was rough, lowered down an octave. "Yes, very hot." He held my waist as he took a few pictures below my neckline. "If I had known you were into body writing, I would have made you write all kinds of stuff on yourself."

"What kind of stuff?"

He brushed his fingers just above my clit and said, "That this is *Hayden's Pussy.*"

I made a low sound, squirming on his lap. "Please let's fuck, I want to… Hayden—*no.*"

I whined when he tugged down my dress, straightening it as he stood up and offering me his hand. "Come on, stop pouting like that. It makes me want to fuck your mouth and we don't have time for that."

He shushed me when I made a grabbing motion with my hands towards his belt. I grinned when he backed away. "Zara, *no*. I won't buy you the most expensive dish here if you keep acting like a sex addict."

Sighing, I sadly tugged down my dress and blushed, thinking that his words were on my skin. "Apparently, you make me act like a nymphomaniac."

He opened the door for me. Cold wind brushed through my bare skin as I stepped out of the cabin, Hayden following me. "I don't know whether it is an insult or a compliment."

"*Both.*"

I yelped when he pinched my butt, making me giggle on his shirt as he wrapped his arm around my waist, walking beside me with a small grin on his lips.

I wish that time would just stop there. With us being playful and happy together on a cold evening.

29

HAYDEN

"Why are you making that face?" I asked, swallowing the taco we had received from the old couple who ran a small restaurant. It looked ancient, and we were the only customers here.

It was our own fault. I wanted to buy the most expensive dish for her but it was made from eggplant and she hated eggplants, so we walked somewhere else until our stomachs kept growling. We found the small restaurant on the corner of the road and walked in without thinking, greeted by the old couple who 'ooh'ed and 'ahh'ed when we mentioned we were there for our honeymoon.

They bought our lie despite our empty ring fingers and even gave us free beer while serving us our orders.

Zara ate the food, forcing herself to swallow it as she thumped her chest, coughing a little and taking a big gulp of beer.

"Was it that bad?" I asked, patting her hand sympathetically.

"It tastes like tears of old people," she grumbled, pursing her lips at the half-eaten taco.

Holding back my smile, I exchanged my dish with her, which was just a salad in some spicy sauce which Zara wouldn't mind chewing through as it did not taste like tears of old people.

"I would offer to say no, thank you, I can eat my food but I can't feel my tongue after eating that." Stabbing the fork on a lettuce, she glanced at me and smiled brightly, "So, thank you for eating that thing. I would kiss you right now, but you probably don't want to—"

I leaned over the table and gave her a peck on her lips. Smiling, I pointed at the salad. "Now eat. We will get something on our way back."

With a pink blush on her cheeks, she took a bite and sighed, closing her eyes. I looked down at the taco and squeezed my eyes shut at that scent. There was beetroot in it. Holding my breath, I fought off the nausea of thinking about the firing as I pulled out the slices of beetroot with a fork.

"You don't like beet?" Zara asked, taking the fork from my shaky hand and clearing the beetroot from the taco.

I shook my head, covering my mouth and nose as she kept the plate of beetroot away and glanced at me. "Thank you," I said to her and ate the tasteless taco in silence.

I tipped the old couple and thanked them for our meals.

"Are you okay?" Zara asked, her hands tightening around my arm.

"I am. Now." I looked at her and said, "I… I don't like the smell of beetroot. It…" I shook my head.

"What?" She paused. "What is it?"

"You don't need to know that, Princess. Come on—"

"If it's troubling you, then I want to know, Hayden."

Her eyes were soft, her voice full of sincerity. I was so thankful that she had not seen or heard anything about what's it like fighting for your own country. I was grateful that she stayed uncorrupted of the real-life casualty and wanting to fight for your life, for the life of your own comrades.

"The smell of beetroot reminds me of the rotting bodies." I said, looking away from her, closing my eyes and trying not to think about those days. "Under the dessert sun with scorching heat, it's all you can smell while trying to keep your head on your shoulder while fighting for your own life."

"Oh, Hayden." Warm hands wrapped around my torso as my tensed body relaxed under her touch. The soft caress of her palm on my back. "I am sorry for making you think of... all of that. It must have been difficult for you. I am sorry."

I hugged her, tightening my arms around her and pulling her close, smelling the shampoo of her hair. "Don't apologize, Zara. I am okay now. *Better.*"

We stayed like that until we heard something shattering behind us. We were in a dark alley, so I put Zara behind me, turning around. There were bins across the small empty road. I held my breath.

Is someone following us? Here?

Zara sighed and dragged me away from there when a cat jumped down the wall, letting out a small squeak of meow.

Even though we were in a brighter street with people around us, I didn't let go of her hand.

Zara

"I DIDN'T ASK FOR THIS." I COMPLAINED TO HIM IN A HUSHED voice.

He slid his eyes over the expensive gold and silver jewellery. "But you had said something expensive, Princess." His blue eyes were clear when he glanced at me. "And I promised I would buy it."

I ignored the burning glance of the pretty employee of the luxurious jewellery store as she stayed standing over the glass counter, bringing whatever piece of jewellery Hayden wanted to see. And he wanted to see *a lot*. From tiny studs for my pierced lobe to anklets. Many dainty earrings, necklaces, and even body jewellery chain. Everything except rings, which I was thankful for.

"But this is… too expensive. I didn't ask for this." I repeated, hating that he would have to spend five figures just to buy something tiny for me. After all, Almas Peninsula was famous for the diamonds. It would be pretty expensive and not to mention that I already had a set of necklace and earrings back at the palace which I had worn once just because it was named after me.

I hope he doesn't see that. It was one of the main reasons I was trying to steer him away from the store, but it was so shiny with white marble floors and lights everywhere that Hayden wanted to come there.

"Hey, look. This is named after you." Hayden pointed at the same set of necklace and earrings I had.

"Haha, really? That's funny."

I might as well wear the damn tiara and tell him the truth.

Hayden frowned at it and looked at me, shaking his head. "Nah, it isn't your type. Please show us something else."

My heart beat increased and palms grew sweaty as I looked away. How did he know I didn't like the style? Just because the designer had named it after a Princess didn't mean that I had particularly liked wearing something that had over ten diamonds on it.

"This is beautiful—*hm*, yes." Hayden held up a dainty golden chain with a small pearl on it, a golden diamond coating the pearl, making it glint in the lights. He looked at me and my neck. "Lean closer, Zara."

Taking a deep breath, I did, ignoring the way the

employees were gushing over us. My cheeks became hot when Hayden's warm breath caressed my neck. He leaned back and straightened the diamond pearl on my neck, gazing at it with a soft gleam.

"It looks perfect. You are perfect."

His white teeth flashed at me, his eyes curling at the corner as my heart pounded in my heartbeat. I couldn't look away from him, the big grin on his face, the softness in his voice.

The employee kept talking about how gorgeous it looked and how old the pearl was and how many labor of hours it took to make the necklace while I stared at my face and neck in the mirror, lightly touching the pearl. It suited well with my skin tone. I liked Hayden's choice. But not for over fifty thousand dollars.

I raised my arms to unclasp the necklace. "It's too itchy," I lied. "I don't—"

Hayden held my hand and closed his around it so that I couldn't move my hand. "No. I am buying it." His eyes turned darker when he looked at me, "Don't remove it and... *behave*."

My cheeks flushed harder as I stayed seated while he wrote a cheque. How he had a chequebook with him was a mystery that I was too confused to solve. I stiffened, trying to eavesdrop on the two employees.

"Did you know Princess is missing?" One of them said.

"What?"

"The Princess of Azmia is missing," she repeated to her colleague.

"*Again?*"

I swallowed the lump in my throat, asking Hayden to hurry. He handed the cheque to the employee while I tried not to gawk at the amount flaring my nose at him. His arm slipped around me, pulling me flush against him as his lips grazed against my ear.

"I am going to fuck you like *my little slut* if you don't stop acting like a fucking brat." My cheeks burned when he smiled at me, his thumb caressing my collarbone as if he was admiring the necklace. "I thought you had some manners, but I think I need to fuck them into you, isn't that right, Princess?"

I was too speechless to say anything. Ever since I was little, I had been taught etiquette, speaking, bowing, eating, walking habits, including how to dance, wield a sword, use a gun, knife, fighting and how to seduce a Royal drink tea and even how to fold a napkin by world's best tutors and personal maids. I had been academically smart and helped Zain, Sultan of Azmia, with a few of his policies whenever I could and read the history of my country with Rahim, arguing smartly with Zayed in political language until he whined to Khalid and yet...

I was speechless. Just because it was Hayden Robert Knight, caressing my skin as if he was in utter awe while gazing at me with his dark sapphire eyes, wanting to bend me over the glass counter with the most expensive diamonds in the world and fuck me on them.

"I think," I whispered, finding my voice too low. "You should hurry."

He smiled, that strange, evil yet sweet smile of his that sent shivers down my spine until my pussy dampened my thong. I didn't know why I bothered to wear them around him when he ruined them without touching me.

"Why not? I have you all to myself for a couple of days." He thanked the blushing employee, who must have heard his sentence, and glanced away from us. He took the large bag with the shop name and dragged me out of there as I smiled at his back.

Finally. It was happening.

30

ZARA

I bit my lip, my stomach nervously clenching. Hayden did not have sex for two years and I was scared that I might not... I shook my head. It was all nerves. It would be good. More than that, because it was him.

He was still holding my hand, his thumb rubbed on my knuckles as we walked on the familiar path towards our cabin. The night air was fresh, smell of ocean wafting in our direction as we crunched through.

"Are you sure, Zara?" He asked, glancing at me. His lashes made shadows on his cheekbones under the moonlight. Leaves rustled with cool wind. I pressed closer to him, have his warmth around me, making me feel safe.

"I am sure, Hayden." I squeezed his hand, admiring how our hands fit perfectly. "Are you?"

"To be honest..." he trailed on when we entered the cabin, closing ourselves from the outside world. Alone in a cozy cabin by the shore. "I am scared of coming too quickly."

His cheeks were slashed with color, watching me with his deep blue eyes. "It's okay," I whispered, kissing the corner of his lips. "You can play with your Princess until you get hard again, *hm?*"

The shade of his eyes darkened, a low coil forming in my abdomen at the heat of his eyes. Like a molten glacier. His arm wrapped around me, pulling me flush against his chest.

"Say that again."

"Your Princess?"

He nodded, glancing at my lips. "Say it again, Zara. It's written on your tits, isn't it?"

I took a sharp breath, remembering the words as my pussy clenched around nothing. "I am your Princess slut, Hayden Knight," my voice was small and soft, warm blood rushing to my cheeks.

"That's right, sweetheart." His fingers brushed against the neckline of my dress. "I am going to fuck you like one tonight. Would you like that?"

"Yes."

I exhaled sharply when his palm thwacked my ass. The low sting melting into delicious warmth, spreading across my heated sex.

"Don't forget your manners, Princess."

Oh, fuck.

Licking my lips, I said, "Fuck me, please, Hayden."

"Fuck you like what?"

He really wanted to tease me, didn't he?

I squirmed, his arm tightening around my waist, keeping me still while his piercing eyes bore down on me. My face turned red when I said, "Fuck me like your Princess slut, Hayden. *Please.*"

His eyes softened, and lips pressed against mine in a slow, soft kiss. "I will, Princess," he whispered. "I will fuck you like my sweet little whore."

I moaned and pressed closer against his hard body, sliding my hands in his hair, unbuttoning his shirt and grabbing him wherever I could. His hands threw my purse somewhere as we clumsily kissed and made our way to the bedroom. Somewhere something fell, but we didn't notice.

We didn't care about anything but each other. The world melting and fading away from us as we panted, staring at each other.

"I want you to wear just this." His hand traced the expensive necklace he had bought me. "And nothing else for me."

I was too dazed with the kisses when he unzipped my dress, turning me around. I stared at our reflection, the dim glow of light in the bedroom making it feel intimate. His tall height looming behind me, his stern face focused as he pulled down my dress.

Hayden frowned. "Your name is stitched on the label…"

Oh shit. Zara. It was one of the dresses that the designer had tailored for me. Of course, it had my name on it because the designer had gifted it to the Princess Zara.

I panicked and said, "Yeah, it's from *Zara*. The brand."

Nice save.

He didn't comment, letting my dress pool around my feet, leaving me in nothing but my drenched thong, the words he had written on my skin and the necklace he had bought for me.

I relished in the way his hands cupped my breasts, looking in the mirror with a wild look in his eyes. "You look so fucking perfect. So beautiful," he murmured to himself, as if he was admiring some art. I shivered when he pinched my nipples, his palm roving down to my stomach, my belly button glinting, and lower until his finger pressed against the stud of my clit, making me buck against him.

"*Shh*," he whispered, kissing my neck. "You belong to me, Princess. Let me play with you for a while."

So I did. I let him play with me for as long as he wanted. Grinding on his fingers, rolling and tweaking my nipples as he gagged me with his fingers while his other hand played with me through the thong.

"So pretty and desperate for my cock, *hm?*" He slid out his fingers from my mouth, lowering them to my waist, sliding my underwear to the side and dipping them inside me.

I met him with no resistance, clenching his digits inside me, throwing my head on his shoulder and groaning his name as he fucked me in front of a mirror, my fingers clenching on his forearms, feeling his muscles tense and his length stiffen with each second.

Pulling his fingers out of me, he laid me down on the bed and before I could take a breath, the sound of fabric tearing apart filled the room. I gasped when I saw him throwing away the lace of fabric that was once my thong. But Hayden didn't seem to care. His eyes and hands feasting on me with desperate, carnal need. Parting my legs, eliciting a low grunting sound and settling himself between me, still fully clothed.

I kissed him, raking my hands down his shirt and ripping it away as the buttons scattered around the bed and onto the floor. Hayden glared at me and his ruined shirt, but I was too busy sliding my palms down his muscles, kissing and tasting his skin.

"That was one of my favourite shirts."

"That was one of my favourite thongs."

He tugged at my hair, kissing my neck. "I would buy you more expensive ones and unwrap you myself from them."

I squirmed and held myself back from saying that I could buy him an entire brand if he wanted. Instead, I lowered my hand down to the vee of his hips and palmed his hardened length, biting my lip at the feeling of his velvety smooth skin. I had taken him in my mouth, but I had forgotten just how girthy he was.

"*Zara...*" he groaned, dropping his head on my collarbone,

bucking his hips in my hand, kissing my nipple while I slowly squeezed him.

"Fuck me, please," I begged him, spreading my legs wider. "I don't want to wait anymore."

Hayden managed to pull himself away and quickly shed his clothes. I watched him through my half-lidded eyes and rubbed my clit in front of him, his eyes pinned between my legs as he quickened his pace, almost stumbling through his boxers.

I would have laughed at the sight of naked Hayden Knight hurrying to get in the bed with me that he stumbled if he had not spread my thighs and replaced my fingers with his hot mouth. His tongue licking my clit, sucking it in his mouth as he groaned, and I whimpered at the reverberations.

"Let me make you cum," he whispered, spanking my pussy with a hard smack as I jumped at the sudden sting of pleasure. His mouth latched on my sex once again, the warmth and molten heat spreading through me as I tugged on his hair, his fingers curling inside me, leaving me breathless as I came all over his mouth and hands.

When I opened my eyes, the black dots blinking away from my vision to find him hovering above me, licking his lips before wrapping them around mine. I hummed, tasting myself on his lips and tongue, sighing when I felt his cock brush against my inner thigh.

"Need... you," I said between the kisses, my pussy sensitive and clenching for him as his tip brushed from my clit to the slicked lips. Coating himself and moaning as he looked down between us.

"Such a pretty pussy," he said to himself, propping a pillow underneath my hips. *Oh God, he was going all in, wasn't he?* "I have wanted to fuck you so bad, Zara."

"Me too." I blurted, "I always dreamt about you."

"Oh, yeah?" Hayden made a low groaning sound, still

rubbing and bumping the head of his cock against my sensitive sex. "Tell me what you dreamt. What I... fuck, what I did to you?"

"You fucked me... came inside me and fucked me again. Your mouth, your words..." I shook my head, "So dirty."

I bit my lip when he spanked my thigh, holding my legs from closing. "I know that it is not safe... but I want to make you full with my cum. Mark you like some fucking animal."

Thoughts of the normal world had left me and all that existed was the carnal desire to be marked by Hayden despite how fucked up that sound. "Mark me then," I begged him. "Claim me, fuck me... make me full with your cum, Hayden."

I gasped, my walls stretching around his tip, but he pulled back, teasing us both. *Torturing* us. He really was a sadist. His fingers glided over my heated sex, spanking me on my clit and rubbing my juices all over me and stroking himself with the same hand.

I was so aroused at the sight of him that I was fondling and squeezing my breasts, pinching the nipples, the cold metal bar of piercing. His eyes averted from my face to my pussy, settling himself over my entrance.

"I want to ruin your pretty little cunt, Princess." His voice was guttural and sexy, the rumbles of it rolling down my body as I arched up, trying to have him inside me.

"Please—oh, *ohfuck*." My lips parted when Hayden slid inside me, my walls stretching around his girth.

"You're so fucking tight and warm. *Fuck*." Hayden was groaning, supporting himself on his forearms when my legs wrapped around his waist to feel him get in deeper. He looked down between us, holding my waist as he gradually moved his hips, my moans getting higher when I clenched him, my legs quivering.

"*Please*," I whispered, not sure what I was begging him for. But he knew what I wanted better than me.

"Almost there, Princess," he murmured, kissing my neck. I felt him throbbing inside me and gasped loudly, digging my fingers into his back when he slid inside me in one deep thrust.

I felt blinded by the light vision, squeezing my eyes shut at the fullness of his cock inside me, his fingers rubbing my clit while he stayed still, whispering sweetly in my ears until I could get used to his size.

His blue eyes were gazing at me with adoration, his thumb caressing my cheek as he pressed closer, making me gasp, clenching him tighter. He made a low groaning sound and pulled out, sliding inside me once again.

My face burnt hearing the lewd sounds of how desperate and wet I was, of how our skin slapped against each other. His jaw clenched when he pulled my legs higher so that I could feel the head of his cock brush against the sensitive spot, my eyes rolling at the pleasure he was giving me.

"You look so fucking beautiful," he whispered, his hands roving over my body when he pulled back. Stroking my neck, the pearl of the necklace cold and rocking with me when he fucked me slow and deep. I mewled when he squeezed my breasts, playing with the piercings.

I could feel his words on my skin. *Hayden Knight's Princess Slut*. I moaned louder, bucking my hips against him, raising them to meet his each thrust when his pace quickened, stroking every inch inside me and filling me up again and again.

I loved every single moment of it. The scent of our musky arousal wafting in the air, the bed squeaking with our weight and the force of Hayden's powerful thrusts, the way he held onto my waist, fucking me roughly, grunting every time I clenched him.

When my orgasm tethered on the edge with his thumb,

rubbing the piercing on my clit, he stopped to spank at my thigh.

"You're not coming without my permission, Princess slut." His voice was smoky and firm.

Hayden

Zara seemed blissed out, her molten chocolate eyes hazy as she peered at me. "Feels too good, Hayden," she whispered, her voice hoarse and sweet that made me throb harder inside her.

I started moving inside her, sighing at the warmth of her pussy surrounding me. "You can hold it, Princess. Only for a little while, yeah?"

She was nodding, her hands clutching the sheets, giving me the perfect. View of her stunning body. Her pale skin glistening with sweat, so in contrast with the dark thick words written across her breasts and stomach. I groaned, rolling my hips and slamming inside her, seeing my name written on her body. The pearl necklace on her slender neck with her pouty red lips parting to moan the sweetest sounds that I wish I could hear every day, morning and night.

My fingers dug into her hips as I got closer and closer to the edge, rubbing her clit and ordering her to cum for me. Her legs tensed around my waist, her body writhing on the bed as I held her when her orgasm rocked through her body, caressing them.

With couple more thrusts, I came, sliding deeper inside her, the spasm of her pussy convulsing around me, her name on my lips. I made a low groan, filling her up as I had promised, squeezing her thighs and leaving red handprints on them as I stayed still, panting.

Zara squirmed, biting her lip when I slowly pulled out. I

looked down between her legs and pushed them over her chest.

"Such a pretty pussy, leaking with my cum, *hm*," I hummed, licking my lips at the sight of her flushed, pink lips, at my seed leaking out of her. She held her legs back when I coated our cum on the head of my cock, moving it around her sex, slathering it over her puffy lips.

Zara groaned, shivering when I kept teasing both of us. Her pussy clenched around nothing, watching me stroke myself at the sight of her naked, sensitive sex.

"*Hayden.*"

"I know, baby." I flickered my eyes from her face to between her thighs. "Your cunt looks so good like this. Glistening with our cum. Let me push it back inside you, yeah?"

"*Pleasepleaseplease.*"

Holding her leg, I slowly slid inside her, just the tip. I rubbed her clit, grinding against the sensitive spot inside her as my abs clenched with pleasure. I was sensitive as fuck from my previous orgasm but I didn't care, I wanted to make her feel good, make both of us feel good.

"I want to make you messy. Have your pussy, your tits, your stomach, everything dripping with my cum. Would you like that, my pretty Princess?"

"Oh, *fuck.*" Zara moaned so sweetly, clenching me. "Yes, please, Hayden. I want that."

"Of course, you do, you pretty whore," I chuckled, spanking her clit lightly making her buck. "You are just my little cumslut, aren't you, Princess?"

"Mhm, yes, Hayden. *Yours.*"

I pulled out when she orgasmed, holding myself against her as I came all over her pussy, coating her in my cum, groaning when some of it landed on her stomach and her breasts.

Fuck.

I laid back on my heels, exhausted, as my thighs trembled. My eyes travelled down her body as Zara basked in the post-coital glow, her nimble fingers running over her tits and her stomach. My eyes darkened when they lowered to her pussy, her face flushing red when she felt just how much I had marked her.

"*Zara,*" I warned her when she lifted her glistening fingers to her mouth and took them in her mouth, peering at me, her beauty spot looking perfect as ever.

I closed my eyes and willed myself to calm down. Taking a deep breath, I opened my eyes and looked at how much mess we had made. But before that.

I ran my hand over her leg, glancing at our juices pooling on the sheets, her sex pink and sensitive. "Are you okay?"

She nodded, a dizzy smile on her lips. "So good." She took a sharp breath when she tried to move her legs, making me worry, but her eyes flashed at me, travelling down to my crotch. "I wish we could have sex again. I want to ride you."

Of course she does.

I kissed her knee. "Later," I promised. "Let's take a bath together."

"Do we have to?"

"Yes, we do. Stop pouting at me before I fuck that mouth."

She pouted more, but I ignored it. She was a brat and threatening her with anything that had a verb 'fuck' made her desperate.

Cleaning myself up in the washroom, I checked the water temperature in the bath and went back to the bedroom. Zara was asleep, her chest slowly rising up and down, her lips parting with a small frown, when I tried to wake her up.

"I can't let my Princess sleep like this, come on." I picked her up, her lips brushing my neck as she moved closer, crooning. "I am going to put you in the bath, okay?"

Her eyes opened as she nodded, pursing her lips when her

naked body sank in the warm water. "Join me?" She asked, blinking up at me with such sweetness that I couldn't say no to her.

So we took a bath together in comfortable silence, her cheeks flushing red when I washed her short hair and cleaned the black ink from her breasts and stomach.

After the bath, we applied cocoa lotion on each other because Zara said it smells better than the one I had and changed the sheets of the bed. Sighing, we snuggled with each other under the blanket.

I liked her. Zara. Her sweet smiles and snarky comments, her love for photography and over-tipping the people working in service, buying thoughtful gifts for her family, her friendship with Ivy and the hidden sort of childish innocence she had about life despite the reality of the world. She didn't hide away from it but tried to look on the bright side, even if there was none.

My stomach flipped at the thought. I kissed her hair as she slept in my arms, wearing the pearl necklace.

I really liked Zara.

PART IV

"Yes, you silly brat. I fucking love you."

31
ZARA

It was our second last day at the Almas Peninsula. I hated the way my stomach was feeling. So I had dragged Hayden into the club. I giggled loudly at something the tan guy whispered in my ear. My eyes blurry with the flashing neon lights.

"I leave you for one second and you are already flirting with someone else." I didn't need to turn around to see who it was. I knew it was Hayden just by his warmth presence behind me and the deep, husky voice rumbling through my ears despite the loud pop music running in the background.

Just his presence made a warm feeling in my stomach, expanding in to my chest and making my heart rate increase. I must be sick. I needed to see a doctor, a cardiologist, and ask them why I was feeling the way I was.

The man across me stiffened, looking over my shoulder and the arm around my waist. I snuggled back into his strong embrace, smiling prettily at the stranger as I leaned my head on Hayden's shirt. His heart beat was normal. He wasn't freaking out like I was. Maybe I had caught a flu.

"I am not flirting with him, honey," I looked at Hayden,

his blue eyes glaring at the man, and slid my hand over his arm that was on my waist. "He was telling me about his trip to Azmia and how he had met the Princess."

He sure has now that she is standing across him, tipsy and horny for the man who was holding her so close.

"Has he now?" Hayden ordered a glass of cold water, ignoring me when I rolled my eyes at him, scoffing at his taste. "That is for you, not for me."

"I should leave—"

"Oh, would you dance with me?" I asked him before he could leave. He had pretty dark eyes, and I wanted to know if Hayden would accept my dance invitation or just watch me with someone else. "He doesn't want to because he is a party pooper."

"Party pooper?" Hayden stayed that in such a deadpan husky voice that I had to stifle my giggle. "What are you, Zara? Twelve?"

I gave him a look and glanced down at my dark tight shorts and velvet bustier top that gave me cleavage. It was a miracle top, it made my girls look pretty.

"Yes, I am on the scale from one to ten."

Hayden cracked a small smile, handing me the glass of water and ordering me to drink it all. I whined at him because the stranger had left without waiting for me and probably already dancing on the stage.

"Do you really want to dance in between so many sweaty bodies?" Hayden asked, wrapping his arms around me when I sat on his lap instead of the stool. His thighs felt warm, the rough fabric of his jeans rubbing against the back of my thighs made it arousing.

I raised my brow at him. "It was your idea to go out and have some fun."

"It was *your* idea to enter this club."

"If you don't want to dance with me, then I will find someone else—"

"No, you won't." His voice was stern as his arms tightened around me, pulling me back onto his lap. "Come with me."

I thought he would take me on the stage and dance with everyone, but I was mistaken when he walked us out of the club.

His hand stayed around my waist. It made my head feel dizzy, staring at his large hand on the curve of my stomach, feeling its warm press that made me want to cling to him and ride him into a dark corner of an ally or make him *kunnafah* in the morning.

Oh, nonono. I don't like this.

"I hated how that man was looking at you."

"Looking at me like what?"

Hayden looked over his shoulder at me. "Like he wanted to kiss you."

I snorted. "I would have stomped on his foot and kicked his nuts if he had done that."

"I am sure you would have."

"You know…" I said after a while, looking at his sharp jaw and the high cheekbones. The way his lips stood out in the stubble, his brows hooded and the perfect way he styled his hair that managed to look tousled and sexy at the same time. I remembered how soft his hair was when he went down on me this morning, waking me up with his mouth while I held onto his hair.

"You look hot when you're angry," I whispered to him, brushing my lips over the shell of his ear and enjoying the way his hand tightened on my waist, pulling me closer.

Hayden didn't reply, color creeping up his neck as we walked through the same route of the cabin. But he took a different route to take us to the beach. Sun had set and sand looked bright orange with fresh, misty wind kissing our bare skin. We could hear the crash of waves as I clutched his arm for support.

I wanted to dip my toes in the warm sand. I swayed, trying to remove the boots I was wearing.

"What are you doing?"

"Removing my shoes."

"Why?"

I threw the one shoe and wriggled my toes, sighing when my foot touched the warm sand. "Because I want to dip my toes in the sand. You should try it too."

He held my arm when I was about to fall, removing the other shoe, and glared at me. His eyes were deep blue, but I had figured his eyes by then. They were a bit annoyed but concerned because his lip didn't have the quirk in the corner and his jaw wasn't clenched, which he did when he was furious.

"Zara, you are drunk."

"Okay, boomer."

He gave me a withering look. "How many drinks did you have?"

"Six inches."

I laughed out loud at his expression and stepped closer, "I am not drunk, silly, I am teasing you." I licked my lips and stared at his eyes, his full lips. "I want to kiss you. I want you to be angry at me."

"Kiss me, but why do you want me to be angry at you?" he asked in between the kisses, his lips warm and mouth tasting like mint. I removed his shirt and ran my hand down his muscled abdomen, peering at him when he shivered and removed his leather belt.

It was a private beach by the cabin, and it was getting late, so I knew no one would be around.

I kissed his jaw and licked his collar bone, moaning in his

skin when his hands squeezed my ass. "I like it when you are rough, Hayden," I whispered

"I know you do, Princess," he said, looking at me with piercing blue eyes when I dropped to my knees on the sand, flickering my eyes at him as my fingers fumbled with his zipper.

"Don't. Get my shirt underneath your knees or they'll bruise." Hayden instructed me as I folded his expensive shirt before kneeling in front of him.

If he ever finds out about my secret or I tell him about it, I will buy him his favourite fashion brand. I had lost the count of how many shirts I have ruined.

I unzipped his pants and cupped his stiffened member through his boxers. Pulling him out of them, I licked at the sight of throbbing veins, his girthy length, and the way glistening pre-cum leaked from his slit, the tip of his throbbing cock red.

I hummed when Hayden wrapped his hand around my short hair. I took him in my mouth, pleasing him with my tongue. By the sounds he was making, slowly thrusting his hips, I knew he loved the way the piercing on my tongue gave an extra sensation to his sensitive underside.

Pulling back, I took a deep breath and licked his hardened shaft, tracing the veins with my tongue until his legs trembled. Hayden held me close and ordered me to part my lips as he fed me his cock. I moaned, my underwear gushing with wetness when I kissed and sucked him, hollowing my cheeks, my hands stroking his balls.

His breathing turned ragged as his other hand caressed my cheek, his fingers moving over my stretched lips, the beauty spot that he seemed to love.

"What if someone sees us like this?" He asked, pulling my head back, his length hard and wet.

"Then let them," I gasped, looking at him through my lashes, my eyes teary. "I want to please you."

His eyebrows raised, "I didn't know you were an exhibitionist."

"Blame yourself for tainting me with yet another kink."

"You really should watch what you speak to me in that fucking tone, Princess slut."

Fuck, I loved it when he was angry with me. Or pretended to be to play with me.

His hand wrapped around my hair as he slid inside my mouth, ordering me to keep my mouth open. He told me to keep breathing through my nose as he slowly fucked my mouth. Hayden grunted, his fingers tightening on my hair when the piercing of my tongue pressed over his frenulum. I closed my eyes and groaned when he jerked his hips, his cock brushing at the back of my throat.

"Oh, *fuck*, sweetheart—I am going to come in your mouth." My toes curled with desire at hearing his hoarse and deep voice. Holding me close, he jerked before coming inside my mouth.

I swallowed every bit of his cum, licking his length clean when he pulled out, his breathing heavy and looking handsome as ever with a wicked gleam in his sapphire eyes. Sun had set over the ocean, and the moon cast a beautiful light over his features.

Wiping the corner of my lip with my finger, I licked it clean. A small sigh escaped my lips when Hayden pulled me up, kissing me soundly. His tongue teased my piercing, making me melt into his arms.

"Let's go back to the cabin," he said against my lips, already picking up his shirt filled with sand and my boots in one hand while taking my hand in other. I laughed when he started running, my eyes taking in the soft waves of his hair, the light in his eyes when he looked at me over his shoulder and the way his back muscles curved beautifully.

His fingers moved swiftly to remove my clothes as soon as we entered the cabin. I exhaled sharply when he threw me on the bed and cried out his name. Spreading my legs, he tore my underwear and before I could scold him, latched his hot mouth onto my pussy.

I fell back on the bed, clutching the sheets which smelt like him, *us*, the lazy morning sex we had that morning following his expert cunnilingus. My legs were shaking and my body was quivering as he fucked me with his fingers, his teeth and tongue playing with my clit and teasing the piercing. I groaned, arching my back when he spanked my pussy, the blood rushing to my lower body and creating heat of the burn as my abdomen coiled tightly for the upcoming orgasm.

Hayden growled. "Come on, Princess. Cum on my mouth."

I whimpered and closed my eyes when he curled his fingers inside me. I came apart on his mouth, holding on to him as my body quivered. When I opened my eyes, the aftershocks of my orgasm rocking through my body as his kisses turned gentle, his tongue lapping up all my juices.

Hayden turned me on to my stomach, my pussy sensitive yet excited about what was going to come next. I shivered when he pressed his hand on my neck, bending me down until my breasts brushed the cold sheets, my ass up in the air. I felt his body heat when he stood behind me, his fingers brushing up my spine.

"Are you okay?"

I chuckled and looked over my shoulder. I was surprised to see that he looked concerned. It was a strange thing to see. Despite how kinky and rough most of our intimate moments were, he always asked and made sure I wasn't hurt, either emotionally or physically. I loved that about him. It made me feel safe and comfortable.

"I will be if you fuck me, Hayden."

He smacked my ass, making me gasp. "Love that filthy mouth of yours, Princess."

Hearing him lower the zipper of his pants, my nerves spiked up, and I clutched the sheets with my fingers. I bit my lip and closed my eyes when he leaned closer, running the tip of his cock down my slit. And then he pushed inside in *one slow thrust*. I moaned, my lips parting when I felt his shaft and girth stretching my pussy with a pinch of pain that came with his length.

Hayden stayed like that for a while, letting me accommodate to his length before he pulled and slammed back inside me. I gasped when my body rocked forward, my erect nipples brushing over the sheets. He groaned, spanking me and fucking me roughly when I clamped him inside me.

"*More*," I gasped when he leaned down, kneading my breasts and pulling at the piercings, pinching my nipples.

His thrusts became slow and deep, hitting the G-spot every time he slammed inside me, his hot breath on my neck.

"Need to see you." He turned me around, lifting my legs to my chest and watching me with his intense dark eyes as my lips parted with each slow thrust.

I couldn't handle it. I closed my eyes and came with a long moan, repeating his name while he rocked inside me slowly, trailing my orgasm as long as it could last. He came inside me after three more thrusts, landing on top of me and breathing heavily.

I took deep, calming breaths and wiped away the tears that had leaked from my eyes when I had orgasmed. *Fuck, since when did I started crying during sex.* I looked at his wavy, chocolaty hair and ran my hand through them. I didn't want him to move. I just wanted to stay like this in our post-coital bliss without the worry of anything else.

But of course, my phone had to ring. I was about to get up when Hayden stopped me with a peck on my cheek.

"Stay, I'll get it for you."

I stared at his naked, firm ass and thanked God for creating a man like him. My thoughts churned to nothing when I sat up, ignoring the burn on my ass and the sweet soreness between my legs when I saw the name on the screen. Ignoring the confused frown on Hayden's face, I declined the call.

"Is everything okay?" He asked, sitting beside me on the bed. He stared at my phone. "Who was that?"

Oh, nothing, it was my brother who also is the Prince of Azmia, Khalid Al Latif. He is getting married in a month and I haven't talked to my family for two weeks so they think that I am missing. Oh, I am sorry, did I mention that I also happen to be the Princess of Azmia, Zara Al Latif. No? Ha-ha, small world. Please don't kill me.

"No one." I stuck with my lie and switched off my phone, lying back on the bed because I was exhausted. "Unknown number probably."

He hummed, lying beside me as we both stared at the ceiling, hearing each other's breath with the crickets chirping outside. My cheeks burned when his knuckles brushed against mine, his fingers entwining with mine as I squeezed his hand.

I am holding his hand! I tried not to freak out. We had held hands many times before. But that felt more intimate than previous other hand-holdings.

"Oh, shit." Hayden sat up quickly, frowning at me.

"What happened?" Did he find out? Did he know Khalid's private number and had memorised it and knew it was him and I was a Princess?

"I forgot to show you something." He checked the time and stood up. "Come on, we still have some time left."

Hayden

"I didn't know you rented... such an enormous yacht," Zara whispered, her words trailing as we walked around the wooden floors.

The smell of ocean air was prominent as well as the wood polish. The yacht stood still in the dark, cold water, docked near the beach. I had remembered to show her the yacht before going back to cabin but as soon as she had kissed me and went on her knees, I had completely forgotten about it.

"Don't you think this is too much just for a day's trip?" Zara asked, trailing her hand over the silky sheets of the bed.

We were in one of the four rooms, which also had a main salon with couches, windows with thick curtains, a religious, a minibar with stools. The staircase led between floors with multiple cabins below decks that made the boat more cozy. It had a wet bar, a hot tub and even space for the cabin crew, but we wouldn't need that as I had a license to drive it.

"Does it feel too much?" I asked, sliding my hands in my pockets. She was wearing one of my tee shirts and her shorts, but she still looked stunning.

"It doesn't. I like it, it is very spacious and has all the necessity even though we are going to be on it for less than twenty-four hours."

Her smile was soft and relaxed as she came up to me. "Maybe I can finally tick off sexy yacht sex from my private bucket list."

"Remind me to ask you more about it." I kissed her forehead as we made our way back to the cabin. "I have a question."

"Shoot."

"What do your brothers do?" Zara stiffened, but kept walking as I glanced at her. "I mean, I would be concerned if my sister went to an island with a stranger. Do they know you are here?"

"Why are you asking me about that right now?"

I stared at her as she kept walking towards the cabin. "I didn't know you didn't want to talk about your family." I shook my head and went after her. "I don't know, Zara. You don't want to talk to me about your family, it's okay. I will wait for you to tell me, but then I think that I know so little about you. Your name is Zara Kent, which is very English, just like your accent and how you had English tutors because you were homeschooled in Azmia. You have two brothers who taught you how to ride a horse and fight, and they seem very rich, but you never mention them even though you have a good relationship with them."

"I have a good relationship with my brothers."

"Okay." I didn't know what else to say. If she didn't want to tell me about her, it's on her. I would not get mad or angry just because she isn't comfortable enough to share it with me. Maybe her parents were neglectful like mine or she had a troubled childhood because she never mentioned her father to me.

"Hayden." Her hand wrapped around me as we stood in front of the cabin. "I am sorry… I want to tell you about my family, about where I grew up, my childhood, everything. But… I can't. Yet. I promise you, I will tell you."

"It's okay, Zara. I don't want to force you to tell me about it."

She nodded and paused, asking me what the big box was about. I followed her gaze and saw there was a big box in front of the cabin with a shiny red gift wrapper around it.

"Did you get this?"

"No, why would I?" I looked at her. "Wait, is it your birthday?"

"No, of course not."

We both stood beside each other as she bent down to retrieve the card stuck to it with a tape.

"When's your birthday?" I asked her, reading the card along with her.

"First January," she whispered mindlessly.

The card read in a sloppy cursive:

Many early happy returns of the day, dear Princess. This is one of the many more big presents to come.

Wait, her birthday is on first January?

"Do you know who sent you this gift?" I asked her. The box seemed too big for a gift. "Why call you 'Dear Princess'?"

My eyebrows furrowed as I glanced between the box and her. Zara had gone still, her face pale.

Shaking her head, she dropped the card and held my arm. "We need to get away from here."

"What?"

"Hayden, please trust me." Her voice was firm but full of nervousness as she dragged me away from the cabin.

"Zara." I took a deep breath. "What the fuck is—"

A wave of heated force flew through us as I slammed over Zara, covering her head with my hand as we both fell on the ground with a groan, the sound of a small blast coming from the cabin.

With a wince, I sat up, ignoring Zara's concerned voice asking me if I was alright. Thankfully, I was behind her and had protected her from the worst of it but my back ached just from the pressure of being thrown over. I cleaned the dirt from the cuts on my arms and glanced at the cabin. Or what was left of it.

The wooden walls were burning, dark smoke floating upwards with crumpled pieces of box and the carpet of living room falling around. My ears were ringing as I looked at the crumbling cabin and Zara.

Her cheek was covered in dirt, her forehead had some blood on it as I tried to wipe it away. My lips moved, and I heard myself,

"Are you okay?"

She nodded, her pupils wide. "I am. Are you?"

I swallowed the lump in my throat and stood up on shaky legs, staring at the aftermath of the bomb blast. Fuck. It had really happened. A bomb blast. From a gift box that someone had addressed to Zara… as *Dear Princess*.

Flashes of memories ran through my head.

That night. The bartender had said it was the Princess's birthday. No one knew how or what she looked like.

Her protective brothers. Expensive dresses. English tutors. Homeschooled. Rich family. Her name on her dress with a black label and golden thread.

The employees gossiping about some missing Princess and how she wanted to get out of the store as soon as it came up.

Not wanting to talk about her family because…

She had the same name as the Princess of Azmia. Zara Al Latif. And the *same fucking birthday*.

"Hayden?" She came up behind me, checking the cuts on my arms and looking at me with her wide doe eyes when I pulled away my arm. "Are you okay? You have cuts on your hands. Let me—"

"You are a Princess."

32
ZARA

My lips parted. His words rang in my ears, creating a sudden feeling of cold that spread over my chest, making my knees buckle as I slowly blinked at him.

"You are a Princess." Hayden repeated it as if it was a disgusting remark, his eyes cold and full of shock and anger. "You are Zara Al Latif, aren't you?"

I didn't reply, dropping my hands by my sides. It was the worst time to talk to him about it when I was planning to make him some meal and then spill my secret. But I didn't know someone was actively trying to kill me by dropping a box of bomb by the cabin.

He knows. He knows I am a Princess.

I squeezed my hand into a fist to stop them from shaking and took a shuddering breath. *As much as I want to explain everything to him, I can't do it now.* We were in danger.

"Hayden, we don't have time to talk about this right now—"

"You are right, we don't. You lied to me and God—*fuck*."

He shook his head and started walking. In the direction of the burning cabin.

"We can't go there!" I called out to him, my legs frozen.

He glared at me over his shoulders. His features were sharp, and I wanted to cower away from the look he gave me. He looked at me as if he didn't know me. I pressed my hand to my chest, my heart pounding. "Oh, I am sorry, Your Highness. But I need to make sure what type of bomb it was and how much is left so I can call someone for help."

"Y-you can't."

His glare turned icier. I was surprised I hadn't turned into a glacier. I took a deep breath and tried again clearing my throat. "It seems like some bad people are after me and if you call someone from your phone—"

"Bad guys will know. I get it." He clenched his jaw and marched towards me, asking for my phone. He wouldn't even meet my eyes or look at me. "I need to make a call."

"Don't tell them I am here, like as a Princess." My cheeks burnt with embarrassment. I wanted to disappear into the forest. "Promise me you will hear me out. I couldn't tell you Hayden be—"

"I get it." His voice was devoid of any emotion and it hurt me that he was pushing me away. "You are a Princess. *Phone*, please."

He said the word Princess like it was a curse. Not the gentle way he would address me before. I pursed my lips from trembling and cleared my throat, hoping that the discomfort in the back of my throat with disappear. My hands shook when I handed the phone to him, watching him type some sort of military code and calling someone. He walked back to the cabin, careful of the small fire as he told the person on the other line what had happened.

My eyes blurred with tears. *I didn't want this*. I wanted to make him *kunafah* and sit across the low table in the cozy warmth of the cabin and tell him about my father. About myself, how I was a Princess. I didn't want him to know the truth like *this*.

Leaves rustled behind me and just as I turned around, someone pressed a cloth on my nose, lifting me up. I gasped, struggling in their arms. *Oh, fuck.* I can't deal with having emotions for a man that I have feelings for, physically recovering from a minor bomb blast, mentally recovering from realising I could be dead if I had been a minute late, then emotionally hurting because the man I liked knew about my secret and hated me, *and* dealing with getting kidnapped all within the span of twenty-four hours.

But even though I tried to stomp and fight back, my body was exhausted and tired, especially after the blast. There were more people than before. My head started swirling as I tried to see the blurry faces, my nose filling up with the scent of something acidic as my vision faded and in a few seconds, so did my consciousness.

"What... her? Yes... blood..."

I kept my eyes shut as I heard the sounds of people walking around me. My head hurt and limbs felt heavy as I stayed still, trying to pretend that I was unconscious. Someone was talking on the phone. My hands were tied up, and I was on some wooden floor.

My nose was itchy with the acid my kidnappers had forced me to sniff, but I could smell the wood polish I had smelt before. The sound of soft waves splashing on the hard metal surface and the cold, breezy wind. It was familiar.

"Is she awake or still passed out?" I knew that voice. The heavy voice of that female. I had heard it before. "Boss wants to talk to her."

I tried not to scoff and roll my eyes. *'Boss' yeah right. Give me a break*.

"Who is this boss of yours?"

I am not sorry. I couldn't stop my curiosity.

I glanced around me, watching two large men—probably the same one who had tried to kidnap me in that parking lot —and three other armed people on… a yacht.

Was there boss that poor that he couldn't afford a yacht or a boat of his own that he had to use the one that Hayden had rented to kidnap a Princess of Azmia? I mean, talk about a terrible villain.

"I knew you were awake—why are you smiling? Why is she smiling like that?"

"Maybe the drugs she sniffed?"

Oh, God, had they drugged me? Khalid was going to have a field day with them.

Focus, Zara. Focus.

Shaking my head, I tried to pay attention. The woman, I realised, was none other than Olivia. Ivy's university friend who I had briefly talked to before meeting Hayden. *What was she doing here?*

"You know, you have been a stubborn pain in my ass for the last two years," she said to me, waving a gun at me.

Do not fucking laugh at her, Zara.

I didn't laugh, but I couldn't hide my grin, either.

"I would apologize, but I am afraid your ass isn't worth remembering if we slept together. Which we didn't, because if we did, you weren't worth remembering, Olivia."

Her eyes narrowed at me and I held my breath when she struck me across my cheek with the flat bottom of the gun. People yelled at her as I felt the warm blood trickling down my ear, pain burning and spreading over my cheek. I wiped it away with the tee shirt and met her hateful gaze.

All of a sudden, I was thankful for my brothers and

Zayed. They had taught me how to behave in a situation like the one I was in. If I ever get kidnapped, how to remain calm, levelheaded and *not die*. They had so much so tried to pretend-kidnap thirteen-year-old me, who had screamed and hit everyone while crying to go back home. I hadn't talked to my family for a week until they bought me a front-row seat to the boy band I was obsessed with personal meet and greet.

I heard one of them say, "Boss wants her alive. Without any bruises."

"Whatever, I will tell him she fell through the stairs."

"Who's this boss of yours?" I asked, looking around and knew he wasn't here. He must be sitting somewhere and waiting for a call because he was a coward. "He isn't here. Pity, I would have liked to negotiate business with him. Not with his minions."

"I swear to God, if she doesn't shut up—"

I raised my chin and asked in a firm voice. "What is the reason behind this?"

The man who was talking to Olivia turned to me. "The reason is simple. Princess of Azmia, you are missing and there's a price on your head to bring you alive and unharmed to the person we are referring to as 'Boss.'"

I nodded. "Please continue." I could see he was a levelheaded one.

"Thank you. As I was saying—"

Olivia, the not-so-levelheaded one, "I have been waiting for a chance to hurt you for so many years. Every time I tried to catch you, you would be one step ahead of me and change your location. From Sri Lanka to Australia to San Diego, out of all places. Did you know I had to befriend that chubby friend of yours just to get—"

"Don't you dare talk about Ivy like that in front of me," I said in a calm voice. "Or I *will* hurt you."

Olivia flared her nose at me. "I can't wait to hear your screams as soon as he has you."

My spine straightened. "*He?*"

"Yes. He plans to keep you. Marry you and hurt you, maybe even breed you to have his children."

"You disgust me," I said to her in my most Princess-like voice. I tried not to let them show the way my body shuddered, thinking about staying with someone who would have such intentions with me.

Just because of my title.

Before Olivia could smack in my face again, I kicked her on her knee. *Hard*. She fell on the wooden floor, slamming her head with a loud *thud* that had me wincing for her. I would have kicked her again if it wasn't for the men taking me away from her.

I relished in her groans, thinking about the accents of the people. They spoke English, but I had heard the same thick notes from someone else. Maybe the kidnappers and their boss were enemies with Azmia? I needed to talk to my brothers, tell them about it, and increase their security. Oh, God, Zain has a daughter, Aya. *What if they plan to harm her, too?*

No, I couldn't just sit around and let these people kidnap me and try to harm my family.

Hayden

IT WAS TRULY UNFORTUNATE. I THOUGHT, HIDING UNDER THE stairs. I not only had to talk to Colonel about the bomb blast but had to watch Zara get kidnapped and follow her kidnappers to the yacht that I had rented and *now* save her.

Frankly, I could have stopped her from getting kidnapped, but I didn't know how I could fight off six people armed with guns and whatnot all on my own. I could, if I could, pull the trigger of the gun, but...

"We should just keep her drugged until we reach there."

That was one of Ivy's friends, or so my sweet sister thought. I was glad that Zara had spoken up and defended my sister, or I was afraid that I would have thrown my shoe at that Olivia woman.

"We can't."

"Why not?"

"We..."

I had knives with me and the combat skills. No guns. I could disarm their guns but I won't be able to use it and the two large men were scary big. I was afraid it would take some time to take them down. Time that could make them harm Zara, or the Princess, *whatever*.

I peered at her scowling face, a firm pout on her lips as she tried to struggle with her ties—*oh, wait*. She had already removed the rope but pretending to do it while everyone kept tabs on her.

That's my Princess.

Shaking my head, I took a deep breath. She was *not* my Princess. I needed to stay calm and get her out of there as safely as I could. The truth that she was a Princess and never once told me or Ivy about it hurt a lot. I had taken her to my suite on the night of her nineteenth birthday and she had let me, pretending to be God knows what. Maybe that was why she had argued about *The Duke and The Princess*...

Rolling my shoulders and neck, I readied myself. I took a deep breath and, focusing on my aim, I threw the knives at the large men, hitting them right on their thighs and calves, missing the fatal artery just by a centimetre.

All the attention turned towards my hiding spot as I rolled over and hid behind another wall. The yacht was still moving as I didn't want to kill or harm the person who was stirring just yet. He could tell us where the 'Boss' was hiding.

"It's her boyfriend." Olivia provided a necessary information as I silently climbed on the upper deck, throwing two more knives at the other two armed men. One missed by an inch, but another struck him right on his arm.

Adrenaline was pumping through my veins as my mind and body readied itself for the battle. Just like previous missions in my life, it was time to save and rescue a Princess. Be her Knight.

Okay, I admit, that was cringey.

I jumped down, straight on the person who wasn't wounded by any of my knives. I slammed my knee on his head, pushing my thumbs in his eyes and throwing him over the railing of the yacht into the ocean as the water swallowed his scream.

Everyone plunged at me and from the corner of my eye, I saw Zara sneaking down and holding the knife in her hand. *God, what the fuck is she doing? Why isn't she going somewhere safe and locking herself?*

I was trying to make sure she was safe and fight off her kidnappers who were, to my surprise, trained well in combat. With a few moves, I had disarmed their firearms and threw two more people into the ocean, but two large men were still onboard, along with Olivia.

Unfortunately, I was fresh out of knives to throw or use as a weapon.

"Hayden, here!"

I turned to see Zara, who aimed and tried to throw the knife at the wooden plank just near my leg. But her aim was pretty bad and struck one man in his abdomen.

"You need to practice your aim," I said, punching him where Zara had hurt him until his knees gave out.

I groaned when his partner wrapped his arm around my

neck, choking me. Exhaling sharply, I kicked the man's head in front of me as he fell unconscious on the floor and focused on not passing out, trying to free myself from the choking hold.

"I hate both of you so much. I am sure the boss wouldn't mind either of your heads as a gift."

I heard someone removing the safety of the gun and ready to shoot.

This is it, isn't it? This is how I die.

On a yacht I had rented to go see a diamond mining field with the woman I liked, now full of kidnappers and a Princess of Azmia who turned out to be the same woman I had developed feelings for. Dying with a choking hold and a bullet between my head. I hope it—

The gunshot rang through my ears and I moved my head to see Zara, my Princess, for the last time.

33
HAYDEN

I was alive. I had realised after five seconds of not feeling any pain in my head or bleeding. The bullet had not struck me.

I slammed my elbow on the ribs of the man behind me. My eyes averted to Olivia, who was standing behind me and clutching her left shoulder, that was bleeding quickly. The gun she was holding fell on the deck with a loud thud as she gaped at the persons standing across her.

Zara. She was the one holding a gun, her face pale as she stared at Olivia. Smoke weaved through the nozzle of the gun as it clattered on the floor, making Zara jump and shiver.

I didn't waste time in throwing all three of them, Olivia and the two men from the yacht. The sound of bodies hitting in the water with a splash was chilling. We were near the shore and the military will catch them before hypothermia could get to them. I tried to ignore the guilt forming in my stomach and walked over to Zara, who was hugging herself on her knees, wearing my tee shirt with blood on the sleeve and her forehead and ear.

"It's okay," I said softly, knowing well it was her first shot and injuring someone like that. "It's okay, Zara, you are safe."

"I killed someone."

"You didn't."

Her arms slowly wrapped around mine as I pulled her closer, sighing in relief that she was safe and unharmed.

"I did. I killed... I killed a human—"

"*Shh*, you didn't." I ran my hand through her hair, tightening my arm around her. "The bullet went through her shoulder, Pr—*Zara*. She will be okay if she survives the hypothermia."

She stayed silent, her body still shaking from the aftereffects. She was handling it way better than me. The first time I had killed someone, I had puked and cried myself to sleep.

"I didn't kill her?" Her voice was so soft and sweet. Like a scared little girl.

I wiped the tears from her face and shook my head. "You didn't kill anyone."

"*Oh*," she sighed, more tears running down her face as she hid herself in my neck. "I am so sorry."

"It's okay." I kept whispering in her ear until she calmed down. "It's okay. You are fine." *You are with me. I wouldn't let anyone harm you. Never on my watch, Princess Zara.*

But I held back those words and kept her cocooned in my arms.

Zara

"Yes, sir." Hayden nodded, his spine straight even though he was talking on a phone. "Of course, I understand. But it is what the Princess wishes. Mhm, do you want to hear it from her?"

I hid my smile and stared at the small dent the knife had made on the wooden deck. After consoling me, we had went downstairs and noticed that the person who was motoring the yacht had also jumped in the water. Hayden stayed close to me as he stirred us to the dock near the cabin.

I had a mini freakout seeing three military cars and two big vans going through our stuff at the cabin with two fire trucks. I was glad to see they had found the entire crew who had tried to kidnap me dripping and shivering and taking them to mini tents. At least they hadn't died.

Hayden had given me a forced smile and asked me to stay in the yacht while he went and talked with some soldiers. Before he left, I had told Hayden that I wanted to get away from there. It felt too crowded, and I needed some time to process what had happened.

"Lucky you, you can stay in the middle of the ocean if you want." Hayden handed me my phone. "Colonel agreed, but there will be soldiers accompanying you."

I frowned at him and looked down at my lap. Someone had offered me some spare sweatpants, which was saved from the fire, and a military coat around my shoulders.

"Aren't you... um, won't you come with me?"

Hayden didn't reply for a moment. I glanced at him to see him staring at me. "Do you want me to?"

"Yes." I blurted and slowly shook my head, "Only if you want to, Hayden."

"Okay," he sighed, sitting beside me, stretching his long legs. "Okay, I will come with you, your high—"

"Please. Call me Zara. Or... whatever you want to."

He looked like he wanted to say something, but someone called him. He stood up and pointed to one of the rooms. "Get some rest. Call me if you need anything." He nodded at me and left before I could ask him if he would join me or sleep in another room.

With slumped shoulders, I locked myself in the room and planted my face on the bed. Despite not wanting to sleep and wait for Hayden, talk to him and explain everything, sleep and exhaustion took over me within few minutes.

34

ZARA

I woke up to someone knocking on the door. A whine tore out of my lips as I sleepily opened the door, slowly blinking at Hayden, who looked way better than me, fresh out of the shower holding a plate of pancakes.

"Didn't you clean up your wounds?" He walked straight in and before I could utter anything, he held my hand and made me sit on the bed. I slowly rubbed the sleep from my eyes with a fist when he came back from the washroom, holding a medical kit.

"You might get an infection if you don't clean your wounds, Zara," he scolded me, his brows furrowing and blue eyes roving over my face. "*Tsk*, such a Princess."

"What's that supposed to mean?"

"Nothing. It wasn't an insult."

"It sure felt like it."

I looked away from him when he leaned closer, gently dabbing away the dried blood from my temple. "I'm sorry," he said after a long silence, applying ointment and a small bandage on the cut on my cheekbone. I relished in the warm press of the pads of his fingers, the soft caress on my skin as if he put anymore pressure, I would break. He held my wrist between his large, calloused hands, cleaning the minor cuts on my arms.

"It is hard to wrap my head around the fact that you are actually a Princess." He whispered, either to himself or to me.

Instead of replying to him, I started eating the pancakes because it was better to stuff my mouth with food than face Hayden and talk to him about everything.

But I couldn't do that anymore. Keep running away from my responsibility when he was in danger being with me, hurting himself and protecting me from the blast and risking his life to save me.

"I am sorry that I didn't tell you about it before," I said finally. "I was... I was scared how you would see me and treat me differently."

"Like what? A human?"

"No. I mean..." I sighed. "I mean that night, Hayden. I was nineteen and bored with my birthday after talking to princes and sheikhs and everyone. I snuck out of the palace to have fun, go to a club and met you. I couldn't just introduce myself as a Princess to you in the middle of the club."

"You had many chances." His blue piercing eyes felt way too close and intimate. I looked away from him.

"I know, but would you have slept with me if you knew I was the Princess of Azmia?"

Hayden clenched his jaw. "No, I would have asked you to dress up and took you back to the palace."

"Exactly." I swallowed the lump in my throat. "Not to mention, I panicked seeing that uniform. I knew I couldn't tell you about me."

"But you *could* have told me," he shook his head. "I would have tried to understand you."

"I thought about telling you but… I got selfish." My heartbeat sped up, my hands getting clammy. "I wanted to pretend that I was just some normal girl and have the chance to enjoy whatever we have… um, I didn't like to lie to you or Ivy or everyone else. But I was so far away from home that I couldn't just tell you who I was without the NDAs and guards and making you feel like a less of a human being than me."

I shuddered, thinking about it. "I wanted to tell you on my own terms. But then the blast and you know… I am sorry for getting you wrapped up in this mess, Hayden. I didn't think you would get hurt because of me."

"Look at me."

His eyes were clear, but there was a slash of cut on his cheekbone. He got hurt because of me. "You don't need to apologise to me for saving you. It was my choice. I think… I think we need to talk more about this."

"Yes… okay."

"Yes." He cleared his throat and looked away. "Finish those pancakes and come downstairs when you are ready. There are two soldiers accompanying us. For your safety."

"Right."

He left without glancing at me, and I sighed at the ceiling. I had written UN speeches for my brother Zain, Sultan of Azmia, and yet I could not utter a few words of apology in front of the man who had saved my life. The man I liked.

"So you had a pet tiger? A living, breathing pet tiger?" Chase, one of the younger soldier, who looked my age, asked me curiously, watching me as I slowly ate the spaghetti Hayden had cooked for lunch.

"Yes, his name was Numair, and he died happily in the shelter in his own territory." I smiled, remembering the times I used to play fetch with him, his guardian watching over us all the time because I was so young he was afraid that he might eat me. But he had never bitten me once, just laid on top of me like a big, lazy cat.

"What was he like?"

"Very smelly and playful. He would paw at my hair, when I had long hair, to play with me. I tried to bathe him once, and he pushed me in the pool once he was clean."

Chase grinned at me. "You must have loved him."

"I did, but my brothers cried the most when he passed away in his old age." I looked at two of them, the way Hayden sat beside me, narrowing his eyes at his colleague. "Don't tell them I told you that."

"Ooo, what are they like? Sultan and the Prince?" Chase leaned in closer, closing his mouth shut when Hayden shot him a glare.

"We are not here to gossip or talk—"

He interrupted Hayden. "Oh, *please*. She is a freaking Royal Princess. The one who no one knew what or how she looked like and we are sitting in her presence." Chase turned to me, his eyes big and dark. "Please, Princess Zara, spill the royal tea."

"Chase Jo—"

I kept my hand on his arm. "It's okay, Hayden. Telling Chase about the time Queen had a spontaneous birthday bash wouldn't hurt anyone."

Hayden raised his brow at me. "You have met the Queen?"

"Of course, I have. She likes me and even sends me biscuits and tulips on my birthday."

"What is the Queen like? Is it true that she drives a stick in her car and—"

"Chase," Hayden gave him a look. "Why don't you check the upper deck? You can talk to the Princess afterwards. We are in the middle of nowhere because she wanted to get away from the chaos on the island."

Chase didn't question or argue with him, standing up and saluting us both with a firm, "Yes, Sir." He went upstairs while I finished my food, the sounds of water and wind whipping tickling my ear. Sun was above us and despite the warmth, the ocean winds were breezy and cold.

"Did you want to talk to the Princess alone?" I asked, picking up the plate and cleaning it in the small kitchen.

Hayden said nothing for a while, standing up and trying to get me away from the sink while I glared at him and took his plate to wash it. He acquiesced and stayed silent as I washed our dishes and kept them on the drying rack.

"Why do you stay anonymous?" He whispered, my cheek tingling when his fingers brushed through them. He didn't touch me, even though I wanted him to. "You are so beautiful. Like a Princess. An angel." He leaned back on the counter, tilting his head at me, his blue intense eyes making me nervous. "In a way, I want people to see how pretty you are, but I am selfish. I don't want to share your beauty with the world."

I took a sharp breath and looked away from him, sitting on the soft cream couch. "*Hayden*," I squeezed my eyes shut. "I have had surgeries to look the way I am today. I didn't... I didn't look like this when I was young. I—" *Was I really going to tell him? Yes, yes, I was.* He deserved to know. The couch dipped beside me and I faced him, meeting his eyes, "I hated the way I looked."

"Why?" He frowned at me as if I had said that I have two heads.

"Mostly because of how my father berated me and... how

I got my nose broken. I am not a Princess. I shouldn't be one, nor I deserve to be one. I was very insecure about myself growing up and it affected me deeply enough that I changed the shape of my nose and stayed out of the public eye."

I raised my gaze from my lap when his fingers wiped the tears from my eyes. I didn't even know I had started crying.

"Talk to me about your father, Princess," he whispered softly. "He must be the reason for hurting such a young, wild kid."

Coldness seeped into my veins just thinking about him. "But he never saw me as one. A child. His daughter or even a human being." I clutched his hand and looked at the wooden deck. "He loved my mother, Isabella Kent. I had kept her maiden name to keep out of the public eye. The night she gave birth to me, my father... h-he tried to bribe the midwives to kill the child if it was a girl."

"*Christ*," he pulled me closer. "Zara, I..."

"They didn't kill me. My mother hugged me to herself and only allowed my brothers and his friend, Zayed, to see me. The midwives were found dead in their home next week. He... he was a monster, Hayden. He killed innocent people because he was a coward to hurt a baby. His own daughter."

I took a deep breath and continued, "When I grew up, I wouldn't understand why he only talked with my mothers, Zain, Khalid, even the guards, everyone except me. Rahim, our advisor, was the only fatherly figure I have in my life. He would spend time with me and my mother whenever he could because Salman Al Latif had banned me from going out of the Palace. He would call me a witch, a monster whenever he would get drunk and find me in my mother's chamber. He would yell and throw things if I accidentally dropped something. He... he was the reason I got my nose broken."

"What the fuck did he do, Zara?" Hayden's voice was low

and hoarse. His hand was quivering, his fingers tightening around mine.

"When I was five, I was walking on stairs with my mother, holding her hand because she trusted me to guide her as she was blind. I was laughing one moment and tumbling down the stairs the next. I... my father had pushed me down wishing I would die."

His hands cupped around mine. My vision got blurry as warm tears burned through my eyes. "H-He really wanted me dead, Hayden. I remember the screams of my mother because she knew I fell, but not being able to find me until the guards ran up to me. He didn't feel any remorse for doing that. No one knows about this, Hayden. Not even my brothers."

His arms wrapped around me, pulling me into a hug as I squeezed my eyes shut, hot tears sliding down my cheeks. His hand rubbed my back as he whispered, "I am glad he is dead."

I nodded, my voice muffled through his shirt. "Me too."

He kissed my hair and wiped my cheeks. "They would have executed me for his murder if he was alive."

"*Hayden...*" I held his palm on my cheek.

"You should have told your brothers about it, they would have helped you."

I averted his gaze. "He used to punish them with lessons, hitting them if they spend time with me or missed a day of combat training even though they were Princes." Swallowing the lump in my throat, I wiped my cheeks with the clean tee shirt, Hayden had given me. "I wouldn't be alive if it wasn't for my brothers."

"Don't tell me that piece of shit tried to kill you again?"

"He did. But... my brothers were there and... here I am."

We didn't say anything for a while, his warm hand entwined with mine. "I am glad you are here," he said after a while. "That you exist and I got a chance to know you, Princess Zara."

I smiled at him and laid my head down on his shoulder. "I am glad that you exist too, Hayden Robert Knight."

"You saved me yesterday."

I frowned. "I think you have it differently. You rescued me and saved me from those people."

Hayden took a deep breath and whispered, "Olivia would have killed me or hurt me if you hadn't shot her."

"I couldn't stand seeing you get hurt because of me."

Hayden pulled away from me and said, "I can't shoot, Zara."

My brows furrowed, watching him stand up, his eyes averting everywhere but at me. "What are you talking about? Hayden, are you okay?"

"I... my last mission in Iraq, I was the only survivor because of a stupid mistake and ever since then, I-I can't pull a trigger." His breathing had increased and his face had gone flush, even his hands were shaking.

PTSD. I knew about it, but I didn't think Hayden ever showed a sign of it except that time when he looked like he would throw up if I hadn't removed the beetroot from his taco wrap.

I stood up and walked over to him, gently touching his hand. "It's okay, Hayden. It's okay."

He exhaled shakily when I wrapped my arms around him, stroking his hair. "It's not okay. I-I could have done better if I could pull a trigger. No one would get hurt. What if I hadn't saved you in time?"

"*Shh*," I hushed him and kept holding him. My neck was getting wet, and I knew he was crying. *This must have been eating him alive.* "It's okay, Hayden. You saved me and no one got hurt."

"I am sorry."

It hurt me to hear how weak his voice had turned. I wanted to take away whatever was making him anxious and worry.

I gently wiped the tears from his cheeks, meeting his dark blue eyes as he gazed at me through his long lashes. My eyes flickered to his lips, my thumbs caressing his cheek and feeling the stubble on his jaw.

"Can I kiss you, Hayden?"

"Yes, Princess Zara."

Leaning on my toes, I pressed my lips against his. Cupping his jaw, I kissed him, sighing at the warmth fluttering in my stomach when he pulled me closer. Hayden swallowed my gasp when he pushed me against the wall, raising me in his arms, ordering me to wrap my legs around his waist.

I got drunk in his sweet kisses, the soft way he licked my lips, kissing my neck and bringing me down on the bed. I hadn't even noticed that he had walked us into the room as I gazed at him through half-lidded eyes, watching him unbutton his shirt.

I removed the tee shirt, sighing with pleasure when his lips wrapped around my nipples, his hands removing and tugging away my bottoms. We kissed and breathed each other name when he slid inside me, holding me close and tight as if I would disintegrate if he didn't.

The world burned away and the only thing existed was him. Hayden hovering above me, his dark eyes soft and warm with tears gleaming in them, his flushed cheeks and the softest way he groaned my name like he was praying.

Only he mattered at that moment as we chased our high, moaning with pleasure, clutching each other's hands and bearing our souls to each other. His eyes were so blue when we exploded together. So full of emotions and vulnerable when tears leaked through mine.

I love you. I love you. I love you.

His hand soothed me, his sweet words, calling me his Princess, calming me as I came down the high. I knew that what had happened was not just sex. At least for me, it wasn't. It was special and overwhelming and something I would cherish forever, even if it doesn't end well.

35
HAYDEN

I wasn't expecting to fall for her. Nope. Never. But like all the best things in life which happen unexpectedly, I fell for her. Even though she was a Princess of Azmia and made the most adorable grumbling sound whenever waking up, I fell in love with Zara.

I was rendered speechless when we had sex the night before. I would call it lovemaking, but it felt more than that. She had cried, and I didn't know whether it was because she felt it too or just the orgasm. I couldn't sleep knowing that the woman in my arms, the woman I adored, would have to go back to her Golden Palace.

"We are going to reach the island in a few minutes," I said to Chase, who was eating the eggs I had made. "Make sure everything is sailing smooth. I will wake up the Princess."

"I can go wake up her, you know."

I looked over my shoulder and raised my brow at him. "We all heard the sounds coming from the Princess's bedroom last night—"

"Chase?"

"Yes, Sir?"

"Do you like your tongue?"

He frowned. "Of course—"

"Then keep your mouth shut and finish the damn eggs."

"Good morning," Zara smiled at us both, her platinum white hair damp from the shower. "What were you guys talking about?" I served the eggs on her plate, melted with butter as she took a seat beside Chase, who was looking at me, wriggling his brows.

"That we will reach the island soon and I was asking Chase to check if everything is clear."

Thankfully, he took the sign and left us alone after greeting Zara.

"How are you feeling?" I asked her, noticing that she still had the pearl necklace around her neck. She was wearing it last night too. It made my stomach flutter and pulse race.

She was also wearing one of my tee shirts. It looked baggy on her and I wanted to give her all the tee shirts she wanted from my closet.

"I am okay, but I am scared to face whatever is going to happen next." Her hand closed around mine over the table. "My brothers would know about the blast by now and... I might have to go back to Azmia instead of San Diego."

I had figured as much. "Isn't the Prince getting married next month?"

"Yes, Khalid is getting married to Valeria, the founder of *Delicate Dew*, the perfume brand." Zara was grinning, a warm glint in her eyes. "I would have never imagined my brother falling for someone who is his total opposite, but they make it work somehow."

"What about you?"

She looked at me, her eyes wide. "What?"

"Do you have any princes or Royals waiting for you back at home?" I really tried not to sound bitter.

"I don't. Most of them are pretentious and the others

want a relationship with the title attached to my name. Not because... they actually like me."

I remembered she had never been in a relationship before. *Was that the reason?* That she could never trust the other person's intention with her and wanting to be with her for her Royal title.

Would you consider a relationship with me?

I was saved from blurting that question and embracing myself when Chase called me on the lower deck. I looked over Zara's shoulder to notice the island appearing closer and closer. The fresh wind whipped at my shirt when I stepped outside and saw a helicopter hovering in the sky, monitoring the yacht with more than dozens of military jeeps and cars waiting for Princess of Azmia.

Looking beside me, I saw Zara's cheeks flush with embarrassment. *Was that normal for her?* So many people caring about her safety and making sure they met all her needs.

Shaking away those thoughts, I asked, "Are you ready?"

She didn't reply when we reached the island, her hand clutching mine tightly.

"Please don't leave me," Zara whispered, looking straight ahead of us.

"With that grip on my hand, Princess, I don't think I would be able to even if I wanted to." I tried to tease her, but seeing so many people in uniform made me nervous, too.

Soldiers in black and gold bowed at her when we passed through them. A dark, expensive jeep was among the other cars with four guards standing beside the bigger tent they had set up. It arched up higher than the other tents and had more security with rifles and guards wearing sunglasses and even ear-piece.

"Someone is here."

"Who?"

"Royal," she replied, pulling me inside the tent.

I wasn't prepared to meet the Prince and Sheikh of Azmia who were talking to none other than—

"What are you doing here, Ivy?" Zara asked, looking between me and her. "Did you call her here?"

Before I could reply, her brother, Khalid Al Latif, said, "No, we had her fly here. Nice of you to show up, Zara."

My hand tightened around her seeing her brother stand up. He was well over six feet four, tailor-made charcoal suit fitting over his broad shoulders, his obsidian eyes glaring at me and the hand on his sister's palm.

He was a well know painter and donated his earnings from the auctions of his paintings to charities all around the world. I had heard of him, of how ruthless yet kind he was, but being in his presence was another thing.

I should have asked Zara if I needed to bow meeting a Royal.

"Sorry to bring you here, sweetheart." Another deep voice said, a man with curly hair and brown eyes who was looking at my sister with a charming smile. "But this is a Royal matter, and we needed to make sure Zara was safe with your brother."

"They threatened me that Hayden was stuck here and he would get killed if I didn't come here as soon as I can," Ivy said, still staying seated on the dark chair, a bunch of papers and files on the table. "Zara, they keep saying that you are some sort of Royal. Tell them that they have you confused with someone else."

Oh, Ivy.

"Oh, Ivy," Zara whispered. "I am... so sorry for bringing this up at such a moment but, they are right. I am the Princess of Azmia, Zara Al Latif."

"Now that we have had our introductions, except for you," Khalid glared at me. "We have important matters to discuss."

"Wait—you are a Princess?"

"Yes," Zara whispered shamefully, looking down at the golden carpet. "I am so sorry for hiding that from you."

"Who hurt you on the cheek?" That was the other man, standing up, tall and lean frame as he glanced at Zara's face. "Nice hair, by the way."

"Can we all sit down and discuss the elephant in the room?" I spoke up. "I am sorry, Ivy, but she will explain it all to you. Yes, Zara has nice hair, but we need to talk about the multiple attempts to kidnap Zara."

I could hear Zara sighing with relief as her hand squeezed mine, Ivy blinking up at us while Khalid kept his eyes on me.

"I heard that you saved my sister."

"Yes, I did."

"Khalid, he is Hayden Robert—"

"Knight," Khalid finished her sentence. Even their accents were the same. The only key difference between them was their skin tone. Khalid and Zayed had glowing tanned golden skin while Zara was pale as alabaster. "Navy Seal Officer who was, *coincidentally*, present on the night of your nineteenth birthday, am I right, Zara?"

Zara stiffened beside me, raising her chin. "I thought we were discussing how Hayden *saved* me from being a potential hostage or getting killed."

"Calm your tits, you two. Sorry, these Al Latif's get angered on little things. I am Zayed, Sheikh of Azmia, and here to make sure everything goes peacefully." Zayed smiled at Ivy, "Could you please excu—"

"Whose shirt is that?" Khalid asked Zara.

Oh God.

"It is Hayden's shirt." Zara said, crossing her arms and glaring at her brother.

I closed my eyes and sighed.

He glared harder, but I didn't let it affect me. "You need to sign some papers."

"Khalid, he saved me. The least you could do—"

He interrupted her. "You are coming with us right now."

He didn't even wait, walking out of the tent as Zara followed him, dragging me with her.

The sun was slowly rising over our head, the weather and the nervousness forming perspiration on the back of my neck as I stayed with Zara.

"I don't want to. You can't even talk to me without—"

Khalid turned around, glaring at both of us as the guards and military troops saw the commotion we were creating. "I am not asking you, Zara. You made a mess and you need to be accountable for it. You are a Princess of Azmia. Start acting like one."

Zara's grip loosened on my hand, color leeching off of her face as she stared at her brother. I pulled her behind me and met Khalid's dark eyes.

"She said she doesn't want to come." I kept my chin high and added, "Even if she did, you are Khalid Al Latif, her elder brother first and a Prince second. Start acting like one."

No one dared to breathe. Khalid tilted his head at me. "This is a family matter and an opinion of a stranger such as you doesn't matter to me."

I had to give it to him. He really knew how to make someone feel small. But too bad, it would not work on me.

"Khalid…"

He ignored Zara and continued, "If she agrees to stay here, then how do you plan to protect her? Guarantee us you won't put a bullet in my little sister's brain as soon as we leave?"

I heard my sister's voice, calling my name and asking me to step back, but I couldn't move.

Zara stepped between us, "That's enough, Khalid."

"Oh, wait," Khalid mocked me. "You can't even pull a trigger, can you?"

36

ZARA

I had never heard my brother utter such cruel things. I didn't even know who he was. He seemed like a different person.

"You can't even pull a trigger, can you?"

My lips parted, hearing him mock Hayden. I didn't even think about what to do next. I just acted on pure instinct. Slapping my brother and trembling with anger and hurt that I felt for Hayden.

"How dare you say that to a person I care about?" I was shaking, my hand stinging with what I had just done as I glared at Khalid, whose cheek was turning pink, not looking at me. "You disgust me for being so cruel to the man I love and the only friend I have."

Tears gleamed in my eyes as I turned away from Khalid. I wanted Hayden. I wanted to hug him and apologize to him—

"Take them away from here," my brother said, his voice cold as he walked away without looking at me. "Zayed, bring her with you or *I will.*"

It happened so fast that I couldn't do anything.

"Don't you dare touch my sister," Hayden sneered at the

guards who were going to hold terrified Ivy. But that wasn't all. More guards came, holding Hayden and trying to take him away.

To where? What were they going to do to him?

"Hayden—*no*," I held his hand. "Stop, don't—"

"*Zara*," Zayed held my wrist, and I hated it, even though his hold was gentle. "They are just going to ask him some questions."

Hayden's blue eyes met mine as he gave me a small smile and mouthed 'Take care, Princess.' I couldn't do anything when Ivy walked away from me, without looking at me, guards and security of Azmia following them into another tent while Zayed took me to the dark jeep.

"Don't touch me." I managed to say, my voice breaking as I tugged my arm away from his hold. I sat in the car, my throat burning as I tried to fight off more tears.

Useless. I am utterly useless. I couldn't even stop them from taking Hayden away from me. I couldn't do anything.

The plane ride home was filled with silence except for Zayed's lively chatter, which he did to himself. I sat as far as I could from Khalid and him in the private plane that had our crest on it. I hated whatever I looked at, no matter how expensive or beautiful it was. Everything covered in our black and golden crest, the champagne which the air hostess had asked if I wanted before stuttering away seeing my face. The flute glasses, the napkins, the plates, everything was branded with the royal crest.

I hate it.

Only the pearl necklace around my neck reminded me that whatever had happened in Almas Peninsula was real. Even when I dyed my hair back to its natural roots in my old room at the Golden Palace, ignoring everyone and feeling utterly lonely wishing Hayden or Ivy would pick up my call. The network didn't seem to work even when I borrowed Safiya's phone to call them.

Two weeks later, I went to Zain's study, finding him writing something on a letter. He seemed surprised to see me. I had ignored him and his wife, Nasrin, when I had entered the palace, shutting myself in my room.

"What did you want to talk about?" Zain asked, leaning back in the chair.

"I don't want to be a Princess anymore."

"This again... I see you are—"

"No, Zain. I want to resign. I don't want to be a Princess."

He looked at me, his dark eyes similar to mine. "You are a Princess, Zara. You can't just quit or resign whenever you feel like it. I wish I could do that. I don't enjoy being a Sultan all the time. I am sure that is how Khalid and Zayed feel."

My nose flared hearing his name. I walked out of the study, not feeling well, and stopped to see Khalid walking towards me, or rather, the study. Just because I had wanted to stop being a Princess didn't mean that they both had stopped being Royals.

"*Zara*," he called me, guilt written all over his face. "I am sorry, Zara." When I didn't walk away from him, he continued in his deep voice, his eyes downcast, "I... I thought of terrible things when you didn't pick up my call. Then we heard the news of the blast and how you were with Hayden. I thought he had hurt you."

My heart ached hearing his name, wishing I could see him, talk to him about how much I miss him.

"And seeing you with him that day, holding his hand... I got overprotective as your brother. I stepped out of a line and... I did a terrible thing. But it made me feel different that you like—*love* someone else. Someone who is not capable to care for you."

I took a sharp breath. "That is not for you to decide, Khalid. Hayden has done nothing but took care of me since the day I met him. It is for me to decide. Not you. Or anyone. But since I am a Princess, I can't make my own fucking decisions, can I?"

"Zara, *no*, I didn't mean it that way. Listen to—"

I brushed past him, my eyes burning and throat aching as tears pooled down my face. As soon as I closed myself in the room, I rushed towards the washroom and puked.

Panting, I leaned back on my heels and cried some more because everything hurt in my body. Hating myself that I couldn't do anything. Talk to Hayden, try to be a better Princess or even a better sister.

That night, Khalid sent me a painting of a sad baby elephant with a small letter of apology. I clutched it to my chest and fell asleep, agreeing to have lunch with the family the next day.

"It is good to see you here, Zara," Nasrin hugged me, her kind dark eyes squeezing my hand as she made me seat on the low table. I had loved her and her glowing dusky skin ever since Zain had introduced her as his fiancé almost three years ago. She had consoled me when I had chopped my hair and treated me like her sister whenever I was troubled.

"You too. Where is little Aya?" I asked her about her daughter and my niece.

"She wanted to braid Valeria's hair—*ah*, there she is."

I smiled at Valeria, taking her in a hug, her red hair woven in a clumsy braid by the little girl who had rushed to her father, climbing onto his lap and demanding to be fed in broken words.

I had missed it. The laughter and banter between the family. Talking to them about their lives, apologising and forgiving the mistakes, promising to be a better person and having the familial bond. I told them about my travels, the island and the little souvenirs I had bought for them.

"I am sorry for slapping you in front of everyone, Khalid," I said when the maids took our empty plates. My ears turned pink with embarrassment, my fingers fidgeting in my lap.

"I deserved it, Zara. I was rude and threatened your friend. Made fun of a soldier, the man you love, because of his PTSD. I truly am sorry."

Before I could forgive him, Zain spoke up, "Wait, you didn't tell me she loves him."

"I-I… don't."

"Your cheeks are red as cherries," Zayed commented. "You love him or you wouldn't dare to slap Khalid like that. By the way, how did it feel slapping him? I want to try it but I love my arm too much to have it chopped off."

"Aw, Zara loves someone," Valeria grinned at me, her green eyes bright. "Is he cute?"

I blushed harder. "Very."

"Have you ever felt the urge to punch him or slap him, maybe?" Nasrin asked, raising her brow.

I frowned at her. "No, why? Never mind. I know you slapped my brother when he came to woo you."

"He scared me and he is pretty annoying to live with."

"Can you stop talking as if I am not here?" Zain asked. "I thought you loved me."

Nasrin replied. "I can love you and get annoyed by you."

"Yes, Khalid has this habit of never keeping his clothes properly and it annoys me too," Valeria said.

Khalid looked horrified hearing that. "You color code

everything, Valeria! I am an artist, I don't like to keep everything color coded."

"But you only ever wear black!"

"I… T-that is not true. I wore a dark grey suit yesterday."

I sighed, glancing at the two bantering couples and Zayed, who was busy playing with the toy car, as Aya sat on his shoulders, clutching his hair in her tiny fists.

Yes, sometimes my family could get annoying. But I loved them.

If only Hayden was here…

37 ZARA

The back of my blouse itched, but Safiya, my personal maid, slapped my wrist when I tried to tug at it. Scowling at her, I ran my hand down the golden gown I was wearing. It was tailor made for Khalid and Valeria's wedding, which was happening at that moment. But my ears hurt from wearing the heavy earrings, the slim necklace and the itchy, intricate fabric of the gown, annoying me every time I moved.

The Court Room was decorated in golden and red and black colors. Flowers and fabric decorations were on every wall and pillars, the throne was empty as Zain, Nasrin and Aya stood together with the wedding couple. Musicians kept playing the soft, lilting song.

My stomach grumbled just as Khalid and Valeria were announced husband and wife. Safiya and an old Royal looked at me when my stomach roared again. I had skipped breakfast because I had woken up late, puking because of the stomach bug that wasn't leaving me alone.

I excused myself and went to look for something to eat. I was in the mood for something sour and sweet—

The Golden Palace rumbled when I stood alone in the

37 ZARA

empty hallway. Screams, angry shouts and gunshots came from the Court Room. Khalid, Zain, Zayed and even Rahim had made the best security plan for the wedding and still... *how was this happening?*

I gasped, covering my mouth when I saw the scene in front of me. All the royals and my family were on the dais behind the throne. The men and women in black with ski masks covering their faces were holding firearms like rifles and pointing at the people who wouldn't follow their commands.

How was this happening?

I scrambled my brain to think of something, call someone for help. Elena. She would help. She was a trained—

I yelped when a large hand held my arm, dragging me towards the Court Room.

"There she is... the woman we have been looking for." The man who was shouting before said to me. His voice was thick and full of malice. His comrade, the person behind me, kept his hand on my back, keeping me still even when I tried to wrench their grip from my hand.

"What do you want?" I glared at him. "You already failed at kidnapping me twice, didn't you?"

"Zara."

I ignored the warning voice of Zain as Khalid pulled Valeria behind him, people in firearms keeping them away from me. More people in ski masks surrounding us. My stomach churned with nerves at the uncomfortable feeling that it would not work out like it always does.

"Well, Princess, third time's a charm, isn't it?" The man across me said, grabbing my chin as I tried to move away. My family was shouting at them, chaos was erupting and I knew I couldn't stay still. Be useless. I couldn't let them harm my family.

I elbowed the person on my back, stomping my foot on

37 ZARA

the ankle of the man holding my chin and lifting my leg to knee him between the legs.

"Not this again," the man behind me groaned, his accent very American, unlike the thick—*wait*.

"Who are you?" I asked him, tackling him on the ground and removing the ski mask from his face. My eyes widened and heart thudded seeing the blue eyes. The same chocolate brown hair and sharp features. "I am dreaming."

"No, you are not, Princess," Hayden tucked a strand of my hair behind my ear. "This hair color suits you more." His eyes looked over my shoulder as he helped me up while I stayed frozen, looking at him. "Why don't you stay here? I will be right back."

I blinked at his back, realising that the people who had entered the Court Room wearing ski masks were none other than our guards and the security provided by Elena, Zain and Khalid's old friend who had worked as a Federal Bureau of Investigation officer.

Why is Hayden here? Why is Hayden fighting and cuffing the men in ski masks, helping us?

"Are you okay?" Nasrin asked me, checking my forehead as if I was bedridden. "Why did you tackle him like that in the middle of the Court Room?"

"Did *you* know about this?"

"No. Zain just told me about it." Her eyes drifted around us, our guards overpowering the men and women who had broken in. "We have been receiving threats of your kidnapping and he knew they wouldn't miss the chance to strike tonight at Khalid's wedding."

"So he pretended to use me as a bait and not tell me that Hayden was in on this?"

"He was going to play all hero and woo you back like Zayed had planned, that's what Zain said. But you hit him on his ribs and—*Imran!* Where are you going?"

37 ZARA

I looked over my shoulder to see Nasrin's younger brother. His brown eyes glanced at both of us. "It's getting too loud in here. I thought it was a wedding not—whatever *this* is. Oh, look, Zayed got tackled. I should go help him."

"I need to talk to Hayden," I said to Nasrin and marched up to him, removing my heels that were hurting my feet.

"Good luck!" Nasrin cheered for me.

"Hayden, we need to talk." I said to him when he sighed, wiping blood from his cheek that didn't belong to him, and glanced at me. There was a large unconscious man in cuffs lying by his feet as he nodded at me, "Yeah, sure, what do you want to talk about, Princess"

Fuck, why is he so hot and handsome? No one should be allowed to look as good as him with a blood on their hand.

"Why are you here? What are you doing here?" I shook my head. "Why didn't you pick up my calls? Why didn't you ever call me? Did you know I was scared that my brother had thrown you into the ocean and that I might never get to see your stupid handsome face ag—"

He didn't let me finish. *Rude.*

Cupping my cheek, he pressed his lips against mine, kissing me and shutting me up successfully. I closed my eyes and held his arms, tasting the sweet musky scent of ocean and wishing I never have to let go of him again.

Hayden pulled away, leaning his forehead against mine as we tried to control our heavy breathing. "You look so fucking beautiful in this." He pulled back, shaking his head as he gazed at me, "Sorry, I wanted to tell you something else, but you look so pretty that I want to kiss you and say... say that I love you."

My heartbeat stopped. I slowly blinked at him. "What?"

Hayden took a step closer, his cheeks slashing with color. "I love you, Princess Zara."

"Do you really?"

37 ZARA

He raised his brow, "Well, that was not the answer I was hoping to hear but yes, *you silly brat*, I fucking love you and I wouldn't be here trying to prove it to you by saving you from the bad guys."

"I never asked you to save me."

"I know you didn't, and you don't need me to save you. But I wouldn't mind staying by your side when you kick ass and occasionally let me help you."

"*Hayden…*" I closed my eyes. My hands were shaking when he entwined his fingers with mine.

"You don't have to say it, Zara. I said it because I wanted you to know that I love you. A lot. Even if you grumble at me, hit me again and tackle me on the ground, I will love you."

His blue eyes were so warm and sincere, his thumbs making patterns on my knuckles. "I… I," I trailed off, my brain closing down and heart feeling heavy as I looked at his eyes. "Look, over you!"

As soon as he turned, I gathered the heavy fabric of my gown and started running in the opposite directions. Nasrin's grin fell when I ran past her, Hayden's curse following me.

"Dammit, Zara. I am faster than you."

I couldn't care. I was scared. Terrified. If I loved him, he would be taken away. Somehow, the people I love always disappear or… die. I couldn't do that. I could love him from afar—

A hand clasped my wrist as I reached the hallways, perspiration forming on my brows when I gasped, tugged around and stumbling into a strong chest of the man I loved. His hold stayed soft as he took deep breaths, his heart beating as fast as mine.

"Don't run away from me, Zara," he whispered, tilting my

37 ZARA

chin at him and wiping a tear from the corner of my eyes. "You are scared aren't you, Princess?"

I nodded, biting my lipid, clutching his shirt in my hands. My knees felt weak, and I felt dizzy.

"I am scared too, love. Of hurting you, of fucking this up and losing you." Hot tears slid down my face when his blue eyes averted from my lips to my eyes. "But I want to try, Zara. For you. For my pretty Princess."

"Hayden…" my voice was a broken whisper. "I am scared that something would happen to you. That you would get hurt because of me or disappear from my life."

"I am glad that you care, but I can protect myself and you, Princess."

"If I… if we do this, do you promise me to take care of me when I get scared?"

"Scared of what?"

"Scared of losing you. I already feel so much for you it will shatter me if something—"

"Yes, Zara." His warm breath brushed against my cheek. "I will take care of you when you get scared, Princess. I will be your Knight."

I blinked at him and pulled away. "That was cringe."

His face fell. "How do I fix this?"

I sadly shook my head and wiped my tears. "I am sorry, I can't be with someone who has such cringeworthy humor—"

"Come back here."

Grinning at him, I wrapped my arms around his neck and kissed him. I ran my hand through his hair and melted into his strong embrace when his fingers dug into my waist. I could allow myself to fall for him and love him.

His blue eyes were gleaming when we pulled away. It was the most beautiful sight I had ever seen. With a small smile curling at the corner of his pink, wet lips. I wanted to wake up to that face and that sight for the rest of my life if I could.

37 ZARA

"I love you too, Hayden Knight."

We kissed once more, grinning at each other, when Zayed burst into the cheering of my family.

"So when is the food getting served?"

THE END

READ EXPLICIT BONUS SCENE HERE
Or type this link into your browser:
https://mailchi.mp/94bc50311f67/trpbonusscene

Thank you so much for reading Tempting Rebel Princess! If you enjoyed reading this book, I would be grateful if you could leave a review on the platform(s) of your choice.

Reviews help other readers like you find this book and are hugely appreciated by authors!

Love always,
Mahi

EPILOGUE

HAYDEN

"I thought I told you to go to sleep," I glared at Zara, her nose in a book as she turned the page, without looking up at me.

"I was waiting for you." She placed a bookmark and smiled at me when I closed the door to her room. Our room since the day I had moved into her room after she had accepted my proposal of marriage.

"How many times do I have to tell you not to wait up for me, Princess?" I walked towards the bed, gazing at her beautiful elfish face. Her short hair was growing longer, reaching her chin. I cupped her cheek, pecking her lips and pulling away before she seduces me to join her on the bed.

"It doesn't matter. I like waiting up for you. So did you make anyone cry today?"

"Only two people."

Removing my shirt, I walked into the washroom, still getting used to the luxurious space, and washing my face. I had already showered at the gym.

After the incident at the Almas Peninsula, Khalid had called me personally and invited me to Azmia one week before his wedding. He had talked to me about Zara, asking

EPILOGUE

for my intention and apologising to me for being rude at our first meeting. I forgave him and he asked for a favour to monitor her during the wedding.

He had shown me their plan of busting the mastermind behind the Library incident two years ago because he knew that those kidnappers were the same. They wanted to get to Zara.

Despite catching most of the people who had broken into the palace during the wedding, we still didn't know who was behind all of it, but we had a few wild guesses who it could be.

I had to leave my life in San Diego if I wanted to spend the rest of my life with Zara. It wasn't easy, but Elena, the ex-officer, had recruited me as a coach to teach her security students.

"You are not showering?" Zara pouted at me as I kept my eyes above her chin level. I knew she had changed into one of her much expensive lingerie that made me wild just looking at her.

"No, because the last time you asked me this question, we ended up having shower sex."

She grinned. "It was pleasant. We should do it sometime, don't you think?"

"Absolutely not, Zara." I changed into grey sweatpants and walked back to bed, humming at her taste in literary fiction and set it aside.

The room was spacious, with a bed big enough for a soccer team and everything carved in golden and red intricate designs.

"Ivy called today."

"What did she say?" Zara asked, getting in the bed beside me, under the blanket.

I glanced at her. "That she will try to visit us before her

EPILOGUE

masters and bring—why are you pouting? Did I say something?"

Zara took a deep breath and sat up on the bed. I swallowed at the sight of stunning mesh nightgown she was wearing. It accentuated her breasts, her piercings and the tiny underwear cinched around her waist.

"Do you... do you not find me sexually attractive, Hayden?"

"What the fuck?" I sat up and showed her the boner that I have been trying to hide. "Zara, of course I am attracted to you. What happened?"

She looked down at her lap and gave me a small shrug. "You turn me down whenever I try to have sex with you. Even when I wear all this and..."

"Oh, Princess," I wrapped my arm around her and lowered my hand to her stomach. "*This...* this baby is the reason why I am trying to control myself."

"I don't understand. How is me being pregnant related to this?"

"Seeing you have my baby, *our baby*, turns me into an absolute animal, Zara. Last week, if I hadn't held your arm while fucking you from behind, you would have hurt yourself... it scared me and I guess, I thought that if we didn't have sex, you and the baby would be safe."

"I wish you had told me sooner about this. I kept thinking that..."

I shook my head, kissing her neck, "You thought wrong, Princess. I love you. Your entire body and your soul. I was afraid of hurting you."

"But you know how much I like it," she whispered, her hands sliding down my abs to my hardened member that throbbed when she gave him attention.

"Zara..."

"Please, Hayden. I need you."

EPILOGUE

I couldn't resist her sweet voice, laying her naked on her stomach and spreading her legs while spanking her ass until it burned light pink.

Zara whimpered when I ran my fingers over her slit, feeling how wet she was. I groaned, spanking her pussy and rubbing the stud on her clitoris.

"You really want me to fuck you like my little slut, is that right, Princess?" I asked, stroking myself over her entrance and feeling her clench around me. She moaned, pushing herself back. "Such a good girl. My beautiful fiancé."

"Hayden!" Her hands scrunched on the sheets when I slammed inside her in one thrust, her velvety walls clamping around me.

Squeezing her ass, I kept my pace, fondling her breasts that were getting heavier and bigger. I murmured sweet praise in her ear, kissing her neck while rolling my hips and thrusting inside her.

I groaned when she came with a sweet broken moan, my cock deep inside her, her walls convulsing around me. I let out a low grunt, releasing inside her. I sighed when I laid beside her, basking in the post-coital bliss with my soon-to-be-wife, kissing her hair, stroking her soft body.

"Hayden?"

"Mm?"

"I love you."

"I love you too, Princess—oh, babe?"

"Hm?"

"I forgot to use a condom."

Zara said nothing for a while. She blinked at me with her brown doe eyes.

"My brothers are going to kill you."

UNKNOWN

I exhaled the long puff of smoke, looking out of the balcony of the guest room. It was a beautiful, sunny day. People were smiling, talking about Zara's engagement as if the attack during the wedding of Khalid and Valeria was nothing.

The people I had hired to kidnap Zara had failed. *Again*. I watched the securities, the woman named Elena had established around the entire Golden Palace. They were following the Sultana, Nasrin Al Latif and her daughter, Aya Al Latif, the Princess. Both of them laughing and running around the fresh cut grass. I had never seen Nasrin grin so freely before.

Too bad I would be the reason for her and others' cries in a few days. I couldn't trust anyone else to fuck up my plan anymore. I would have to do it on my own.

"Is there anything I can help you wi—"

Turning around, I offered a small smile to the maid. "No, thank you. I was just watching the Sultana and the Princess playing in the gardens."

The maid's smile was genuine. "Ah, yes, Princess Aya has wrapped everyone around the palace in her little hands.

Sultan and Sultana are very careful with the security. You must know that, Prince."

I let out a soft chuckle and put out the cigar I was smoking, walking towards her. Her smile washed off when I brushed my knuckles on her cheek. She seemed too young to be working in a palace full of royals.

"What's your name?"

"Iesha, P-Prince... I-is there—"

"*Shh.*" I pressed my finger on her lips, her dark eyes widening. Her fingers clutched the long skirt she was wearing, a thin veil of fabric covering her blouse. I gently tugged at it, her brows scrunching in fear. "Only speak when I ask you to, beautiful Iesha, and you'll be rewarded."

Her slender throat bobbed as she swallowed nervously. I bared her curvy frame to me, raking my eyes over her rich brown skin, smooth and tawny. I could eat her alive if I wanted to. She was perfect. Her nipples were hard and poking through the fabric of her white blouse. I rolled the sleeves of my shirt to my elbows, pacing around her, removing the pin holding her dark hair and letting them fall over her back in waves.

"How old are you?" I asked, tipping her chin towards me when she wouldn't meet my eye.

I was a bastard, yes. But I still had the morals of a gentleman when it came to innocent women like her. Of course, those morals wouldn't have been seen in front of Zara if I had her.

"N-nineteen."

I let go of her chin. "So young and working in a Palace as a maid?"

"It is my honour to serve Sultan Zain and his family—"

"*Kneel.*" I glared at her, pouring myself a glass of whiskey from the golden tumbler.

Her brows scrunched. "What?"

"Don't make me repeat myself, Iesha. Kneel on the floor."

I took a sip of the sweet alcohol, refilling it before prowling towards the beautiful, scared girl.

"What do you dream of?" I asked her, standing so close to her, her eyes peering at me from her long lashes. It pleased me to see her acquiesce without any squabble. It wouldn't have mattered. I would have made her kneel if she had followed my command or not.

She licked her lips. "Maids like us don't have many dreams, Prince."

"Such a fucking shame, isn't it?" I asked, toying with the tendril of her hair, tugging at it lightly. "Zain—forgive me, Sultan Zain offers you a place to stay, allowing you to work as a maid until you get old. Tell me," I leaned down, looking at her dilated pupils, "Would you like to be a Princess, Iesha?"

Her eyes widened, "Y-you don't mean that y-you want… you want to marry—"

At least she was smart.

I smiled at her, brushing my thumb over her bottom lip. Such a pity that an innocent girl like her would have to play a pawn in my game. "Yes, Iesha. Be my Princess. Marry me."

Say yes and help me destroy Al Latif family. Help me bring down Azmia.

"I-I don't know, Prince. You are… you are *you* and I am just a maid."

"Then stay with me for a night and then you can decide, *hm?*"

I didn't let her answer. I parted her lips and poured the whiskey down her mouth, watching her neck bob as she swallowed the alcohol. Her body jumped when I threw the glass away. It crashed, shattering into thousands of pieces just as I claimed her lips, pushing her down on the floor and tearing her blouse open, the hooks flying away.

I thought about vengeance and the way Zain had married

Nasrin, Khalid had killed my men, and how Zara was taken away by her fiancé. I thought about the royal family, their roof I was staying under while fucking Iesha, pinning her down by her throat and wrists as she cried and whimpered and begged for more.

I thought about their downfall as I came. Blood coated the insides of her thigh when I pulled away, panting down at her. I pulled out a handkerchief from my silk trousers and wiped her clean. She was a beautiful mess. Her clothes disheveled, her hair mussed up with tears drying on her cheeks.

"I will marry you," Iesha said, her voice a broken whisper. "I want to be a Princess,"

I hovered above her, brushing my fingers on the rough bite marks across her ample breasts. Maybe I had been too rough for her. Poor Iesha.

"I promise to make you happy, just like this, Princess Iesha." I purred in her ear, pushing her on her knees, lying through my teeth as I held her long skirts above her ass.

She whimpered into the Egyptian rug when I slammed inside her, groaning and squeezing her ass, muffling her sounds of pain and pleasure with my hand on her mouth.

Just a few more days until Azmia is nothing but ashes.

PREVIEW OF CHARMING HANDSOME SHEIKH

ZAYED

"You are going to pick up the phone and bend over that sink for me like a good little witch." I said and unbuttoned her pants when she tried to pull away.

"I-I can't—"

"Then I will." I accepted the call and turned it on the speaker. My other hand found her lacy underwear and pushed my finger against the wetness between her lips.

She whimpered, squeezing her eyes shut when we both heard the soft voice. "Hello? Elena?"

I closed her mouth and hissed in her ear, "Stay quiet or he will hear how good my fingers feel inside you."

Elena glared at me, her eyes full of lust, anger and hatred. *Good.* I wanted her to hate me. Hate me when I rubbed her needy swollen button through her wet panties. Hate me as I peeled her jeans from her toned, long legs. Hate me as I looked at her and held the lace in my hands, ripping it off of her skin with a tear. Hate me with a burning passion of lust when I cupped her where she was burning hot and told her to answer her call.

EXCLUSIVE CONTENT

Want more exclusive content? You can sign up for Mahi's Patreon to read steamy one shots every Saturday!

As a supporter, you get access to early drafts, exclusive VIP content, deleted scenes, deleted chapters, cat pictures and YOUR NAME in the Acknowledgements of my books.

www.patreon.com/mahimistry

PREVIEW OF TWISTED THERAPIST

IVY KNIGHT

"I am so sorry, Aiden, the traffic was so bad," I heaved, taking support of my knees to control my breathing. So much for dressing up in cute dress, applying light makeup and curling my hair in waves just for the session. I wiped down the sweat from forehead and straightened up, daring to peek at him.

Aiden looked like he always did. His face stern and no emotions showing on his face. His eyes travelled down my body and I held in my shiver when they raked over my bare legs.

He made a dramatic point of checking his wristwatch that cost more than the car that I drove and hummed. "We will talk about your tardiness after the session. *Sit.*"

I quickly sat down and drank some water, the breeze of the air conditioner cooling my skin. The session started, and we made usual talk about my day, what happened that week or if anything exciting happened that I wanted to share with him.

"How did your journaling go?"

We talked more about the days where I would write two-three pages a day or days when I could barely write a paragraph. He listened to me and asked questions when I would stop talking, urging me to drink water and keep going.

"Do you mind if I see what you've written?" He asked, his dark eyes soft.

My muscles tensed as I met his obsidian eyes. They ran over my body and noticed how stiff I had become. My eyes lingered on his crisp white shirt, stretching over his shoulders, the sleeves rolled up to his elbows with a dark-coloured tie. Maybe it was my imagination when I thought his eyes had stayed far too long on my chest and my legs. I shuffled in my seat and tucked the strand of my hair behind my ear.

Aiden's eyes flickered to my face, and he closed them for a moment, as if he was taking his time. He finally said, "You don't have to if you don't want me to read. I will understand and respect your privacy."

I licked my lips, trusting my instinct. "I-it's okay, I don't mind. You can read it."

I handed him the diary, frowning at the ruffled separate pages that I had shoved between them. He silently read the entry of my first day while I squirmed in my seat. I may or may not have drunk too much water, so I excused myself to the washroom.

When I came back, I could feel the change in the air. Aiden was sitting on the couch, but his posture was stiff. He barely addressed my presence when I sat down in my seat. I saw the diary was placed beside him and his jaw was clenched.

"Is everything okay?" I asked, my voice small.

He finally looked at me and the corner of his lips twitch. Leaning back on the couch, he said, "Yes, I suppose you could say that. I want to ask you something, Petal, and I want you to be honest about it."

Frowning, I nodded.

His eyes darkened, and he said in a stern voice, "Use your

mouth."

"I—*um*, yes, Dr. Aiden."

I didn't know why I *felt* the need to address him seriously.

"What were you doing this morning?"

My eyes widened, my heart pounding in my ears. I glanced at the diary and it struck me. Those ruffled pages. *Shit, shit, shit.* After journaling every day for a week, I wrote my fantasies regarding Aiden, my brother's best friend, on different torn pages. I always tucked them back in the diary, reminding myself to pull them out before I brought it to the session. But I was in such a hurry that I had completely forgotten about them.

Did he read it? I hope he didn't. I would rather eat raw broccoli than have him read all those pages.

Looking away from him, I lied and carelessly shrugged my shoulder, "I was meditating."

I mentally winced at my lie. He had tried coaching me to meditate, but I could never do it.

He is right. I am a terrible liar.

Aiden raised his eyebrows. "Is that so?"

I didn't like the tone of his voice. He seemed serious, and I prayed that the ground would swallow me up. He waited for my answer, crossing his arms over his chest. I got distracted by the way his biceps bulged, the veins on his forearms getting prominent.

He noticed me staring. I glanced down at my lap, twiddling my thumbs. "Y-yes, Dr Aiden, I was meditating and I-I focused on my breath like you taught me—"

"Why are you lying to me, Ivy?"

My head snapped at him. I shook my head, "I-I am not lying."

Aiden tilted his head and my throat went dry when he said, "Then why did I hear your voice moaning my name when you orgasmed with your fingers inside your pussy?"

PREVIEW OF DON'T DATE YOUR BEST FRIEND

KIARA

"If you don't want to kiss me then . . . let's swim."

"Yeah, sure."

"Naked."

"*What?*"

"I always wanted to try skinny dipping." I pursed my lips and said, "And I really want to get out of these clothes."

When I thought about it, I wasn't feeling self-conscious about my body when it came to him. Yes, he had seen in me in bikinis and accidentally walking in when I was busy writing something on my Post-it in my underwear and bra. But I was never self-conscious about what he would think of me or my body. I did have stretch marks, but I wasn't uncomfortable about them. What I was most worried about was *myself*. If he got naked and my hormones spiked up, I didn't know if I would control myself and not jump on him.

Gosh, I sounded so bad in my head. Not to mention, my best friend would be the first guy I would ever see naked. *Way to go, Kiara.*

His voice was strained when he said, "What if someone catches *you* . . . me, both?"

I moved my damp hair over my shoulder. "We will be in the pool, Ethan. And no one can see us from the living room." I smirked when I said, "Unless you want to watch me while I swim, you can stay here."

The thought of Ethan watching me with his intense green-blue eyes while I was swimming naked in the pool sent a delicious shiver down my core.

His eyes darkened and he looked away, probably thinking the same when I noticed red blush creeping up his neck and making his ears and cheeks flush. *Cute*.

I prodded, "Come on, Ethan. Don't be a chicken . . ."

"*Fine.*"

He stood up, his tall frame towering me. I forgot how to breathe when his dark eyes seared me, slowly trailing down my body as if he had all the time in the world. His voice was rough when he said, "Remove that sweater first."

I raised my eyebrow at the sudden change in his demeanour.

Ethan said, "You have an extra piece of clothing than me."

I grinned. "Who said I was wearing any underwear?"

I loved the way his pupils widened in shock, surprise and then they were clouded by scorching desire. Biting my lips, I whispered, "I was messing with you."

Holding the hem of the sweater, I tugged it up and removed it. I straightened my damp hair and shivered. But it wasn't because of the cold air.

His eyes averted down my breasts, which were barely covered by the ivory lace bralette. As it was wet, he could easily notice my hardened nubs, which were begging for his attention.

We were crossing a dangerous line right now. And I knew neither one of us wanted to step back.

"Your turn," I managed to whisper.

ALSO BY MAHI MISTRY

Have you read them all?

Alluring Rulers of Azmia Series

Dirty Wild Sultan

Filthy Hot Prince

Tempting Rebel Princess

Charming Handsome Sheikh

Alluring Rulers of Azmia Complete Series Books 1-4

The Unfolding Duet

Don't Date Your Best Friend: Best Friends to Lovers

Don't Date Your Ex Best Friend: Second Chance Best Friends to Lovers

The Unfolding Duet Books 1-2

Dominating Desires Series

Twisted Therapist: Brother's Best Friend Age Gap Romance

Tempting Teacher: Student Teacher/Dad's Best Friend Age Gap Romance

Scan to easily access all of my books:

ACKNOWLEDGMENTS

To all the kinky readers, who blushed reading this romantic erotica and raved about this book to others. You guys are one of the best people I know. I am grateful for your love and support. Thank you for taking time to read Zara and Hayden's story and share it with the world. It means a lot to me.

To Ama, for being the best accountability partner and encouraging and cheering me with support when I thought I would never finish this book. You are the sweetest.

To my family and my cats for always believing in me.

To all my beta readers, proofreader, arc readers, bloggers and book lovers, bookstragramers, I couldn't have done this without you.

Thank you to everyone who accepted the ARC edition of this book and helped me share this book with the world.

If you enjoyed reading this book, please don't forget to leave a review. I would really appreciate it. It helps find more readers like you and they are very important for authors!

ABOUT THE AUTHOR

Mahi Mistry has been writing since she was in middle school. Soon, she fell in love with writing passionate, steamy romances. Her stories have elements of humor, suspense and character development. Mahi's main purpose in her life is to make one person happy every day, even if that is a stranger reading her book and rooting for the main couple or her cats by giving them extra treats.

She enjoys simple things in life, like spending time with her family and friends, cuddling with her cats, reading and writing drool-worthy characters while sipping on hot chocolate from the wineglass to validate herself that she is actually an adult. She is an avid reader of fantasy, romance and thriller books and thinks writing about yourself in third person is atrocious. She firmly believes that cats rule the world.

www.mahimistry.com

www.ingramcontent.com/pod-product-compliance
Lightning Source LLC
LaVergne TN
LVHW091704070526
838199LV00050B/2270